The Scent of Corruption

Alaric Bond

The Scent of Corruption
Alaric Bond

Copyright © 2015 Alaric Bond

Published by Old Salt Press, LLC

www.oldsaltpress.com

978-1-943404-02-5 (print)
978-1-943404-03-2 (e-book)
Library of Congress Control Number: 2015908622

The cover shows a detail from
"A British Man of War before the Rock of Gibraltar"
by Thomas Whitcombe (1763- 1824)

For Tony

By the same author

The Fighting Sail Series:

His Majesty's Ship

The Jackass Frigate

True Colours

Cut and Run

The Patriot's Fate

The Torrid Zone

and

Turn a Blind Eye

The Guinea Boat

CONTENTS

The Scent of Corruption

Chapter One

The last thing Lieutenant King wanted was to be interrupted. His day had already been long and taxing enough, and there were no further duties scheduled until dawn. He would rather forget all about HMS *Prometheus*, along with any responsibility he may have as one of her officers. Nevertheless his visitor probably deserved a second glance, even if there was nothing ostensibly unusual about him.

He was dressed as a seaman but not smartly so, and certainly not in an off duty Jack's more usual shore-going rig. Instead of a tape seamed, bright buttoned jacket he wore a plain round affair, along with the more common shipboard attire of chequered shirt, and baggy canvas trousers. The latter appearing to have been sewn aboard ship and owed more to practicality than style. His hair was cut short, in the modern manner, with no queue, and beneath was a face tanned to the degree only many years at sea can achieve. He was also carrying the ubiquitous tarred hat that might be found in any lower deck man's possession.

Lieutenant King considered him through a slight haze that had more to do with the gin he had already drunk than the parlour's smoke-filled atmosphere. His visitor could be here on duty – a hand sent from another ship, or even one from the past but, despite his mildly inebriated state, King was reasonably sure he had never laid eyes on the fellow before. He told himself he would have remembered and, now that he looked more carefully, wondered if there was actually something different about the man. Something that said, however conventional the appearance, this was no normal lower deck hand: even his opening question had proved that.

"What manner of position are you seeking?" King replied at last, taking care to enunciate his words clearly above the babble of the busy room, while willing his brain to clear.

"I'd be happy to ship as a regular hand, sir," the seaman told him.

King considered the stranger's clear and annoyingly sober eyes. There had been no trace of a waver, and it was unusual for a regular hand to meet an officer's gaze quite so directly. Yet the seaman, who appeared slightly older than himself, was not giving any impression of impertinence; quite the reverse, in fact.

"Do you have experience?" King asked. It was like looking a gift horse in the mouth: despite a period of active recruitment, *Prometheus* remained desperately undermanned and any addition to her crew, be they able, ordinary or landsman, would be welcomed. But the visitor's demeanour intrigued him and he wanted to know more.

It was partly the way he stood, in all respects a seaman, with head respectfully bared, yet there was no sign of an earring. His voice was also unusually well rounded, almost genteel. And he had sought King out in the parlour of a hotel: The *Earl of Essex* was little more than a pretentious boarding house admittedly, but still considerably above the standard most lower deck men would feel comfortable entering. That much at least was decidedly curious but, strangest of all, he wanted to serve aboard *Prometheus*.

There was nothing wrong with the ship, King hurriedly assured himself; a seventy-four gun line-of-battleship fresh from refit and about to join the Channel Fleet – worse postings existed undoubtedly. But then neither was she a frigate set for a cruise, when excitement and prize money might be expected. And if he had wanted to volunteer to serve his Majesty, why had the man not applied to one of the several Rondys nearby? There he would have been greeted far more warmly, and could have taken his pick of the bounties, both official and otherwise, that were bound to be on offer.

"I've served in the past, sir," the visitor assured him: King's silence had obviously caused concern and his glance fell away for the first time. "In *Hector*, and *Suffolk*, then I was in *Adamant* and saw action at Camperdown. After that there was a spell ashore, followed by two years in *Wakeful*."

"I was at Camperdown," King remarked and, despite the words being slightly slurred, he spoke them with pride, in the way that most who had served with Duncan would. But, if this was a veteran, he seemed almost ashamed of the honour, and King was becoming more intrigued by the second.

"I don't mind being rated landsman, sir," he added, as if frightened King might lose interest. "Not if you already have a full complement, though I can hand, reef and steer with the best of them."

King glanced down at his current drink. It was one in what was surely destined to become a series, and had remained ignored for longer than any so far that evening. But suddenly the hotel's rightly acclaimed Hollands held little attraction for him, and he wished himself sober.

"We might take an extra landsman," the lieutenant conceded, loftily. "Though, if truly skilled, would prefer an ordinary or able hand, and should gladly rate you so."

The man's expression relaxed, although it was to one of relief rather than pleasure. "But, forgive me," King continued. "You do not come across as a regular foremast Jack."

Again the man's glance fell away and he even looked mildly ashamed.

"What is your name?" King persisted.

"Ross, sir," the seaman replied smartly enough. "And I can hold my own as able, if you put me to test."

The lieutenant scratched at his head; to return to the ship with a willing hand in tow would do his personal standing no harm at all, especially in a place like Tor Bay, where such things were almost unheard of. And he was sadly aware his status aboard

Prometheus had been slipping consistently of late. The new ship, larger than any King had previously known, excited him, and it was good to be walking a deck again after so long ashore. But he was finding it hard returning to life as a sea officer, and his time on the beach had encouraged a lot of bad habits, one of which he was indulging in that very evening.

"How long have you served as an able seaman, Ross?" he asked, and noted the man's immediate swallow.

"I have yet to, sir, but am familiar with the duties."

"As an ordinary hand then?"

Ross shook his head. "I've no objection to being rated landsman, sir." he muttered.

"What was your last position?"

"In *Wakeful*, sir?" It was very nearly prevarication, and King nodded impatiently while the seaman drew breath.

"I was her first lieutenant," he replied at last.

* * *

Of all the places in *Prometheus,* the forepeak was one of the more remote; a fact that had been very much on Thompson's mind in his selection. And security remained a major concern as he slipped down the companionway before stepping quietly along the orlop. It was late enough for the idlers to be off duty, so he had to be especially careful. In one hand he clutched a canvas pouch, while the other held a small bottle filled with water. He could have found himself a lantern, but a moving light would have attracted attention, and attention was something Thompson wished to avoid.

He walked slowly and carefully past the powder room and forward magazine, using the occasional lanthorns that lit the ship's low-beamed underworld as a guide, then paused at the top of the ladder that led down into what he was starting to regard as his own private space. There was no sight or sound of movement beneath, and the only scent was that of stale bilges, damp wood and rats: it was perfect. He dropped easily down the well worn rungs until his bare feet touched a deck that had not seen sunshine since *Prometheus* was built. Turning to larboard, he found the small glim

4

and firesteel he had left behind. With two strikes a feeble yellow flame appeared, which he quickly transferred to the lantern, and an eerie glow was cast on Thompson's surroundings.

About him lay all manner of broken fittings and discarded iron work: items that did not deserve a defined home elsewhere, or were of limited value. To anyone accustomed to Royal Navy order, the place looked decidedly disorganised, but it suited Thompson's purposes perfectly. He waited until, drawn by either light or noise, a young woman appeared from the depths. The amber rays caught her face, and Thompson smiled. Flickering shadows danced upon her and he was struck, once more, by a rare and natural beauty.

Yes, she was certainly a prime catch, he decided. The hair, which hung long and unkempt, might have looked better properly dressed and arranged, but draping over her shoulders as it did was enough for a simple man. And the long smock Thompson himself had provided was surely as attractive as any fine dress or ball gown, especially as the occasional tear gave tantalising glimpses of the body within.

"What cheer, little one?" he asked gently, rising up and extending a hand in her direction. She took it with caution, allowing herself to be guided towards him as if invited to dance. He led her to the centre of the space and seated himself on a stack of old wardroom panelling, presumably left over from the refit, while she rested awkwardly against a coil of worn, ten-inch hawser that had yet to be turned into oakum.

"I've brought you some scran," Thompson informed her, indicating the small canvas pouch. "There's salt horse, two onions, an' a bottle of fresh water."

The girl reached forward to take the bag but Thompson held it up and out of her grasp, his yellowed teeth shining in the poor light. "Ain't you forgettin' yourself?" he asked. "A man likes to be thanked, don't you know?"

She glanced down and gave a sigh of resignation before turning her attention back to the seaman. Bending forward, she kissed him, firm and long, upon the lips and, if she minded the hand that felt its way beneath her shift, there was no indication.

When he had finished, both bag and bottle were passed across and she fell upon the food. Thompson watched while she ate, grinning with pride and occasionally nodding in encouragement.

"Are you warm enough here?" he asked. The girl grunted, her mouth too full to reply. "'Cause I can get you a blanket else," Thompson added, with the air of a generous benefactor.

"I ain't cold, but don't like the rats," she told him at last, before laying into the chunk of salted beef once more.

"Can't do much about that," he told her, philosophically: being so close to the bilges, rats were inevitable. "But if you keeps out of their way, they shouldn't bother you unduly."

"They run over my legs in the night," she said, before biting again.

"Then I'll get you that blanket," he promised. Such a task would be relatively easy, certainly more so than providing any further clothing for his treasure.

"I got to go now," he told her when she had finished. "But will come back afore the afternoon watch tomorrow." The girl's eyes shone in light from the glim, but her face was void of expression.

"How long will I have to stay here?" she asked.

Thompson shrugged. "That's hard to say. Ship's due to sail in just o'er a week; if anyone finds you before, you'll be put straight ashore, and no mistakin'."

She seemed to understand.

"But once we are underway, things will be different," he assured her. "You can come on deck, and dress proper. Meet the captain and behave like a real lady."

"You said you was the captain," she objected, although her words lacked conviction.

"I said I was acquainted with him," he corrected, pulling himself up to his full height. "We have spoken twice, and shaken hands."

"But we are going to Portugal?"

"Oh yes, we're going to the Tagus," the words were clear but Thompson closed his eyes as he spoke them. "We'll be in and out like a fiddler's elbow: can't avoid it on our present run. And you shall be put ashore there, if that's still what you wants – though maybe I can visit when we calls in the future?"

6

She nodded silently in the dim light.

"Very well then." He rose to go.

"Won't you leave the light?" She was now staring at the flickering flame that had already started to smoke. He shook his head.

"Can't do that; it would give you away eventually," he said, smiling conspiratorially. "And we don't want that now, do we?"

* * *

The following morning, Lieutenant King entered the magnificent wardroom of HMS *Prometheus* to find it filled with bustle, noise and the scent of breakfast. It was, he supposed, one of the advantages of serving aboard a two decker: in *Scylla*, his last posting, the space allocated for senior officers – perversely called a gun room – had been smaller, and with a low deckhead that was always catching him out. And in addition to being cramped, the place was dark and stuffy, lacking the generous stern windows *Prometheus* provided. A fifth rate frigate also carried less than half the number of cooks and stewards a seventy-four boasted, yet there were no more than five additional mouths to feed. It was just a pity the increase in personnel had not added greatly to the quality of food provided: actually it was the very reverse.

Prometheus was on petty warrant victuals at present, getting most of her daily provisions fresh from Brixham, and it was surely reasonable to think little could be done to spoil such excellent fare. The current wardroom staff managed it, however. From what King could gather, the warranted cook that was supposed to provide for both wardroom and great cabin had simply disappeared during a trip ashore. And without an experienced hand at the helm, the eclectic assortment of stewards and pantry-men spent far too long in argument and confusion. Made meals were either served cold or burnt to a frazzle, fresh milk seemed to turn in the course of a day, and there had been several truly monumental disasters, such as their commissioning dinner, when the roasted goose presented for Caulfield to carve was found to be red-raw and bleeding. Efforts were being made to secure a trained man, and King supposed their present staff would improve in time but, until they did, he remained cautious about what was ordered.

He seated himself in his usual place at the long table and gestured briefly to the steward who offered him his customary boiled eggs, a meal that King judged to be the safest form of cooked breakfast. He had been on duty since first light and was in need of both food and drink even though the headache that usually accompanied his early morning routine was thankfully absent.

"I've a letter from Adam Fraiser on St. Helena, Tom." Michael Caulfield's voice broke into King's thoughts. He spoke conversationally from the head of the table; a position that confirmed his place as both first lieutenant and president of the wardroom mess. King looked towards him cautiously; Caulfield's words had certainly sparked his interest, but the younger officer hid a guilty secret. Several mysterious dark marks had appeared on the half deck overnight. No one could tell what they were, or who had made them, but no amount of holystoning or spirit of turpentine would encourage their departure. It was only a question of time before the first lieutenant was made aware, and King doubted Caulfield would be quite so affable then.

"Adam Fraiser?" he asked lightly, while reaching for the bread basket and helping himself to one of the fresh, shore-baked rolls that the wardroom stewards had yet to find a way to ruin. "Is he well?"

"Well enough," Caulfield grunted. "Though his wound still pains him and he seems to have crossed the hawse of some superior vicar in Jamestown. Here, you may see if you wish."

Caulfield tossed the folded paper along the long pine table. It landed in front of King who collected it and opened the single page so he could read whilst eating. Fraiser had been the sailing master in two ships he and Caulfield had served aboard. A dour Scot who knew and understood the way of seas and oceans only marginally better than he did the hand that created them, Fraiser had lost a leg in action, and opted to retire to St Helena during their last commission. King's eyes ran over the neat, clear writing while he reached for the pewter teapot, filling his cup, then sweetening with sugar almost unconsciously. There had been a time when the old

8

man had been closer to him than his father, yet as King read the crisp and detailed descriptions of life on the remote outpost it was with scant consideration. Fraiser had been left in the care of Julia Booker, a girl King had known during their stay, though not quite as well as he would have liked. But there was no message from her, or even a specific mention and, as the three letters King had himself sent remained unanswered, he was forced to concede that his hopes for a future together should really be forgotten.

The eggs arrived. King switched his attention from Fraiser's note to tackle one with a spoon and, if he tapped the shell more firmly than the task warranted, it had nothing to do with his thoughts. Julia was a wonderful woman, and he had honestly believed they could have been happy together: it was surely a pity she did not agree. But the cure for regret was readily available, and, despite the hour and his unusually clear head, King had the sudden urge to forgo his tea and call for something stronger.

Several of the officers present were new arrivals and would hardly turn a hair were King to call for a rummer of gin. He looked about for a steward then noticed Donaldson, the bloated and ruddy captain of marines who was already halfway through a bottle of hock, his usual accompaniment to a bloody breakfast pork chop. In a hard drinking age, the wine was by no means extraordinary: Donaldson would finish that bottle as well as another of claret and be tapping the brandy long before supper. But one look at the marine's heavy, reddened jowls as they slurped at the smudged glass was enough to quell all desire, and King reached for his cup of sweetened, milk-less tea instead.

"Fraiser seems to have settled well enough," Caulfield boomed from the end of the table. King forced himself to concentrate on his words before more thoughts of Julia could lead him further astray.

"Indeed," he agreed, then, struggling for something to say, added: "Though it is to be expected; the island is a beautiful place, and he is in good care."

"Care that is every bit as beautiful as good," Caulfield agreed, catching King's train of thought in a manner the younger man had not intended. "I fancy there are worse ways and poorer company in which to see out a life than in the charge of the enchanting Miss Booker."

King glanced sidelong at the first lieutenant who, despite their difference in status, was also a friend. At the time he had harboured suspicions that Caulfield was equally struck by Julia, yet now the man could speak easily and without a hint of regret. He turned his attention back to the eggs. It was strange how easily other people survived deep emotion, while he took even the most trivial of matters to heart, dwelling on them until they became totally out of proportion. Strange and more than a little annoying: he was quite certain such a defect in character, and he could view it in no other way, made life that much harder to live.

King finished the first of the eggs, which had been hard boiled, and found the second, a brown, to be hardly cooked and barely edible. He wondered for a moment how whoever was in charge of cooking the things could be so inept in their duties and almost made to complain, when the memory of those stains came back to haunt him. King was well aware that he was hardly the epitome of efficiency at that moment, and with *Prometheus* still in the early days of her commission, there was much slightly amiss. Perhaps the correct boiling of eggs might not be so very important.

Movement ahead caught his attention and he looked up to see Davison, the second lieutenant, seat himself opposite. The two exchanged the briefest of good mornings. They had only been living in close proximity a matter of days, yet already it was clear they would never become friends.

"Brought us a fresh hand, did you not?" Davison asked, with more than a hint of condescension as he reached for the teapot. "And an experienced man, by all accounts – how did you chance upon such a prize?" The habitually smug expression grew suddenly wicked as he added: "Been frequenting the nanny houses, have you?" in a softer tone.

King did not elaborate. Davison was actually ten months younger, but had sat his board and obtained appointment as a lieutenant a whole year ahead of him. Consequently the bright, assured and annoyingly handsome cull was rated second lieutenant to his third, despite the fact that King had served with both Captain

Banks and the first lieutenant throughout several previous commissions.

"Would that be an able seaman?" Caulfield asked, overhearing.

"Indeed, sir," Davison confirmed in a louder voice. "Fellow by the name of Ross: he has been allocated to my division. I've yet to speak with the boatswain but fancy we might rate him able."

"Excellent," Caulfield mumbled through a mouth now filled with soft tack.

"Of course we have yet to see how he performs," Davison continued. "But I'd chance we may have landed ourselves a regular fo'c'sle man, and the Dear knows we've few enough to speak of."

King wriggled uncomfortably in his seat. The volunteer from the previous evening had asked for his history to be kept secret and, in his slightly fuddled state, King had agreed. But now, in the company of fellow officers, he wondered if it had been the right decision.

There were a number of reasons why a man might be broken at court martial: by their very nature, such tribunals varied greatly. And often those assembled on foreign stations were made up from a small selection of available officers, many of whom may have known the defendant well. Such knowledge meant they could be lenient and indulging, or the exact opposite, and the mere fact that Ross had been treated harshly did not automatically imply guilt. He might simply have found himself in the wrong place at the wrong time, or become the victim of a senior officer's spite. But once stripped of his rank and having little understanding of life ashore, even an experienced man may be left with no alternative other than to ship as an ordinary hand.

Then again, Ross might equally turn out to be a bad apple: someone keen to fill a seaman's mind with twisted truths and resentment. Since the Quota Act of '95, and the vast number of educated criminals consequently sent to serve afloat, the general level of understanding had risen considerably forward of the mast. An average seaman was now not quite so gullible or naïve, while the lower deck remained just as notorious as a place where rumour and tattle-tale could multiply faster than any bed bug. To introduce

Ross, who was both bright and potentially brim filled with resentment, into such a fertile environment might prove other than the bonus it appeared.

But on reflection, King thought not; there had been something about the man that struck him at the time, and did so again even as he considered the subject. Broken he might have been, but Ross retained an air of competence and respectability that would have been drummed into him throughout his progress from cockpit to wardroom. Every officer lives with the eternal fear of mutiny and, however low he may have fallen or unjust his treatment, King sensed that Ross was not one to cause trouble.

"Did you say his name was Ross?" Donaldson broke in from the other side of the table. "Knew a Ross when I were stationed in India." King's body went cold, but he looked across with an expression of apparent interest. The red faced marine was well into his fifties: old to be no more than a captain, and at sea. But despite the rheumy eyes and a constant need for alcohol, Donaldson had travelled extensively. For all King knew, he might well be acquainted with Ross, in which case the little charade was to be guessed relatively early in play.

"Factor in Bombay," the older man continued, before reaching for his glass once more. "Though he also kept the finest set of polo ponies east of the Hooghly."

"A trained hand is welcome, Tom." Caulfield said, ignoring the marine. "Would that you could find us more; we still need three score at least if *Prometheus* is to sail with any confidence in ten days' time."

"I was speakin' with Cook of the *Tonnant.*" It was the slightly hesitant voice of Lewis, a former master's mate who had recently passed his board and was their fifth lieutenant. King had served with Lewis in three previous ships, the first being an antiquated sixty-four, where Lewis was rated an ordinary hand. King was the first to notice his potential and had taken quiet satisfaction in watching the man's progress ever since. "He says they're still a hundred short," Lewis continued. "And in danger of groundin' on their own beef bones."

The remark drew sympathetic mutterings from all at the table.

12

Tonnant, a fine, eighty-gun ship – Toulon built from Adriatic oak – had been captured during Nelson's action at Aboukir Bay some years ago, and now boasted Edward Pellew as her captain. He was a man almost universally respected and even loved by his men, yet his ship lay at anchor not five cables from *Prometheus,* and with about as much chance of putting to sea as a Cheapside punt. Britain might only have been at war a matter of weeks, but all present understood the damage that had been done months, and possibly years before.

"It would have been better were the Navy maintained to the same degree as the army," Caulfield spoke quietly but to a series of knowing grunts from those at the table. During the uneasy peace, most of Britain's fighting sail had been stood down. Working ships with seasoned crews were paid off, freeing their people to take more lucrative berths in traders and East Indiamen. Consequently, when conflict resumed and warships became needed again, precious few were available to man them. In March, a hot press had scooped up every available Jack, be they willing or otherwise, along with any landsman who gave the slightest indication of being trainable. The short term effect had been sound enough; ships so recently laid up in ordinary were able to sail in record time, and the seas Britain relied upon for both trade and protection were soon within her control once more. But barely three months later there were few seamen of any type to be found, save those already on the other side of the world and aboard merchants. Industries, such as fishing and coastal transport had almost ceased to exist, while any returning John Company fleet was set upon by the pressing tenders, seizing men who had been asea for years and turning them over to serve in the Royal Navy. All would settle in time but foresight, and a less parsimonious government, would have kept more warships in service and avoided such confusion.

"We should have news of Benson afore long," King said, breaking the silence that was a rare commodity during wardroom mealtimes. Benson, the fourth lieutenant, had taken a party of trusted hands inland on a mission that fell somewhere between a recruiting drive and kidnapping, and was due back with his haul the following day.

"Aye, with luck he could bring us a dozen or so," the first lieutenant agreed. "But they are likely to be weavers or other poor wretches made seedy by the factories. Trained hands is what we need; more like that Tom brought us last night."

The murmur of agreement spread about the table, and King's eyes fell. Caulfield's words had embarrassed him in a strange way. However sure he might feel of Ross, the man had yet to prove himself, and he only hoped the first lieutenant's confidence was well placed.

* * *

When a ship is at anchor, lieutenants do not take charge of a watch; that responsibility passes to senior warrant officers. And so it was that Gabriel Cartwright, master's mate and a man with over thirty years' sea-going experience, had been left in control of one of his Majesty's line-of-battleships while her people were at breakfast. Such a duty was probably the closest Cartwright would ever come to command although he was not altogether sorry. Since joining his first ship as a third class volunteer, he considered he had done all right for himself. From being the lowest of the low – what some of the cruder members of the lower deck referred to as a powder monkey – he had risen to senior warrant rank and, in truth, was only one step away from being a commissioned officer. But sitting a board had never been one of Gabriel Cartwright's ambitions. There would be too much book learning: as it was, he struggled with many aspects of navigation. And the prospect of compiling journals, keeping the necessary logs, and conforming to officer etiquette filled him with disgust as much as trepidation. Even if he were fortunate enough to fool a bunch of post captains into granting him a commission, then trick another into taking him aboard his ship, there would be far too much responsibility for his liking. And it would come with little in the way of recompense.

Cartwright earned over three pounds a lunar month, which was less than half that paid to a lieutenant. But much of the difference would be eaten up with expensive mess bills, and Cartwright could live quite simply in the cockpit. And, as the

14

senior master's mate, he was also in charge of the midshipmen, which gave him more than enough power and prestige, should he crave such a thing. Besides, sea-going berths for lieutenants were relatively rare, whereas an experienced warrant officer was always in demand. If he kept his current rank he would be likely to find employment for the rest of his life. He was quite content with his station, and reasonably happy to die in it, although perhaps not in the very near future.

But even with such a lack of ambition, it was still good to walk along what Cartwright told himself was the weather side of the quarterdeck – the breeze being too light and fickle to be certain. To stand at the break, hands stiffly clasped behind his back, and look down on the deck beneath. To consider those ship's boats not in use, which were stacked neatly on skids before him, then raise his eyes slowly, taking in all of the mighty foremast that, even with topmasts set down, towered way above until it quite hurt his neck to look. And to assure himself that, in theory at least, the third rate line-of-battleship on which he stood, her and every one of the mighty cannon she carried, was currently under his sole command.

The hail from the forecastle lookout rudely interrupted Cartwright's private fancies. A shore boat was heading for them and the 'Aye Aye' bellowed in response told him there would be an officer aboard. Cartwright glanced down to the larboard entry port where all but the most senior would be expected to enter. He was still not unduly worried. The likelihood was his visitor simply carried a message from the port admiral, or maybe it was one of the dockyard supervisors with ideas above his station. But even if the boat contained the Admiral of the Fleet travelling incognito, Cartwright would not be unduly moved. It was one of the benefits of his rank; in difficult situations there was likely to be someone more experienced to take control, and they were usually no more than a summons away.

But it might not be a bad idea to meet whoever was coming, he decided, as the boat hooked on to *Prometheus'* mainchains. Cartwright eased himself down the quarterdeck ladder; he was by no means stiff, old or rheumatic, but of late had not been inclined to rush some things that had been more easy when a lad. Mr Midshipman Steven, one of the young gentlemen under Cartwright's care, was already at the entry port and talking to an unknown midshipman who had presumably been one of the occupants of the boat. The two lads stiffened slightly and shed their boyish grins as Cartwright approached.

"Mr Dickson here is from the receiving ship, Mr Cartwright," Steven said. "They've hands for us."

"Not so many, I fear," the second midshipman added. "*Prometheus* has only been allotted three, but all are seamen, mind."

"Three ain't going to do us much good," Cartwright grumbled, although it was clear that any ill feeling was not directed at the boy.

"They took a bundle out of a transport with a homebound convoy," the visitor told him. "And from the same ship, so Mr Robson said we should divide them 'twixt every vessel at anchor."

"Otherwise they'd have all gone to *Tonnant* I suppose." Cartwright snorted, glancing across to where their more illustrious neighbour lay a few cables off.

"She's even worse off for hands," the lad agreed. "But Mr Robson said this weren't a happy bunch, and wanted them split as much as possible."

"Very well," Cartwright sighed. "Send 'em up an' let's take a look."

When they did, the three seamen did not appear so very remarkable. All were well dressed, clean, and appeared healthy; one even carried a ditty bag and, to look at them, few would have guessed they were being brought aboard *Prometheus* against their will.

"Welcome, lads." Cartwright was well aware that little would be gained from antagonising pressed men further. "We're glad to have you aboard, and sorry for the necessity."

On closer inspection it was clear that two of the newcomers had faces like thunder, although they regarded the master's mate in apparent acceptance, but the third was still too angry to make eye contact. Cartwright ignored them, and took the proffered paper from the regulating midshipman. He signed against the three names and handed the receipt back. The new hands would come round – he knew that from many years' experience. And every man present was equally aware it was not down to Cartwright that they had been dragged from a cushy berth to serve in a man-o'-war. Or that such a diabolical act had occurred just when England had hove into sight, and their wages were almost in their pockets.

"Very good, Mr Dickson," Cartwright muttered in the manner in which he had been addressing young midshipmen for what seemed like an eternity. "We shall take them from here. Thank you for your efforts, and kindly remember us again in the future."

The lad touched his hat, flashed a grin at Steven, then disappeared backwards through the entry port, leaving the warrant officers looking at their new recruits.

"We're for the Channel Fleet," Cartwright told them, not unkindly. "So there'll be a better chance of a home port than aboard most ships. And the captain's a good officer who has taken more than his share of prize money in the past."

The news had little impact. It was common knowledge that a home port did not necessarily mean shore leave, rather the opposite: such a privilege being far more likely to be granted where there was less chance of desertion.

"What say we gets you below and you can meet up with the pusser?" Cartwright continued lightly, his gaze inevitably shifting to the third, who was still glaring at the distant horizon. "Then we'll settle you in a mess and sort out any kit you may be a-missing."

The first two seemed compliant enough. Most seamen would be pressed at least once in their careers and considered it a pitfall of their chosen path: an occupational hazard, to be offset by prize money and the certainty of enough drink to see them partially anaesthetised for at least some of the day. But the third had still to accept his fate, and Cartwright knew he would give trouble even before the man made his move.

When it came it was sudden, but lacked ingenuity. An abrupt lunge for the larboard bulwark and, with the agility of his type, the newcomer was over the side and had apparently disappeared before they knew it. Cartwright exchanged glances with Steven as a loud splash marked the man's landing, and the two officers strolled laconically across to peer over the top rail.

"Belay that," Cartwright grunted to the marine posted at the main channel. The sentry, who had been quick to raise his musket at the prospect of enlivening a dreary watch, lowered the weapon reluctantly and gave an audible sigh. "But you can keep an eye on those two," the warrant officer added, pointing over his shoulder with his thumb.

The man in the water had recovered himself to some extent and, in the main, was staying near the surface. But like the vast majority of seamen, he was plainly unable to swim, and Cartwright supposed it a measure of his desperation that such a means of escape was even considered. The boat that had delivered him still lay close by, and the young midshipman directed it over to the now struggling fugitive. In no time the sodden body had been dragged, dripping yet still objecting, into the sternsheets.

"Are we going to try again?" Cartwright asked when the man had been sent up the entry port steps for the second time and stood on the main deck once more. "You can do that as often as you wish, but we'll always get you back. And there'll be some not quite so lenient as me."

The seaman seemed to accept Cartwright's logic and finally met his gaze. The two considered each other for a second or so, then the warrant officer tipped his head towards where the remaining two recruits were standing.

"Get yourselves below, and we'll say no more about it." he said. Cartwright was fortunate in always choosing his berth, but he had been around pressed men long enough to appreciate something of their despair. And scant good would be served if the newcomer was called up on a charge – some might say a sound flogging would deter others, but if a man unable to swim was prepared to try and make it half way across the harbour, there was surely little that would truly discourage him.

"Get that mess swabbed up," the master's mate told a nearby hand when the men were gone. A sizeable puddle of seawater had been left as a reminder of the incident: the sun was sure to burn it off in no time, but Cartwright would prefer to avoid any need for explanations. He knew he had bent the rules in not reporting the attempted escape, but felt there was reason enough behind the action. And, as he had been in nominal command of the ship at the time, the decision had surely been his to make.

Chapter Two

"Starboard watch be ready," Simmonds, the boatswain's mate, warned the deck in general as mess tables were cleared of all traces of breakfast, and men prepared themselves for labour. The short and slightly stout petty officer watched them for a moment, then sauntered over to the nearest group and sought out Flint, the seaman who led them. "Chips says your lot may as well continue where you left off yes'day."

"Right oh, Mr Simmonds." Flint turned to Ross, the new man in his mess. He appeared to be a regular seaman, but there was something fragile and strangely vulnerable about him, and Flint had already decided he needed careful watching. "We been on caulkin' duty the last three days," he told him. "So don't wear anythin' you was akeepin' for Sunday."

Ross had only been on the lower deck a matter of hours and was still getting used to the dramatic change in conditions. Sleeping in a hammock slung in tiers between other men had been a very different prospect from his former accommodation, while merely being aboard a king's ship again, yet excluded from the quarterdeck and command, made his fall from grace that much more apparent. But he was grateful for the information, and pulled his second pair of trousers from the ditty bag.

"Bit of luck we'll see it finished this watch," Jameson, who was one of the younger members of the mess, muttered to no one in particular.

"Aye, but there's plenty more for you after that," the boatswain's mate commented loudly. "We're about as ready for the sea as my wife's mother – though I might be wrong in that, as they do say witches float."

There was a ripple of appreciative laughter from the mess, and they formed up all the more readily for work. Ross had already noticed Simmonds. He might be a petty officer, but the man remained very much one of the hands and understood them as well as he did their humour. In his former life Ross had known such

20

men existed: indeed he had fully appreciated their importance to the efficiency and well being of a crew. But this was the first time he had seen one in action, and from the lower deck's perspective. Even from such a brief example he could tell that the boatswain's mate was solid, and maintained good discipline. And it would be delivered with the tact and understanding that no commissioned officer could hope to emulate from their exalted position.

This was just one of several similar revelations: in the last few hours Ross had learned far more about the average seaman than he had in nearly fifteen years at sea. Such insight would have been precious until only a few months ago but now, with no chance of his ever walking a quarterdeck again, it was of dubious value. And, considering the amount he had to learn about his new life, pretty much a waste of time.

In fact, the faster he stopped thinking and acting like an officer the better. One thing he had always known about the lower deck was their ability to detect forgeries. The majority of everyday scoundrels would be tolerated, but thieves, cheats and liars drew very short shrift. Should it be discovered that he was once a lieutenant, in itself a heinous crime, and had attempted to cover the fact up, banishment to the ignominy of a pariah mess was the very least he might expect. Consequently the sooner he could get his new status accepted by the other men, the better.

"I'd thought you a topman," he said to Jameson, in an effort to strike up conversation. "Why then the caulking detail?"

"Just lucky, I'd chance," the young man replied with an ironic smirk. "The barky needs more work below than aloft, so I don't gets the option."

Ross felt a little easier for the exchange, even if Jameson's answer was slightly worrying. *Prometheus* must be far shorter of hands than he had first thought. That, combined with the number of small jobs and adjustments needed; tasks that should not have been necessary after the ship had been in dockyard hands, must be causing her lieutenants countless worries. He consoled himself with the thought that this was the first time since his court martial when he was actually glad not to be a lieutenant, and that such problems were now someone else's to solve.

"Aye, we've more than enough to do, and no time to do it in," Flint agreed laconically.

"Just what degree of re-fit has she seen?" Ross asked mildly.

He was changing his trousers; the white ducks bought from a Brixham pawnbroker and worn the previous night were of no great quality but remained his best. They were still slightly damp from that morning's holystoning, but would be completely ruined were he to wear them whilst working with hot pitch.

"How do you mean?" Jameson asked sharply, and Ross brought his mind back to the real world.

"Well, aren't there various forms?" He began hesitantly, conscious that the rest of the mess had quietened to hear his reply. "A minor repair would only see the ship docked a few months, whereas a full refit can be several years' work."

One of the others that Ross had barely met was treating him to a quizzical look. "And you want to know what the dockyard has done to her?"

"Aye," another agreed, fixing Ross with his stare. "Why would you be asking that, I wonder?"

A cold thrill ran down the new man's spine as he realised his question had overstepped the mark. Even when an officer, Ross had known that few seamen thought beyond their immediate world. He hurried to make amends. "No reason," he said. "Other than she's fresh from dry, yet we seem to have a deal to do in putting her straight."

"But those dockyard mateys never were up to much," Flint said soothingly, and the tension eased. "And since Old Jarvie started messin' with them, they gone a whole lot deeper."

"Aye, bent as a fiddler's arm, they were," another seaman added. "But at least you knew where you was with them. Now they still robs you blind but no one can tell how or where."

The last man to speak was a round faced cheerful sort with remarkably few teeth: Ross remembered him from the previous night, but could not recall his name. He knew the words to be true, though; it was hardly two years since he himself had been supervising *Wakeful*'s commissioning. And he didn't need any reminding of the corrupt ways of those in power.

"Well that's as maybe, but you still got a foredeck to caulk," the boatswain's mate interrupted. "And the sooner you're up on deck, the sooner you'll finish. There's rain expected later, and we don't want to get all wet now, do we?"

* * *

The picture was an incredibly good likeness. It had been sketched by the rector's wife in crayon but, although smartly framed and with a generous border, was still almost too small to display. It also showed his son in baby clothes, whereas John was almost a lad now, and would soon be in britches. But as Sir Richard Banks walked about the great cabin, so much larger and more comfortable than the captain's quarters in a frigate, he quickly found the ideal place. It was by the transom knee, where it would hang well enough next to the slightly more professional portrait of Sarah, his wife. He held the sketch up and nodded to himself noting, with approval, that there was even space for further pictures should it be required.

He placed the sketch back on the already cluttered table, and peered once more into the wooden packing case. It was one of many his wife had sent down from their Hampshire home and seemed to contain mainly personal effects. Some he was familiar with, and had already accompanied him to sea for many years: others were purchased by Sarah at his request, with the remainder being small gifts apparently included on her initiative.

He picked out his old velvet housewife, bought when he was first commissioned as a lieutenant, and laid it to one side. In it would be his tortoiseshell comb, various brushes, scissors and a somewhat bent tooth pick. Next there was a brightly polished wooden box, which must be the new razor he had requested. He opened the lid and glanced inside; there were actually seven matched blades, one for every day of the week, and each set in identical carved bone handles. They were smart, and obviously of a very high quality, but a box of razors was an unnecessary extravagance as both he, and his body servant, were perfectly capable of maintaining an edge.

Glancing into the crate again, he scowled slightly, before bringing out a succession of small bottles. Most were hair oil, scent or other such potions and clearly Sarah's attempt at seeing he was well cared for. Banks placed them in a neat line: he had never used perfume or powder and, even though he was now a senior captain, had no intention of starting.

At the bottom of the case was a collection of books; he picked up several and skimmed the titles before dropping them back. Novels and poetry: whatever had she been thinking of? Sarah had sailed with him in the past and really should know that diversions or amusement of any kind had no place in the life of a fighting officer.

Then Banks remembered he had been resting for over a year, and possibly his wife now saw a different side to him. It had been his first extended time ashore both as a husband and, latterly, a father. But while he was relearning social skills at the dining table, and discovering the joys of parenthood, his new command had been in the hands of an Admiralty dockyard. In consequence he now felt rusty and ill-prepared for the task ahead, whereas the tool he was to use had, in theory at least, been cleaned, honed and sharpened to perfection.

HMS *Prometheus* was by no means freshly built but, at over sixteen hundred tons, she was undoubtedly large and, when Banks had first paced about her lower decks in the company of his first lieutenant, he had wondered quite what they were taking on. Laid down almost thirty years ago, the battleship's timbers were massive, compared with those of the fifth rate frigate he had last commanded, while her main armament – two full decks of eighteen and thirty-two pound long guns, with additional carronades to forecastle and quarterdeck – was more than sufficient to claim her place in the line-of-battle. It had been like inspecting a cathedral, when he was used to country chapels, and Banks had been suitably humbled.

But despite her time in dockyard hands, there was still an inherent smell of rot in the bilges and both men were quick to notice many small jobs that should have been attended to, but instead had been botched or simply ignored. From speaking with other captains, Banks already knew this to be common: Lord St Vincent's recent reformations might have been intended to eliminate corruption in his Majesty's dockyards, but their performance had undoubtedly been weakened in the process and it was universally agreed that both the standard of repair, as well as materials used, were far inferior.

Banks wondered, not for the first time, if he had made the right choice in accepting the line-of-battleship. His recent exploits had earned him a deal of credit with the Admiralty; if he had chosen to stand by *Scylla*, his old frigate, he might well be in the middle of an independent assignment by now; maybe even a cruise. Britain's declaration of war had taken Bonaparte by surprise coming, as it had, at a time when almost the entire French merchant fleet was at sea. There would have been fortunes to be made for those in the right place, and he had undoubtedly missed out on his share. But Banks was not a greedy man and had already done well with regards to prize money. Ignoring earlier accomplishments, his recent reward for taking one French fifth-rate, sinking two corvettes, and recapturing a Company packet in the South Atlantic had been substantial, and would keep his family comfortably for many years to come. Besides, he had wanted a ship-of-the-line; perhaps it was age, or maybe even marriage and parenthood, but the cut and dash of a frigate no longer appealed and he preferred the sheer might his present command gave him.

He looked about as he thought. The captain's accommodation in *Prometheus* was truly sumptuous, with a fine spread of stern windows, a separate sleeping area, and quarter galleries the size of many officers' cabins. His servants, who were numerous, had access to a pantry that would shame most domestic kitchens, while the long dining table that was more or less permanently set up in the great cabin, could seat twelve in comfort and still allow room for other furniture as well as waiting personnel. The spell on land with all that it entailed had made Banks appreciate such luxury and there was no doubt he had also grown portly, both in mind and body. The slight belly that was a new acquisition would doubtless reduce with active service, but attitudes and expectations were a different matter.

He knew he was no longer a frigate captain; those days had long passed. Smaller ships were for young men; they might be more likely to see action, but little can truly be achieved by capturing a merchant or sinking a privateer. The proper role of a frigate remained to bring fleets of warhorses such as *Prometheus* into contact with those of the enemy: it was such encounters which made a difference and truly decided the outcome of a war.

However, much of his time was likely to be spent on blockade, while enemy shipping, though possibly in sight, would remain tantalisingly out of reach and protected by fire from shore batteries, should he steer too close. And with a dangerous coast ever present – ever ready to trap him and his ship with treacherous shoals or an uncharted rock, it would be no holiday. Blockade duty was also slow and monotonous, taking its toll on both fabric and men; a constant crossing of the same tightrope might become commonplace in time but the inherent danger remained and, as he returned the perfumes and lotions to join the books in their crate, Banks knew he would have no energy to waste on such nonsense.

He turned from the box, picked up the picture of John once more, then replaced it rather guiltily on the table as his body servant entered the great cabin.

"There are some more personal things here, David," he told him. "See to them, will you? Most can go in the quarter gallery or my sleeping cabin; the books I am not so certain of."

"Those bookcases we have are already filled, sir," the young man told him seriously. "But I can ask Chips to make up some more; maybe they could go in the coach?"

"Do that, will you, but don't give it importance, I am certain Mr Roberts is busy enough with the ship working up." Indeed the carpenter and his team, which represented one of the larger departments in a third rate, would be fully employed for some time to come and Banks had no intention of diverting him merely for the storage of books that would never be read. He indicated the picture of John with elaborate casualness. "But if he could send a hand to fix this next to the portrait of Lady Banks, I should be obliged. There is no urgency, however."

"I can rig that for you, sir," David told him cheerfully, picking up the picture and smiling with genuine affection at the boy's image. "Won't take no time at all."

"Thank you, I would appreciate that," Banks muttered, grateful, yet again, to have an efficient man at his side. David was a former slave, freed on his voyage to St. Helena roughly two years ago. Since then he had proved a loyal steward, both on the journey back, and in the house Banks and Sarah had taken near Southsea. In all that time David had never undertaken anything beyond him, and the more Banks grew to know the man, the more he was impressed by his many skills.

"Have the rest of the cabin stores been taken aboard?" he asked, and the servant gave one of his customary full grins.

"Oh yes, sir, though we have more than expected. Her ladyship has added items not requested, and we have a deal too much of everythin' else. There is coffee, preserves and dried fruit to supply much of the ship and I've had to store some wine in your sleeping quarters, as the sailing master says the spirit room is expected to be filled by the time we sail."

It was so like Sarah to be doubly sure he was well provided for. His personal livestock had yet to be delivered and Banks dared not guess what she had ordered there, or where it would be put.

"I am sure you will cope, and do, of course, use any space you require."

"Very good, sir; I shall see to it."

As soon as he was alone, Banks slumped down on the easy chair that was another unrequested addition from Sarah, and wished all his problems might be confined to finding storeroom. Ignoring the work needed correcting her shoddy repairs, *Prometheus* was desperately short of men, and those she did carry seemed to be mainly landsmen or ordinary hands. All could be trained up, of course, but that would take time, and they were still seventy or so actual bodies short, with little likelihood of correcting the deficiency before they were to sail. Fortunately he had a good set of officers, with many known to him through two previous ships, while those sent to supplement what would be the largest wardroom he had ever commanded carried excellent references.

He relaxed against the upholstered back of the chair that was surely much too comfortable for shipboard use. Glancing at the deckhead, Banks noted the heavy timbers supporting the poop above. They seemed unnecessarily substantial for what was in effect a light platform, and one that did not even boast a single gun. The beams seemed to sum up *Prometheus* perfectly: she was as tough as they came, and might as easily have been hewn from granite as the solid, seasoned oak that actually made up her frame. Most single deckers could out-sail her on a bowline but, with the wind on the quarter and a pleasing sea, the old girl would still show a fair turn of speed. Once they had a full crew and had attended to her deficiencies, she should be able to stand up to anything the weather could produce, while the two decks of heavy cannon could deliver a punch capable of sinking whatever was foolish enough to chance too close.

He found himself smiling slightly at the thought and, poorly prepared, ill manned and untested as she was, realised he was already becoming attached to his new command. There would be discoveries to be made and doubtless disappointments to come but, even after so short a time, Banks felt confident in his line-of-battleship and knew she would never let him down. He simply hoped to be in a position to return the favour.

* * *

"If it's men you're a wanting, I know where some can be found." The woman's voice was low but clear, and Lewis, on his way below and with his mind somewhere else entirely, found himself stopping to consider her words. She must have come from one of the victualling hoys, and really should have stayed in the vessel – women visitors only being encouraged aboard H.M. ships as guests of officers, or when the wedding garland was raised. But Lewis knew from one look that she was of the kind well able to take care of herself. Short, thickset and dressed in an aged watchcoat, the woman stood solid on the half deck as if ready to resist any form of opposition. And her stare was bold and direct; with penetrating eyes that shone white in contrast to the grime on her face. There was a job to be done; she would do it, and no one was going to stop her.

"If you know of trained hands I should of course be interested," Lewis said, cautiously. "Perhaps you would wish to speak with our first lieutenant in the wardroom?"

"I'll stay where I am, if you don't mind, Captain," the woman replied. "If they sees me going below the talk will follow: I'm not proud of what I'm doing and could be held to account. But if we speaks here it might be about anything or nothing."

Lewis considered her further; indeed any person acting as a crimp – one paid to secure men for the Navy – was not likely to be popular. But there was something refreshingly defiant in the woman's manner, and he guessed that what she did was not for financial gain.

"There's folk in these parts what takes liberties and don't know where to stop," she continued, guessing further explanation was needed. "I don't mind free trade if that's what it truly is, but cannot cope with those what deals with the enemy."

Mention of the term struck a chord in Lewis' mind and now he thought he understood. Free trade was the euphemism usually attributed to smuggling. The woman's hoy was probably delivering the blankets they had been expecting; it was quite possible her business was being affected by the runners, although Lewis could not immediately see how.

"Alf says I shouldn't be speakin' so, but what's wrong is wrong and owlers is undoubtedly evil," she said with quiet feeling. "Takin' the wool I used to buy and sendin' it to the Frogs is bad enough. But when they brings back all manner of tawdry lace an' the like, we can't compete."

"Owling?" Lewis questioned. "Surely not from here?" Now he was fully aware of the risk the woman was taking. If she truly intended to crimp members of a smuggling gang, a good few might definitely disapprove and their objections would not be confined to verbal protests. But owling, the illegal exporting of wool and woollen goods, was more an east country crime.

"Oh they does it in the west, sure enough," she stated firmly. "It's not much of a hop to Guernsey, or even France if you times it right, and such goings on is taking all my supplies as well as messin' with what customers the factories 'as left us.''

All knew the smuggling trade was rampant, but this was a side effect that Lewis had never considered.

"An' it ain't endin' there," she continued. "Word is they're taking gold with them now an' all. English gold what they're sellin' to the French for a profit. An' with us expectin' to be invaded at any moment – there's something plainly not right.''

Yes, he could certainly sympathise there, but with bullion attracting premiums of up to thirty per cent, Lewis supposed there would always be those who would take a profit, even if it was their own country that suffered. But how that might gain more men for *Prometheus* was another matter entirely.

"There's a meeting this evening," she added, guessing his thoughts once more. "I can tell you where and when. You should net the whole mob, every man Jack of them. And Jacks they shall be," she added with what might have been a smile, "if that's what you're after.''

* * *

The girl, and she was hardly more than that, had not spoken and barely moved since Thompson's visit of the night before. The cramped and stale forepeak had been her home for all of three days although time meant little in such a private world. She had spent much of it sleeping like a cat, making up for the almost constant vigilance of the previous week. Occasionally bells were struck and unknown voices would bellow "All's well," from various locations in the ship. These bothered her little, even if the sentiment could not have been further from the truth.

It was probably a mistake to have gone with the seaman in the first place: she could see that now. But after such a time of fending for herself in the streets of Paignton, it had been good to find someone so strong and assured. Someone willing to take care of her, and with a boat bound for Portugal, or so he had said, when asked: that was a major point in his favour.

Lisbon was the closest thing to a home she knew, and the only place where things could be put right. People knew her there, good people who must at least understand the situation even if they did not approve of it. It was also somewhere she was confident of being fed and sheltered, certainly for as long as it took to catch up with James.

As soon as the bulk of a massive warship appeared from out of the darkness she had known herself duped. Thompson was no captain, that was obvious from the start, although she could imagine the sailor having a degree of authority in something smaller; perhaps a merchant, or even a privateer. But such a huge vessel as *Prometheus* was bound to be officered by gentlemen, and by no stretch of the imagination could Thompson be considered so. The fact that he lacked breeding had also worked in his favour in winning her confidence, though; all too recently she had been given more than enough cause to mistrust those of higher status.

And it had been midnight, on a small boat, in the middle of a crowded bay: there was little she could do but go along with his wishes. Besides, after sleeping in doorways and losing most of her possessions to the street thieves and cut-purses, her new home had not seemed so very terrible a place. It was at least private and offered far more in protection than she had been used to for a while.

At that moment two men could be heard walking by on the deck above and she automatically froze. One addressed an unheard remark that caused the other to laugh. Then, as their footsteps gradually faded, she found she could breathe once more.

There was a good deal of doubt in her mind as to what would happen were she discovered. Thompson, the man who had turned from friend to captor, might string yarns of having her up on deck and dining with the captain, but she wasn't as green as she was cabbage looking. Without doubt this was a ship of war, and everyone knew women were as welcome aboard such vessels as stones in a boot. But still she hoped to see Lisbon once more; he could not have been so very wrong about that. All the man had to do was get her off as easily as she had boarded, and everything would be well again.

A rat scuttled across the deck just beyond her feet. Despite what Thompson had been told, the things hardly bothered her now; she had become almost immune to them. Just so long as they kept away, they could be tolerated and even when she had awoken to find one nestling against her belly, it had not been so very shocking. In truth, she had gone through such a lot in the last few weeks that much which would normally have sent her into fits of hysterics was being endured in a way she would never have expected.

Her parents were both British but for many years had been nothing more than increasingly dim memories, and she knew no other world than the sun-backed town on the banks of the Tagus. She had been in full time service, so never ventured on the water, and it had taken quite a bit of persuading from Master James for her to even clamber aboard the stately and undoubtedly grand Indiaman.

The ship was one of many calling at the port on the way back from the East, and James had been especially clever to secure a cabin. It was small, dark and stuffy, but totally theirs to enjoy and seemed like heaven. Until then, her life had lacked ambition; she carried out her duties, even to the extent of enjoying some; especially those that involved food. Such work felt natural to her, and the extent of her dreams was that one day the change would come from serving girl to cook. But when she found herself courted by the youngest son of her employer, all foolish aspirations were forgotten.

And James had wooed her so well, and with such tenderness and respect: for the first time she felt herself truly of worth. They had barely more than kissed before boarding the ship and, with no time to explain or give notice, both of them were suddenly out in the middle of the ocean, her old world and its strange security left many miles behind.

It wasn't until they were safely underway that she began to realise quite how young James actually was – hardly older than her, in fact. But even that did not matter greatly: with him being so understanding and compassionate, she truly felt blessed. There had been no bells to answer, no chores to attend, while the tiny cabin became the closest thing to paradise either of them could have imagined. It was only a few days later, when the sea had started to turn wild, that things began to fall apart.

She had thought herself pregnant. To be absolutely accurate, even now she was not certain either way. But the constant sickness seemed so similar to symptoms a girl she had worked with complained of, she was soon convinced. James tried to reassure her with tales of an illness he called *mal-de-mer*, and told of how many succumbed to it. But, on the only occasion she had been tempted up to the fresh air on deck, none of the more seasoned passengers seemed in any way affected. That made her fate seem more certain still, and then James began to grow far less loving.

The Indiaman had finally come to rest in a nice little bay that looked just like the England she had been told of. By then the weather had started to improve, and her symptoms abated as she allowed herself to be put into another small boat and rowed ashore. And James had been nice again; handed over two golden guineas for her to buy the secret wedding dress, before arranging to meet that afternoon by the quay to continue their journey. They would be in London within a week and married soon afterwards; that had been the last thing he promised and even now, in circumstances that must surely contradict, a part of her continued to believe it.

But he had not been there and, with most of the money spent on white lace and linen, she soon realised herself abandoned. The wedding dress had been the first thing stolen: from then on her life just dissolved. She still had severe doubts about Thompson; he had altered her situation to some extent, but had yet to improve it, and at times was far less loving than even James at his worst. And much of what he said had already turned out to be lies but, if there was some truth in them being bound for Portugal, meeting with him might yet turn out for the good.

* * *

Flint's mess consisted of men of differing ages and experience. Ross soon decided that, although he was probably one of the older ones, and knew as much theory as any, he was the least well practised. He had served as a lieutenant for almost eight years and, until recently, his major concern had been the gradually decreasing chances of being made Commander. Now he was simply one of many lower deck hands and would never see further advancement. He might know more of navigation, writing up a log, or setting a watch, but in terms of pure seamanship, everyone else was streets ahead of him.

His mess had assembled at the foot of the main companionway as the bell began to strike and were half way to the upper deck before it finished.

"Fo'c'sle's the problem," Flint told him as they emerged into the full sun of a June morning. "Payed the seams over old oakum, they did, the robbers. Job looked fine, but started to weep as soon as we was in the basin."

"Downright liberty," Ross exclaimed, genuinely shocked.

The was a hint of laughter from one of the men behind and Flint gave Ross a sidelong glance. "Aye, that's as maybe," he agreed cautiously. "So now it's all got to be picked out an' begun again, just so they could move the barky on a day earlier."

Ross followed Flint along the main deck and up the forecastle ladder. Much had been cleared away; both chase cannon were missing, and there was a distinct lack of the down lines and halyards usually found in the area. But instead the deck was crowded with the paraphernalia of caulking. Oakum lay in roughly rubbed lines, and there was a positive pile of metal prickers, pullers and various sizes and types of caulking irons, together with waste tow, pitch kettles and mysterious brown glass bottles, sealed with metal stoppers. A brazier smouldered beneath a small cauldron and the air was already rich with the smell of hot pitch and spirits of turpentine.

To starboard, the strakes were scraped clean, with neat dark lines of fresh pitch dividing them, while those to larboard lay covered by a tarpaulin. As Ross watched, Jameson and another hand removed this to reveal the ragged and uneven edges of three un-caulked planks next to a bank of several that had been rather poorly sealed. Three of Flint's men immediately set to, teasing the tar and old oakum out of these, while another stoked up the brazier and two more started to heat the long handled metal loggerheads that would be needed to keep the fresh pitch warm.

"Have you a hand with a caulking iron?" Flint asked Ross. "If not, you could make yourself busy as a sweeper."

"I've not used an iron before, but have seen it done," Ross told him seriously. "And would be glad to try, if you give me leave."

"Good of you, I'm sure," Flint grinned, collecting a wooden mallet and handing it across. "And you may consider my leave granted."

Ross took the maul feeling mildly foolish; he really must modify his way of speaking or become a laughing stock for the entire mess. Kneeling down, the deck felt hard through the thin cloth of his trousers, but he was far too concerned with the job before him to worry about anything so mundane. He had seen caulking done a thousand times, and knew the procedure well, although this was his first opportunity to actually attempt it.

Filling the gaps between strakes with tightly packed hemp helped preserve the rigidity of the deck, and thus stiffened the ship itself, while a fresh coating of pitch would make all sound and watertight. He collected a long sausage of rubbed oakum from the pile, and laid it over a freshly cleared seam. Pickling up an iron, Ross tapped it gently with his mallet, watching as the twisted fibres were forced into the void. It was actually a simple and satisfying procedure, and soon he found himself making distinct progress along the line.

"Keep all tight and even," a voice told him from above, and Ross took this as encouragement – had he been making a total ham of it, Flint would never have just stood there commenting. For the first time in an age he actually began to enjoy himself, and there was even a modicum of satisfaction in the work; another thing that had been distinctly lacking in his new life until then. He finished the seam, and looked along it with critical satisfaction, before shuffling back to the next, giving those with the caulking kettles room to work.

"Nice effort, that," an anonymous comment came from the direction of the brazier. "Reckon that man was born to be a caulker."

Mildly encouraged, Ross addressed himself to the new seam.

It was tighter, and he decided would not need quite so much oakum, but still the amount he took was slightly too great. The residue spilled out, although Ross felt confident it could be pressed back in place, and collected the hammer. But his iron slipped on the excess fibres, and he struck his own hand painfully.

Ross said nothing, even forgoing to swear as he was not totally certain what oaths or profanities would be in keeping with his new status. But the voices from afar could be heard quite plainly.

"Did you see that?" one asked. "The cull struck his paw a nasty."

"Aye," another replied, with a distinct lack of sympathy. "Ask me, it were a downright liberty..."

Chapter Three

"Butler," the master at arms repeated thoughtfully as he indicated the space where he must sign. "Thought I recognised the phyz – we was aboard *Vanguard* together, 'less I'm much mistaken." The seaman, who was still slightly damp from his dip in the harbour, pulled a sour expression. Not much more than twenty four hours ago he had been on the books of a homebound transport, with no intention of ever serving in the Royal Navy again.

"An' I remember your face an' all, Mr Saunders." he said, with a slight emphasis on the title. "Thought to have seen the last of it though, as you did mine, I've no doubt. Never did get on, did we?"

The master at arms retained his customary set countenance, although the memories were coming back and they were not all bad. "Well that's as maybe, but there's no cause to open old wounds. It seems we're to be shipmates again," he said, checking the entry. "And might as well make the best of it."

Butler handed back the pen and went to move away. He supposed the Navy had caught him: he had made his mark on the muster, and there was very little to be done other than accept matters. But meeting with a former shipmate, even one as miserable as this particular Jimmy Leggs had encouraged him to some extent, and he turned back to the master at arms with a more contrite expression.

"Look, I know we've had our differences, and none of this is down to you, as such, but I've just come back from a trip to New 'olland, and ain't seen my home nor nothing."

"Is that right?" Saunders asked, his eyes ever cold.

"True as I'm standin' here," Butler assured him. "Pressing tender caught us off Berry Head, stripped the barky of her crew, and left a bunch of useless ticket men in their place. We ain't even docked, an' all I've got to show for two years' work is a Navy promise."

"That's sad," the master at arms assured him, although few could have guessed his true feelings.

Butler eyed the warrant officer cagily. He held out very little hope of his story being accepted, but even this one final try was worth the effort. "Last time I saw me wife she were with child," he continued. "It had been a straight passage out, so there weren't no mail waiting for us in Sydney, an' we never called back – the chit'll be walking b'now."

"That's probably the case," Saunders agreed sagely. "And likely with a brother or sister or two ta keep it company..."

Butler was now glaring with pure hatred.

"I'm not sayin' I don't feels for you," Saunders said, his tone softening slightly as he noticed the man's change of expression. "But you won't find many aboard who ain't got some form of sorry tale to tell. With any nous you'd have volunteered whilst aboard the tender. Every pressed man gets the chance, and there'd have been clink to send your woman. As it is, you're pressed, so won't see a glimpse of coin for six months or more. And no one says you 'as to like it."

* * *

Lieutenant Lewis glanced at the front door of the tavern with a mixture of apprehension and loathing, before ducking back behind the wall of straw once more. This was not his favourite duty; he had disliked being a member of a press gang when a regular hand and, after several years of advancement, found being forced to lead one no more pleasant. But now he had reached the dizzy heights of lieutenant, Lewis also understood the necessity.

Should *Prometheus* remain in her undermanned state she would not be able to sail: it could hardly be more simple. And the ramifications went deeper. For a captain to be revealed as unable to raise a crew would be a very public black mark against him, with the stigma being shared equally amongst the officers he commanded. Lewis, whose uniform was both new and unpaid for, would be lucky to find another seagoing berth. Half pay when not employed was a newly acquired luxury, but one that would not see him far, or free of his current level of debt.

So, unpleasant or not, the work had to be done and, if the

38

information obtained from the old woman was correct, at least they should come away with a good number of able men. And there might be added consolation in the knowledge that he was also solving another problem. If there really was a gang of smugglers meeting tonight, he would not only be claiming valuable bodies for the Navy, but also eradicating a few of the parasites that currently sapped the lifeblood from his country.

As a sea officer, Lewis would hardly be affected by a reduction in what the public liked to call free traders, while most who benefited from his actions might probably never know, or recognise the fact. But the old woman would. They had not spoken for more than five minutes, but Lewis hoped her business would survive. And, being of a genial nature, the concept of two birds being killed by one stone appealed, even if he were only to benefit directly from one.

He and his men had been watching the place for over an hour from the privacy of the livery stable across the lane. From their point of view, it appeared a normal country inn; one of three in the village and, being less than three miles from the sea all were strongly biased in favour of the sailing man. It was even likely that the landlord came from similar stock; many, if not most, lower deck hands harboured a desire to open just such an establishment if their luck turned. And it was not so far fetched a dream; with prize money a constant possibility, it might take little more than a single afternoon's work to acquire the necessary funds. Maybe just a minor action, or the luck to be on hand when an enemy convoy was taken. Or simply snaring a single rich merchant when theirs was the only ship in sight.

The seaman's share of any prize would be notoriously small, when compared with that paid to commissioned and flag officers, but these were desperate times, and of late more than a few enemy vessels had been caught carrying cargoes of unheard value. Even a tiny portion of such a capture could turn a tidy sum. Such riches might come at less than a couple of hours' notice and, however slow or bad the official pay, knowledge of the possibility was all that kept many foremast Jacks from utter despair.

Once the lucky man was so provided for and his premises

secured, be it pot house, inn or tavern, he could say goodbye to the sea for ever. As a freeholder, he would be legally immune from the press, while his past experience must make the place a favourite amongst other salty types. Often these would be men equally lucky in funds, but with ambitions that extended only as far as several nights' complete oblivion. They would be pleased to empty their purse into the hands of a former shipmate, spending their hard earned coin in an orgy of wanton excess that covered every one of the primary deadly sins, with a few more thrown in for good measure.

Knowledge of what a beached seaman liked best could make a landlord comfortably off, and many were content to be so, even at the expense of their former colleagues. Once established and with staff installed, the business could just about run itself, and had the advantage of being totally legal. And, for those who wanted even more and did not mind a little risk, there were further ways in which additional wealth could be achieved.

Smuggling was the most logical. Many of the usual seaman's skills were required, as was the raw courage and outright temerity common amongst lower deck men. Substantial funds could be made with relatively little risk, the force of revenue officers and preventive men being so small in times of war that a determined runner was more likely to encounter shipwreck or foundering than seizure.

And from what Lewis' informant had passed on, this was one such instance. Being so near to a naval base, the tavern would have been regularly visited by the press, so any seaman found inside was likely to carry a protection. But now that it was growing dark, and most honest souls were on their way to bed, if not already inside, Lewis was reasonable certain of finding a rich haul of men ripe for impressment. And these would be bright, alert, fit young men, rather than the landsmen or fools that had made up much of the press gang's haul of late. For, by their nature, smugglers were not only acquainted with the sea, but enterprising enough to make a sizeable living from it.

Lewis was about to take a further look, but quickly dived back behind his cover as yet another visitor approached. This one was riding a horse; the third to have come so, and he tensed once more in case the animal should be brought over to shelter in the yard. But it was a pleasant enough night, and the beast was left to steam companionably next to its fellows. In time of war, for an ordinary man to afford a mount was as clear an indication as any that his business was lucrative. Lewis drew comfort from the thought they would not be arresting paupers, but rich men of business who were probably deserving of such a fate. He motioned briefly to Clement, a boatswain's mate, who was the official look out, then settled himself down with the rest of the men to wait.

His watch told him there was less than a quarter of an hour to go until the time when all should have assembled. The other seamen were yarning quietly while Chivers, the midshipman, checked the priming of his pistol for the ninth time that evening.

"Will we be takin' them on to the Rondy, sir?" one of the men chanced. Lewis turned to see it was a seasoned hand, and one he had served with in several other ships before.

"No, Jenkins," Lewis replied softly. "I don't intend keeping any on land for longer than we need." The others drew near to hear as he continued, and Lewis supposed it as good a time as any for a final briefing.

"Remember we want seamen, not gentry. They may well be free traders, but we ain't gobblers or landsharks and look only for those who will be of use aboard ship."

There was a murmur of understanding from those about him, and Lewis wondered if they knew of his other reasons for avoiding the ringleaders. Anyone smart enough to place themselves in a position of authority was likely to dodge an impressment order with ease. Some may even be lawyers or magistrates themselves: it was not unknown for men of all manner of business to indulge in such a lucrative venture. He had documentation that entitled him to seize able men; even taking free traders was perhaps stretching the point, although any overstepping of authority might also be excused. Men caught smuggling were frequently sent for five years' service with the Royal Navy on conviction. It was conceivable that *Prometheus'* commission would be shorter so, in effect, Lewis was doing them a favour. But a well set up individual, be he doctor, lawyer or even a tavern keeper, might not see it in quite the same light. And, given access to a court of law, they could bring charges against Lewis or the captain for false imprisonment.

No, it was better to go for the ordinary workers; the common hands who would be of more use, cause less trouble and probably be a good deal more skilled into the bargain. He would whisk them back to the ship, where any protest could be received in private and relative safety. There were two dockyard carts standing by, and the horses were reasonably fresh: with luck, all should be over within the hour, and they would be well on their way back to *Prometheus*.

"Two more walkers," Clement whispered, and Lewis raised himself up to look once more. That would make eighteen, by his calculation. He had little room for more on the wagons; some of his men might have to run alongside as it was.

"Very well, form up, and check your equipment."

They rose slowly, flexing stiff limbs, and some began to shake out their sand filled coshes with professional swagger, slapping them against horny hands and grinning to each other in anticipation. Lewis was far happier for his men to carry such weapons; to his mind they were infinitely preferable to the belaying pins favoured by many. Handled properly, the business should be orderly enough but if it came to a fight, seamen were inclined to use force without consideration. A heavy blow from a cosh might well cause unconsciousness, but the same stroke delivered with the solidity of what amounted to a heavy club could easily kill.

Each man was also equipped with a cutlass, while some carried pistols. These were unlikely to be used: even if drawn, it would amount to an admission of defeat or, at least, unforeseen resistance. Those seized usually went easily enough at first, and could be trussed up and removed relatively quickly. In time they might try to escape, and it was not unknown for friends to learn of their impressment, and attempt to free them. That meant the journey back would probably be the most dangerous part of the procedure. The three miles they had to travel gave ample time for accomplices to be raised and an attack organised. Then it may well come to cold steel or even firearms.

"If all are ready, we shall begin." Lewis spoke softly, well aware that it was not customary to phrase an order in such a way, although press gang work was somewhat apart from the usual shipboard discipline. In the next few minutes every man would be looking after the other but, unlike a regular action, they must exercise control. There was no enemy here; instead it was hoped that whoever they seized would someday become a friend.

They walked silently out of the yard and across the darkened street. Without a direct order, Jenkins, Todd and Harrison broke off and made to secure the rear, while Sanderson and Jeffrey stayed behind with the carts, and stood ready in the lee of the stables. All had carried out similar raids on previous occasions and most actually enjoyed the exercise. But every one of them was also well practised and, as Lewis strode forward boldly and rapped on the heavy wooden door, he was quietly confident. There was the customary silence from within, then a small crack appeared and a cautious eye peeped out.

It took no more than one kick from a well aimed boot to throw the door back in the man's face. Lewis stood to one side, allowing his men to stream past, then followed, almost casually, in their wake. Inside it was the usual scene: upturned tables, a rush of bodies, the tinkle of broken glass and, all too often some woman drawing attention to herself by screaming, crying or defending a favoured man: occasionally all three. Lewis watched with the eyes of one who had seen it all before. He was unable to approve or condemn; his job was simply to make sure everything reached its logical conclusion, and with as little trouble as possible.

* * *

Captain Banks read the message one more time while waiting for Caulfield to join him in the great cabin. It was a nonsense, of course; their deployment had already been changed once, which explained why Sarah was so many miles away in Southsea when *Prometheus* lay at anchor in Tor Bay. And now this – it was late in the evening, and he was not in the mood for such tomfoolery. The thump of a musket butt drew his attention from the paper as his sentry announced the first lieutenant's arrival.

"It's not the Channel Fleet," Banks said, by way of greeting, handing the order to Caulfield who was in shirtsleeves and appeared as if he may already have been abed. The first lieutenant looked uneasily at his captain as he took it.

"Came by a messenger from the port admiral not five minutes past," Banks said incredulously. "And after we were told it would definitely not be the Med."

When *Prometheus* was released from the dockyard, barely three weeks ago, she had indeed been destined to join the Mediterranean Fleet. Sarah had taken a house close to Portsmouth, to be on hand during the rare occasions when the ship might return to England, and all aboard were looking forward to spending the next year or so on the magical inland sea. Then, with almost unseemly haste, *Prometheus* had been switched to service with the Channel Fleet. It had not been a popular move, and the knowledge that the entire commission would probably be spent on blockade duty, either polishing the enemy coast with the inshore squadron, or sailing aimlessly back and forth as part of the main force, had not been appreciated by officers or crew. They had made for their new home within two days, limping along the south coast, desperately undermanned, to finally set their hooks in the mud off Tor Bay, the base for what were colloquially known as the Channel Gropers. And now – now it seemed the original plan was to stand, and once more *Prometheus* was Mediterranean bound.

"Under Admiral Nelson," Caulfield commented, with a modicum of respect as he handed the paper back.

"Indeed," Banks agreed. "It will be an honour I am certain, and he will doubtless do every bit as good a job as my Lord Cornwallis. But why the change?" he questioned. "We have already lost time and continuity in switching berths, and are drastically undermanned in consequence. Yet now the Admiralty wish us to sail almost forthwith!"

"We are more than seventy short," Caulfield replied automatically. "And all should be trained hands, were we to have the choice."

"Benson should be back on the morrow," Banks remarked. "And Lewis is out at present – with luck he may bring back a smuggler or two."

"But that will not make up the deficiency," Caulfield replied softly.

"Well, there is nothing for it: I shall have to petition the Admiralty. They cannot expect me to recruit efficiently if my ship is constantly switched and no time allowed for the process. Why, it says here we must be ready to join an India convoy from Thursday – that gives us less than two days, when we were expecting ten. Most of the repairs needed will hardly be completed by then and that is not accounting for our lack of hands."

Caulfield said nothing. He was probably more acutely aware of the problems than his captain; as executive officer, the fabric and manning of the ship was directly under his control. Positions for first lieutenants were by no means plentiful and, if he failed to present a workable command, he would not find another, and neither could he expect to make that all important step to Commander. However, the fact that he was potentially worse off than his captain hardly eased the situation, and he doubted he had ever seen Banks quite so angry.

"But of course, I cannot," the senior man sighed after a moment. "They would merely laugh, and say the fault to be mine, then ask if the ship were above my mark."

"We may run into a homebound convoy," Caulfield suggested. "Or even be able to recruit at Gib. There are always those released from the hospital, and they often hold men from foundered vessels, to say nothing of exchanged prisoners."

"There shall be precious few of the latter this deep into the war," Banks replied glumly, although Caulfield's remark had consoled him to some extent. The tiny outpost to the mouth of the Mediterranean was certainly a potential source of hands, and both men had pleasant memories of the place.

"It will be good to see a bit of sun, though," Caulfield continued. "After our time in St Helena, and the winter we have just endured, I must say I could use a tanning."

Banks snorted to himself, and regarded the piece of paper once more. Serving in the Med. also meant far fewer chances of home leave. At least with the Channel Fleet he may have expected to see Sarah every year or so. But Caulfield was right, it would be a more pleasurable place to serve, and with that spitfire Nelson in command, action was far more likely. He just had to solve the current problem of manpower.

* * *

Most of Lewis' predictions proved to be right on the mark. The parlour of the tavern had actually contained twenty men and, with the speed and efficiency in which his team performed, all were taken by surprise. A few, who had arrived barely minutes before, put up some semblance of resistance but, when matched against the combined might of trained and eager seamen, it soon fell to naught. And those who had been present for some while were well into their cups, and simply viewed the press gang's arrival with bemused interest. Lewis had no idea what the smugglers were planning for that night but, with a full moon due, it could hardly have been anything too adventurous, not when a good proportion were having difficulty in keeping upright. Once the initial protests were stifled, the captives had been trussed up and herded outside, then heaved aboard the waiting carts.

Now though, as the two wagons and four horses trundled his catch through the darkened streets of Brixham, Lewis' prisoners were becoming slightly more ambitious. All had their wrists firmly tied behind them and the removal of boots and belts meant that any attempt to run would be slowed. As an additional measure, a length of half inch line had been threaded through each pair of manacled arms, looping the groups together in a way that would make escape all but impossible. But they had not been gagged; somehow Lewis could not bring himself to give the order and, on such a quiet night, that might have been a mistake.

Most of his captives were clearly felons, and to his mind deserved not an ounce of clemency. But it was one thing to drag a drunken man from his home and occupation, however illegal, and quite another to stuff his mouth full of oakum, as one seaman had suggested, or simply bind a length of tow between his lips. He might easily choke, and a charge of murder awaited any officer heading a press gang when their actions ended in death.

And so they stayed, secured but vocal, as Lewis stumbled along the narrow street next to the second of the carts, his eyes watching the two banks of houses and small businesses that lined each side. Lamps were appearing in the upper stories as moans and calls from his prisoners brought attention to their plight. A window was forced up several doors ahead, and the contents of what appeared to be a necessary pot tossed out and over the leading cart to a mixture of cries from those hit, and shouts of glee and approval from the rest. Lewis supposed the act might equally have been a comment on the Navy or smugglers, but in either case the local populace clearly knew what was afoot.

The road wound on for less than a hundred yards, then there was a mile of open country before the short spell of forest that spanned the outskirts of the naval dockyard. There, at least, they might find shelter and, once his tiny convoy was free of the small town, Lewis would take a seat up next to one of the drivers. But until then, manoeuvrability of command seemed far more important than comfort, and he was content to stay following the carts on the ground.

More shouts came from the upper rooms of the buildings, but these were simple insults; nothing had been organised and, as the final house was left behind, he began to grow more confident. Reaching up, he hauled himself aboard the second cart just as Chivers, in the driver's position, encouraged the horses on. A seaman helped him aboard, and Lewis clambered past the wriggling bodies of his captives, stepping over the driver's box and seating himself next to the midshipman.

There was a strong moon rising, and the road ahead was hardly dark. They were in rough scrub, with little high vegetation, although Lewis could make out a line of trees that seemed to block their path in the far distance.

"We'll be back at the barky in no time," Chivers informed him casually. They were off ship and the lad clearly felt in no need of the formalities expected when a warrant officer addressed one of commissioned rank.

"Aye, that's so," Lewis, whose roots also acknowledged no such distinction, agreed. "But there's a while to go yet, so keep your eyes skinned."

The midshipman urged the cart onwards. Clement, who drove the leading team, came from farming stock and was setting the strong pace Lewis had directed. It was surely better for the horses to tire nearer their destination than be held back in what was doubtless the more dangerous area. But on other matters Lewis was not quite so certain.

They had taken far more men than he had intended. Twenty was really quite a haul, and there were three who he doubted should really have been included at all. Two, by their apparel, might even be gentlemen, or men of business unlucky enough to have been caught with the rest. But Lewis' instinct said otherwise; for true gentry to have been found in such a low place indicated a degree of wrong doing. They might equally be venturers: men of means who made good money by financing smuggling operations. The third appeared to be a cook; he was certainly dressed in such a fashion, although it was not unknown for some to adopt a hasty disguise if seizure became likely. Consequently there could be problems back at the ship: warrants might be issued, and a few forcibly released, with the possibility of a fine or some other censure for his pains. But, on an open and well lit path, and with a goodly distance to travel, such trouble almost sounded attractive: however hard things might turn out, at least he would be safe, and amongst friends.

The road was rough and must have felt uncomfortable to his prisoners, the majority of whom were lying prone and relatively quiet as they bounced on the hard wooden bed of the carts. There was no time to address that either; the surface would improve in time, while bruises and scrapes could be attended to later. For now they must simply make all speed; that and hope nothing appeared to delay them.

It proved to be in vain. The first sight of pursuing horsemen came about a minute later, one of the seamen seated at the rear of Lewis' cart giving the alarm as they were half way between the village just left and the wall of trees they were all too slowly approaching. Lewis glanced back and saw the dim outline of several mounted riders heading hard for them. He reckoned there were ten, maybe twelve, only just less than his own force but, mounted as they were, the enemy would be so much more manoeuvrable. There was also the additional problem of a divided command. Clement, in the first wagon, appeared bright enough, but did not have the intellect to act independently whereas Chivers was little more than a boy.

"We've company astern" he bellowed to the first cart, and noticed the boatswain's mate turn back and raise one hand in acknowledgement. "Maintain your way, and prepare for boarders," Lewis continued, speaking to the men in general. "Any with pistols, save your powder until they are close, and then aim for the horses."

It was a futile hope, and Lewis had no illusions: those under his command were as hard as they came and would think nothing of killing any legitimate foe. But they could also be sentimental fools and, when ordered to kill what they would doubtless consider innocent animals, most would baulk. A horse made a far larger target, however, and for as long as Lewis' force could keep moving, their enemies remained a threat only while they were mounted.

A pistol ball whined past, some feet from his head, but Lewis was almost pleased to hear it. Their pursuers were still some distance off. Any shot was as likely to hit one of the prisoners as his men, and it would be impossible to reload whilst at the gallop.

Chivers was bringing the reins down hard upon his horses; the beasts had begun to tire and would be looking for the chance to slow at any opportunity. Lewis glanced back; his pursuers had halved the distance between them and now could be made out far more clearly. He forced himself to count and was fairly certain there were eleven, with most, apparently, armed. Forward, the oncoming trees seemed no nearer, and the shelter they offered would probably be of dubious benefit. Lewis swallowed as he braced himself for what was to come.

"Want me to take a pot shot at 'em?" A round faced, toothless seaman asked, raising his pistol in enquiry. Lewis shook his head, struggling to remember the man's name. Was it Harris? Henderson?

"No," he hissed, temporising. "Wait for them to draw nearer!"

Harrison, that was it. Lewis twisted himself on his seat and tried to look back before deciding it was too great an effort, and instead clambered from the driver's box while drawing his own gun.

Another ball sped past, this time far closer; it had caused Chivers, on the driving box, to duck and may have fazed the horses. Lewis stood uncertainly on the rocking cart and stared at the oncoming force. If he had brought some marines with them it might have been a different matter. The British Brown Bess was a reliable piece: a group of men so armed, and practised in reloading on a crowded deck, would have accounted for that little lot in no time. As it was, most seamen viewed firearms as boarding weapons and, given the choice, usually chose a cutlass, half-pike or tomahawk instead. They would certainly fire the things readily enough, but were unlikely to take accurate aim, preferring to press them into the stomachs of an enemy, when a miss was less likely. Their cutlasses might prove more effective: most were drawn now and held firmly in each man's right hand, while those equipped with pistols, which were probably of more immediate value, clutched them in their left. The first horse was drawing closer to the tailgate of his cart, and the rider began to take deliberate aim with his own weapon.

Lewis fired quite instinctively, only realising afterwards that the target had been the man rather than his mount, and he had ignored his own instructions. The job was done though and the rider fell sideways, leaving his animal to veer off into the night. A small cheer from the seamen greeted the result, and Lewis grimly accepted that no horses would be shot that evening.

And then none of it appeared to matter. Bullets seemed to be flying in all directions as horsemen approached on either side.

"Faster!" Lewis shouted, moving over to cover Chivers' right. "They're gaining on us!"

The midshipman struck wildly with the reins, but to little

effect; their horses were either exhausted or determined not to give any more. And then, amid a succession of pistol shots from the British seamen, their pursuers were upon them.

One, close alongside, brought his sword up to slash at Chivers. The attacker was at a disadvantage though, being on the starboard side of the cart, and Lewis was able to hack sideways with his own hanger before any damage could be done. Sensing his rider hurt, the horse shied away, but another soon came to take his place. Lewis was leaning out to strike once more when that one also fell back, this time struck by a bullet fired from the leading cart. Another shot slammed into the wooden frame between him and Chivers, miraculously missing both, and then the lieutenant's attention was drawn to something amiss ahead.

To larboard, a rider had drawn level with the wagon's horses, and was attempting to rein the beasts in. His actions were only partially successful but the pair's natural synergy had been disrupted, and Chivers, flapping wildly with the reins, was hardly helping. But there was no doubt the cart had slowed, and was starting to be left behind by the other; soon Lewis would have all the attackers to contend with on his own. It may mean Clement would make *Prometheus* with at least some of their captives, but that was not an arrangement he was prepared to accept.

Harrison, the toothless seaman next to him, was still clutching his pistol. Lewis snatched it from him by the barrel and was about to take aim when he noticed the hammer resting redundantly against an open frizzen and knew it to have been fired. Instead he flung the thing, with a mixture of rage and intent, in the general direction of the man who now sat almost astride the cart's larboard horse, and was pleased to see the empty weapon bounce satisfyingly off his head. The blow, which must have been considerable, had no immediate effect but, as he and Harrison watched, the fellow soon began to sway and, accompanied by a roar of delight from the seaman, finally fell between his own mount and the cart's horse.

Chivers regained control, and they seemed to be travelling faster as the horses fell into step once more. Lewis looked about. They were still being chased, but the number had dropped considerably. Then the sky darkened, and he realised they were finally in the depths of the forest.

The track had also narrowed: hedges brushed against them on either side. He drew a sigh of relief; for as long as the path stayed as tight, they could not be overtaken, while it would be far easier for his men to reload their pistols on the back of a cart than for those mounted and riding at speed. Something of this must have occurred to their pursuers who fell back almost immediately, and soon the two wagons were left to continue alone.

"Anyone wounded?" Lewis called out, to no response and, for the first time in what felt like ages, he drew a full breath.

"Reckon we was lucky there, weren't we, sir?" Harrison enquired with a gummy grin and Lewis nodded. He reckoned they were.

Chapter Four

The rain that had been predicted by Simmonds held off until the following morning and then fell with a vengeance. Individual drops descended in force to test the caulking or devised other, more ingenious, ways to get below, while those less ambitious gathered together to wash across the decks in wide and abundant rivers. Dales and scuppers soon became full and began gushing out untidily, carrying away layers of newly applied paint, while the fresh running rigging became swollen and impossible to reeve. Any cleaning, painting or paying still to be done on the open deck had to be abandoned, with the hands being sent below to work instead in stuffy storerooms or cabins. And all the time those officers who had been informed both of *Prometheus'* new destination, and her revised departure date, swore testily at what men they did command, while privately wondering where more might be found.

But there was good news as well; Benson's excursion had proved far more successful than they could have expected. Earlier that morning the fourth lieutenant had returned from his recruiting drive bringing with him five experienced hands along with seven landsmen, three of which had actually volunteered. The able hands were man-o'-war trained, having recently returned from a thirty month commission in a frigate, and apparently spending their accumulated wages over a two night binge that ended with them before the local assizes. All five had shown spirit to begin with but now seemed resigned to their fate, whereas the landsmen were still so bemused by their situation and surroundings as to be positively docile. The receiving tender had provided three more the previous morning, two of whom were already settled, but Lewis' lot from the night before were not quite so amiable.

There had almost been a riot getting them aboard and, even several hours later, some of the more lively were continuing to object. Caulfield supposed he would have to go and listen to their complaints eventually but for now was content to let them expend their energy below, where the more violent were safely contained in bilboes. But however much trouble they were causing, he readily acknowledged that *Prometheus'* most junior lieutenant had done well.

Two of his prisoners needed to be released almost immediately, and left threatening to return with injunctions for the rest, but such legal niceties would take at least three days to produce, and the ship should be well out to sea by then. And those still held appeared experienced seamen in the main; just the kind they were after. Even their overly expressed anger at being taken showed character that only needed to be channelled to good advantage, and the first lieutenant made a mental note to alert the captain of Lewis' performance. A commendation from him would mean much to the lad, who had not held a commission for more than a couple of months and would be feeling his way for some time.

But that still left them short of the five hundred or so lower deck hands that was their ideal wartime complement. It was not a massive deficit; ships had sailed with far smaller crews, but one that Caulfield was at a loss to know how to rectify. *Prometheus* was well provisioned, the only other commodity lacking being fresh water and, as he looked out at the appalling weather through the chart room scuttle, the irony did not appeal. Once that was aboard, they might sail, and the first of the lighters was expected that very afternoon. He had placed his pen down and was rolling up the watch list he had been studying when there came a tap at the door. One of the midshipmen poked his nose through the crack.

"Captain presents his compliments, sir, and might he speak with you when convenient?"

Caulfield grunted an assent to what amounted to a royal summons, and slipped the watch list under his arm before leaving the tiny room. He had a feeling it would be needed.

* * *

"We have new messmates for you, Flint," Cartwright announced as he approached the head of the table. He had three contrasting men

54

in tow, and each viewed their new home with differing levels of interest. Dinner, the mail meal of the day, had just been eaten, while the first issue of spirit was still warm in their bellies. So those of Flint's mess were in a genial mood, and they in turn examined the newcomers with a collective, and amused, curiosity.

"Butler has joined us from a transport," the master's mate continued, indicating the first. "Carrying lags out to the colonies he was, so will be used to mixing with a better class of folk. He's a seaman through and through, though, as is Billings, who can surely hand reef and steer, even if he may not have done so for a spell. And Potterton here seems more suited to preparing scran, though none the worse will be thought of him for that."

The men were certainly diverse: the first two could easily have been father and son. Butler was hardly in his twenties yet had broad shoulders and a deep chest that suggested a good store of strength, while his slim waist and clear eyes showed him to be supremely fit: perfect material for a topman. But the look was sullen and he was obviously there against his wishes. Billings was the very antithesis in shape, having allowed himself to grow plump to the extent that he even boasted a slight paunch. What hair remained was turning to grey and he had the look of one heading for an early old age. Placed together, it was like looking at opposing ends of the same life, while Potterton differed again.

The man possessed an ageless quality that placed him anywhere from thirty-five to sixty. As with the other two, he was clad in the standard seaman's attire that would have been freshly issued, but in his case it he wore it with an air of competence and dignity. Either the jacket had been especially tailored to fit, or he carried it well; the white duck trousers were hauled up so they hardly brushed the deck and his neckerchief was neatly tied. But even if he was undoubtedly the smartest, a lubber could tell there was little of the mariner about him.

The rest of Flint's mess eyed them critically from the security of the group, each sitting comfortably to one side of their table, while the newcomers stood more uncertainly at the head. All three had damp hair and the scent of men recently washed and were loaded down with a filled ditty bag, as well as two brand new hammocks.

"So make a space there," Flint said in mock desperation. "These are our mates now and, given time, you might even get to like 'em."

Those seated slid a few inches towards the spirketting, leaving just enough room for Billings and Butler to squeeze onto one end of a bench with their dunnage piled before them, while Potterton lowered himself more elegantly opposite, and placed his belongings carefully on the deck. Ben, the third class volunteer and boy of the mess, replaced the keg he had swept aside when Cartwright arrived, and reclaimed his rightful place at the head of the table. It was a position he regarded as one of seniority, even if he was alone in such an opinion.

"So where've you washed up from?" Jameson asked the two newcomers facing him.

"I'm from Marldon," Butler told them in a quiet voice. "Small village not ten mile from here. Got snatched by a pressing tender yes'day even'."

"Transport was it?" Flint prompted, remembering Cartwright's words.

"Aye, homeward bound. We'd been out best part of two year, an' I were expectin' to be snug with my wife and chit b'now."

There was a rumble of understanding, mainly from those who had been recruited in a similar manner. If they had been members of the gang seizing him, little mercy could have been expected but, now that Butler was effectively one of them, most were prepared to sympathise.

"You won't find it such a bad berth," Flint said gently. He had been pressed in the past himself, and knew all too well the anger and frustration that Butler would be going through. The feelings passed soon enough, but that did not make them any more agreeable while they lasted. "We've a fair bunch of officers," he added. "And the captain's as level as they come."

"I served with your Jimmy Leggs in *Vanguard*," Butler told them, using the traditional slang for the master at arms, "He were a bastard then and, from what I gather, ain't changed a jot."

"It's a bastard's job," Flint replied simply. He was eyeing the newcomer with a mixture of compassion and concern. There was no doubting Butler was carrying a fat tail; this might be down to having been pressed, in which case he would probably work up to be a first rate member of the mess. On the other hand he could be a troublemaker, and better ditched at the first opportunity.

"Aye, I'd chance you're right," the new man allowed. "We actually rubbed along well enough but..."

"But you'd prefer to be at home?" Flint asked.

Butler's mask of thunder seemed to melt, to be replaced by a reluctant smile, and Flint breathed more easily.

"An' what about you?" he asked the more portly Billings.

"I'm a man of business," the second newcomer stated loftily. "And was about to undertake a financial investment in the Three Tuns of Galmpton, to add to my other ventures."

"Oh aye? Nanny house, is it?" Cranston, one of the gunners, asked with rude interest.

"The Three Tuns is a catering establishment of the highest standard," Billings replied stiffly, his gaze remaining wide of his fellow men. "Probably one of the finest in the county: Potterton here is one of the cooks and the concern has an excellent reputation." The third new arrival inclined his head slightly at the mention of his name, but made no comment. "My associates will have lodged the appropriate protest and you shall not take it amiss if we are soon gone, I am certain."

I remember you from last night," Harrison's fat face beamed in the half light of the gun deck. "I were in Mr Lewis' party: you was as drunk as David's sow."

"My companions and I were interrupted in the middle of a small celebration," Billings stated loftily. "The invasion was totally without cause, and there will surely be action taken."

"Hold hard, there: you said this one was a cook," Harrison pointed at Potterton. "If that's so, he might 'ave a case and could be set free, but I don't see what chance you got."

"Are you the freeholder?" Jameson, the topman, asked.

"It is a shared enterprise: I was about to join the board of owners so should never have been seized."

"But you're not a freeholder?" Jameson repeated and received a sullen shake of the head in reply.

"I do own business," Billings admitted. "But not property."

"Press rules don't recognise business owners," Flint said coldly. "But they knows all about seamen," he added, looking pointedly at the faded tattoos that covered both the man's lower arms.

"I might have served once," Billings glanced down, hurriedly attempting to stretch the short sleeves of his jacket and, when he spoke again, much of his assumed importance had disappeared. "But that was a while back. Last ship I were in carried a Dutchman out of Bombay. That was in 'ninety-eight an' the prize money changed me for the better. But I haven't worked a deck in years," he added defiantly. "An' don't intend starting again now."

"Word is we're sailing on the morrow," Flint's tone remained dispassionate.

"Not with me aboard," Billings said, as he examined his fingers. "Nor Mr Potterton, if he knows what's good for 'im."

"I understand you have requested legal representation," Ross this time. He rarely spoke at the mess table, but already the others had learned to listen when he did. "So is it right to assume the officers are aware of your status?"

"They's aware all right," Billings replied, finally deeming to look down from the nearby beam, and his glance naturally falling on Ross. "Young fellow named Davison, but he were far too clever and didn't want to pay no notice."

"Aye," Cranston agreed reluctantly. "They're so light of hands no one cares who they takes."

"Well their minds may be changed when I bring legal action against the captain," Billings said, with some of his previous manner returning.

"Can he do that?" Ben, the boy of the mess, asked.

"Any man may bring suit against illegal impressment," Ross replied gently. "And Mr Billings is quite correct, a successful action can indeed result in compensation."

"So how come you knows so much about it?" Harrison demanded suspiciously, leaning forward towards Ross to give his question extra weight.

"Let's just say he does," Flint said firmly. He also harboured doubts about Ross, but sensed this was not the place or time to voice them.

"Only it won't do him no good," Greg, one of the gun room stewards, added importantly from further down the table. "Not unless he can actually get ashore and see a lawyer."

"How do you mean?" Jameson asked.

"You won't get many legal folk being allowed aboard a ship about to sail," Greg explained. "And I can't see anyone letting Billings off to go meet with his 'six an' eight-pence'."

"But would he get compensation? I mean – if he were pressed illegally," Jameson persisted.

"That is a possibility," Ross allowed. "But he would need a cast iron case and, yes, a lawyer would usually be involved."

"Money promised for tomorrow is no better than that owed from yesterday," the steward explained enigmatically. Greg knew both his numbers and letters, as well as several words in French and, until Ross came along, had considered himself the educated one in the mess. "The only time coin's worth a light is when it's been paid out, and sitting in your hat."

"Well I ain't interested in government money, past, present nor future." Billings grumbled, his previous lofty stance crumbling further. "I got right on my side and just wants to get back to me own fire, and leave the Navy far behind."

"You'll find a few round here what thinks the same," Flint told him dryly. "But when the hook comes up tomorrow, they'll be sailing just like the rest of us. And all the right in the world won't make no difference."

"And how do you feel about this?" Jameson asked Potterton.

All eyes fell on the third newcomer, whose expression remained impassive.

"We have made our objection," he said with quiet dignity. "And will doubtless be released if an error has occurred."

"Well I'm not so sure I wants to go back to sea." Billings declared, conscious that he had lost the group's attention.

"You seem to think you have a choice," Flint told him.

"They can't keep us aboard this ship forever," he blustered. "I shall continue my legal objections at the first British port we touch."

"Then you'll have your work cut out," Harrison gave a toothless smirk. "This ship's bound for the Channel Gropers; we could be years on blockade duty, and will be kept aboard if called back to port. The next time any of us touches dry land the war'll probably be over. That's if the capt'n don't try something clever, and we ends up running into France first."

"We ain't bound for the Channel Fleet," Flint said, switching his attention from the newcomers. "Ain't you heard? There's been a change of plan: it's the Med. for us."

"Is that right?" Harrison asked, amazed.

"Aye," Greg confirmed. "So there's much more chance of shore leave. And when we gets some, Billings can try his luck, if that's his intention. There'll be English lawyers a plenty at Gibraltar, Malta, even the Tagus, if I'm not mistaken."

"The Tagus?" Thompson repeated, almost jumping with surprise. He had been dozing gently at the far end of the table, head resting against the spirketting and all thoughts centred on the welcome that awaited him in the forepeak. "That's Lisbon!" he spluttered. "Who said anything about us going to Portugal?"

"I've sailed with the Med. fleet afore, an' so has Jameson." Flint assured them. "We spent a tidy time there back in 'ninety-seven – or was it 'ninety-six?"

"But the Med. Fleet?" Thompson questioned with disgust. "When did that 'appen?"

"I heard the or-fisers in the gun room talkin' over breakfast," Greg told him proudly. "Bin switched yet again, we has; joining Admiral Nelson, or so they says."

"Those Johnnies bagged a fortune in prize money after Aboukir Bay," Harrison agreed from the other side of the table. "Would that we'll be half so fortunate."

"But I'm not sure I wants to go to Portugal," Thompson grumbled.

"Blimey," Flint raised his eyes to the deckhead in mock despair. "We got another one."

* * *

"As soon as we finish watering I propose to single up to the starboard bower," Banks said. "Then be ready to sail as soon as the convoy appears; with luck we may even catch the afternoon tide."

"When are they expected?" Caulfield asked. The two were sitting comfortably enough at the dining table in the captain's great cabin; the spacious surroundings were far more opulent than either had known in previous ships yet they had already become accepted and ceased to be noticed.

"Any time after mid-day," the captain replied. "I understand they were becalmed off Portland yesterday even', though the wind has picked up since."

"Are we not to await them in the Channel?" Caulfield asked, but Banks shook his head.

"Three of their number are coasters, and will be leaving the convoy for Tor Bay. When these are sighted we can up anchor and be sure of meeting the main convoy before they make Start Point. 'Tis a sizeable force, I believe."

"And we stay with them as far as Gibraltar?"

"Thirty-eight degrees north, to be specific. But shall certainly call at the Rock where, I trust, more hands will be available." He relaxed in his upright chair glancing, only briefly, at the far more comfortable affair that sat in the corner of the cabin. "Tell me, how many are we short?"

Caulfield spread the sheet of paper out on the warm, mahogany surface. "We can rate eighteen more able or ordinary from what was brought in yesterday," he pondered, "and ten landsmen – one of whom is a trained cook, which may prove useful. That leaves us approximately forty lacking of our minimum complement. And, of those, twenty-five at least should be trained."

"Topmen?" Banks asked.

"Ideally, yes, though we have sufficient for now. I would prefer some to be better prepared however, and there are few to spare."

A man must possess both youth and experience to join the elite band of hands who work aloft, and these seemingly

61

conflicting blessings meant topmen positions were the hardest of all to fill.

"Well, there is nothing more we can do; certainly in the time," Banks mused. "But at least our petty and warrant officers are well prepared. Some of the landsmen may prove worthy, and we can make more of them cruising the Med. than on some Godforsaken blockade."

"What think you of our chances with my Lord Nelson's fleet?" Caulfield asked. It would have been a bold, even a daring question from most executive officers, but the two had served together for many years and knew each other well enough for such a degree of latitude.

"I really cannot say," Banks replied simply. "The Med. is a troublesome place for sure. A few years back we were forced to abandon, and yet not so very recently it became the site of a most famous victory. Now the French have been cleared from Egypt there is perhaps less importance on the station, but still I would chance it to be filled with enough excitement for those that crave such things." As he spoke he drew his eyes away from the picture of his baby son that had already been fixed on the nearby beam. "And Nelson has fared well in most of the actions he has led. Should he remain true to form, I cannot see any of us becoming bored."

* * *

His meeting with Ross had sobered King in a literal sense. The newcomer, once an officer of at least equal status to him, was now finding his feet on the lower deck. Of course he had still to speak privately with the man, and could have no idea of the enormity of his crime, or why such a disgrace had been laid on the head of a commissioned officer. But the very fact that one could fall so low was a firm enough warning, and King had resolved to improve both himself and his performance.

He had never been a paragon of virtue; there were plenty of incidents in his past that might have brought him down, had they been given sufficient importance by the captain, or the attentions of a particularly harsh court martial. And with his marital problems apparently blighting the last few years, King's naval career had been allowed to run unchecked for far too long. Ross might be guilty of anything from insubordination to bedding an admiral's daughter, but King was reasonably certain that, whatever the crime, he himself would be capable of the same, and might suffer a similar penalty just as easily.

And so it was that his evening gin sessions had ceased, while greater attention was being paid to both his duties and general appearance. Collars now sat stiff and clean against a smooth chin, his boots shone and he gave orders from a clear head and without ambiguity. Some of the other officers, especially those who had known him in the past, may have noticed the improvement, and in such a public world it was probably significant that no mention had been made of the change. The only one who voiced an opinion on the subject was Keats, his servant, whose life had been forced to alter just as radically, leading him to grumble and gripe about the extra duties to any fellow marine who would listen.

But even after a bare few days of the new regime, there was no doubt that King himself felt the better for it and, when he mounted the quarterdeck after the main meal of the day, and gathered with the other officers in the warm sunshine that had finally replaced the rain, he was not only ready to see the ship to sea, and start the commission proper, but actively looking forward to the prospect.

"Any sign of the coasters?" he asked the first lieutenant tentatively. Barring the ship's surgeon, Caulfield was probably his closest friend. In the past they had discussed ship's business in a casual manner that was almost on an equal footing. But what could be allowed aboard a frigate was less acceptable in a ship-of-the-line and, with the date of Davison's commission effectively coming between them, making King the third, rather than second, lieutenant he was now less sure of his position.

But Caulfield replied affably enough. "Nothing as yet," he said. "Though I have doubled both main and fore lookouts, and doubt the bilges have ever been so dry since she were built."

There was the faint scent of cigar smoke in the warm air.

Donaldson was puffing purposefully on a black cheroot nearby and, with the majority of *Prometheus'* wardroom complement sipping sedately at cups of coffee and making polite conversation, the atmosphere on the quarterdeck was more of a social gathering than a warship about to put to sea.

Davison was holding a china cup, his smallest finger pointing delicately away, as if ashamed of using so crude an implement. "Mr Brehaut still in the bilges, is he?" the second lieutenant asked, with a smirk, of no one in particular, and there was a titter of light laughter. Brehaut, the sailing master, was one of the few not present. He had already revealed himself to be obsessive about the ship's trim, and spent most of each watch adjusting stores to ensure *Prometheus* was riding to what he gauged to be her best level. The recent introduction of seventy tons of drinking water had inevitably set his calculations awry, and the time since had been spent frantically ordering entire tiers of provisions moved, in the hope of gaining their previous equilibrium.

The bell rang out seven times and King was just considering returning below as his watch officially began in half an hour, when a foremast lookout broke into all their thoughts.

"Deck there! Three brigs coming round the headland to the nor-east."

"And steering to weather Thatcher Rock," another voice, this time from the masthead, added in an apparent effort to justify his existence.

"That sounds like our signal," Caulfield said to the deck in general. "Mr Chivers, my respects to the captain and advise him of the situation if you please. Gentlemen, may we go to stations for leaving harbour?"

The polite words started a thousand different chain reactions: junior officers were summoned and, in turn, bellowed at those beneath them, while all dispersed to their appropriate places. King made his way forward to supervise the raising of *Prometheus'* remaining anchor. They had singled up to the starboard bower some while earlier. All that remained was for the remaining seventy hundredweight of iron that currently sat deep in the mud and sand of Tor Bay to be lifted clear, then safely stowed away without anyone being killed or seriously injured, and they might sail.

King took up position on the forecastle. Looking aft, he saw Banks appear from his quarters under the poop and give a nod to Caulfield. The boatswain's pipes instantly began to scream, a signal was made to the port admiral; orders rang about the deck while hands flocked aloft and marines unfixed their bayonets and stamped away from the posts they had been jealously guarding throughout the time *Prometheus* had been at anchor.

They had the gentle off-shore breeze and a compliant tide: it would be a simple matter to weather Berry Head and leave what was a wide and accommodating harbour. And actually raising the final anchor should prove no more difficult; with a clear head and his newly regained self-assurance, King was quietly confident of the manoeuvre. Water streamed from the huge twenty-one inch cable as the ship gently crept forward under topsails. Then it was 'Up and Down', and the huge weight was being borne by *Prometheus'* main capstan aft.

Now a wave to the quarterdeck was all the signal needed; they were finally free of the land, further canvas could be released, and the ship herself allowed to roam wherever she pleased, even while the dead weight of swinging iron was still being painstakingly hauled up through the dark waters.

Everything was in order, the way it should always be in the Royal Navy and King was feeling suitably smug when Adams, one of the newer midshipmen, appeared at the head of the forecastle ladder. The boy had an anxious look on his face as he scampered along the deck towards him, finally coming to a stop so abrupt that his hat fell off and had to be retrieved from the scuppers by one of the hands.

"Mr Cartwright's respects, sir, and would you be so kind as to come?"

King couldn't think why the master's mate, who was responsible for supervising the nippers and drying the sodden anchor cable, would require his attention. If a man had been injured, the surgeon was the person to send for, and the capstan was still turning at a creditable rate.

"What is it?" he demanded, conscious that the lad had, quite unintentionally, broken his happy mood.

"It's in the forepeak," the midshipman replied, his eyes almost completely round in wonder. "They thinks they seen a ghost."

Chapter Five

His eyes were accustomed to the bright light of a sunny afternoon, and the contrasting darkness of the orlop took some time to penetrate. King stepped off the lower companionway and turned aft towards where he trusted Cartwright and his party would be found. To one side the larboard anchor cable, raised that morning, hung loosely over the drying racks, while the sodden starboard line was snaking down unattended from the messenger and lay, muddy and dripping, in an untidy heap on the deck. King looked about but no one was present and, grunting with annoyance, he turned forward again, ever conscious of Midshipman Adams who bustled about his heels like a hungry puppy.

"What the devil is it, Mr Cartwright?" he asked, as the bulky form of the elderly master's mate finally came into view. He was standing by the entrance to the Gunner's store room amidst a cluster of heavyset, but pale-faced men who gathered about him as if for support.

"It's down below, sir," the man explained, somewhat embarrassed and pointing foolishly at his feet. "In the forepeak. Jenkins saw it first, and a couple of others, then I caught a glimpse m'self. White, it were," he added, almost in wonder.

"And you think it to be a bogeyman?" King asked directly. Cartwright was a good twenty years his senior and a seaman through and through. He would have no hesitation in going aloft in the fiercest of storms, leading a boarding party, or quelling a brawl between the most vehement of foes. But, as with so many of his kind, one mention of the spirit world, and the man was like a babe in arms.

"I don't know what it was, Mr King," he replied, his weathered face contrasting oddly with an expression of naïve fear. "But what I saw certainly weren't natural."

"You don't think it might have been a stowaway?" King asked, in mock concern. To his mind that was far more likely, and hardly an unusual occurrence. Any ship leaving harbour is liable to attract an irritating number of unofficial passengers. And to compound the annoyance, they often turned out to be female, when an extra hand would be of far greater use.

"It's a possibility, sir," Cartwright conceded, while starting to look slightly shame-faced.

"Well, whatever you have found, I doubt it to be hostile," King snapped, advancing and glancing down to the darkened depths of the forepeak. Quite why the place had not been searched prior to leaving was another matter entirely. Davison led the starboard watch, which had been detailed for the task. But that was something to be addressed later; first he must make his own inspection.

"Below there," he called, stepping cautiously down the ladder. "Come out. I shall do you no harm."

A shape moved at the far edge of the chamber, just as he reached the deck. But it did not step into the faint shaft of light that came from above, and King swallowed. Now that he found himself effectively on his own it was not quite so easy to be blasé. After all, enough ghosts had been seen elsewhere for them to have some credibility. And a warship, with all the distress, disease and death it must attract, was bound to be a suitable home for at least one troubled spirit.

But this was nonsense, the stuff of childhood fancies, and with him a king's officer. Drawing a breath, he clenched his fists before shouting up for a lantern, then tried to focus on the dim form before him.

"I'll do you no harm," he repeated more gently, as he thought. "But you may not stay here; far better accommodation can be found elsewhere."

It was probably a person, he assured himself; and a woman at that, so he need not be afeared. And, should it turn out so, she would belong to one of the lower deck hands. Warrant and senior petty officers might apply to the captain for their wives to accompany them, sharing their accommodation and being victualled in exchange for light duties. Banks had already agreed to the presence of Mrs Roberts, the carpenter's wife, and shown himself lenient in similar cases in the past. Not every admiral approved of the practice of course, with many viewing members of the opposite sex as something between an unnecessary distraction and instruments of the devil. And there were even those who refused their officers permission to marry when on foreign stations, although such examples were becoming fewer with the passing years. But for a common hand to bring his partner, be she legal or otherwise, was another matter entirely, and one that was rarely sanctioned.

King remained motionless, as did the vision, so much so that he began to wonder if there was really anything there.

At no time in the current commission had the wedding garland been hoisted aboard *Prometheus.* Several women had attempted to take up residence on one of the gun decks, and two contrived to make the dark recesses of the lower their home for more than three days. They were found eventually, of course, and sent back in the next shore boat although, as the days lessened before *Prometheus* was due to sail, the divisional lieutenants and midshipmen were supposed to be more sensitive to the possibility of anyone else trying the same thing.

A lantern was handed down to him and, by its warm light, King eased himself closer to the figure. More could be seen now: and it was definitely a person, one below average height. Yes, undoubtedly human, probably female, and possibly a child. He took another step noticing that, even though it was not unduly cold, she appeared to be shivering.

"Come," he said, extending a hand, and speaking in the softest of tones. "Come, we shall take some food, and find you a place to be warm."

The figure moved forward by barely a pace but it was enough, and King could see her more clearly. She had a round, pleasant face, marred only slightly by the matted strands of long, dark hair that stuck to the sides of her skull and reached down to well below the shoulders. Her feet were bare and she wore the briefest of what might once have been either a white shift or some form of thin dress and, even in the dim light it was obvious, very little else.

"Send down a blanket," King ordered, only slightly raising his voice, and he noted the mutterings of confusion that his words created.

"Do you have a friend aboard?" King asked gently. "A husband, perchance?"

"Not a husband," her voice was barely more than a whisper and, with the creaks and groans of a ship gathering way, King had difficulty catching the words. "But I knows a man; Thompson. He brought me here."

Thompson. King sighed: he knew him as well. Not exactly a bad sort, but one that always looked for the main chance.

"You will be well cared for," King assured her as a soft lump fell to the deck behind with a thump. He turned, collected the blanket, and held it out. "Take this," he said. "Then we shall find you something hot to eat."

She seemed to come to a decision before making a dash forward and wrapping herself deep within his arms as if he might offer shelter as much as warmth. King reached over and pulled the blanket tight about her, suddenly conscious that he had not been embraced so for quite some while. The girl leant into him, her body frail and vulnerable and for King to hold her close was every bit as natural as the silent tears she soon began to shed.

* * *

Prometheus left harbour on a light, offshore breeze which strengthened and backed more easterly as the coast was left behind. It was little more than ten miles to the rendezvous point, but their masthead picked up the tail end of the convoy in under an hour and, in two, they had crept up to windward of the main body and were making their number together with that day's private signal.

The convoy's senior naval officer was Ford, an admiral Banks had known briefly when he had been a post captain. Old and somewhat crusty then, Ford now flew a proud blue flag at the mizzen, although most of his peers considered him lucky to have escaped being yellowed.

The force he commanded was significant, however. In addition to *Prometheus*, there were two other line ships, both also

70

being seventy-fours, as well as three frigates and a number of smaller, un-rated vessels that would have most of the work to do in chivvying up the slower or less responsive members of the convoy. And the escort's charge was no less impressive. Nine stately Indiamen of the larger classes; noble ships, built to carry wealth, power and influence in whatever form it was needed, be it general cargo, arms and equipment, or manpower. Together with the more numerous smaller traders and a handful of less impressive vessels that were already having difficulty keeping up, the total value of the convoy could be measured in millions.

"Flag acknowledges, sir," Lewis reported, his head buried in a small, but thick book. Chivers, one of the signal midshipmen, was holding the deck glass on the flagship and whispered something in his ear which set the pages turning. "Then our number - 'take station two leagues to leeward and astern of me'," the lieutenant continued with a hint of incredulity and an accusing look at his informer.

"I think that might be cables, Mr Lewis," Banks said in a markedly flat tone, and both officers blushed visibly. "But the wind is blowing the signal away from you," the captain allowed, before turning to the sailing master beside him on the quarterdeck. "Mr Brehaut, if you would be so kind..."

The senior warrant officer touched his hat and stepped forward. Banks moved away slightly, and might have been considering the nearest merchant, but was actually watching Brehaut intently.

The Jerseyman had first joined *Prometheus* at Portsmouth and carried excellent references from his previous captains, several of whom were known for being hard to please. As a man he was presentable; relatively short in stature, and lightly built, with frank blue eyes and a look of constant concern. But Brehaut was also modest: the fact that he spoke French fluently had only come out by accident, with a genial nature which soon made him a popular addition to the wardroom. The sailing master had also guided them from Spithead to Tor Bay without the help of a pilot or any hint of trouble.

That had been navigation, though; something an academic

71

may excel in: to conn a strange vessel with an untried crew through a crowded fleet would be a test of his innate seamanship, and many would judge such a skill every bit as important. Banks had been spoilt by his predecessor, Fraiser: a seaman of the highest standard. It would take someone of considerable talent to impress after such an example.

Brehaut's first command was bellowed through the speaking trumpet with perhaps not quite the force most would consider necessary. But it was a sensible order nevertheless and, as the forecourse was taken in and the ship ceased to gain on the convoy, settling to a speed fractionally slower than that of the surrounding shipping, Banks began to relax.

Two East India Company monsters were forereaching to either side; the captain noticed Brehaut consider both, but keep *Prometheus* on a steady course that allowed them plenty of room to pass. Then, when the danger was cleared, he had the helm put across, and *Prometheus* began to cut a diagonal course across their wake.

Banks acknowledged that this was probably the most dangerous part of the procedure. None of the watch keeping officers had handled the ship for more than a few tricks, and to estimate the difference in speed that might be expected of *Prometheus* when turning from being close hauled to a broad reach was probably beyond all of them. Brehaut had extra canvas in hand, but even re-setting the forecourse would take time, and there were close on ten large ships bearing down on them. The captain was also aware that most of the merchants were commanded by Company men; trained seafarers in the main, but not known for endangering their charges unnecessarily. They might easily view the warship heading across their path as a hazard, and start taking unnecessary avoiding action that, in turn, would endanger others.

But either Brehaut was in luck, or his intentions were both obvious and unambiguous, for *Prometheus* was allowed to reach clear water off the flagship's larboard quarter without a major incident. Then all that remained was for her to lose way, allowing all to forereach until the required distance had been attained, then drop the forecourse once more and adjust canvas to bring her to convoy speed.

Banks drew a silent sigh of relief. The ship, her crew, and Brehaut had performed perfectly; failure in any one might not be considered a disaster as such, but would hardly have been the best start to a commission, and no captain can give of his best while being unsure of any aspect of his command.

Brehaut reported the ship in position, then replaced the speaking trumpet in its becket before turning from the binnacle, his task apparently accomplished. Banks noticed that, apart from a slight flush to his pale cheeks, he did not seem unduly moved by the episode, and took a place next to Caulfield and Davison without a comment to either.

"Very good, Mr Brehaut," Banks told him. "That was well done indeed." The commendation was formal and almost a platitude, but in this case meant with total sincerity.

* * *

"As to the state of any pregnancy, I would not care to speculate," the surgeon said, washing his hands in a pewter basin. "Though if so, it must be precious early and I would say you are much underfed. You may also be suffering from some form of chill – there is perhaps a trace of fever, but no more."

Manning turned and surveyed his patient again. She was sitting back on the plain deal table and drawing the light gown about herself once more. He had not seen his own wife, Kate, for over a month, yet several years of married life, and many more dealing with the meat that comprises a human body, enabled him to view the woman with total objectivity. Certainly she was undernourished; the bones on her upper arms, legs and ribs were far too prominent, and he had noticed the obvious signs of an empty stomach during his examination.

"Were you to wish it, I may be able to start investigations as regards the possibility of a foetus, though you will appreciate that a line-of-battleship is hardly equipped for such tests." He gave a reassuring look. "But from what you say I would diagnose a simple case of sea-sickness. You have had no recurrences after setting foot on dry land?"

The girl shook her head and Manning's face relaxed. "I thought not: it is a certain remedy."

He moved across the sick berth and opened a locker. "I do not have much in the way of clothing I'm afraid." He pulled out several shirts and a pair of canvas trousers. "These may do for the present, and of course you may keep that gown. You will doubtless be able to make more of them later. There are two men aboard who act as reasonable tailors, I am told, and will be happy to oblige if you are not so skilled."

"Am I staying then?" she asked, turning on the table and allowing her bare legs to swing down.

"Most certainly," Manning replied. "For now at least. We are deep into the English Channel and cannot turn back." He was about to add 'for a mere slip of a girl', but his innate sensitivity saved him. "But you will no doubt want to wash," he said instead. "And may do so here, if you wish – it is probably more private. I shall send to the galley for hot water."

"Where are we bound?" Her voice was fragile, but Manning noticed she had actually gained a little colour in the last minute or so. The thought of being set ashore must have been playing on her mind and, as he considered the trusting expression, he wondered if she were inclined to act younger than her years.

"We are for the Mediterranean, my dear," he told her. "And will be calling at Gibraltar; you may be permitted to land there if you wish, though it will be the part of the captain to confirm any arrangements."

"And Lisbon? Shall we be going to Lisbon?"

Manning paused on his way to the sick berth entrance. "Yes, I recall you did say it was your home." He opened the door no more than a fraction and murmured to someone in the dispensary beyond before closing it firmly once more. "The water will be coming presently," he explained. "As to Lisbon I cannot rightly say; once more, it is the captain you will have to speak with on such matters. But we have been with the Med. Fleet afore, and the Tagus was a useful station then, so I would certainly not rule it out."

* * *

He had not engineered the situation; it just so happened that King found himself in the great cabin with the captain when Ross was sent to request the latter's presence on deck. It was a minor matter; Banks would soon return, and they could continue to discuss the starboard watch bill, so King remained standing by the large table, but indicated for the seaman to remain also.

"We have not spoken," King began awkwardly. "Not since the day you volunteered."

"That's right, sir," Ross agreed.

"You are settling down?"

"Well enough, thank you, sir," the seaman replied with little feeling. "My mess seem a decent bunch," he added.

King had arranged for the former officer to be with a seaman who was one of his personal favourites.

"I have served with Flint in a number of ships," he told Ross. "Lieutenant Lewis started in his mess as an ordinary hand: you may progress as well and could achieve your former rank, who can tell?"

Ross said nothing, but now his eyes were set directly ahead as if he were being questioned, and King felt he had inadvertently stepped over an unseen line. "You know you may ask me if there is any way in which I can help," he added.

"Thank you, sir, but I shall be able to manage." The reply came quickly: then Ross seemed to soften. "But your concern is appreciated."

"This is a perilous life, and no one can be certain of the future," King continued carefully. "I know nothing of your personal circumstances, but think the majority of officers have been guilty of at least one trivial error in the past: I mean one that would have seen them in peril, were it discovered."

"But few are come down upon quite so heavily as me," Ross added, with a wry look.

"And what caused such an act?" King asked after a moment or two. "Not that you need tell me," he hurried to add. "Every man's history is his own to keep private."

75

"Aye, I would say so, sir." Again that look. "Whatever the status he may have attained." Ross seemed to consider, then continued. "But I am happy to tell you, Mr King; my secret has been kept so far, for which I am grateful, and I would gauge that adding to it will not be too great a burden for you."

King gestured silently, and Ross began.

"My commission was revoked earlier this year. It was by court martial; my last vessel, *Wakeful* had run aground off Crump Island and was a total loss."

King remembered reading the first news of the incident, and being struck by the irony of the ship's name when it was surely wrecked by the inattention of whosoever had command. But there was nothing unusual in a vessel foundering; far more Royal Navy ships were lost in such a way than to enemy action. And the act might well have mitigating circumstances, in which case it would attract little more than a reprimand. There had been no subsequent notice of any eventual court martial verdict, however, and King had disregarded the matter.

"I did try for the merchant service; they are short of hands, and thought to find myself a berth as a junior officer or mate. But the India Company seem thick with the Admiralty, neither did any private owner want a man who could not pay attention. And so it was the R.N. or starve – which was why I especially sought out a member of *Prometheus'* people that evening."

"Indeed?" King asked. "Why so?"

"Captain Banks has a fine reputation," Ross replied. "I read of his engagement with the French squadron off St Helena on my journey home; it was as fine an action as ever I had heard, yet none of his officers were known to me. And at that time the word was you were bound for the Channel Fleet, which has an honourable commander, and is set a goodly distance from the Caribbean."

All made perfect sense, although King was still in doubt regarding the court martial verdict. Ross came across well: it seemed strange that one so apparently sound and reliable should have been broken. "I am saddened to hear your tale," he said, "though wonder that the blame for the loss of any ship can be wholly attributed to a single officer."

"I said all I was permitted to at the court martial," Ross' voice was flat and without emotion. "*Wakeful* was nought but a brig and I her only lieutenant. The watch had been mine when she ran aground, but Commander Harker was determined to try for a faster passage and took the conn. And he was a favoured man: the other officers owed their positions to him, and one was the son of an admiral."

It was not such an unusual scenario, although King remained silent.

"Then we had the presiding captains," Ross continued relentlessly. "Most were close to Harker or his cronies and, when it came to the call, all seemed content for me to take full responsibility."

"I see," King said finally, and he surely did. He had never come across Harker personally but the man appeared as one with more connections than skill. On a foreign station, where the eye of the public and a far off Admiralty could easily be distracted, it would have been little trouble for influential friends to whitewash a popular commander. And with a presumably friendless lieutenant on hand to bear his blame, all could be neatly sorted.

Such were the problems of serving in un-rated vessels. Though more power and responsibility rested with their senior men, and a man might learn and progress more quickly than aboard battle-wagons such as *Prometheus*, the risks were also that much greater. Had Ross been backed by a loyal band of officers, Harker could not have passed the blame so easily. But, when it came down to one man's word against another, and the captain was well connected, it was clear who would come in second.

"Once more, I am sorry," King sighed, "and can only repeat my earlier offer. Should a chance present for you to be promoted, or singled out in any way, I will not hesitate to take it."

"Thank you, sir," Ross said, with a little more feeling this time. "I appreciate that though it was made plain to me by the court president that I may not expect to progress."

"You cannot accept promotion?" King questioned.

"No," Ross told him sadly. "That path is now forever closed to me."

* * *

Ford might have been an uninspiring captain but, now that he was an admiral and in command of an entire fleet, he certainly did not lack energy. No sooner had *Prometheus* joined the convoy than a general change of course was ordered, and the signals continued with annoying regularity for the rest of the evening.

Individual merchants were commanded to keep up, or maintain better station, with their naval escorts often being sent to enforce the order. This meant there were usually one or two warships either crossing the convoy or leaving their own post unguarded while they chivvied a back marker, causing no end of consternation to the officer of the watch in every other vessel. And the admiral was also setting a breathless pace. *Prometheus*, being fresh from the yard, was able to keep up under topsails, courses and staysails, but there were some of the older Indiamen, those who had already made three Eastern trips and were close to the end of their useful life, that were having obvious problems.

The convoy commodore, an aged HEIC officer named Spice, had protested, sending a series of poorly composed signals that were decoded with ill suppressed amusement by Lewis and his team. But Ford was having none of it, and clearly intended to use his rank and position to the fullest extent. His enthusiasm even extended to refusing the usual request for a reduction in sail as the sun began to dip towards the horizon. It was a habit most passenger carrying merchants practised if travelling independently and had almost become traditional when in convoy. The previous rigid sailing order was relaxed to give a slightly larger margin of error between each ship, but there was no lessening in speed and the convoy's pace, which at times exceeded seven knots, was maintained throughout even the darkest hours.

After two days of such a regime, there was no doubting the standard of sailing exhibited by certain members of the convoy had improved considerably. Brehaut, *Prometheus'* sailing master, was also pleased to note they had recorded a truly creditable distance, and were out of the relative confines of the Channel.

The following afternoon he stood at the chart room table and surveyed the situation. There was a change of course due and, with the wind having backed more to the west, he expected it sooner than later. Brehaut looked once more at the series of small pin pricks that marked their progress up to that point. It might be prudent to warn the captain of such an event, and even pleasant when proved correct, as he undoubtedly would be, although Brehaut was never one to court a good opinion and certainly did not seek approval or promotion.

Since leaving his native Jersey and joining the Navy twenty-three years back, his aspirations had been met in full. For all his professional life, Brehaut's only wish had been to become a sailing master; to him a position that epitomised seamanship at its best, and he did not want for more.

"Admiral's signalling a change of course, Mr Brehaut." The midshipman's voice had followed the slightest of taps on the barely opened chart room door and was punctuated by its sudden closure. The sailing master was unsurprised at the lad's brevity. His rank, though one of the more important in the ship, was considered less than any of the lieutenants, all of whom carried commissions drawn out on parchment, as opposed to his simple paper warrant. And it was not uncommon for midshipmen, who made up his principal students when it came to teaching navigation and general seamanship, to treat him initially as something between a schoolmaster and a jape. All aspired to wardroom rank, so could hardly take a man invited to berth there out of courtesy, rather than right, with any gravity. But Brehaut had served in many ships and knew the importance of his role would be proven in time. And he was also confident that any youngster who finished the deployment would do so with far more respect for a sailing master's duties.

He moved out of the darkness of the chart room and on to the quarterdeck. The heady sun had already chased away every sign of an earlier shower and the day was fast becoming uncomfortably hot.

"Flag orders sou'-sou' west, Mr Brehaut," Cartwright, one of the master's mates, told him as he stepped up to the binnacle. "Captain's aware, but will not be attendin'," the warrant officer added.

"Very good," Brehaut replied, after a nod to Davison, who was the officer of the watch.

"And the commodore is repeating the order," the signal midshipman reported with a grin. "Just so as we knows he's still livin'."

South-south west was most definitely the fastest course, even if it would take the convoy perilously close to the west coast of France and, more importantly, the numerous islands and shallows that littered it. Clearly the admiral was putting everything into a quick passage, and did not appear unduly worried about endangering his precious convoy in the process.

"Prepare to alter course," Brehaut said, although the warning was unnecessary; all on the quarterdeck and most of the duty watch were aware of the situation, and what was about to happen. It was not a complex manoeuvre, like tacking or wearing, but still must be carried out well and Brehaut calmly collected the speaking trumpet from the binnacle as they began to wait.

The signal midshipman now had his glass trained solely on the flagship as every man stood ready. All were prepared to act, and intended doing so in a manner that would do their ship credit. They might have many untrained men aboard, but those with skill would cover and nothing must cloud the crack reputation they were all determined to establish for *Prometheus*. Then, after what seemed like an appreciable time but was actually less than thirty seconds, the young voice shouted "Down!" as the flags were whipped away.

Brehaut roared out the orders, *Prometheus'* helm was put across, and her braces adjusted as she took up her new course with all the composure and aplomb expected of a Royal Navy third rate line-of-battleship. About them, some of the merchants began chasing their prows. Others showed flapping canvas while, in one case, a foreyard refused to move, forcing the Indiaman concerned to fall out of station. But *Prometheus* and her sailing master had done their duty with competence and, as he recorded the time and change of course on the slate, Brehaut was content.

Chapter Six

"Scran's a good deal better," Marine Captain Donaldson commented through a half-filled mouth. "Has someone shot the cook?"

"Something upon those lines," Dawson, the purser, agreed. "And we may blame Mr Lewis, here," he continued, nodding towards the lieutenant seated opposite.

Lewis looked up absent-mindedly at the mention of his name and was surprised to see all at the wardroom dining table smiling benignly at him.

"Nabbed us one of the finest cooks in the West Country," Marine Lieutenant James agreed, with evident respect.

"I did?" Lewis replied, blinking.

"Rather," the marine confirmed. "Queer little man to speak to, but knows his food – shaken them all up in the pantry, so he has. If he keeps the same heading, we'll soon have a kitchen to be proud of."

Lewis had noticed the improvement in wardroom fare but was totally unaware of any responsibility for the transformation, and felt suspicious of the sudden attention.

"Fellow you took from the The Three Tuns," Dawson prompted. "Calls himself Potterton."

The name meant little to Lewis, but then even the raid on the tavern was little more than a distant memory.

"Too used to the good things in life for my liking," the purser continued. "Always pestering me for wardroom supplies, and I tells him that's a completely different department. But you can't argue with the result; this is the best lobscouse I have tasted in years."

"Well, we should offer you a vote of thanks," Donaldson said, raising his glass in approbation. "Damned fine show, Lewis. Damned fine."

* * *

"Her name is Judith Kinnison, she is nineteen years old, an orphan by all accounts, and hails from Lisbon," King announced.

"But not Portuguese?" Banks questioned. He had seen the girl in passing and not been struck by any obvious foreign traits.

"I have no idea where born," King replied hesitantly. "But she claims to be English, as was her family. Although she also states her father to have been a Scot; it is all singularly vague." He shifted uneasily on his chair.

Actually the interview with the girl had disturbed him greatly. Since that last, disastrous, meeting with his estranged wife, King had been keeping away from females of any description. Even Mrs Roberts, the carpenter's wife, a woman with the face of a mule and a demeanour not so very different, was given a wide birth. But Miss Kinnison had awakened much of the urges he had considered successfully stifled, and to discuss her now, dispassionately and in front of his captain and first lieutenant, was strangely disconcerting. King was a seaman, and would have preferred another subject to have been chosen.

"She believes him to have worked in the diplomatic service, though any connection is tenuous," he continued, manfully. "There are no surviving relatives that anyone is aware of. Lord and Lady Shillingford brought her up in their Lisbon house, though it was the servants who cared for her in the main, and she joined them in their work on reaching an acceptable age."

"So what brought her to Tor Bay?" Caulfield asked.

"Well, that is where it becomes even more of a puzzle," King confessed. "The girl is confused and speaks only of travelling in a big ship. And the surgeon said she were afeared of being with child."

"And is she?" Banks asked.

King shook his head. "No, sir. Mr Manning thought it more likely the symptoms described to be nothing more than sea-sickness."

His audience erupted into sudden laughter which took King, who was now deep into the story, by surprise. Caulfield even added something along the lines of wishing all such cases were so easily cured.

"I would say that the girl is no half-wit," King continued, now decidedly flustered. "But then neither is she inordinately clever."

"And she was transported in a big ship?" Caulfield asked, still chuckling.

"That is what she said," King confirmed.

"Well, it was likely to have been a ship," Banks' expression was now more controlled, even if King suspected he still found the situation annoyingly amusing. "And we can probably assume it to have been big..."

"I believe it was," the young lieutenant agreed earnestly, conscious that he was now blushing slightly behind his notes. "An Indiaman, I would chance, though she claims not to know the name, and will not say that of her travelling companion."

"If he abandoned her in Tor Bay I'd judge it misplaced loyalty," Caulfield mused. "Perchance enquiries made at the Shillingford house might tell us more?"

Banks shook his head. "Be that the case or not, we are bound to this convoy until thirty-eight degrees north. And then must make for Gibraltar before seeking out *Victory* in the Med. I can authorise no diversion in order to repatriate some fool of a girl who cannot remember much beyond her name."

King swallowed; he sympathised entirely with the captain's predicament, but that did not ease his situation any. As the officer who had discovered the stowaway, it had fallen upon him to represent her, and he would far rather have been given a different task.

"Well, there is no more to be said now; if chance presents to transfer the wench to an Indiaman, we must take it," the captain continued. "But I will not delay the convoy any, and neither shall I request a diversion to the Tagus." He turned to King. "You have found her accommodation?"

"She has been sleeping in the sick berth," the lieutenant replied. "But I had assumed would eventually lodge with Mr and Mrs Roberts."

"The two of them have space hardly bigger than the chart room," Caulfield muttered. "And I wouldn't trust that badger

Roberts to share with anything female, even with his witch of a wife in the offing."

"No indeed," Banks agreed. "Both gun room and orlop would be equally unsuitable, and we have no schoolmaster or chaplain to take her under their wing. It will have to be the wardroom."

The two lieutenants regarded their captain with more than a hint of incredulity. Although supposedly manned by gentlemen, the senior officers' accommodation could be a very basic environment and hardly suitable for the introduction of a solitary young woman.

"Would that be entirely appropriate, sir?" Caulfield questioned.

"Is anywhere in a ship of war?" Banks replied. "I could oust Roberts from his cabin and let her share with Mrs Roberts alone, but fear such temptation would not be good for the people's morale, and there would undoubtedly be a problem with the heads. No, the wardroom it will have to be. The chaplain's quarters are currently being used for storage, I believe; have them cleared, and she may be suited there."

King and Caulfield exchanged glances. In the past they had shared smaller spaces with several women; it had not been ideal, though manageable. But *Prometheus* carried a larger staff of officers, so the ratio of men to a single female would be higher.

"Perchance her presence might improve the language and behaviour of some of the newer officers," Banks continued, warming to the idea, and seemingly oblivious to any problem he may have introduced. "And, who knows, could even prove a cure for Captain Donaldson's incessant flatulence."

* * *

As the commission rolled on, a reasonable level of routine and order became established in most departments. The carpenter's was perhaps the first, luck having provided Roberts with a team of trained men who needed little instruction and were already cooperating in a way more common at the end of a voyage. Stevenson, their sailmaker, was almost as well served, as was the ship's cook; a man named Stone. In the latter's case, this was more than fortunate. Stone was an experienced seaman of advanced years who had lost a leg at the Battle of Copenhagen, although this was his first experience of feeding several hundred bodies, three times a day. But though he might know precious little about catering, Stone was an expert when it came to organising men, and the high proportion of landsmen aboard *Prometheus* provided a rich vein of experience for him to recruit from. Other areas were not quite so well served however, with the afterguard, gunners and topmen showing the main deficiencies. They were faults that would take time to rectify and caused more than a degree of worry amongst the lieutenants.

But summer had now become firmly established and, as *Prometheus* headed ever further south, she was warmed by a sun that seemed to grow in strength by the day. With the wind constant and in the north-east, this was indeed perfect sailing weather, even if few of her officers, be they commissioned, warrant or petty, had any mind to enjoy the conditions. From breakfast at eight bells of the morning watch, to down hammocks, twelve hours later, the ship was in a near constant state of exercise, with topmen almost continually aloft, while the rumble of gun trucks and shouts from the quarter gunners seemed to echo throughout every waking hour.

And the regular drills had other, positive, side effects: *Prometheus'* officers were also finding their feet. The majority had served aboard other ships in their current rank and needed only to adjust to the peculiarities of their present vessel. But for Lieutenant Lewis, until recently a master's mate and once a common seaman, it was his first experience of wardroom life, and the change was more difficult to embrace.

Small matters, such as having a marine as a personal servant, and dining at a different hour, with formal toasts, superior food, and a seemingly endless supply of alcohol, were relatively easy to adjust to. It was the authority his new found status attracted that he found more disconcerting. Even as a senior warrant officer, he had remained on familiar terms with the men. He was of their stock, after all, had lived their lives, and knew all their requests and excuses as well as the reasons behind them. But now he was officially a quarterdeck officer there could be no such intimacy.

Men he had known well, and even messed with in previous ships, would only exchange a formal knuckled salute in return for an amiable smile, while anything from a specific order to a polite request was treated with the ultimate respect, and responded to instantly. Lewis supposed he would find such attention to be usual in time, and remembered providing as much to commissioned officers in the past. But still the distance between his old life and the new was disconcerting, and not completely welcomed.

Meanwhile, on the lower deck, Ross was making adjustments that were almost exactly diametric. The incongruity of carrying out duties only ever ordered in the past took some while to accustom to. And having to look after himself when, even as a humble volunteer he had a hammock man and shared the services of a steward, was also a new experience. Then there were other, greater adjustments: for all his time at sea, Ross had been in small ships and considered officers' accommodation to be cramped. But the worst encountered was nothing compared to what an ordinary hand had to endure. And further than simply lacking personal space, he found he must learn the subtleties of what was, and was not, acceptable to men who lived in such close proximity to each other. How dirty bodies, incessant snoring or any other unsociable habit was soon jointly identified and corrected, while confidences and simple friendships became valued and respected every bit as much as those encountered in more gentlemanly circles.

But still progress had been made; each week one man from each mess was voted cook, a thankless duty that involved drawing the daily allowance of raw food from the holders and ensuring correct amounts were given. It was something Ross had done with an impeccable fairness that drew silent approval from his fellows, and he had been selected more than once. And other skills, from tying simple hitches with one hand and in the dark, to mending clothes and chewing, rather than smoking, tobacco were coming to him gradually. His informal education also had fringe benefits; new found knowledge was developing alongside scantly remembered muscles that ached at night but proved far more solid the next day. And hands, previously soft and without character, now became efficient tools, if mildly ingrained with the honourable stain of hard work. He felt his waist reduce and upper arms broaden; a four hour shift aboard a hammock gave far better sleep than any time previously spent in a cot, and the fellowship found in his lower deck mess was undoubtedly superior to any wardroom atmosphere previously known.

His fall from grace had been a disaster, and nothing could stop Ross yearning for the feel of a quarterdeck under his boot. But life on the lower deck was not the hell he had imagined. And in time, he felt, may even become acceptable.

King was also adjusting to the world of a large ship of war, while starting to positively benefit from his reformed ways. His abstinence from alcohol had heralded a dramatic improvement in both performance and attitude, while the private knowledge that he was no longer abusing his body gave a satisfaction that was in danger of making him smug.

Life in a third rate's wardroom was very different from the frigate gun rooms he had been more recently accustomed to. The amount of space was still hard to comprehend, and seemed to make getting to know the intake of fresh faces a more lengthy business. A few he became familiar with straight away: others took far longer and Marine Captain Donaldson was one of the latter.

The older man's loud voice and dominating ways seemed to saturate even such a large living area. And in the brief pause following Donaldson retiring, and before the deep, stentorian snores began, he found he was not alone in drawing a sigh of relief. On the other hand, Second Lieutenant Davison, undoubtedly his superior, yet almost a year younger, and as fresh faced as many of their midshipmen, took acclimatising to in a totally different way.

But the hardest of all to accommodate was not one of King's fellow officers. In fact the person in question was entitled to no rank whatsoever, and yet dominated his thoughts when really there were far more healthy matters to consider.

Despite any reservations they may have held, the girl settled remarkably well in the wardroom. Judy, as she came to be known, was apparently used to unusual living conditions at the

Shillingford house, so close proximity to the opposite gender was no novelty to her. And in time, as *Prometheus* and the rest of the convoy headed steadily south, all the senior officers became accustomed to having an additional female servant, for she was determined to earn her passage in some way, attending to them.

The other stewards accepted the help readily enough; none more so than Potterton who, despite his deferential appearance, was a true firebrand when it came to running an efficient pantry. He quickly noticed a fellow spirit: the girl had an obvious talent for dealing with food in any form and with her help the quality of *Prometheus'* catering rose further. Meanwhile other members of the wardroom staff, already far happier now they were working for a professional, took her under their collective wing. Most were many years her senior and treated the naïve Judy with a mixture of paternal care and professional appreciation, while simultaneously maintaining a wary eye for any common sailor who attempted too close an association.

And, as most officers mentioned at some point, she did clean up remarkably well. To eyes starved of female company, Judy looked particularly fetching in a crisp white steward's shirt and round jacket above her plain dark half dress sewn from slop cloth the purser had provided. While there had been no temptation, King's enforced celibacy had been relatively simple to maintain, but with the distraction of her wandering about his living space at all times, his thoughts had become harder to keep on the task in hand. In the past, any desires that proved too persistent could be saved for the evening and then drowned in a surplus of alcohol but, with strong drink forgone, and a pretty face and figure constantly in attendance, King was finding a clear focus harder to achieve, although he was helped in no small way by an unlikely source; the other officers had also noted her charms.

All treated Judy differently, as would befit their various personalities, from the polite, almost sisterly affection exhibited by Marine Lieutenants Swift and James, through Benson's more equal and gentle teasing, to the overt leering of Marine Captain Donaldson. Even Caulfield, the balding and prematurely middle-aged first lieutenant, who most automatically assumed to be immune from feminine appeal was not unmoved.

But Caulfield and King had served together for far too long for there to be any subterfuge; the younger man could easily detect subtle differences in attitude when the first lieutenant was attended by Judy, rather than a regular wardroom steward. And King found such discoveries strangely reassuring: however wrong it might be to be interested in the young girl, he was evidently not the only man guilty.

* * *

"This is something you have to see," Thompson told Butler and Jameson as the afternoon watch was dismissed.

"What you found then, Thombo?" Jameson asked. He and Butler had spent almost the entire afternoon aloft in continuous drill and the prospect of the second spirit ration of the day, supper, and then rest was far more attractive. Besides, in a ship that had been at sea a fair while there could hardly be anything new to discover.

Thompson said nothing in reply, but merely beckoned them to follow as he made his way along the upper deck towards the forecastle.

Jemmy Ducks, the elderly man detailed to caring for *Prometheus'* prodigious stock of poultry, was clearing out pens: a job that seemed to take up most of his waking hours. He looked round at the trio as they approached, and Jameson noticed the subtle change of expression on the oddly angelic face.

"What cheer, Jemmy?" Thompson asked, while flashing a look of shared mischief to his two messmates.

The old man stayed silent, but stopped work, and rested back easily on his haunches as he regarded his visitors.

"Been a busy day has it?" Thompson persisted. "Jameson an' Butler here have been aloft, and I was at gunnery practice. But how's the life of an idler: keepin' track of them hens, are you?"

"I been clearing the coops," Ducks replied solidly. "I keeps them clean for the officers' birds."

"I'm sure you do," Thompson agreed. "And it's a fine job you make of it."

Butler and Jameson exchanged glances; both would have preferred to be somewhere else and found little sport in teasing such a one as Jemmy. But Thompson, it seemed, was determined to show them more.

"You do good work, Jemmy. And it's only fair you gets some recognition," the seaman told him. "So I brought you a present."

Two clenched fists were offered up and slowly opened in front of the elderly face. In one palm was a small silver coin, while the other held a tattered note.

"Now here we are, Jemmy," Thompson continued. "Either is yours to keep – there's a fine English pound, or a shiny, silver groat – which will you have?"

Ducks raised his gaze from the money to the seaman standing over him, and then back to what was on offer.

"You can take one," Thompson prompted. "But not both. Come on, you old cuff – Harrison says you've done it 'undreds of times afore."

The rheumy eyes were now set on the money and there was an awkward pause. Then, faster than could be seen, the groat was snatched from Thompson's grip, and pressed deep into the man's pocket.

"Seems he does that every time!" Thompson said in triumph as he turned to grin at his companions. "Always the groat, never the pound."

"And what would you have done if he'd taken it?" Jameson asked.

"Get it back off him," Thompson told them simply. "I can't afford to go tossing money away."

"But you let him keep the groat," Butler pointed out.

"A groat's neither here nor there," Thompson replied loftily. "An' it were worth it just to see 'im bobbed."

The old man had turned back to his work and, as the three walked away, began knocking soiled straw out of the coop once more.

"Half the larboard watch has tried it," Thompson continued in hushed wonder. "An' he's never once taken the pound."

"I am surprised," Butler commented, although his tone said otherwise.

"Aye," Jameson agreed. "He's a chub, and no mistakin'."

* * *

And so the convoy sailed relentlessly south, with Admiral Ford urging maximum speed at all times; a policy that prevented any physical communication between ships, and forced some of the smaller, unofficial, members to fall by the wayside. Once free of both the constraints and protection of the Royal Navy warships, these independent vessels could set their own pace, although many undoubtedly fell victim to the line of faint shadows that constantly haunted the pack.

This was the flotilla of enemy privateers that kept steady pace to the north of the main body, and on the very edge of the horizon: predators stalking the herd, waiting for one, possibly not so fit, to present themselves as prey.

On the night when, by Brehaut's unspoken estimation, they had been taken far too close to the rocks off Ushant and were about to enter Biscay's uncertain seas, Ford authorised a force of smaller warships to deal with the followers. What followed appeared to be a splendid fight, and one that resulted in two of the privateers so afire that the night sky was lit spectacularly, even dazzling those on deck in the darkened convoy several miles off. The escorts returned, bloodied but victorious, the next morning but it took little more than four days before the number of stalkers was as before.

And then, when the storms of Biscay appeared, one threat was swapped for another and no consideration could be given to enemy activity. *Prometheus* was not alone in discovering many items previously considered secured to be less so. She lost small pieces of equipment; both the galley stove chimney and one of the stern lanterns were washed away, never to be seen again, and the pinnace that sat on the spar deck amidships was cleanly stove in by a fiddle block falling from the foremast. Simply remaining in contact with what had become a widely spread jumble of ships became an impossible task, and there was no question of keeping anything like their prescribed station. And after such a time on shore, even seasoned members of the crew were liable to exhibit what soon became known as 'symptoms of pregnancy', and it wasn't until the far, north-west corner of Spain was rounded, and the convoy finally began sailing more peacefully down the coast of Portugal, that order was finally restored.

Their sinister followers failed to re-appear, clearly having a set hunting ground that did not extend so far south, but that did not mean there was no longer any danger from pirates. Each day brought them nearer to the Barbary Coast, a particularly evil stretch of land to the north of Africa that was infested with all sizes and types of warship. Some, the larger ones, were known to prowl quite deep into the Atlantic, and made a rich living from ships similar to those *Prometheus* protected.

As a stately two decker, tackling smaller enemies was not strictly in her remit; far better to leave such matters to lighter escorts: the brigs, sloops and frigates that were faster and so much more manoeuvrable. But, as all the officers were aware, should *Prometheus* fall in with a corsair as an enemy, it would be a difficult action to carry off well. A handy little gun boat might run rings around the ponderous battleship and, if a merchant fell victim while supposedly under her protection, they would be held up to ridicule by all.

But no pirates were spotted and, as they came increasingly closer to the line of latitude where they might finally bid farewell to their charges, there was a noticeable lightening in the attitude of most officers.

All were now yearning to be released from the convoy; to say goodbye to the constant tension of chivvying obstinate civilian masters, some of whom seemed hell bent on self destruction. To see an end to taking orders from superannuated admirals who delighted in making contrary signals while apparently glorying in their power.

And soon they would be free: soon their prow must turn for Gibraltar and, soon, *Prometheus* could take on her correct role as a warship, sailing in a mighty fleet with others of her kind. Then her overall command would shift to that of Admiral Nelson, noted firebrand and born fighter, and such a change could not come too early for most on board.

But when it did arrive, they were all taken by surprise.

Chapter Seven

"We are steering damnably close to the Burlings," the sailing master said in disgust.

King had the watch and turned to him. "The rocks to the north of the Tagus?" he asked, surprised. "We have already worked out to sea; do they still stand in our path?"

"Not exactly," Brehaut conceded. "More to the south-west, and will doubtless be in sight presently. By my estimation we should pass within a couple of miles but, with this wind, and the manner in which some have kept station so far..."

He left the sentence unfinished; Brehaut did not approve of Admiral Ford, or anyone in authority who took unnecessary risks, although it was probably unwise to say as much out loud, even to one as trusted as King.

The convoy's navigation had made the sailing master uneasy for most of the journey, being as it relied far too much on detecting seamarks and coastal points, rather than sun and star sightings. And on the occasions when they were forced further out to sea, direction became worryingly vague. During the mad dash through the storms and tempests of Biscay, they had apparently been surprised by the northern coast of Spain, which was a concern in itself. There might have been some excuse for the last incident; a blanket of cloud had made shooting any celestial object all but impossible. But simple dead reckoning had told Brehaut they were off course, and for several hours he was left with the dilemma of when he should alert the captain. Fortunately the land was spotted in daylight and good time, so no ships were lost; but since then the admiral had only seemed happy when the Portuguese coast was visible off their larboard beam, and *Prometheus'* sailing master remained uncomfortable.

"Oh I dare say we shall clear all well enough," Brehaut grunted. "We have done so with every hazard to date, though the Burlings are known for being hard to spot, and I should be happier to leave any lee shore a little further beyond the horizon."

The ship was on a broad reach, showing topsails, staysails and forecourse, and easily maintaining the speed that Ford also appeared to find so essential. And what Brehaut said was correct: even while standing by the binnacle, his memory of the chart was almost as good as having it before him. To be certain was never a bad thing however and, as any good sailing master eventually becomes almost pathologically cautious, Brehaut was about to leave the deck and check when a call came from the masthead.

It was land, presumably one of the outcrops of the treacherous rocks the locals called the Berlengass and, as he had predicted, well enough away to be of no immediate danger. But there was more: a further complication.

"I can make out what looks like a ship set down upon it," the lookout added a few minutes later.

Brehaut and King exchanged glances, and both waited while a midshipman with a glass was sent up to check and make a full report.

"It looks like a liner: something of size, at least – maybe an Indiaman," the lad began hesitantly. "But a good deal larger than the rocks about her. And she is partially dismasted."

"It would appear someone has already discovered your hazard," King told the sailing master laconically, but Brehaut made no reply. To him any vessel running aground was too sensitive a subject to be taken lightly.

"She's an Indiaman, right enough," the midshipman continued when they had drawn closer. "Not of the largest class, but firmly aground."

"Too far off to be one of our current charges, surely?" King murmured.

"Oh I should say so," the sailing master agreed. "We are the stern escort, but any of the convoy's ships would need to be spectacularly off station to manage such a feat."

"Then I think Sir Richard should know," King replied, with only faint reluctance. It would mean disrupting the captain's meal; by tradition he dined an hour later than the wardroom, but Banks insisted on being informed of anything out of the usual, so could hardly blame King for obeying his standing orders.

95

By the time the captain appeared, most of the convoy were also aware of the beached Indiaman, and several had even made a mild, but unilateral, turn to starboard to be sure of not sharing her fate. Banks waited patiently on the quarterdeck while the admiral sent admonishing signals to his errant charges, and then *Prometheus'* number inevitably came up. They were the sternmost escort of any size and it was of no surprise that they had been chosen to investigate.

"What is our exact position, Mr Brehaut?" Banks asked formally.

The sailing master touched his hat and approached the captain. "Thirty-nine degrees, twenty-eight minutes north, sir," he replied with commendable efficiency. "I shall be certain to note that in the log."

"Do that, if you please, master," Banks replied. "There is what appears to be an Indiaman caught on the rocks off the Burlings," he continued. "We are to see if we may haul her off."

All knew Brehaut had been present throughout, but still it seemed appropriate, and even polite, for the sailing master to adopt a look of mild surprise.

"I should be obliged if we might close with her," Banks continued. He had dined well and phrasing the order in the form of a request suited his mood.

"Shall we be rejoining the convoy subsequently, sir?" King asked, as Brehaut directed *Prometheus* onto the course that had long since been stored ready inside the sailing master's head. King knew both the captain, and his moods, well enough to guess the question would be tolerated.

"That depends upon a number of factors," Banks told him. "The most important being the condition of the wreck. She may be derelict and empty, in which case we might simply stop for a look see, before returning to the others. But if any form of salvage is possible it shall take time, and will not be aided by the current wind."

Indeed, lee shores were to be avoided, and the thought of the complex manoeuvring which would undoubtedly accompany a rescue attempt, was enough to cause any seaman concern.

"But with our departure point hardly more than two hundred miles off," Banks continued, "I rather think *Prometheus* may have seen the last of Admiral Ford."

"We should close with the wreck in under half an hour, sir," Brehaut reported as he rejoined them by the binnacle. There was a definite lightening in atmosphere and, conscious of it, the sailing master looked from one to the other. The captain carried what might be called a self-satisfied expression, while King was grinning openly and, as *Prometheus* steered away from the constraints of the convoy, Brehaut found that he too was in a better frame of mind.

They were heading for a hazard that had already claimed one victim, and there were likely to be difficult and perilous manoeuvres ahead that must be carried out in a contrary wind. But at least three of *Prometheus'* officers were facing the future in far higher spirits.

* * *

There was light enough for the time being but rescue, if indeed it were possible, would not be quick or easy. An hour later, *Prometheus'* quarterdeck was alive with officers: even her marine lieutenants, as well as the gouty old Captain Donaldson, were amongst the group that lined the larboard bulwark as the ship stood off to windward, about half a mile from the wreck. The breeze had dropped slightly, but would remain a hindrance if anything too ambitious were attempted. And it was still summoning sufficient breakers to dismantle the grounded merchant even as they watched.

"Indiaman, though not a large one; probably under five hundred tons," Caulfield said decisively. He went on studying the hull through the deck glass for a while longer, then added, "I'd say she were from the earlier southbound. Might have fallen by the wayside, or have been intending an independent course to the Tagus. But whatever, she won't be travelling further under her own sail."

The last part was especially true. The Burlings jutted out more than ten miles into the Atlantic and seemed to be composed entirely of granite. The merchant, which by her only partially dismantled state could not have struck more than a day or so before, had been fortunate in selecting an area with marginally less rock, and her hull was still holding together. But impact must have been made while she was under full sail: her fore and main topmasts had carried away, and were now draped forlornly over the forecastle, while the mizzen, which might not have been carrying appreciable canvas, was still intact, and stood stock still, indicating the ship to be securely beached.

Banks, who was also studying the wreck through his personal glass, had reached very much the same conclusions as Caulfield. And only when the condition of her fabric had fully been assessed did he allow his gaze to wander on to those still crowding the decks. Of these there were a goodly few, some seamen, currently attempting to cut away the damaged spars, but also a fair number of passengers – civilians – shore-dressed men and, in one case, a woman who would have no connection with the sea, and were desperately waving hats and coats in *Prometheus'* direction. It was as if they were certain the proud Navy ship would otherwise miss their plight, and leave them abandoned.

"What think you?" Banks determinedly looked back to the ship and spoke as quietly as the conditions allowed. "Would we be able to haul her off?"

"I should not wish to try, sir," Caulfield replied firmly. "With the wind as it is, we might as easily discover ourselves sharing her fate, and would doubt that hull to be in any condition to swim."

Both men said no more, but diverted their eyes from the imploring civilians as *Prometheus*, with backed main and a watchful quartermaster, was slowly carried past and to the south. A further outcrop of rock was visible off their larboard bow, and Banks could tell Brehaut was itching to take her about. He gave a nod to the sailing master and soon the ship was gaining sea room, in preparation for tacking back to the north, and sweeping in again.

"No, it would be foolishness in the extreme," Banks agreed when they were on the opposite tack and passing the wreck once more, although now a good deal further off. "Even were we able to take her under tow, we might lose our own masts in the process, and there is no guarantee she would hold together."

And there was something else, something that Banks was hesitant about even mentioning, if only due to some insane fear that it might bring bad luck. Were they to try, and fail, *Prometheus* would be landed with a sinking ship stuffed full of vulnerable beings. A vessel of such a size could be expected to require a crew of at least seventy. Passengers were less easy to estimate; the better class of traveller would naturally choose the larger, more stable Indiamen, but even if she carried a minimal number, several trips with the ship's larger boats would be necessary to carry them off. To rescue all in one go from the water, and on the very edge of a lee shore, would be asking too much, and many would inevitably drown. The captain's eyes unwillingly drifted back to the pleading figures aboard the wreck, only to be diverted as soon as he realised what they were doing.

No, Banks decided; he could only attempt a gradual evacuation: they would use the launch, with both cutters. He muttered the order, and preparations immediately began to free the boats from their berths on the spar deck.

The cutters were excellent sea craft; even under oars alone, they would be fast and stable but, being a mere twenty-five feet in length and with a beam of under seven, could carry less than the more stately launch. The larger boat would be the devil to handle though and, if filled to capacity, was more likely to find herself swamped. He would need sound men in each; lieutenants, as opposed to midshipmen and even then, those he felt he could trust.

"Mr King, you will command the blue cutter, Mr Lewis, the black. Mr Davison, you shall have overall charge in the launch. Tell your crews off, and prepare to leave at once."

The officers responded instinctively, touching their hats in acknowledgement, before moving towards the break of the quarterdeck. Banks paused; he would have liked to send Benson in one of the cutters, but the man had suffered badly from seasickness during Biscay, and a spell in an open boat might easily reawaken the condition. Had that not been the case, King could have led in the launch, which would have been infinitely preferable. Davison, the second lieutenant, had not given him cause for worry as such, but the captain was still watchful of the man. He had yet to prove himself and, when it came down to it, appeared far too young for his present position.

But he knew King and Lewis were sound enough. Banks had sailed with both in previous vessels and over several commissions; they could be trusted to keep their heads, even if Davison were to lose his.

Prometheus duly reached the end of her northward leg, and Brehaut began taking her round to starboard with the two cutters lying ready for when the evolution was complete. The ship could then heave to, and allow both to be swung out, followed by the launch, already cleared of the small pinnace that usually stowed inside her. Banks estimated all three boats should be in the water within ten minutes, and bearing down on the stranded Indiaman in fifteen. He reached for his watch, just as eight bells were struck, making the effort redundant. Four o'clock; the hands would have to wait both for supper and their second issue of spirit. But they could still get all back on board, along with as many survivors from the wreck as could be rescued, before dark. And it should be a simple enough operation, he assured himself. There was really nothing to worry about.

* * *

King's cutter had provisions for eight oars, but only four held her steady as the short, twin masts were erected. Chivers, the midshipman he had detailed to accompany him, was at the bows, supposedly supervising the operation although, as most of the cutter's crew had been at sea before the youngster was born, none appeared in need of his wisdom. King, manning the tiller himself, kept the boat's stern to the wind. He glanced across to where Lewis, in the black cutter, was slightly behind in raising his masts, and also noted that Davison's launch had only now been lifted on the stay tackles. Being a heavier load, the launch required top burtons rigged to the fore and main topmasts; it must then be transferred to the yardarm tackles, and finally lowered onto the water. King knew the procedure was likely to take a while longer, whereas the cutters would be ready to put off for the wreck at any time. He pondered, unsure if it would be politic to wait for the younger man, who was also his superior officer and in overall command, then gave a private sigh. He had not even begun what promised to be a complex and dangerous rescue operation, and had already found a dilemma.

Lewis' thoughts were clearly running along similar lines, though. King noticed the fifth lieutenant looking to him for guidance and, in turn, began searching *Prometheus'* busy decks for some sign or indication. All were far too busy with the current operation; he might close with the ship and seek advice, but such caution was verging on indecision and neither quality figured highly in King's nature. Both masts in his boat were secured now, he gave a nod to Chivers and a wave to Lewis: the twin lug sails were run up with all the speed he could have hoped for and, as the heavens suddenly opened and rain began to beat down upon them, the cutter took to the wind. In no time they were bearing down on the stricken ship, and King was already soaked.

As they drew closer, more could be seen of the Indiaman. The hull was wedged at an acute angle on a bank of rock that seemed to be the only area of land where jagged edged boulders were not so prominent. Basically she had run aground, although a small channel remained to leeward that was regularly filling and emptying, and might just be large enough to allow a boat alongside.

Despite the wind, the rain, and what lay ahead, King still found himself pondering on the cause of the Indiaman's predicament. Inattention on the part of the officer of the watch was the classic finding in such situations, although it was commonly accepted that such a verdict was frequently misleading. An absentminded lookout, or some fool at the lead was far more likely to be the actual culprit, even if the blame ultimately fell on an unfortunate lieutenant. King's mind automatically drifted to Ross, and it was with an effort that he brought it back to the job in hand.

Whoever was to blame, the Burlings had accounted for many such vessels in the past, and to remain in what was relatively good condition, the ship could not have been there for more than a few hours. The Indiaman might even have struck in broad daylight and been deliberately run aground. It would have taken considerable skill to place her so, when razor like edges of granite to either side were ready to tear the bottom from her on impact. And why anyone should attempt such an exploit was a mystery; surely, if that had been the intention, the crew would have hauled in their wind before striking?

But now set, and apparently immobile, the merchant was taking a pounding and beginning to show signs of breaking up. Much of the crown glass had disappeared from her ornate stern, part of the starboard quarter gallery was crumbling and there were visible cracks along and above the wales that suggested the hull itself had twisted. With both the fore and main masts effectively lost, her boats could not be launched conventionally, although a spirited team were doing their best to manhandle a pinnace amidships. As King's boat drew closer he could see the small craft poised, stern first, over the windward top rail, and watched it fall, apparently unchecked, into the swirling waters beneath. There was then the briefest of pauses before the incoming rollers accounted for it.

The boat's destruction was not without benefit however, and had actually served a useful purpose. As soon as the waves collected, lifted, and smashed the frail vessel against the big ship's hull it was clear the narrow avenue between the Indiaman's leeward side and the rocks was the only viable route for a rescue. With the constant but regular change of water level, it would not be an easy approach, but still infinitely preferable to coming alongside to windward. King had also learned that, though the merchant's crew were hardly of the highest order, they did not lack enterprise: something that might prove useful in what was to come.

There was no sounding rod aboard the cutter although such an unwieldy device would have been useless in the current conditions, as the channel was visibly filling and clearing with encouraging regularity. King ordered the sails down, then pointed forward, indicating to Chivers, stationed at the bow, and Flint, who pulled stroke, that he intended to ease the boat into the Indiaman's lee.

The oars picked up their speed, and the boat surged forward, but there was a dwindling gap of less than twenty feet of eddying water between ship and shore, and they would have to manhandle the tiny cutter beyond the merchant's quarterdeck to bring her to a place suitable for transferring survivors.

"Way enough," King called, as they rode in towards the gap on the head of a wave. Then, at the last possible second: "Boat your oars!"

He might have been fractionally late as Chivers yelled "Steady, there!" when the starboard bow's sweep struck the merchant's side. Then each man unshipped his oar, and used it to fend the boat off against rock or hull. Between them they could hold the cutter stationary as the water beneath ebbed and flowed, but forward movement was almost impossible. Someone in the Indiaman must have noted their predicament, as a fall was tossed down. The midshipman secured it forward, and they were dragged into the wedge of space that gave them precious, if temporary, shelter.

It was even narrower now, and the boat grounded every twenty seconds or so, before rushing up the side of the Indiaman, only to fall back and hit what must have been solid rock beneath.

"I can take twelve," King yelled above the din of crashing waves, screaming women and bellowing animals that was surely more suited to a believer's concept of Hades than any beached merchant. A line of faces stared blankly down at him from the big ship's larboard side. Actually he had already decided they might manage fifteen. With a crew of ten, counting himself and Chivers, that was just conceivable for such a boat, and in the present conditions. But he had no wish to risk breaking the cutter's back with too much weight on the first attempt.

An agile young man scaled down the side of the ship, finally landing in the stern between King and Flint. He was dressed as an officer, although King could not place the flamboyant uniform.

"David Carroll, of the *Belle Île*," he announced in a strong Irish accent. Then, meeting the lieutenant's surprised eyes directly, added: "We greatly welcome your assistance, sir."

"Are the passengers ready to disembark?" King asked. This

was only one of many questions that came to mind, but the small boat would not stand up to endless punishment: it was important they took whoever they could and moved off, to give Lewis a chance.

"Indeed they are," the Irishman replied. "I have organised a fair mix of civilians and crew for each load."

King nodded approvingly; that made sense; it might be sentimental to rescue all the passengers first, but to crowd their cutter with unskilled landsmen would be downright foolish. And he had no wish to command a boatload of hysterical wives.

At a wave from the officer, two seamen descended. One, a lascar, was wearing robes that were totally impractical, and needed to be tucked up into his girth in a manner that was both awkward and undignified. When the passengers followed, the women were no more elegant, being lowered on a mixture of boatswain's chairs and bowlines, and needing to be guided aboard the constantly shifting boat in a flurry of cloth, lace and bare flesh.

But King soon learned he could leave the embarkation arrangements to Carroll, and concentrate instead on keeping his boat clear of lethal obstructions. The Irishman proved worthy of the trust, arranging for a seaman to be alongside every group of civilians while chivvying both with a mixture of good humour and authority that seemed to draw any hint of danger from the situation.

"Take a couple extra?" Carroll asked, when all had been accommodated: King considered his load. There were bodies crammed next to each of the rowers, with more huddled miserably between. In theory, a couple could be squeezed in, but their freeboard was already low. Besides, there was still the dangerous passage back to *Prometheus*, and the cutter was now grounding with a worrying thump.

"No," he snapped. "We shall return presently, and another two boats will be calling before."

The officer seemed to understand, then looked up and bellowed: "One more, Charlie!"

King was about to object when Carroll made a leap for the ship's side, and landed expertly on the upper sill of a gun port. In a few more slick moves he had clambered back aboard the Indiaman, his place being taken by a flushed and overweight woman who seemed liable to burst at any moment.

"Very good, be ready to ship your oars!" King shouted, when she was seated. They were being pulled back and into the turmoil again, with whoever was supervising the towing waiting sensibly for sufficient water beneath them. Then the boat was clear and free to be hit by breakers once more; the painter was cast adrift, and the tiny vessel left to wallow in the boiling seas.

Oars at the bow were pressed against the Indiaman's counter where the name, *Duke of Cambridge*, could be read. The cutter was painstakingly manhandled round, with Flint, and the man immediately behind, ready to fend off against nearby rocks if need be.

"Out oars!" Again, the order could have been mistimed, but King considered there to be room enough to gather speed, and so it proved. The current was now thrusting them hard against the merchant's side, and he held the rudder over as each rower dug deep into the maelstrom for a purchase. Slowly they gained water until the waves were cheated and, rather than rolling the cutter sideways in a threat to tip her over, broke with far less effect over the prow. Within thirty seconds a considerable distance had been gained, and some of the seamen were attempting to rig the sails. King glanced back; Lewis' boat had been backing water behind them, and was now intending to copy their example in approaching the lee of the Indiaman. Further off, Davison's launch seemed to be in more confusion. She was in the water but stood close to *Prometheus*, which was hove to, and slowly being swept southwards. The launch's single mast was in the process of being stepped, but had apparently jammed at an angle and the boat, under-loaded with what was obviously a minimal crew, was leaping and shying like a young foal. King relaxed the cutter's rudder and felt her sails take the wind, then began aiming for a point a good way ahead of the drifting battleship.

"Very good, ladies and gentlemen," he said, glancing once more at the selection of moon-like faces that stared back at him in hope and wonder. "Welcome aboard, you are now guests of the

Royal Navy."

* * *

The cutters made five trips each and were far more successful than the launch, which failed to complete even one. After Davison's first, almost disastrous, attempt, Banks was forced to call him back; despite her size and greater capacity, the boat was not ideally suited to such conditions and proved more of a liability than an asset. It was possible that someone in command with more experience, or perhaps a stronger personality, might have made a better fist of things, although the captain felt no blame could be placed on the second lieutenant's young shoulders. And still the rescue could be considered a success, even though it took almost until nightfall and, at the end, King and Lewis looked to have aged a good ten years.

Between each run, *Prometheus* emptied the boats of their human cargo before being obliged to wear round, head back, and then tack at the northernmost leg of the circuit. There the cutters, which had been towed behind her, were released to ply back for more and the entire procedure could begin again. It was a laborious business, hardly helped by the warm but continuous rain that kept all comprehensively sodden, or the effects of almost constant concentration that started to play strange games with their minds on the latter trips. Over a hundred and ten souls were recovered, however, which apparently amounted to all aboard the Indiaman, and every one of *Prometheus'* men returned safely, if a little bedraggled.

Throughout the rescue, the same young man who had boarded King's boat at its first visit was very much in evidence. If not briefly with one of the cutters, and calling the survivors down to embark, he remained on the Indiaman's deck carrying out a similar role. And it was not an easy task. To ensure a boat had the correct number of trained seamen aboard: even deferring a mother and child in their favour, took an iron will, with authority to match and King was impressed. In the past he had found Company officers, though different in outlook from those of the Royal Navy, to be of a reasonable standard. But Carroll who, by his youth, could hardly be more than a cadet or junior mate, had a natural ability to command that was worthy of any ship's master.

The survivors were taken aboard the battleship where they gathered in unhappy groups; with passengers divided between great cabin, wardroom and gun room, while ordinary hands were accommodated on the gun decks which, though some were slow to realize, actually represented their new and permanent homes. *Prometheus'* generous proportions came in to their own: though she was undoubtedly crowded, there was none of the strain common when smaller vessels become overloaded. She rose to her extra human cargo with a capacity that was apparently endless as more and more damp and disheveled unfortunates were dumped upon her decks, each carrying their equally pathetic parcels of luggage and, in one case, a small dog.

That the Indiaman apparently held no senior officers caused King to ponder. Even during the rescue, while the boats were being towed back to the north by the battleship, and their crews were grasping what rest they could, the fact bothered him. But his mind remained on the job in progress, and it wasn't until he was safely back aboard *Prometheus* that he was able to give more attention to the thought.

A ferocious towelling, followed by fresh clothes as well as two cups of hot, sweet tea did much to restore him. But, when summoned to report to the captain and first lieutenant, King was still relieved when Banks immediately brought the subject of officers up.

The great cabin and coach had been given over to the care of survivors, so the three were squeezed into the small partitioned room that usually served as the captain's sleeping quarters. Cot and attendant furniture had been removed, and a full sized mess table installed, but still there was precious little space, while the noise of passengers equally crammed beyond the thin screen bulkheads was very apparent.

"No one of fifth officer status or above," the captain confirmed, with an air of wonder. "Neither are there any India Army men, which is a strange occurrence in itself when a number seem to be almost mandatory on every Eastern voyage. It is as if anyone of rank had been spirited away prior to her running aground."

"Possibly it is a case of cause and effect," Caulfield commented dryly. "Were senior officers present the accident may not have occurred."

"There was a young man, Carroll, I think his name," King said readily. "He was of great assistance during the rescue, and may shed some light on the subject."

Judy chose that moment to enter with a tray of tea which she set down on the table before them. She gave King, who she clearly regarded a special friend, a very obvious smile.

"Thank you, Kinnison," Banks growled in a manner far more gruff than he would have used had she been a man. "Be so kind as to pass the word for a Mr Carroll; he is amongst the survivors, I believe."

The girl nodded seriously, and left.

"It is a shame we could not salvage any cargo," Banks said when she had gone. "Even in outward bound goods, there'd be a tidy sum upon those rocks."

"Neither were we able to burn her," Caulfield agreed, then asked, "Were there animals aboard?"

"Yes, but they were accounted for," King told them. "The same man who organised the passengers saw to their despatch."

Caulfield and Banks said nothing in response, but King was well aware of the debt he, at least, owed the young officer.

A tap on the door heralded the arrival of the Irishman.

"Good even' to you gentlemen, and my thanks for agreeing to see me so promptly," he said, squeezing into the small room and nodding politely at King as he took a seat.

"I understand you were extremely active during the rescue, Mr..."

"Carroll, sir," the man beamed. "Indeed I was, and am grateful for this gentleman's assistance," he looked towards King, "as well as the other officer. And especially appreciate the care you have given my men."

Carroll must have been able to dry himself to some extent, but was still wearing the same uniform that King had noticed in the cutter. Looking again, it appeared even more outlandish; a bold red jacket and cream shirt, over blue trousers; without doubt a dramatic contrast to the usual East India Company livery. Such clothes made him appear something between a cavalry officer and a coxcomb: unless King had seen evidence to the contrary, he would have written the young man off as an aspiring nonentity.

"They will be well provided for," Banks assured him. "And any that wish to take service with the king, especially welcomed."

"I think there will be few enough to do that, sir," Carroll replied lightly.

"Well, if we promise not to persuade them too hard," Banks agreed. He knew, as well as any present, that only a fool would volunteer for the Royal Navy when an Indiaman's berth was infinitely more snug and profitable. But they were many miles away from the nearest English port, and with their ship currently being pounded to a wreck, the men would have little choice. And to Banks, such an influx of trained hands was a gift not to be turned down.

"I don't think you understand, sir," Carroll continued, more seriously. "We carry privateer papers; they should be treated as prisoners of war."

Banks, Caulfield and King looked uncertainly to each other, their expressions suddenly frozen.

"Prisoners of war?" Caulfield questioned.

"Indeed, sir." Carroll now looked equally confused. "Why did you not know of it? Your Indiaman was a capture of my ship, the *Belle Île*; I was in command of her prize crew.

Chapter Eight

Flint was cold, wet and hungry. He had missed both his afternoon grog as well as that evening's meal and with a banyan day, when no meat would be served, due for the morrow he was desperate to get some food inside him.

"I saved you some salt horse." Jameson gave him the welcome news as the older man slumped down in his usual place at the mess table. "And traded your tot for a bottle of blackstrap with Greg."

Flint nodded appreciatively as a platter of cold, dark meat was dropped in front of him, to be followed by a dark, unlabelled bottle. The stopper was only half in; there was no doubt that the thing had been refilled on several occasions, and might contain just about anything. But it was a well known fact that drink was the fastest way of filling an empty belly, and Flint bit the cork out and spat it expertly into his left hand while raising the bottle to his lips with his right.

"Good, is it?" Thompson asked, solicitously from the opposite side of the table. The man was only a short time into a twenty-eight day loss of spirits for smuggling Judy aboard, and could expect no supplement from his mess mates, as any caught would face double the punishment. Still he drew a masochistic pleasure in watching another enjoying the drink.

"It'll do, Thombo," Flint replied briefly.

"We's taken quite a few aboard," Harrison lisped from the far end of the table. He was known as a notoriously slow eater, and still struggled with the last of his duff. "Reckons the old girl'll be up to full numbers afore long."

Flint's mess was not unusual in being light of a few bodies, and Harrison was quite right, they could expect more joining, although Flint was too intent on tackling the cold salt beef to comment. But when he was finished, and the grease had been wiped from his face with the back of a hand, he was not surprised to see Cartwright, the master's mate, once more standing at the head of the mess table with a group of seamen clustered about him.

"Just got you down for the one, Flint: Molony here," he said, indicating a slightly built, short haired man with a squint. "Come to us from the East Indiaman, so will probably appreciate a bit of high livin'," the petty officer continued. "I'm sure he won't be disappointed..."

The group moved on to the next mess, leaving Molony standing alone. But space was soon found for him on the benches, and Flint graciously passed his bottle across.

"It's kind of you, so it is," Molony said, after taking a moderate swig. "Never been as cold and wet in my life, and doesn't the wind just kill yer?"

"Must be your first trip to the East," Butler, the hand seized from the homebound transport, commented. "If you'd made it as far as the Cape you'd know what a wind can really do."

"Well, I wasn't intending on going such a distance," Molony replied. "Just a few more miles an' we'd have been snug in Cádiz."

"Spain?" Flint questioned. "Why would a John Company vessel be so bound?"

Molony grinned. "Because some devils of privateers had captured her," he told them.

"Then you can hardly be a regular East India Company hand." Butler stared at Molony in wonder.

"No, I have to admit, that I am not," Molony agreed, swigging once more.

"So were you part of the prize crew?" Ross was first with the question that was just springing to everyone's lips.

"Indeed I was," Molony agreed, cheerfully enough. "Though no one seems to have smoked the fact. Born in Clonakilty, but I've been serving with the French since 'ninety-nine. And if you did but know it, you're all drinking with the enemy."

* * *

"So you are a French corsair?" Banks asked, after nothing had been said for several seconds.

"I serve as prize master in a French privateer, sir." Carroll's tone was even and quite respectful. "Though am Irish myself, as are all of my people. Our ship, *Belle Île* took the *Duke of Cambridge* a little to the north. The Indiaman had become separated from her convoy in a Biscay storm."

"And the senior officers?" Caulfield asked, with the air of one who already knew.

"Regrettably the captain, and two of his mates were amongst those killed during the capture, I believe the rest still to be aboard *Belle Île*," Carroll confirmed. "As well as a few of the more notable passengers that Captain Agard, my commander, felt better accommodated there. We were making a run for Cádiz, when we struck those rocks."

With Spain still a nominal neutral there would be no official blockading force on the port. And even were it not the base for the privateer herself, Cádiz would prove convenient for anyone wishing to quickly and quietly dispose of a large merchant vessel and her cargo.

"Our prize crew was not sufficient for the size of vessel," Carroll went on. "And it appeared the India Company quartermaster decided he would rather take the ship onto rocks, than remain my prisoner. Sure, I cannot blame the man; more attention should have been paid to him; we were remiss."

Mention of Carroll's associates appeared to prompt Banks, and he dropped the pen he had been toying with.

"Your men are still mixed with the East India seamen?" he announced, momentarily horrified.

"So they will be," the Irishman responded without emotion. "All are Irish so may not have been noticed, though they will do you no harm, and are doubtless grateful for the rescue."

"You will point them out to me without delay," Banks informed him.

"I shall be happy to, or can provide a listing of their names if you so wish," Carroll agreed. "But you have nothing to fear from them, Captain. Without your help we would have been dashed to pieces on those rocks, there is little doubt of that."

Banks seemed little assured, although he did allow Caulfield to take up the questioning.

"Your ship, would she still be in these waters?" he asked, with elaborate casualness.

"Now that I would not know," Carroll replied, more guardedly. "And frankly, neither would I tell you if I did. She is the *Belle Île* as I have said, and hails from Lorient. More than that you must discover for yourselves."

There was silence as all considered what had been said, and King suspected his thoughts were running on a similar course to those of the other officers. Lorient was all of six hundred miles to the north-east. Other, more local, ports must be used to supply and maintain the privateer during her cruise. Therefore it seemed likely she was treating Cádiz as a victualling point, although Carroll would have been a fool to have admitted as much.

"Can you tell us her strength?" Caulfield asked, with little hope.

"I may say she is of no danger to this fine ship," Carroll replied, his eyes twinkling slightly.

"Well, we shall be keeping a sharp look out, nevertheless," Banks continued, collecting the pen once more, and starting to fiddle with it in his fingers. "And if we are lucky enough to sight her, shall do all we can to bring her to battle."

"Captain, I would expect nothing less," the Irishman confirmed.

* * *

Of the seventy-seven seasoned hands rescued from the wreck, only fifteen turned out to be Carroll's men. The rest were pressed aboard *Prometheus* and, even though they exhibited differing levels of enthusiasm, ranging from resigned acceptance to outright hostility, there could be no doubting the following day's sail drill was more efficient. Further practice with the great guns then resumed and, with at least one battery being exercised at most hours of the day, the rumble of carriages was once more constant throughout the ship. The additional men also filled every available space in the messes and, when combined with the passengers accommodated in the great cabin, as well as a screened off portion of the upper deck, *Prometheus* soon became a crowded and noisy place. But at least her officers now had the material to create a proper workable watch list and, as Caulfield, King and Davison left the cramped confines of the chart room where the third version had just been drawn up, it seemed they had the basis of a fine crew.

King's mind was on this, and little else as he followed Davison across the quarterdeck. So much had happened in the last few hours that a good deal had been forgotten and, when the second lieutenant turned and stopped him with the back of an elegantly placed hand, he was more than a little taken aback.

"There was something I had been meaning to bring up," the young man said. King glanced down at his chest, then up and into Davison's eyes. There was the slightest flicker, and the hand was withdrawn.

"You wished to speak to me?" King asked coldly. The fact that the second lieutenant was both younger and apparently less experienced than he was had been enough to make him cautious from the start. But, and ironically for the same reasons, he had gone out of his way to be polite, even though Davison's arrogant manner annoyed him greatly. However, the more he grew to know the officer, the more King became convinced that, not only did he have genuine cause for dislike, but there was also something inherently unpleasant about the lieutenant.

"I wished to mention yesterday's rescue," Davidson said, as if it were the most obvious talking point there could have been.

"Indeed?" King questioned, while his mind instinctively ran back through the previous day's proceedings. "And which particular aspect?"

"I think you behaved most disgracefully," came the icy and unexpected reply.

Now King was both confused and angry. Those hours spent dodging breakers in uncertain shallows while trying to convey boatloads of seamen and frightened civilians to safety had not been enjoyable. That they were over, and he had carried out his duties to the notable approval of the captain, was gratifying. And, if Banks were happy, King could see no reason for censure: certainly not from the jumped up little marionette that now faced him.

"You are well practised in small boat work, I fancy?" Davison continued. Caulfield had moved on, leaving the two of them standing in the middle of the crowded quarterdeck. Brehaut was holding a class in navigation nearby, the ship's wheel was being managed by a quartermaster's mate and two timoneers, and Benson, who had the watch, stood close at hand, but still King felt strangely isolated and more than a little wary.

"Not especially," he replied. "Certainly no more than most officers of my age."

"I heard different," the tone was accusatory although, for the life of him, King could not think what sin had been committed. "I heard that your speciality was such, and many exercises and even actions have been carried out in cutters and launches under your direction."

"In my last few commissions I served in frigates," King retorted. "And sure, when the choice was betwixt me and Mr Caulfield, it were usually myself chosen. But I fail to see..."

"Then my original assertion stands," Davison interrupted. "You are a seasoned small boat man, yet were content to see me given the launch, when I have little experience of such vessels."

"Now look here," King began, but younger man would not be silenced.

"You failed to warn me it were blatantly unsuitable for the work in question. Neither did you offer to go in my stead, or relinquish your cutter as a more suitable craft for directing the operation. In short, you did not support me in the way a superior officer might expect. I was made to look foolish; the more so when that newbie Lewis was so publicly acclaimed."

"Lewis has not been a lieutenant for more than a couple of months," King was now genuinely angry although his voice actually lowered in both pitch and volume as he spoke. "It was his first such action, and yes, he did well, and should be praised for it."

The two men's faces had become dangerously close. "Lewis still has the stink of the lower deck about him," Davison hissed in reply. "And might find himself back there soon enough, if he is not so very careful."

"It was the captain who appointed you to the launch," King responded. "If you have a concern, belike it should be taken up with him. As for Lewis, he has the makings of a fine officer, and one I am proud to serve alongside."

"Well, I do not wish to associate with either of you," Davison replied in a far clearer tone. "Any further attempts to discredit me will not be ignored: I shall be left with no other option than to call upon my family connections."

* * *

The following morning saw them once more heading south, but with the Portuguese coast sensibly out of sight, and under a racing sun that was fast clearing every trace of bad weather. *Prometheus* sailed easily with a steady north-westerly on her quarter; the watch on deck, their duties temporarily accomplished, were stood down and Banks, who had been present since dawn, was unaccountably happy.

As a general rule, seventy-four gun line-of-battleships were herd animals that rarely travelled alone. So, on accepting command of *Prometheus*, he had naturally resigned himself to few independent missions until he attained flag rank. But here he was, sailing a wide blue ocean with the only other vessels in sight being a cluster of fishing boats several miles to larboard. And not only that, he had a well found ship, provisioned for three months and with much of her rushed or inadequate refitting work now rectified. They had also managed to make up their deficit in numbers in a most unexpected way; more to the point, the fresh intake included a rare proportion of fully trained seamen, while most of the landsmen already taken on board were learning fast and would soon be making a worthwhile contribution. There were still a number of prisoners on the orlop that needed careful watching, and that fellow Carroll remained very much in evidence, although neither presented a true problem. Sadly the same could not be said for several former passengers from the *Duke of Cambridge*.

Almost as soon as they were dry the captain had started to receive complaints about their lack of personal effects or, to be more accurate, the reluctance on King and Lewis' part to recover

116

vast bundles of luggage. Banks had remonstrated, pointing out that no lives had been lost in the rescue, but he was not experienced in dealing with Company factors or lower grade civil servants and there was no doubting that some had been offended. The fact that he had given up part of his own precious space was apparently ignored; the great cabin and coach having been wordlessly accepted as communal accommodation, while he moved into his sleeping quarters, yet still they were not happy.

The ship's officers were also enduring a measure of discomfort; wardroom, gun room and cockpit had been filled to overflowing, while several complete families were berthing in screened off accommodation on the upper deck. All parts of the ship seemed to be plagued by especially noisy children, and that damned dog had turned out to be a pathological yapper.

He didn't wish for a quiet command; King was currently exercising the larboard upper batteries, and there were shouts and whistles from the boatswain's party working aloft, but these were natural shipboard sounds. Babies crying, children screaming, and the noise of domestic pets fell into a very different category, and had no place aboard a man-o'-war.

But a few day's fine sailing would solve all such annoyances and Banks was determined not allow negative thoughts to destroy his good temper on such a lovely day. Those not required on board would be simply landed in Gibraltar, leaving *Prometheus* in a fine state to sally forth in search of Nelson and adventure.

Some of the children were causing a nuisance even as he spoke. Three boys, one temptingly close to service age, had ventured onto the hands' sacred forecastle. They were soon chased off by an indignant boatswain's mate who roared and swung his starter with equal impotence. Banks stopped in his pacing to watch, and told himself that John, and possibly even the sibling Sarah was predicting when he left England, would be up to similar tricks in no time.

The bell rang, bringing forth the usual reports from each station, and the captain flexed his shoulders. Aft, his servant David should have his breakfast waiting. It would be laid out in his sleeping quarters with due formality, and was probably growing cold even as he thought of it. But the morning sun was unusually pleasant on his uncovered head and that, or possibly some more subtle force, was enough to keep him standing on the quarterdeck.

A flock of large birds many miles from land flew low over the ship. He watched them as they passed, each taking turns for position at the head, before changing course as if by private signal, and finally disappearing into one of the few clouds that daubed the crystal sky. Then there was no further excuse, and he was in the act of turning back for his quarters when a cry came from the main masthead.

He paused instinctively; the lookout might only be reporting the hourly change, but any intelligence from that sensitive station was enough to interrupt most actions, and this time it did turn out to be information worth hearing.

"Sighting on the starboard bow!"

Lewis had the watch, and Banks said nothing when Adams, the duty midshipman, was sent aloft with a glass strapped about his young shoulders.

"I have her more firmly now," the lookout reported, as the lad arrived. "She's three masted and steering to cross our prow."

Few ships carried masts higher than those on *Prometheus,* while even some that did had smaller hulls and far less fire-power, so the heading was hardly significant. It would also have been the logical course were a vessel set deeper in the Atlantic be making for the nearby port at Lisbon. Still Banks was hoping for more and felt himself rooted to the spot, despite the scent of what he guessed must be his very own bacon wafting forward from the pantry.

But when it came, the news was inconclusive; even with the aid of a glass, Adams had little to add. The ship, as ship she undoubtedly was, would remain hull down for some considerable time and, while running before the wind, her topsails were almost side on and gave little clue as to nationality, purpose or intention. *Prometheus,* sailing several miles behind, was by no means setting records; the sighting would cross her bows some considerable distance ahead, and might even be preparing to enter the Tagus by the time she reached that spot.

A muffled scream came from aft, followed by the same inane

laughter that had already been heard several times that day and could surely only originate from an imbecile. Banks guessed the passengers in his dining cabin were at breakfast, and some of the younger ones were making their presence known. The thought of eating his own meal in a stuffy room, separated from such a din by the thinnest of bulkheads, was not appealing and, despite the relative disappointment of the sighting, remaining on deck seemed much the better option.

"Ask my steward to prepare breakfast here, will you?" he murmured to a youngster nearby. But, before the message could be delivered, David had already appeared along with two wardroom stewards who carried metal trays that smelt delightfully of coffee and fried bacon.

"Mr Lewis, would you care to join me?" he asked, as the food was presented tantalisingly close to the men at the wheel, and the young officer quickly assumed a look of genial expectation. The table that Banks generally used for cards then appeared, along with several of his dining chairs and soon he, Lewis, Benson, who had just happened on deck at the appropriate time, together with Franklin, the oldster midshipman who could have given all save Banks several years, were sitting comfortably in the warm sun and enjoying a splendid meal.

The bread was only just soft enough to be edible but, soaked in fat in the cockpit manner, still made a fine dish. Banks noted that the meat was heavily smoked and just to his taste. Presumably Sarah had chosen it, and he wondered that she should have noticed his liking. David poured coffee; he collected his and examined the cup with interest. It was another reminder of home; part of a delicate service that also showed Sarah's concern for him. The china was exceptionally thin, and had been privately condemned as too light for shipboard use. But the memory reinforced feelings that were really best forgotten and, even though his drink was still scalding hot, Banks found himself gulping deeply.

"Deck there, sighting is changing course." The information came as a welcome interruption and the captain's thoughts were brought back to the present as he took another mouthful of breakfast. "She's coming to larboard and adding t'gallants," the midshipman added.

Both the extra sail and change of course must have been caused by sighting *Prometheus*. Banks dropped the rest of his roll back onto the plate and absent mindedly licked at his fingers before standing and collecting the hat his servant proffered.

"Mr Lewis, you will oblige me by summoning the watch below," he said, clearing his throat, and wiping his mouth with his handkerchief.

The lieutenant, with whom he had so very recently been enjoying breakfast, was now also standing and bellowed an order that in turn prompted a series of shrill pipes to disrupt the entire ship. Banks placed his hat firmly upon his head, signifying that he was now on duty, as a rush of feet came up the main companionway. Equally summoned by the call, more officers began to assemble on the quarterdeck with Caulfield, who appeared with the rosy red flush of sleep still apparent on his face.

"We have company to the south-west," Banks told him flatly. "Three masted, and clearly interested in us."

"Any colours?" Caulfield asked. The captain shook his head.

"No, but you will oblige me by hauling down our pennant directly."

The first lieutenant flashed a look to Franklin, then collected a glass, even though the sighting was still well beyond their horizon.

"It is probably nothing more than one of our frigates," Banks continued as the long, flowing bunting that was a permanent fixture at their masthead was taken in. "But the last thing they will expect to see is a third rate sailing independently and, if this be the privateer, I would prefer they thought otherwise."

An Indiaman travelling alone was a far more common sight, and presented quite a juicy prospect for any ambitious predator. *Prometheus* might be larger than the majority of long distance traders, but not all: of late some truly massive ships had started to appear, many rivalling even three-decker proportions. Most were armed to some extent, and would make a difficult catch but they also regularly carried a fortune in cargo and, if this was the same ship that had taken the *Duke of Cambridge*, its captain had already shown himself to be no laggard when it came to attempting large prey.

"We are carrying John Company colours aboard, I assume?" Banks asked, as a plan began to form in his mind.

Caulfield had no idea and Stevenson, the sailmaker, was duly summoned.

"Flags of every nation, sir," the petty officer confirmed. "An' some what 'aven't yet been thought of. We got a Trinity 'ouse as well, 'long with a Royal Standard, if you was interested."

"The East India Colours will be sufficient, thank you," Banks told him crisply. "Be sure they are for the northern hemisphere."

Stevenson knuckled his forehead and was about to go when Banks stopped him. "And do we have a spare forecourse?" he asked.

"Yes, sir," the man responded instantly. We have two fully made sails, and enough canvas for further if you wishes."

"And do they have a man-o'-war's roach?" Banks demanded.

Stevenson seemed to hesitate, then his face dropped and he gave a slight shrug. "They do, sir." he finally admitted. "I could make up another of merchant pattern, though it would take a fair spell."

"No, we do not have the time. Thank you, that will be all." Banks turned to Brehaut, newly installed at the binnacle. "Master, you will oblige me by taking in the forecourse."

Brehaut's expression was not quite so revealing as the sailmaker's had been, although evidently the request still came as a surprise.

"I wish to disguise us as an Indiaman," Banks explained, testily. "And a man-o'-war's roach will reveal our true identity as plain as a full broadside."

"I-indeed, sir." Brehaut stammered, as the large company flag was bent to a halyard and raised above them. There were numerous differences between *Prometheus* and an Indiaman that might not be quite so easy to hide, but Banks trusted few would be visible from such a distance. And if his measures only enticed the enemy in for a closer look they would have served their purpose.

"We will not be in clear view for several minutes and have that time to rig other disguises," Banks continued, speaking to the quarterdeck in general. "If you have any thoughts, gentlemen, they would be welcomed."

"Might we not strike the mizzen topmast, sir?" King, who was one of the new arrivals, suggested hesitantly. "It could signify damage taken in the recent storm, and give us cause to be travelling independently."

"A worthy idea, Mr King," Banks replied. "Though, if our friend here is who we suspect, I would prefer to maintain our sailing abilities. "But I should like as many lascars as we carry to be on the upper deck," he continued. "And any that can go aloft, so much the better; otherwise they should simply make themselves plain. Meanwhile, gentlemen," he added, once more addressing his officers generally, "You might consider adopting watchcoats and, despite the hour, I think we could extend the courtesy of the quarterdeck to all passengers."

"The passengers, sir?" Lewis questioned. One of the few stipulations the captain had made was for the quarterdeck to be out of bounds until the end of the afternoon watch.

"Indeed, the passengers," Banks confirmed. "If any have access to those umbrella devices, so much the better." Then, after a moment's thought, "And tell them they are welcome to bring their children."

* * *

By mid-morning the sighting was in plain view from the deck, and becoming less of a mystery by the second. It had changed course yet again and, after allowing *Prometheus* to close, was steering to keep pace with the battleship, less than two miles off her starboard bow. Standing on the forecastle, King studied her with interest through his personal glass. She was a warship without a doubt; single decked, probably under four hundred tons, and would probably have been considered a sixth rate if on the British list. He brought the glass down and closed it with a snap. This was slightly more than extreme range though: even if the captain were in a position to fire a full broadside they would be lucky to score a single hit, which would inevitably pitch low. And once that were done – once *Prometheus* had shown her true identity and power – the enemy would simply bear away and be gone, with never the chance of a stately battle-wagon catching such a lithe craft.

"French, is she, sir?" King turned to see Ross, the seaman who had volunteered to him at Tor Bay, standing close by. It was good to notice the man appearing more at ease: he held himself with greater confidence, and had lost some of the awkward, bewildered look that, to one who knew his history, marked him as an object of pity. And King could tell his fingers were simply itching to take hold of the glass.

"Would you care to inspect?" he asked, proffering the telescope. There was an argument against too much information reaching the lower deck, and King knew that, by handing an able seaman his glass, he was breaking with protocol, especially as the ship was likely to see action shortly. But he could hardly ignore his private knowledge of the man, and did not think any officer on the quarterdeck would notice.

"Yes, a Frenchie, plain as day, sir." Ross murmured, focussing the small telescope. "Rig gives her away and she ain't sturdy enough for a Spaniard. Ask me, the captain's going to have to play a pretty tidy game if he wants to lure her close."

King wriggled uncomfortably and looked about, but no one was in direct earshot and the seaman's words had been quietly spoken. "She is plainly not certain of our identity," he muttered in reply. "Should they be convinced we are indeed an Indiaman they would have closed with us by now. But then no Frenchman of such a size would allow a British liner to come into range, and we are on the very edge of it."

"And all the time are drawing nearer to the Tagus," Ross seemed to agree, although he continued studying the sighting. "But were we running for port, it would not be raised by nightfall, and that is when most privateers strike."

"Privateer?" King questioned, looking hard at the man. "You do not think her a national ship?"

"I do not, sir," Ross replied directly, and with surprising confidence. Nothing had been said to the men about the possibility of Carroll's vessel being in the vicinity, or her size and power. The

123

sighting was without doubt of foreign build, but equally had not raised an ensign, so might still be of another navy entirely, yet Ross seemed to have taken it for granted that this was the ship in question.

King thought on. There were a number of Royal Navy vessels that had started life on other slipways, and a sleek and elegant hull, coupled with tophamper that was mildly over-sparred did not necessarily mean they were regarding an enemy. But mainly it intrigued him as to how Ross could tell if the vessel in question belonged to the state, or a private owner.

"You would not say she was a *fregate-de-eighteen* then?" he asked.

"No, sir," Ross remained adamant. "She is less substantially built – I'd say our friend was armed with nothing heavier than twelves – apart from maybe some heavier short-range pieces."

King said nothing. He was relatively familiar with foreign shipping, but still would not wish to judge between two classes of frigate from such a distance.

"You will have noted the gun deck, sir," Ross continued, sensing interest. "A national ship would have no more than thirteen a side, along with smashers on the quarterdeck and maybe a couple of fo'c's'le chasers. But I think you will find the main battery has more," Ross added, handing the glass back.

King gave the man a doubtful glance, then set to focussing his telescope on the sighting. The distance did not make accurate counting easy, but eventually he was forced to concede that, rather than the thirteen ports he had been expecting, there were indeed fifteen.

The mere fact that a Frenchman was over-gunned did not come as a great surprise. Such a practice was common to most continental navies, in the same way as lengthened spars aloft, and the main reason why many French captures were down-rated in ordinance when adopted for British use. But that was in the actual weight of the guns, King reminded himself, not their number.

"There are an extra four cannon in the captain's quarters," Ross continued. "The French Navy hate cluttering up a commander's private space. But a privateer would have no such inhibitions, and are inclined to mount every ounce of armament they can squeeze aboard."

King was impressed, and not just by the man's knowledge. Ross had pulled off a remarkable feat by imparting the information in such a way that his superior officer was not offended. "So, she is a Frenchman, a privateer, and will attack at nightfall," King summarised blithely, and the seaman nodded seriously in reply.

"That's about it, sir," he confirmed.

"I'm obliged to you, Ross," King told him after a moment. His mind was racing. All that the man said made perfect sense, yet to have him repeat it to the captain might bring forth a number of questions that neither of them would wish to be asked. But then King was not the type of officer who would steal another's theory and present it as his own.

"I shall not mind your passing my thoughts on, sir," Ross must have read his mind and was barely whispering now. "Indeed, I wish you would so do."

King continued to think: Ross' frankness and honesty was commendable, especially in one who had not been well treated by the service. "Very well," he said, almost with regret. "But I shall repeat my promise, and hope to see you off the lower deck as soon as it may be fitting."

* * *

Two hours later, *Prometheus* was a very different ship. Brehaut was to meet with his midshipmen charges and take the customary noon sightings but, as he stepped onto the quarterdeck, he looked about in mild astonishment. Banks had cleared for action when no reply was received to their private signal, but it was not just the absence of bulkheads and smoke from the galley that indicated the change.

Aloft, lascars had taken many of the topmen's places, and were perched easily at the crosstrees, tops and yards, their robes tied back but still fluttering faintly in the slight wind. From the forecastle came the doubly incongruous screams of children as they were encouraged in a raucous game of tag by a group of indulgent hands, while *Prometheus'* poop and quarterdeck were filled with the bonnets and gowns of factors' relations. The officers had also undergone a change and now broiled in heavy brown coats more appropriate for cold weather, or appeared unusually casual in plain, shirt-sleeve order. To starboard, and so placed as to be obvious to anyone aboard the privateer, two red trousered lads who were still serving John Company cadets had secured themselves to the shrouds and were ostentatiously studying her through their telescopes.

"She is still showing no colours then?" Brehaut asked of Davison, who had the watch.

"Indeed not," the second lieutenant confirmed. "Though that is scarcely unusual. Mr King seems convinced she is a Frenchman and a privateer to boot, despite her being uncommonly large for the type. None of those from the Indiaman can support him, however, as they were taken during the night. Myself, I would not be surprised if our companion turned out to be on passage to Lisbon, or even Gibraltar and of no danger to us whatsoever. Why the captain might even be playing a jape, and could shortly raise the union flag."

Brehaut said nothing. As sailing master, his concern was the managing and navigation of the ship. He had little knowledge of naval protocol, neither did he wish for any. And both King and Davison had been known to him for a similar length of time. But, even though the latter was superior in seniority, he knew which was more experienced, and whose opinion he valued more.

"Mr Lewis," Banks called, his voice cutting into a dozen conversations. "You would oblige me by repeating the recognition signal for our previous convoy yet again."

Lewis touched his hat, gestured to the midshipman and within a minute three small flags were running up *Prometheus'* main, followed by a single red ensign at the fore. It was a procedure they had already performed twice and still no answer came from the frigate. Instead the mystery ship continued to hover just beyond the range of any gun *Prometheus* carried.

"Very well, Mr Caulfield," Banks said with either resignation or suppressed excitement. "I think by now a merchant master would assume the sighting to be up to no good. Direct the passengers below, if you please. They may be accommodated in the gun room. The prisoners are well guarded?"

"I took the liberty of moving them from their quarters on the orlop, sir," Caulfield said, after whispering a command to Benson. "They are now secured in the for'ard hold, with those of Jenkins' mess standing guard; they won't bear any nonsense."

Now every available midshipman was rounding up the civilians in preparation for seeing them below. It would by no means be palatial accommodation, but at least offered safety from splinter and shot.

"Very good," Banks replied. "See to it that the passengers are also supervised." He was remembering an occasion when a civilian had been mortally injured, despite every precaution taken on his behalf. "I don't want to see any private individual off the orlop for as long as the action continues."

"Yes, sir." Caulfield's face appeared wooden, although Banks was sure he also recalled the incident.

Brehaut, who appeared to have lost his students, raised his sextant and began to make practice sights of the sun, gradually lessening the masking lenses until the glowing orb could be viewed clearly and for some time without damaging his eye.

"Glass dry," the duty marine sang out, but eight bells would not strike until the sailing master signalled true noon and there were still several seconds to go. Slowly, almost imperceptibly, the sun hovered about the horizon, being forced into such a position by the series of prisms. Then, as soon as he noticed any variation, Brehaut called out.

"Noon, sir!"

Banks replied with a curt: "Make it so," the bell was struck eight times, and *Prometheus'* new navigational day could begin.

Usually such an occasion would have coincided with the first issuing of spirits and a change of watch, as well as dinner for seamen and junior warrant officers, the scent of which would have been colouring all their thoughts for some time. But on this occasion there was a strange silence, and one made even more apparent by the absence of noisy children.

The relative peace was welcomed by the captain: it enabled him to think. What King had said made sense; a French privateer, as he was now totally convinced his opponent to be, would certainly prefer to attack in the dark, when several fast and murderous strikes might be expected to wear down even the boldest of Company ships. Such an action may allow *Prometheus'* lower deck guns to come into play more readily, but a smaller, more manoeuvrable opponent would find greater benefit in the darkness, and the added confusion must count heavily against them.

Instead he had to lure this particular foe within range of his lower deck guns during daylight; something that would call for particular cunning and not a little risk. And no small part of the plan would include effectively ignoring his main guns until the time came when a full broadside, one that must ultimately reveal *Prometheus'* true identity, could settle the matter permanently. Before then he must rely on his secondary armament: the carronades and maybe a few eighteen-pounders that would give him only a limited advantage over what was bound to prove a faster and more agile opponent.

Even in daylight, *Prometheus* was liable to take damage and men could be injured. Some might die: the likelihood was strong, in fact. Such a sacrifice would be justified if the Frenchman were eventually taken, but what if he were unsuccessful? What if this turned out to be a long drawn out action, one with an extended butcher's bill to match, but ultimately doomed to end with the privateer smoking his ruse? He supposed the waste of men's lives might not be taken so very seriously by some, but already knew such a failure would haunt him for the rest of his days. And time was not on his side: he really could not afford to continue the action after darkness – that might spell disaster.

Chapter Nine

On the lower gun deck, two hundred or so men and boys stood ready to serve *Prometheus'* main armament. The ship had beaten to quarters some while back, and now most of Flint's team, which included several from his own mess, were at their starboard piece. But none were comfortable, and neither did they seem particularly happy.

There was less room than usual. In a ship where no deck was longer than a hundred and seventy feet, all were used to living crowded lives and such an inconvenience was accepted when unavoidable. But that was not currently the case, as every piece in *Prometheus'* main armament was still, annoyingly, inboard.

Normally the great guns would have been run out by now, leaving a far larger area for those who were to serve them. That was not the extent of their problems however: the cannon being inboard meant all ports remained closed, so the men crowded within were also denied light and fresh air, as well as news of the action.

The ship had been manoeuvring for several hours, with no heading held long enough to be considered a change of course. It was clear that intricate games were being played above; games they were not privy to, and their annoyance grew with each heave of the deck. The captain might have grounds for such unconventional behaviour: it might be a ploy – a tactic that would see the British ultimately successful – that, or the lower deck had simply slipped his mind. But whatever the reason, *Prometheus'* lower ports remained securely shuttered, and the near solid mass of humanity within was left cramped, panting, and very much in the dark.

As if to emphasise their situation, the deep rumble of long guns being run out on the deck above had been heard some time ago. Since then, all below had been imagining men of the upper battery stretched out in more spacious surroundings as they relaxed in the cooling afternoon breeze and casually regarded the enemy.

Meanwhile the more important weapons, and a thirty-two pounder must surely be regarded so, sat loaded, primed and otherwise prepared for use, with their servers apparently forgotten.

A call came from above, and was soon repeated by Davison, the second lieutenant, who stood by the main companionway further aft and was in overall charge of *Prometheus'* lower deck armament.

"Target will be for'ard and high!" Chivers, one of the midshipmen, took up the order, his voice high with youth and excitement.

Forward and high – at least that spoke of action, although even then the men were not placated. Every long gun in a Royal Navy warship was kept loaded whilst at sea, but the servers on the lower deck had already been instructed to draw the standard single round shot from the weapons under their care. It had been a lengthy and awkward business, made no easier by having the ports closed, and one that enhanced their feelings of injustice as the chance of a deadly spark was very real. But both batteries were now reloaded with bar shot: and the order, however much it might have been expected, did not go down well, and lowered morale still further.

It meant they would be aiming at top-hamper – a Frenchman's trick which did not find favour with British gunners. Besides any irrational prejudice against aiming anywhere other than their opponent's hull – their usual practice, and something they considered more manly – no fine degree of accuracy would be possible. Each gun captain was suitably proud of his craft, but there could be little skill when using such ill-shaped projectiles as bar shot. They would simply have to train their pieces in the general direction of the enemy's masts and trust the murderous linked balls to do their mischief. Bar shot was undoubtedly effective, but the result somehow lacked the satisfaction of a well aimed broadside of round.

"So we knows roughly where," Flint grumbled as the ship gave yet another heave in response to a savage turn. "And at what... Any danger of finding out *when* we're to fire, Mr Chivers?"

"All in good time," the midshipman replied, recalling a phrase used against him a dozen times since joining the ship. "Until then, keep them ports shut. Captain wants the Frogs to think we're an Indiaman, and you wouldn't get no Company ship sailing with a lower deck stuffed full of thirty-twos."

"If he wants them to think we're an Indiaman, why don't he just pay us John Company wages?" an anonymous voice enquired, to a rumble of appreciative laughter.

"The last Indiaman I was in carried guns a plenty," Thompson, who was a designated loader on Flint's team, mused. "Only they called them cannonades. Ruddy great blown out things they was; something like a cross between a smasher and a proper gun, with all the disfavours of both."

"Aye, no good for nothing, they're not," another ultimately agreed. "All wind and noise but no result – bit like Thombo after too much burgoo."

"Most were stowed in the hold," Thompson continued, riding the laughter. "Took us a couple of hours to rig 'em if we thought pirates was about, and then it were anyone's guess where the shot would go."

"Well these are Navy guns," Chivers replied with more confidence than he currently felt. "And are going to come as quite a surprise if what we've raised turns out to be a Frenchman."

"Frenchman or Irishman?" It was Cranston's turn to grizzle. "All them prize crew seem to be Paddies."

"Makes no difference to me – or Sweet Sue here," Thompson said, patting the cascabel of his weapon affectionately. "If they turn out enemies of the king, she'll deal with either, sure as a gun." The man's sour expression suddenly cleared. "Sure as a gun!" he repeated with obvious glee having never heard the joke before, while those about him rolled their eyes or grimaced indulgently.

Another call was heard, this time more tense and urgent, and all conversation immediately ceased.

"Stand by there," Lieutenant Benson, who was second in command of the main battery, ordered. "The enemy's on the move."

Once more there was silence, then a low creak told how *Prometheus* was also altering course.

"Steady, lads," Flint spoke softly to his team. The waiting had already gone on for several hours, which was far too long. He was starting to feel the well remembered tension of action and knew some of his men were not as seasoned as him. And even he had been tested beyond his limit in the past; it was several years back, and there were circumstances that had grown more mitigating with time, but still he remembered the raw terror, and knew how easily it might return.

They were only facing what amounted to a frigate, but a well placed twelve or eighteen pound ball might still punch through a third rate's bulwarks, and shot or splinters from an inferior enemy could be every bit as deadly as that fired by a three-decker. "We'll be in action soon enough," Flint continued, more to himself than anyone else. "An', when it starts, all will feel a darn sight easier."

Some of the men picked up on his words, and there was the flash of grins as the mood began to change. A few even began to joke amongst themselves when the tension lessened further. Then the singing began.

It came, slowly at first, and apparently from the very depths of the ship herself, making every officer present, from lieutenant down to quarter gunner, look to each other in concern. None on the lower gun deck were responsible, and the ship's medical team, who had laid out their wares and would be waiting for their first customer on the orlop below, were not known for hosting mess nights. The passengers, and any other supercargo, were gathered aft, but the sound came from further forward. And it was men's voices, singing a song that some on the lower deck might have heard before, but few had ever sung.

"It's the bloody croppies," Thompson called out both in revelation and anger. "Them what we saved from the wrecked Indiaman, an' turned out to be traitors."

The song continued, muffled slightly by the four inches of gun deck planking, but still loud enough for all to hear. They may be captured and secure, but it was the sound of their enemies, defiant even in defeat, and the very presence of it was disquieting to men about to go into battle.

* * *

"I've a request from Jemmy Ducks, sir." Caulfield told Banks with a hint of awkwardness.

"Indeed?" Banks was mildly surprised. Jemmy Ducks was the traditional name given to anyone who looked after a ship's poultry and, to his mind, *Prometheus'* particular holder of the title was not the brightest of sparks. He did possess an instinctive talent for the creatures under his care however and, considering the very real concession Banks had already made on his behalf, it was surprising that he should have been bothering the first lieutenant.

"I gather the livestock hands are looking to him as a spokesman," Caulfield continued, aware, as was his captain, of how close to mutiny this sounded. "They appreciate their charges have been spared, but wonder why the animals might not be fed or watered. Ducks says none can survive for long and will start to complain shortly."

Banks sighed. In saving the livestock he was contravening the normal practice of despatching live animals when a ship prepared for battle. So soon into the voyage, *Prometheus* was filled with beasts of every description; too many to be easily butchered and simply jettisoning them over the side would have upset both passengers and the sentimental element on the lower decks. To compromise, Banks had reasoned they might even be of use, hence his depriving them of provisions. The mystery ship was still some distance off but, if anything would convince an enemy they were an Indiaman, it must surely be the sound of mooing cattle, clucking hens and grunting pigs.

"Tell him it is better for them to starve for a day than the alternative," Banks said harshly, before dismissing the subject and concentrating instead on the vessel off their starboard bow.

* * *

"Why can't you keep your people quiet?" Judy asked impatiently.

"They do no harm," Carroll replied. "No man is trying to escape, nor physically interfering with the action in any way. And there are enough of your soldier boys on hand to see they do not, if any have a change of mind."

"They don't need to make such a row, though," the girl maintained, adding a sniff for good measure.

"Ah, yes," Carroll smiled beguilingly. "But then we come from a musical nation; singing is natural to my countrymen, as well as being a basic human right. Sure, I could not stop them from doing so no more than I could their breathing."

"It's upsetting the children," Judy sulked. Indeed, of the ten she was attempting to care for, all but three were in tears, although it was doubtful if a group of men singing rebel songs at the other end of the ship was actually the cause.

"If that is the case, then I am truly sorry," Carroll flashed his dark eyes dangerously. "Shall I help you keep them amused? I might show them a trick or two. Would they care to see me break my arm?"

"Break your arm?" The girl was less certain now; it was an extraordinary thing to say, yet the man's presence was powerful and oddly hypnotic. "Why should anyone wish to see that?" she added weakly.

"It usually attracts attention," the Irishman responded modestly, before bending forward, and seeming to draw the youngsters towards him. "It's a very weak arm I have," he told them confidentially. "And takes nothing at all to make it... Snap!"

Now all in the crowded space were captivated; even the two uniformed marines who stood guard rested back on their muskets to watch.

"Just a simple tap in the right place," Carroll continued softly, chopping at his upper right arm with a flattened palm. "And it crumbles..."

He then grasped the hand with his left, and appeared to tug the limb free. The arm slid several inches out of the loose sleeve to gasps from the children. It was a simple enough trick, but done well, and certainly caught the youngsters' imaginations, all of whom were now quiet in fascination. Some of the adults laughed, and even Judy unbent enough to smile.

"Aye, but I have plenty more fobs if you're interested," Carroll beamed good naturedly as he waved the restored limb to reassure any that might have been in doubt. "Would you care to see me make myself disappear?"

Now the children were firmly entranced. The looks of wonder and anticipation were soon replaced with confusion though, as all the funny man did was count to three, then place his hands in front of his face.

"I'm gone, and none of you can see me," his words were muffled and both eyes remained firmly covered. "And now I'm back," he continued, revealing that fetching look once more. "And you'll all be wondering how I did it."

There were calls of complaint, then some of the youngsters laughed out loud, and even a few of the adults grew cross before finally seeing the joke. But Carroll had won them over: no one could hear the singing any more and neither was there any crying.

* * *

Ross ran his fingers through the raw fibres of lambswool that were fixed to one end of his flexible rammer. To the other, a wooden block would see the charge was finally pressed home but what was colloquially known as the sponge performed a far more vital function. When soaked in water and used correctly, the lambswool mop ensured a barrel was wiped free of all burning embers before the next cartridge of powder was inserted. Both tasks were entirely down to him and, although a long way from the responsibilities he had carried when a lieutenant, Ross was conscious of an obligation to the men about him that actually felt more real.

Were he remiss in his work, it would be Thompson's arm that was blown off. Ross had only known the man a brief time, but they had been messmates for all of it, and both felt a natural affinity for the other. It was the same with every member of his mess, as well as those of the gun crew; a spirit of true camaraderie that had been definitely missing during his time in a wardroom.

This came as a surprise, but was only one of several – the intense fear he was feeling at that particular moment being another. It had been present throughout all the hours of waiting, and was something else Ross supposed he would have to get used to as an ordinary hand. In the past he would have been on deck, or at least remained informed of the circumstances; down here in the darkened depths of the lower battery, it was a very different proposition.

Ross had seen action on several occasions and only once, as a young midshipman, had he been truly frightened. But now, in the confines of the cramped gun deck, with Irishmen's songs and the cries of starving animals ringing about his ears, he was going through the same emotions as when a boy. *Prometheus* had yet to receive a shot or fire one in return; the action could barely be thought of as begun – which probably accounted for much of his feelings. The monotonous, inharmonious drone from below was growing louder if anything, and all about seemed affected. He guessed there was little anyone could do to stop it, although the distraction was such that he would have had no hesitation in ordering the prisoners gagged, or worse, were the responsibility with him.

"Bloody load of Micks," Thompson grumbled. "Someone aught to learn them to keep quiet, so they should."

Soon all the gun crew were venting similar opinions, and Ross found their words comforting. He even went to voice his own thoughts on the subject, but found his mouth to be unusually dry.

"All right, that'll do," Flint said, quietening them gently. "Let them sing their lungs out if that's what gives them the jollies. It's not going to make no difference, we're still gonna take their ship." He looked about at his men, and Ross thought his eyes might have settled on him. "And don't any of you start to get the shivers," Flint added as an afterthought. "I told you, it won't be long."

* * *

On the quarterdeck, Banks was of the same opinion. He had done all he could to close with the enemy, but the wind was steadily failing: a rare occurrence for those latitudes and one that was proving more than a little annoying. With her size and weight, *Prometheus* was at a distinct disadvantage in light airs, and found herself severely out-sailed by the smaller, but decidedly potent, privateer.

By now, no one had any doubt she was indeed Carroll's former ship. Large for the type she may be, but there must be a hundred like her laid up in countless French ports, while seasoned hands eager to serve at sea rather than rot ashore would be ten a penny. A vessel of such size and strength would also be more effective in tackling the larger Indiamen, as well as handier when dodging a blockading inshore squadron. Then Banks remembered they had probably been making Cádiz their base, and with Spain still ostensibly neutral, there were no sanctions on any of her ports. The privateers might ply their wicked trade all about the Portuguese coast, snapping up merchants separated from convoy, or chancing a solo run. They could also see off any unrated Navy ship, while proving a tough opponent for much that was larger. And all the time with the convenience of a free and friendly harbour close at hand, one that no blockading force was able to starve of supplies.

Almost any merchant they encountered could be seized, carried and offered up for auction within a week, the latter under the very eyes of the British. And with so many potential victims at sea, the owners would become rich, encouraging others to speculate in similar enterprises, at a cost to Britain's economy that would be devastating. His government could object to the use of a Spanish port, although all the protestations in the world would have little effect. But should Banks be able to lure them close enough to his guns, the whole escapade would end now, and without further loss. It was something he must attempt, even though it meant risking his own precious ship.

And risk there was; he could not deny that. However much larger she may be, and whatever fire-power *Prometheus* possessed, the *Belle Île* had a distinct advantage over her in both speed and manoeuvrability. And they were fighting at sea, a medium with a habit of correcting inequalities with bad luck or misfortune. It was not unknown for a powerful frigate to take a line-of-battleship; little more than five years ago Pellew had accounted for the *Droits de l'Homme* off Plozévet and there were examples a plenty of larger ships being subdued and carried by cunning and lucky captains of smaller vessels. As a former frigate man himself, Banks knew all that would be needed was to let the enemy too close to a vulnerable section, then the loss of rudder, or an important spar could redress the odds considerably in the Frenchman's favour. But he also had to allow them near enough to use his great guns to their maximum effect. It was a difficult balance, and one he found harder to judge as the time wore on. And all the while he was painfully aware that, should the unthinkable happen and his precious *Prometheus* end up the prize of a private ship, he would never walk a Royal Navy quarterdeck again.

But whether it was right or wrong to encourage close action, the privateer was proving less than compliant in his efforts, and the lack of a decent wind was certainly no help. Banks had attempted all manner of manoeuvres to tempt the Frenchman in, but all had proved fruitless, with his quarry remaining in contact, but tantalisingly at the very extreme of his main guns' range. Currently she was lying prow on and apparently in irons, with *Prometheus* creeping slowly towards her. Were they allowed to travel much further, Banks would have the advantage, and may even be able to yaw, before landing a sizeable amount of shot on the Frenchman's fragile bows. But he was not so much the fool as to think them easily beaten, and was soon proved right. As he watched, the *Belle Île*'s jib was brought back to the wind. Then, when still more canvas was released, the frigate tacked to starboard, before surging forward in the gentle breeze as if to show her clumsy opponent just how easy such a manoeuvre could be.

Banks resigned himself to the prospect of continuing to conn his new command in a failing wind for a while longer. He had yet to get to know *Prometheus* properly, but already could tell the enemy had her measure in agility: any move he attempted was inevitably signalled well in advance, while the privateer seemed able to skip from one tack to the other almost on impulse. However, he still had that tremendous fire power hidden away and it would only take one mistake to allow him to deal a significant blow which must surely see the privateer at his mercy. They were no longer sailing under the Company flag; that had been struck some while back, to be replaced with the newest Navy ensign they possessed. He had hoped the enemy would consider the exchange a double bluff, and so it had proved.

He gave a quick glance to Brehaut, who was standing ready at the binnacle, then another to check his own canvas. *Prometheus* was riding under topsails, with a couple of staysails and a jib for good measure and no more would be added. The next logical sail was the distinctive forecourse, which must mark her very definitely as a man-o'-war, while any difference in speed would not be sufficient to catch such a slippery foe. The privateer had drawn ahead and was hauling in her wind, allowing *Prometheus* to forereach on her once more. Soon she would wear and make a pass across their own bows – it was the same manoeuvre the enemy had carried out several times already, but on this occasion Banks was determined they would not get away with it.

"Ready larboard, upper deck only, and remember the firing order," he bellowed, and received an acknowledgement from King standing in the waist. Of the battleship's larboard upper battery of eighteen-pounders, all were run out, but only eight would actually be fired, an act that would hopefully maintain the fiction that *Prometheus* was indeed an Indiaman. Most merchants of such a size would carry some serviceable cannon, with the remaining ports filled by 'quakers': wooden gun barrels that appeared genuine from a distance, and were designed to fool an enemy into thinking her fully armed. By firing a reduced broadside, Banks hoped the *Belle Île* might be further convinced, and the irony that real cannon would be emulating imitation pieces was not lost on their grinning gun crews.

"Prepare to lay her to starboard, Mr Brehaut," he added, in a voice barely louder than the din of bleating cattle, and the sailing master growled out a clearer warning to the quartermaster. Then, as the frigate was starting to swoop down upon their prow, Banks gave the word.

"Port your helm!" Brehaut ordered and the ship began to turn, throwing the aim of the gun captains, while those at the braces fought to keep pace with what breeze there was. A shout from forward heralded the crack of shot glancing off the battleship's hawse, followed by the rumble of a full broadside from the privateer. Those were no pop-guns, Banks told himself, The frigate was well armed, but range was in his favour and he trusted *Prometheus'* timbers to be strong enough to deflect such a blow without sustaining serious damage.

King bellowed from the waist, and the battleship's reduced broadside was released with a clatter of fire that came as an anticlimax to anyone familiar with her true capabilities. It too was at extreme range, though and almost all of the British shots went wide or fell short; an act that, though unintended, would have enforced their subterfuge still further. But it was good to finally hear the guns in use, and Banks was just anticipating being able to reap the benefits of his action when the Frenchman surprised him yet again.

Turning apparently within her own length, the *Belle Île* momentarily presented her stern, but was wearing round and making to starboard before the British could reveal their heavy cannon, or lay her remaining secondary armament far enough forward. Banks grunted to himself; his opponent was certainly lithe and he wondered when she would become tired of such games, or if his simple hoax would ever be revealed. The noise of *Prometheus'* broadside seemed to have encouraged the animals, who were now making a truly raucous din forward. Soon the racket must be audible to the enemy, and Banks could think of no better disguise for a fighting ship. A close and considered inspection would reveal their true status, of course, but he trusted the enemy was manoeuvring too far off for such a luxury and while he kept his lower ports closed, and the smallest of doubts remained, the action would continue.

But not for much longer. He was rarely one to believe in sixth senses or intuition, but still felt a conclusion was close by. That exchange had been at extreme range, but at least they had finally fired. It was still some time until darkness and the battle, such as it was, had already lasted for several hours. But no action can continue forever, and a feeling deep inside told him the privateer was not intending to draw things out for very much longer.

Chapter Ten

And so it proved. The frigate completed her turn and came back as close to the wind as she could bear while *Prometheus* continued, now with the breeze on her beam. Lisbon, with her batteries and the likelihood of Royal Naval support was growing steadily closer, although the sun was also beginning to head for the horizon. Both commanders were running out of time. Banks could not continue manoeuvring, when any merchant captain worth his salt would choose to run, while the privateer was starting to risk being interrupted by the appearance of another vessel, and so be cheated of her prize.

"It is my duty to inform you the enemy is gaining the windward gauge, sir." It was Brehaut who spoke and, of all the ship's officers, he was the only one allowed such a liberty. A quick glance from Banks confirmed that there was no implied criticism: the man was simply doing his job as sailing master in advising him of the situation. And, in the majority of engagements, it might not have been the best of tactics, but Banks felt he knew what he was doing.

His plans had never involved releasing *Prometheus'* lower deck guns on the hull of the French ship: such an action would likely wreck her for sure. When the chance was finally given, it would be better to aim for her tophamper – something easier to achieve when sailing to leeward. And giving up such a tactical advantage should fit in with his imitation of a merchant captain.

The enemy was still a good mile off their quarter, but plainly preparing what the French commander intended to be the fatal blow. As they watched, the frigate tacked neatly and was adding royals as she began to charge down upon them.

It was like waiting to be set upon by a particularly vicious, if small, dog, Banks soberly decided. The enemy would continue to advance, gaining speed all the time, then either fly down the length of *Prometheus'* hull, relying on superior speed to keep them safe as they dusted her decks with grape or, more likely, turn at the last moment, peppering the British ship's stern with a close ranged broadside. But for Banks, the time for bluff was very definitely at an end. This was where he played his trump card, and must accept the consequences.

"We shall be turning to larboard," he said with certainty as the *Belle Île* began to throw a large white cloud from her stem. "Pass the word to Mr King, then Mr Davison and Mr Benson on the lower deck," he added, speaking directly to the most senior midshipman in sight. "I want a solid broadside from the upper deck; all guns are to be fired, make sure Mr King understands that." With luck the upper eighteen-pounders and carronades would do considerable damage and hopefully delay the enemy in manoeuvring further. "As soon as our shots are received, the lower deck may open ports and run out their pieces, but not before. Ask Mr Davison to ensure every captain has adequate time to take aim: and emphasise that the target is to be their masts. And remind him I require an accurate rather than a fast response."

Franklin touched his hat briefly and then was off. It was proof of the importance of his message that Banks sent the older man although, even without word reaching them, he trusted his lieutenants to know their duty. This was his only chance; as soon as those lower ports opened, revealing the terror within, the *Belle Île* would run. His gamble was that *Prometheus* could cause enough damage to make escape impossible.

* * *

The message arrived, and was duly passed on to all on the lower gun deck. Flint had led the five elite members of his team that covered both weapons to their larboard gun some while back, and now all were ready with that piece.

"So what do you think we shall see?" Harrison asked and Flint knew himself near the end of his temper.

"I know as much as you," he snapped. "But masts are to be the target, so be ready to whip that quoin out if I says. We took a nasty to larboard earlier: it's clear the Frogs are no shirkers when it comes to using their cannon."

"Slip the bolts and clear ports, but keep them lids tight shut," Davison's voice erupted from aft. With darkness, heat and what was a now a constant bellowing from hungry animals, coupled with the din of Irish prisoners bleating out in song, it was a scene that would not be out of place in any nightmare. But now something positive was being called for from them, the gun crews felt far easier. "Be ready to reload with bar once more," the young lieutenant continued, his voice now raw with shouting. "With luck we'll get a second in."

"That would be a luxury indeed," Flint murmured to himself. "Target's a frigate: if the main course don't settle her, they're hardly likely to stick about for a pudding."

Then the ship began a sudden turn, and some of the less experienced amongst them lost their footing as the deck heaved to starboard.

"Least that shut the animals up," Thompson commented.

"And the Micks," Harrison agreed.

Thompson went to add a rejoinder when Benson's voice cut through.

"Cast loose and provide!" Then, a little more gently: "be ready for the word, lads..."

Though officially second in command of the gun deck, the older man was markedly more controlled than Davison.

Their larboard port lids were now cleared of the oakum that sealed them and began to sway with the rolling of the ship. Even such a slight movement allowed tantalising shafts of light into the gloom, while side tackles were secured and train tackles locked on to the eye bolts at the rear of each powerful weapon. Flint carefully removed the lead apron and lock cover from his gun, and eased the hammer back to half cock. Cranston, the second captain, had collected a line of smoking slow match and was twirling it in the air to redden the end. It would be used in case of a misfire and, although primitive, was more reliable than any flint on steel. In the curious silence the faint shrill of a whistle could just be heard; then the deck above apparently exploded in ear splitting cacophony.

The noise echoed about the lower battery for some time; it was far louder than the upper deck's previous broadside and a few of the newer servers were open mouthed with shock, while others looked accusingly at their own pieces. Davison was yelling something which was being repeated by Benson but, even without hearing the words, Flint knew what must be done.

A wave at Cranston was enough to open the heavy port that had been shielding their gun, allowing late afternoon sunlight to flood into the darkness they had become accustomed to. The sudden light dazzled the deafened beings within and added to their confusion, but a sound brain was not required to haul on a line, and the beast that was Flint's larboard cannon was soon run out to take its first look at the enemy.

"That's close enough for a Chinaman," Flint said, in quiet appreciation as he viewed the oncoming warship. She was considerably less than quarter of a mile off, and still heading for them at a goodly pace. Shot from their upper decks had peppered her fore topsail and course, and it appeared as if a jib had been cut down. But her major spars were unaffected and, unless they could cause serious damage in that department, she would soon be bearing away, and gone.

Prometheus was continuing to right herself after the turn, and Flint paused, his left hand in the air, while two of the gun's permanent team eased her across with their handspikes. From further forward the deep throated crack of two cannon firing simultaneously went unheard as Flint fixed his mind solely on keeping that pyramid of sails in his sights. Then, measuring the degree of roll, he actually shoved the quoin a little deeper under the cascabel. The ship paused considerably at the top, and that was when he intended to fire. Guns were erupting on both sides now, but still the enemy ship claimed all his attention. The Frenchman was starting to turn, and would soon be beating back, and making her escape, but there was time enough for this one shot, and Flint was not going to waste it.

"Clear the gun," he yelled. Then, stepping to one side himself, waited for the uproll to begin. The firing line was actually pulled just before she reached the climax; there was a momentary pause, a flash from the priming, then the gun spoke with a terrible roar and it was a sound that would rebound about all their minds for the next few hours.

Carriage wheels squealed as the dead weight was hurled back, to be checked by a groaning breech rope. Then the tackle-men took charge: Cranston yelled for the sponge and Ross was quick to plunge his sodden lambswool mop into the still smoking barrel. Men stood by with powder, shot and wads in an effort to have the gun reloaded in the least possible time but Flint, glancing at the enemy through the gun port, already knew the action to be over. Theirs was one of the last shots fired, and there could be no guarantee it was responsible for what had occurred. But the nett result was unequivocal.

"She's hit, and hit good," Thompson shouted as he returned from delivering his cartridge of cylinder powder.

Flint made no reply: he could see as much from his position by the cannon's smoking breech. The enemy's fore topmast was lying in a tangle across her forecastle, having been cut down by the hail of flying metal. Her main topgallant mast had also fallen and, despite the wind that was finally rising once more, escape was now impossible. The French might surrender, or could wait to be boarded, but there was no doubting that single broadside had won the battle, and the privateer was effectively theirs.

Chapter Eleven

"That's a sight and no mistaking," Lewis said in unaccustomed garrulity as *Prometheus* beat closer to the stricken ship. As fifth lieutenant he had charge of signals as well as the quarterdeck and forecastle carronades. The latter had taken all of his attention for some time, but he now had a fine vantage point to view the lower decks' work.

In addition to the damaged fore and main masts, *Belle Île*'s bowsprit had also suffered; her dolphin striker hung loose from the jib boom and her forecastle was draped in a mass of line, canvas and splintered wood. The damage looked particularly unsightly on what had been such a trim craft, but there was no time for aesthetics; the enemy had yet to surrender and could still cause them serious damage.

"Larboard battery, stand ready!" Caulfield's voice cut through the babble of excited chatter from men and officers alike, and the order was repeated to King on the deck below, as well as Davison at the main battery. "Target the hull."

"Battery's reloaded with bar, sir." a quarter gunner reported to Lewis, who looked uncertainly towards Caulfield.

"Very well, let it be," the first lieutenant replied. "We may still cause sufficient devilment, and, with luck, shall not have to fire."

And, as they drew closer, a further broadside certainly seemed to be unnecessary. *Prometheus* out gunned the smaller ship several times over although, with a tattered ensign still flying from her jack, there was nothing to stop Banks pounding her to a wreck, should he feel so inclined. Then an officer on the enemy's quarterdeck waved his hat; their flag was slowly lowered, and a cheer began to flow from deep within the British ship.

Banks watched with a relief that was strongly coloured by exhaustion. He had been on deck since before sunrise and it was now late afternoon. A chunk of stale soft tack and some bacon was the only solid food eaten in that time, although what he craved most was peace and a chance to sit down. And, as the tension slowly ebbed from his body, he supposed it had been no great victory: few of his fellow officers would think anything of a two decker taking a frigate. But they did not know of the failing wind, his untried ship, and those doubts that, even after the battle was over, haunted him still.

Caulfield was offering his hand, and he shook it absent mindedly; of all aboard *Prometheus*, the first lieutenant was probably more aware of what had been achieved that day than anyone.

"Cutters and launch, if you please, Mr Caulfield," Banks said in return. "Initial boarding party of marines, then a prize and repair crew under two officers."

"Very good, sir," Caulfield replied. "Who is to command?"

Banks paused. "Mr Davison and Mr Benson: they may select three midshipmen, and one of the master mates." He would prefer to have sent King, who had more experience of boarding captures but, as second lieutenant, the honour should fall to Davison.

"Boatswain and carpenter will be needed also," he continued, as *Prometheus* drew closer still, and the damage they had caused became more apparent. "And alert Mr Manning." There were dead men visible aboard the Frenchman, with doubtless more wounded below; as far as he was aware, his ship had not suffered a single casualty, and the realisation put their victory into perspective.

Banks turned away from the sight, momentarily disgusted. He might have frightened himself with thoughts of what was at risk, but having more recently been a small ship captain was probably to blame for that. In reality, the triumph they had won was due solely to one major broadside and an enemy too greedy to leave well alone – he gave himself no credit for subterfuge, or the many hours of manoeuvring that had led to that single knock-out blow. But the time had taken its toll, and he would not be the only one to feel tired.

"Secure from action stations, Mr Caulfield, and have the galley stove re-lit." he said, flexing his shoulders stiffly. "Then you may pipe Up Spirits – and see to those bloody animals."

"You do not care that your boat has been taken?" Judy asked Carroll. For the last four hours the two of them had been entertaining ten lively children in the stewards' room, which now bore a close resemblance to a domestic nursery. And their charges, finally weary after being treated to a succession of japes, tricks and numerous other boisterous activities, were sleeping peacefully in the midst of an extended game of 'Dead Donkey'.

"Oh I care very much indeed," the Irishman assured her as he accepted the mug of hot tea she proffered and rested back against the ship's scantlings. "Indeed, it is a disaster for me in many respects, the most being financial."

"So it was your boat then?"

"Ship," he corrected gently after sipping at his drink. "But no, she did not belong to me outright. I had a share in her, which cost my family everything we owned and more. A few days back, when we took your *Duke of Cambridge,* I was looking forward to a life of wealth and luxury, but now that appears to have been lost forever."

"You have a family?" she asked, with poorly assumed nonchalance.

"I have," he admitted. "Father and two sisters in Galway, though I have not seen them in more than three years."

"And yet they lent you money..." Judy said, with more perception than Carroll expected.

"Sure, am I not the same man they knew when we lived together?" he replied. "And money is not so very difficult to move, even in war time, although it helps if you have some to begin with."

"What will you do now?" she asked and he shrugged.

"That will depend very much on those who hold me. My ship carried a *lettre de course* so I trust the privileges of a normal prisoner will be given when I am landed. In the last war, most were exchanged; this new fellow Bonaparte may have different ideas, but I hope to be back on French soil before so very long."

"You wish to go back to France?" she seemed surprised. "But

Ireland is your home."

"Ireland *was* my home," he corrected. "And indeed, where my family still are; but there is little left of the old place, and I should not wish to live under English rule."

"You do not care for the English?" her voice had grown more cautious.

"I do not care for some," he corrected. "But others I may grow to like in time."

For a spell neither spoke as they sipped at their tea, although both found themselves taking the occasional glance at the other as if by chance.

"And what of you?" Carroll enquired at last. "You will be returning to Lisbon?"

"It is the only home I know," she replied. "And the only place where I have friends."

"And presently it bears not more than a few miles off our larboard bow," the Irishman mused. "Was not the captain willing to set you ashore there?"

"Lieutenant King said he would make a request," she said, brightening slightly. "Apparently it would be possible, without delaying this ship hardly at all. He was to take a boat – a cutter, I think. Run me to land and then rejoin the ship later. It seemed the ideal solution and I was so grateful, but with things as they are..."

"Well I'm truly sorry to have upset your plans," Carroll told her, and they both laughed. "But I would chance you shall find yourself back in Lisbon soon enough," he added. "If that is where you really wish to be."

"Oh I do not mind wherever I ends up," she said with frank conviction. "Just as long as there is someone close who cares for me."

* * *

"As I see it, we have a number of options," Banks told the group of officers. They were in his sleeping quarters once more, but this time crammed about the small, baize-topped card table, that was proving far more practical than the larger mess furniture had been.

149

And it was less than twenty-four hours later, yet much had been done. The captured frigate boasted a fresh fore topmast, the replacement having been transferred from *Prometheus'* spar deck that morning. It would take the rest of that day and most of the next to rig shrouds and yards, then set up a new main topgallant and repair the bowsprit. But much of the patching to the hull and superstructure had already been attended to, and there seemed little reason why both ships might not set sail before the following night.

However, despite what was undoubtedly good progress, and the fact of his recent victory, Banks was finding it hard to evoke either energy or enthusiasm. His head ached: the pain had been increasing steadily since early morning and was now on the verge of becoming unbearable. His mouth also felt uncommonly dry and, despite a night in his cot that had only been interrupted once, he was in sore need of rest. As with all commonly fit people, Banks detested being even mildly unwell, and rejected the notion that his ailment could be down to overwork. To his mind, the strain of the past few days would be considered nothing to most sea officers, and should have been carried off without a thought.

But there was no question that he was suffering and, once he had accepted the fact, the doubts began. Perhaps it was becoming a father? Perhaps he was just not fit to command such a huge enterprise as *Prometheus?* Or perhaps he was simply getting too old? But, whatever the reason, Banks was definitely not feeling quite the thing that day.

"I have spoken at length with *Belle Île*'s captain," he continued, "who initially proved less cooperative than his subordinate, Mr Carroll." Banks' mind went back to the conversation. Despite commanding a mixed crew that included a good many Irish, Captain Agard had refused to admit any knowledge of the English language. Fortunately Brehaut was on hand: the Jersey born sailing master had spoken French all his life, and soon punctured that little bubble of obstinacy to the extent that Banks was finally able to speak with the man without an interpreter. "It would seem to have been a relatively new venture," Banks told them. "And the *Duke of Cambridge* was the first ship taken, which explains the large crew and such a high proportion of officers."

Any ambitious privateering venture would provide for potential prize crews and it seemed *Belle Île* was no exception. There were nods of general agreement and King looked as if he might be wanting to ask a question, but Banks hurried on. Usually he welcomed comments from his officers, although on that particular day he would rather the meeting was simply over.

"Which brings us back to where we should make for," he continued resolutely. "I understand from Mr Brehaut that we are currently less than six hours from the Tagus, and obviously shelter may be found there." The pain was causing his mind to wander and, as he tried to focus on the task in hand, his eyes flashed round the group seated elbow to elbow at the table before him. They consisted of all his lieutenants, as well as the sailing master and Marine Captain Donaldson. Each, apart from Brehaut, nodded quickly in agreement as his gaze met theirs, but Banks found he had lost his thread and was forced to pause and collect his thoughts before starting again.

"The Tagus, yes," he repeated. "Calling there is certainly an option."

It was a wide, yet sheltered harbour, and the anchorage had been a Godsend to the Mediterranean Fleet for some while. Just how a captured prize would be dealt with was a different matter, however. Banks was no expert in international law but had read enough of previous cases to make him cautious. With Portugal a neutral country there may be no end of legal wrangles; though apparently French, *Belle Île* had been using a Spanish port and, for all he knew, might even be registered in Cádiz. If so he could be forced to release his prisoners and return their ship; a thought that momentarily appalled him, and made the headache worse.

"Or, of course, Gibraltar is also well within reach." He forced himself to adopt a slightly more optimistic tone. Indeed, given a favourable wind, the tiny outpost might be raised within three to four days, and probably not more than a week if all turned contrary. That option brought up another highly significant question though: were they prepared to travel so far with the liability of a captured ship?

The actual vessel did not present too much of a problem but, with almost two hundred of her crew as prisoners, and a further contingent of passengers and officers from the Indiaman to cram between both ships, it was not an especially joyous prospect. In fact, to him, and given the way he felt at that moment, it seemed utterly impossible. But then Banks also knew he was under the weather, and all would appear so much easier once his damned headache passed.

"Were we to attempt such a journey, I would suggest the following," he persevered, although even as he spoke the words, he realised there was only really one option.

Gibraltar would undoubtedly be their destination and, as for him making a suggestion, the days when he would proffer or propose ideas had ended when he moved away from frigates. Now, as captain of a line-of-battleship, a far more positive attitude was called for. But Banks equally acknowledged that he wasn't at his best, and many of the officers before him were also friends, so there was little harm in dressing his orders up in a modicum of politeness.

"We clear the capture of prisoners, and accommodate all aboard *Prometheus.*" It might have been his imagination, but the room seemed to have suddenly grown uncommonly hot, and there was a faint haze in the air not noticed before. "Secure quarters can be built into the orlop, which incorporate the former midshipmen and warrant officers' berths, with any vulnerable stores or provisions moved accordingly. Captain Donaldson, the prisoners would be in your care, with the marines maintaining an all-watch guard."

The bovine officer's permanent flush deepened slightly at the mention of his name, but he did not seem unduly perturbed by the responsibility. Banks regarded him for a moment, focussing on the red nose that seemed, if anything, a little larger than normal, before deciding that not so very much could go wrong.

"Sixty trained seamen could then be transferred to the capture, under the command of two commissioned officers and whatever master's mates and midshipmen they may require." The headache was growing worse now, but he struggled on manfully.

"Passengers can be divided between both ships: the most being taken aboard our prize while those of standing being suited in the great cabin aboard *Prometheus*." He could foresee some of the *Duke of Cambridge*'s more pretentious travellers objecting to being forcibly accommodated aboard a recently captured Frenchman and, however bad he might be feeling, didn't wish to ruffle feathers unnecessarily.

The officers before him seemed agreeable while Banks' pounding brain tried to detect a fault. But it was a reasonable scenario, and he could find none. With just a sailing crew aboard, space would not be at a premium in the prize, and sufficient men could be retained aboard *Prometheus* to provide protection for both ships, should such a thing be required.

"Well, I would judge that a workable scenario; if anyone has any comments, I shall be delighted to hear them," Banks concluded, his focus travelling unsteadily about the faces before him.

But, even as he waited, the captain realised he did not wish to hear more. Usually, and when his head was feeling normal, proposals or remarks were welcomed from his deputies. On occasions they had proved valuable, and were often adopted, at no loss to his prestige or position. Now though, not only did he not want to hear from the assembled company, he also doubted if any action or intelligent comment could be made on what might be said.

But fortunately no one spoke, and Banks was secretly relieved. There would inevitably be problems constructing the temporary accommodation to house so many prisoners; well, they had an experienced carpenter in Roberts, who led a capable team: let them deal with it. Likewise, isolating the hazardous stores, such as spirit, paint, pitch and powder, from the reach of any captive set on self murder; there were plenty of sensible officers available to deal with such matters. Passenger space aboard *Prometheus* must be limited to the great cabin and coach, and it was likely that more would wish to stay than could be suited, while the French victuals served in the privateer were bound to offend the taste of some sent aboard her. But he would have two commissioned men on hand,

and they should be able to handle any such crisis without reference to him.

Thoughts of the officers to be chosen prompted him to consider further and, as no one was apparently interested in gilding his lily, Banks' aching mind turned to this final issue.

"So, who is to go?" he asked rhetorically. There might have been expressions of mild concern on the faces of King and Caulfield, but these disappeared as he spoke, and every lieutenant looked back expectantly. Davison and Benson had been the boarding officers who accepted the privateer's surrender, with both supervising repairs up until that time. But Davison had already complained about the fourth's lack of ability, something that had hardly come as a surprise to Banks.

He had previously noticed his second lieutenant's tendency to hold high expectations, and equally that he was rather too keen to blame others for what were possibly his own deficiencies. Banks regarded both as symptoms of youth and inexperience. Without doubt, Benson and Lewis had much to learn, but they were keen to do so and, under the guidance of someone more seasoned, would probably benefit from the experience.

Davison was not that man, however; despite anything his references might say, the days when he could command respect through ability rather than rank were still to come. And Caulfield could also be discounted: with so many prisoners to guard, as well as a reduced crew, his organisational abilities were needed aboard *Prometheus*. Which only left King.

The latter had commanded prizes in the past and was not wanting in ability or initiative. Actually he might easily have led the prize crew, with Benson or Lewis as support. But no, that would never have done; Davison was bound to see a junior man being given the posting as an affront and was known to have important friends: men of influence who might someday be useful to Banks' own future.

He mused, caring little that all in the tiny cabin were waiting for him to come to a decision. Then the ideal solution presented itself; one that would solve all problems while leaving him free to dismiss his guests and get some rest. He would post Davison as lieutenant in command with King, admittedly the more experienced, in support. To his throbbing mind there was little wrong in such a combination and, more importantly, the meeting could be called to a close.

Once all were gone, Banks would ask David to rig his cot and, with the way he felt, perhaps the surgeon should be sent for. But first, he hoped, a short sleep might set him to rights.

* * *

"It's a mild fever," Manning told Caulfield in the dispensary, which was probably one of the more private parts of the ship at that time. "I have administered a draught of Peruvian Bark, and taken eight ounces of blood. He is currently asleep and it is best if we allow him to remain so. His servant is giving excellent attention."

"Are there any other instances?" the first lieutenant asked. News of his captain's sickness was bad enough; were the illness to spread to other members of the crew, it could spell disaster.

"Yes, though mainly amongst the marines." Manning scratched his head thoughtfully. "None of the Indiaman's former passengers are reporting symptoms, which surprises me as I would have guessed them to be the cause. Their medical man appears to be a fine practitioner, and is Edinburgh trained. I am glad to say he does not suspect typhus, but believes the malady to be nothing more than a minor chill, which should not prove life threatening. With luck and good care it may even pass."

"Could you estimate how long that might take?" Caulfield was not in any great hope of an answer, but at least the captain's life did not appear in danger.

"I should say no more than a week," Manning replied.

A week: in such a time they could have raised Gibraltar, or found themselves in action with an enemy fleet. But at least much had already been done as far as planning was concerned. Both ships would soon be ready to sail, and the carpenter's team were finishing the improvised cells on the orlop.

"Very well," Caulfield said, with sudden decision. "Then we

should make for Gibraltar without delay. We can start transferring passengers and captives at first light and square away shortly afterwards. You will keep me informed of developments with the captain?"

"I shall indeed," Manning confirmed. "As well as any further patients that might present."

* * *

"Well, it's hardly the grandest of pitches," Thompson said, dropping his ditty bag and hammock onto the deck at their allotted space. "Not for a single decker."

Being entirely free of cannon, the berth deck of a frigate was usually spacious to the point of being draughty, and the sixty or so hands selected to sail the prize had been expecting far more in the way of accommodation. But the lesser passengers would be making their homes aft of a canvas screen, rigged rather hurriedly between main and foremast, and the seamen were pragmatic enough to know that stealing their space was likely to be the least of the civilians' crimes.

"When's that lot comin' aboard, then?" Harrison asked, eyeing the barrier with mistrust.

"Almost immediately, I'd say," Flint replied. "What with the Frenchies an' all, it were getting like a cattle market aboard the barky."

"Well, at least we got the galley fire," Thompson, who liked his comfort, muttered. "An' the 'eads."

"An' it'll only be a brief while," Flint agreed, glad to find a positive comment. "Three or four days, at worst, then Gib. an' all her wonders."

Those detailed to the prize had been drafted in messes, the theory being that men already acquainted and in most cases used to working together would be of more use aboard a strange vessel. Such a consideration was even more important when dealing with ships of the third rate and above, where crews were seldom less than five hundred and could frequently rise to almost double. But of all of Flint's mess, only Jameson and Butler were recognised topmen, which was the obvious requirement when sailing an alien ship. Consequently, the others would have to reconcile themselves to acting as members of the afterguard or even waisters.

"She's a tight enough craft," Butler said as he placed an appreciative hand on one of the overhead beams. "With a bit of luck, they'll buy her into the service."

"Why should you care if they do?" Billings asked suspiciously.

Butler gave him a sideways look. "Because they'll be needing a transit crew," he said. "And I, for one, don't intend spending the rest of my days beating 'bout the Med."

"Anyone checked out the ballast?" Thompson asked of nobody in particular.

"Should we need to?" Ben, the lad of the mess, asked innocently.

"Far too many Frenchies been aboard this tub for my liking," Thompson explained. "They got a nasty trick of burying their dead in the shingle."

"This was a privateer," Ross spoke softly, but with his usual authority. "And only recently out of harbour so you have nothing to fear."

"Aye, there'll be no bodies rising up in the night and strangling you in yer 'ammock," Harrison chuckled, running his hands up Thompson's back and grasping him playfully by the throat.

"Oh, I ain't afeared o' nothing," Thompson lied, as he struggled free of his mate's embrace. "It's just not a very nice habit, that's all."

* * *

Judy examined the jar that Carroll had passed to her earlier that morning. She had already been able to use some of the powder, but there was still a good deal of it left. Davie had said it would do no harm, but she was not convinced. And neither was she certain the stuff would go unnoticed. Slipping some into one of the ship's coppers would be no problem; Stone had boasted about cooking up a spicy lobscouse for the marines that day, and such slop could hide any amount of strange flavouring. But the officers' food was different, and commissioned men's palates were likely to be more sensitive than those of marines. She had tried some on the captain's devilled kidneys without him apparently noticing, but then neither had he been seen since. There was even a rumour that Sir Richard had taken to his cot, although that might just be tattle-tale. She opened the lid, and sniffed at the white powder within; it looked quite innocuous – similar to sugar although, when a finger was cautiously dipped in, it tasted anything but. Still, there were plenty of kidneys left over from the ration bullocks which Potterton had allocated for tomorrow's wardroom's breakfast. And she had promised Davie the stuff would all be used as soon as possible.

Chapter Twelve

"As officer in command, I shall be taking the captain's quarters," Davison announced when they had finished their inspection of the privateer. There were a number of items he had found fault with, none of which were King's sole responsibility, although the young man had made each sound like a personal affront. But it was the last statement, made on the half deck when they were as close to being alone as was possible, that really raised King's ire.

"Indeed?" he asked sharply. "It was my understanding that we were to share the great cabin. Space must be found for the master's mates and midshipmen, and there are several families with young children aboard, as well as single women who require private accommodation."

"Female civilians can berth together; they are not our responsibility and middies will take the cockpit: it is what they are used to, after all," Davison replied. "Likewise the master's mates. Claim a cabin in the gun room for yourself, by all means. I trust the screaming babies will not take too much of your sleep."

King went to speak but Davison had already turned on his heel and was gone.

"Am I to put your dunnage in the great cabin, sir?"

It was Keats, his servant: the man was approaching under a pile of luggage that included King's watchcoat, sword and spare clothing.

"No," King told him. "My quarters appear to be in the gun room."

* * *

Caulfield stood by the binnacle of *Prometheus*. It was four bells in the afternoon watch, the passengers who had been persuaded to leave were already embarked in the prize, while all prisoners, apart from Carroll, who had given his parole, were secured in their newly made pens below. And every man in both ships had been fed – in itself a major undertaking, and one that took a good deal longer in the frigate, whose stove had proved a mystery to the cook's mate sent to master it. The British amongst them were still slightly groggy from the effects of their mid-day spirit ration, but there were several hours of daylight left, and no sense in delaying longer.

"Very well, Mr Brehaut," the first lieutenant said, with more formality than was usual. "You have a course; kindly make sail. Mr Lewis, you may signal the prize to that effect."

The bunting broke out on the larboard main halyards and was brought down just as *Prometheus'* topsails were released; an action copied by those aboard the frigate as near simultaneously as could be managed: Davison was clearly intending to impress. The wind, strong in the north-west, began to fill the canvas and, as forecourses and jibs were added, both vessels eased into motion, with the battleship taking station to windward of her charge. Caulfield felt the deck heel only slightly beneath his feet, and listened with satisfaction to the creaking of spars, rigging and hull as *Prometheus* took life. This was not his favoured position; he was used to being second-in-command and had to admit, preferred to be so. There had been a time when the role of captain appealed, but that was some while ago, and he knew himself too old now. But Banks was lying in his bunk with a temperature hot enough to fry an egg and, as no one better equipped to carry out the task was on hand, Caulfield felt he might cope – at least on a temporary basis.

And it really should be for the briefest of periods; a day's good sailing would see the journey time cut significantly and, by then, he should have grown more used to being ultimately responsible for two ships and nearly a thousand lives. But still it was not a duty the first lieutenant enjoyed, and he could only wish it over as soon as possible.

* * *

As it turned out, all went agreeably enough for the first few hours: it wasn't until the following morning that Caulfield's troubles began. They had spent a peaceful night: the traverse board consistently showing speeds of over six knots, and he was looking forward to having logged a considerable portion of their journey by the noon observations. And after a shaky start, the prisoners were also behaving themselves. At first their officers, especially the privateer captain, caused a measure of trouble, but this was swiftly calmed, and by an unexpected ally.

None, apart from Carroll, would agree to give their parole, so Caulfield was left with no alternative other than to incarcerate them with their men. This was not popular, but with space at a premium, he had no option. Fortunately the Irish prize master came to his aid: he had no idea what words of persuasion Carroll used, but the nett result was a peaceful ship. It was all he required, and the first lieutenant felt grudgingly grateful for the man's intervention.

More men had presented with the mystery illness but, for the moment at least, they could manage, while the captain's condition seemed to be progressing steadily. His fever remained high, but there were signs of waking and Banks' servant was sure of improvement.

Consequently, when he settled down to breakfast in a wardroom finally cleared of passengers and children, Caulfield was feeling mildly optimistic: a mood that was heightened by the smell of devilled kidneys and what might be mutton chops that came from the officers' pantry. He reached for the wardroom copy of a newspaper. It was over two months old and had already been well thumbed, but there was only Captain Donaldson and his subaltern at the table, and the first lieutenant preferred to read the thing for the umpteenth time than make small talk.

But before he had even been able to order his breakfast, the first signs that matters were not to continue well made themselves known. Donaldson had dined slightly earlier, and was sitting at ease, enjoying the last of his customary early morning bottle of white wine, when an odd change began to overtake him. Caulfield watched over his newspaper as the man's almost constant flush suddenly lightened, before reverting to an even darker puce. Then his half-filled glass dropped to the table and he lifted both hands to his head, while letting out a guttural moan.

"Whatever is the matter, man?" Caulfield demanded as Marine Lieutenant James rose to attend his superior.

"Damnedest pain in the head," Donaldson slurred, still pressing at his temples. "Can't see straight, and my mouth's gone as dry as a drab's kiss."

"You'd better see him to his quarters," Caulfield said to James. "And pass the word for Mr Manning."

Until that moment there had been no more instances of fever amongst the officers, and Caulfield had even come to hope they might be in some way immune. But if anyone was to succumb, he would have guessed it to be the old soak. The first lieutenant watched as, in the arms of James and one of the wardroom stewards, Donaldson allowed himself to be eased upright and, still moaning pitifully, dragged backwards the short distance to his cabin.

"Would you care for breakfast, sir?" Judy, the girl steward, asked from close by and Caulfield looked up in surprise. He had grown accustomed to having the woman about, and there could be no doubting she made herself useful. But still the sight of a pretty face was enough to disconcert him, even on the best of mornings.

"What's that?" he asked sharply, while tearing his glance away from those finely shaped breasts that had surely been presented far too near to his face.

"I was offering you breakfast, sir," she answered. As one well versed at both table service, and the irascibility of gentlemen before breakfast, Judy always appeared self possessed although, on that particular occasion, Caulfield noticed her lip was trembling slightly.

"What is available, Kinnison?" he enquired, a little more gently.

"We have mutton loin or kidneys," she replied. "An' there is some tommy soaked in cow's milk that has toasted up nice."

A roar came from Donaldson's cabin, followed by the sound of someone retching. Judy seemed to wince, while the first lieutenant tried to ignore the chest that was still being held tantalisingly close to his face.

162

"Did you say kidneys?" he asked vaguely: Caulfield was an officer of the old school and had always been particularly partial to offal.

"Yes, sir. Devilled, and served with fried onions," she confirmed, although her attention appeared to be elsewhere and there was now a definite flush to her cheeks. "Or there's fresh loin chops from the gun room pig what died last Tuesday."

"What did Mr Donaldson have?"

"He took the kidneys," Judy answered instantly, adding: "but the pork looks nice, an' 'er death were natural," with half a smile.

"Oh, very well, bring me that," the first lieutenant sighed, before holding up the paper to read, and tearing the thing neatly down the middle.

* * *

In the captured frigate, King was also enjoying breakfast. What was actually a substantial gun room now felt quite small when compared to the massive proportions of *Prometheus,* and the space they did have seemed a good deal more crowded. He sat at the head of a table that was filled with at least three generations of passengers, with the youngest making themselves known by crawling about the deck, and occasionally encountering his feet. The food was good, though. A few of the wives seemed to have formed some sort of catering committee and, using discovered cabin stores and a good deal of ingenuity, had taken it upon themselves to organise meals for all of their number, as well those officers berthing in the gun room. Consequently he had eaten his fill of scrambled duck eggs, served with particularly dry sausages which were not in the least unpleasant, and a form of flat bread that tasted as if it had been freshly baked. There were also jugs of chocolate, not usually King's favourite of morning drinks, but very acceptable. The drink was far thicker and stronger than any he had tasted before and left him with an effect not unlike that felt after taking too much coffee. He had just finished his second cup when Hughes, Davison's steward, pressed his way through the crowd of chattering civilians to speak with him.

"Captain's compliments, sir and he'd like to see you in his quarters." Hughes might have been speaking directly to King, but the servant's attention was elsewhere and the man appeared fascinated by the still heavily laden table.

King suppressed a grin; he supposed that, as the officer in charge of a prize, Davison might conceivably be referred to as a Captain, but it was stretching matters slightly.

"Very well, my compliments and I shall join him presently," he replied, returning to the remains of his meal.

"He did say it were urgent, sir," Hughes whispered, conspiratorially. King raised his eyes and considered the servant, who had the grace to look abashed, before returning to his breakfast.

* * *

But whatever his aspirations, the second lieutenant was still senior to him and not more than five minutes later King found himself standing in front of a seated Davison. The younger man was also dining, but alone, and at a table that was all but bare. He waved his hands dismissively at his near empty plate.

"I should have saved some for you, King," he said, with a complete absence of regret. "But Hughes said he could find little in the way of cabin stores, and we do have several days' sailing ahead of us."

"I have already eaten, thank you," King replied stiffly.

Davison eyed him suspiciously for a moment, then indicated the chair opposite.

"Cartwright has the watch at present," he continued as King seated himself. "And does a fair job. I think he can be trusted."

King thought so as well: the master's mate had more seagoing experience than the two of them put together, and was undoubtedly competent enough to stand a watch.

"And we can allow Adams and Steven to do likewise."

Now that was another matter entirely. Both midshipmen were in their teens and ideal as supporting officers. Either would also have the sense to call him or Davison should an emergency occur, but at sea the time to summon a superior is a luxury that cannot be guaranteed. Far too often action must be taken immediately, and King doubted they had the combined experience to handle every crisis.

"They should not be needed," he said, temporising. "If each of us take a trick, that will mean none work more than one out of three." King could tell from the blank look that his words were not being accepted by Davison, but continued despite this. "Counting dog watches, we will always get at least six hours off duty, and usually eight."

"As captain, I shall not be standing a watch," the younger man told him bluntly. "But, as I have already stated, with Adams and Steven's help, we shall not be stretched."

King shook his head. "But that is not right," he found himself saying. "Sir Richard placed you in command of the prize crew: that hardly constitutes being a captain."

"Do you not regard me as your superior officer?" Davison asked with feigned concern. "I would be happy to present my commission, if that is required. You will find it significantly trumps your own as far as the date is concerned."

King shook his head. "I do not doubt your seniority," he said. "But am certain Captain Banks did not mean for you to behave thus."

"Whether he did, or whether he did not is hardly your concern," Davison continued. "But we shall say no more about it for now. You may relieve Cartwright at eight bells and, obviously, send for me if the need arises. And please remember that it would be more fitting if I am addressed as sir by all my officers. Now," he added with a look of great condescension, "will you take tea? Hughes says there is little else, I'm afraid."

King rose stiffly. "Thank you, but I have a pot of rather fine chocolate awaiting me below," he replied. "Sir."

* * *

Manning's concern was growing steadily. Not only had two officers now fallen victim to the mystery ailment, but more of the lower ranks were being presented to him with every hour that passed. And it had not escaped his notice that a high proportion of them seemed to be marines.

He told himself that such a situation was understandable: when men sleep, mess and work together, illness is bound to spread more readily. And if this made the general caring for the prisoners more difficult, that was hardly his concern. But Manning had just reported to Lieutenant Caulfield that, of *Prometheus'* force of seventy or so marines, more than twenty five were currently considered unfit for duty. This was a high proportion and, even though his own responsibilities extended no further than the health and welfare of the men, Manning could not help but be concerned.

Apparently measures were being taken; all marines had been relieved of servant and steward duties and put to work watch and watch about to keep the prisoners exercised and fed. They still had slightly less than the minimum it took to guard such a number, however, and there was no guarantee that the current rate of attrition would cease. The first lieutenant had supplemented them with ship's corporals and boatswain's mates – men used to enforcing discipline, and not afraid to do so. But since then more seamen had started appearing amongst the surgeon's patients, and Manning was concerned that mixing regular hands with those already infected would escalate the epidemic further.

He collected yet another volume from his personal library that included works by Blane, Trotter and Gillespie, and rifled through its well thumbed pages. The symptoms were reasonably defined but none exactly fitted those of a recognised ailment, and he began to wade once more through chapters that he now knew almost by heart with feelings of increasing desperation. At the back of his mind lurked the spectre of Gibraltar Fever; a highly infectious condition known to haunt the citadel and renowned for being both quick and deadly. But *Prometheus* had yet to even sight the rock and the Indiaman had also been outward bound.

On making enquiries he had discovered the *Duke of Cambridge* to have left Blackwall barely three weeks before, so should not have been carrying anything more exotic than traditional shipborne ailments. There were lascars amongst her crew, however, and they would have been transferred directly from a homebound ship before entering British waters. It was a common practice amongst Company vessels wanting to avoid government regulations on shipping foreign hands, but one that might prove disastrous on this occasion. The native seamen, now heading back to their home without touching British soil, could easily be carrying all manner of diseases, and he would have laid the blame firmly at their door, had they not appeared to be apparently immune to the malady themselves.

It was all so terribly confusing, and yet Manning sensed there was a simple solution, if only he were given time to think of it. He wished he might speak again with the Company physician who had transferred to the prize. Chances were high that he was also experiencing similar cases by now, and they may do better by comparing notes. He might request a boat – something the first lieutenant was bound to allow, although that in itself would increase the chance of spreading the disease still further.

He sighed and changed his current book for another; one that spoke more of gastric ailments and, although such symptoms were only a part of the problem, he supposed it might shed some light on the subject. One thing was certain: a good three days' sailing were needed before they raised Gibraltar, and the time spent in between was not going to be uneventful.

* * *

But not everyone was under such pressure. Unbeknown to Manning, there had been no outbreaks of illness aboard the prize and those seamen transferred from *Prometheus* were actually enjoying their spell aboard the former privateer. As confirmed man-o'-war hands, there was something novel in crewing a ship purely for her sailing abilities, with no concern for practice at the guns or small arms. Even being set to working as waisters or members of the afterguard, heaving at braces and trimming sails while chattering passengers did their best to distract or encumber them, did not ruin their enjoyment.

"Bit of a breeze blowin'," Harrison sniffed the air expectantly as they came on deck with the new watch. "With luck that yellow haired frizzy will wear her white dress again."

Flint eyed him thoughtfully as they formed up on the half deck. "Why should you care about a passenger's clothing?" he asked.

"I spent most of yes'day's af'noon watch on helmsman duty," Harrison told him smugly. "An' most of the time she were bent over the leeward bulwark, yarning with her husband. Wind kept lifting her frock up: lovely, it was. Ain't seen so much leg since Admiral Worthington's lady got stuck in the boatswain's chair. Lucky Seth Marne were my oppo. or we never would 'ave kept a regular course."

"It's a funny thing about old Seth," Flint agreed. "Women's legs never did do much for him."

"Watch on deck, stand to!" Clement, a boatswain's mate, called and the new men brought themselves up to something approaching attention for the start of the next four hours of duty.

* * *

The prisoners made their move just after two bells in the afternoon watch, when most of *Prometheus'* crew were still recovering from two pussers' pounds of salt beef, plum duff and the quarter pint of spirit that had preceded both. Marine Lieutenant James, who had been visiting Donaldson in the sick berth, was actually on hand and one of the first to die: the bayonet of a Bess, recently wrestled from the arms of one of his own men, accounting for him with silent efficiency. Other officers were also caught napping, in some cases literally; Bruce and Sutton were asleep in the midshipmen's berth when they were run through with boarding pikes, while Simmonds, a boatswain's mate caught in the aft cockpit, at least had time and sense to shout a warning before meeting his end under the edge of a looted cutlass. But the cry had little effect; by then the contingent of twenty prisoners about to be escorted up for air and exercise had already overpowered their guard before releasing the rest, and soon most on *Prometheus'* orlop were well aware the deck was no longer their own.

On receipt of his parole, Carroll had been allowed a cabin in the gun room and was seated at the warrant officers' dining table, checking the list of prisoners' names with the first lieutenant, when both men heard the first sounds of insurrection. Caulfield looked to the Irishman who gave a shrug of incomprehension, then they both turned to see five wide eyed men burst through the outer door and come crashing into the room.

"Rise, citizen," one shouted to Carroll in a strong Irish accent. "The orlop is ours; we are currently fightin' for this an' the upper deck. Once they are taken we may claim the ship!"

Caulfield stood and made to reach for his sword, but the weapon was safely in his cabin on the deck above, and one of the men pressed him roughly back down on his chair, holding him there with the flat of a cutlass blade. Carroll raised a hand and silently pointed at two of the penned off cabins that ran down both sides of the gun room. The rest of the privateers understood at once and divided into separate groups, before surging forward, kicking the thin doors to splinters, and blasting into the tiny rooms. Swift, a marine lieutenant, was dragged out almost immediately and stood, shaken and fuming, in open shirt and loosened britches. Of Abbot, the gunner, there was no sign; the men exited his cabin without comment, although one appeared to have fresh blood on his sword.

"There'll be no more of that," Carroll stated firmly, noting the weapon. "We are privateers, not pirates; contravene the letter of marque and all will end up on the gallows."

The men appeared suitably shamefaced and took to securing the two officers using a length of line that had been used to hang drying laundry by the warrant officers' bread bins. Caulfield, still seated, felt his wrists bound tight behind him. Then two turns about his chest and another round his ankles meant he would remain secure for as long as his captors wished, while Swift was simply hog tied and left to wriggle uncomfortably on the deck.

"Where is Agard?" Carroll demanded.

"The captain is outside," another replied in English, through a strong French accent. His teeth gleamed in the poor light. "He is about to lead the attack on the rest of this deck."

"Then we must not delay," Carroll said decisively, and went to leave.

"But your parole!" Caulfield's shout caused him to stop and look back.

"Ah yes, my parole," the man laughed briefly. "I was quite forgetting," he added. Then flashed his eyes, and was gone.

Chapter Thirteen

Outside, the scene was of terror and confusion. In the half light of the lower gun deck, vague figures could just be made out as they fought desperate and individual battles. Some wielded cutlasses or boarding pikes, others simple gunners' tools, awkward beneath the low deckhead, while a good few of either side preferred the bare fist fighting they were used to, laying into their opponents with all the science of a Saturday night brawl. There were shouts, calls and the occasional scream and it was clear that no order would be established until one side was seen to hold the upper hand.

"Davie!" the girl's thin voice sounded incongruous in such surroundings, and Carroll looked round in annoyance as Judy came running down the aft companionway towards him.

"Go to the gun room," he told her firmly. "Find one of the cabins and lock yourself in."

"But I must come as well," she protested. "You promised!"

"I shall join you shortly," Carroll snapped, then snatched at the boarding cutlass being handed to him by one of his colleagues. He had taken a step away and was about to enter the fray when the girl's hand stopped him.

"Come back with me," she pleaded, hanging on to his arm. "I'll not lose you now!"

"You will lose me forever if you do not let me go," he said, with heavy irony. "Now back to the gun room." The others were already deep into the fight, and he wished beyond anything to join them. But she was looking at him with that set expression he had already learned meant her mind was made up.

"Let me come with you," she insisted, even as he tore her hand from him.

"Go, Judy, go I say!" his voice was far louder than he had intended, and her face registered surprise. "I shall return for you directly, once the ship is ours, but for now be gone!" And then his expression softened. "But my promise will still hold, and you have already done far more than I could have asked."

* * *

In the prize, midshipmen Adams and Steven were sharing the watch and standing, with wildly assumed confidence, to either side of the binnacle. Both ships had made good progress that day and, with the wind holding steady on their starboard quarter, there was mercifully little for either to do. Meanwhile King, who had handed over the conn all of two hours ago, remained on deck and was currently forward, on the forecastle. A faint smudge of land was steadily becoming more visible off their larboard bow, and he was staring at it intently through his personal glass.

King knew this to be Cape St Vincent, and that they were close to the site of the fleet action he had witnessed over six years ago. *Belle Île* was sailing half a mile to leeward and a cable behind the battleship to give both maximum advantage from the wind and, for some time, he had been waiting for a signal from Brehaut that would take them further out, to round the treacherous promontory. Despite what he had said to Davison, King was reasonably sure the midshipmen would be competent enough to see the ship onto a new heading, but nevertheless had decided to remain on deck, if only to be available should they encounter trouble.

However, the order to change course was now considerably overdue and King was growing restless. The sun still burned bright; visibility was near perfect, and they would weather the cape easily enough on their present heading. But it was so unlike the usually cautious Brehaut to delay, that he turned his glass on *Prometheus* in case a signal had been missed.

"Port the helm, lay her four points to starboard!" King bellowed, surprising himself and those about him. The hands on watch had been gossiping sleepily in the shade of the starboard gangways while those passengers stoical enough for the early afternoon sun were either beneath the lee of the quarterdeck barricade or sheltering under a patch of canvas spread across the main shrouds. "Summon the watch below," King roared, as he thundered along the gangway, while beneath him the waisters and afterguard stirred themselves into action.

"Is there a problem, sir?" Adams asked, his young face filled with concern for what the two of them may have missed.

"Indeed, but not of your making. Summon the cap..." he corrected himself. "Summon Mr Davison, if you please. Mr Steven, kindly escort the passengers below."

There were no officers from the Indiaman on deck, they being far too accustomed to an early afternoon's rest, but several appeared soon enough as the ship changed course, and were present when a flustered and angry Davison stomped out onto the quarterdeck.

"What the devil do you mean by all this?" he began, after a single glance about him. "Why, steering as we are, we shall run aboard *Prometheus*. Quartermaster, starboard your helm this minute!"

"Belay that," King yelled, although the men at the wheel were less than fifteen feet away and Davison a good deal closer. "Small arms for all, and prepare for boarding. Gentlemen, if you are able, we should appreciate your assistance as well as that of any of your servants," he added, turning to two nearby Company officers who were blinking in the unaccustomed sunlight.

"King, have you lost your senses?" Davison demanded. The prize had settled on her new course and was bearing down on the two decker with every second bringing them closer.

"*Prometheus* is taken," King snapped in explanation. "Or, if not, there is certainly an uprising aboard."

"Taken you say?" Doubt clouded the younger lieutenant's expression, and he took the proffered glass from King, turning it on the two-decker that was rapidly nearing their larboard bow.

"Dear Lord," he said after a moment. Then, after lowering the glass and looking directly at his second in command, asked: "Whatever are we to do?"

* * *

The battle for the lower gun deck was not going well for the British. Taken by surprise, and at a time of day when they were more used to rest than violent action, the watch below had only become fully alert to the danger when hoards of yelling men came pouring up the companionways. And their attackers were well equipped, having previously raided both small arm stores on the orlop. *Prometheus'* regular crew were not without weapons, however. Purpose built, in the form of the ready-use cutlasses, half-pikes and tomahawks that were set on beams or in stands about the masts, as well as the more improvised gunners' tools of handspikes and worms that also lay to hand. Yet even so armed, many were quickly overrun by what proved to be a resolute and determined enemy. A cluster of stalwarts still fought several desperate actions further forward but they were outnumbered and, as Carroll and the French captain looked on, it seemed no more than a matter of time before they would have control of the largest area in the ship.

"We have done well," Agard muttered to his prize master. "Although there is still much to do."

"Indeed," Carroll agreed. "And those on the upper deck will now be aware. We can expect a counter attack at any moment."

He was right; the remainder of *Prometheus'* crew had certainly been warned, and were already on the offensive. Leading a party of his own men, a shirt-sleeved sergeant Jarvis was first down the wide, but steep, aft staircase. The stocky NCO reached the deck before ducking down as an erratic volley of musket fire bit into the backs of the fighting privateers. Then his marines laid in with their bayonets, while more of *Prometheus'* seamen, variously armed with boarding weapons and belaying pins followed close behind. Carroll flashed a look at Agard as they drew back behind the relative safety of two thirty-two pounders. Even weakened by illness and taken by surprise, the British could still overpower them. And now they were fully alert to the danger, as well as being under proper command, the situation could quickly turn sour. He watched as two Frenchmen nearby fell to the lunge of marine bayonets and decided the disciplined force would prove a far more substantial enemy. But there were others who had taken sanctuary amidst the guns and Carroll knew that, as with the British, a bit of order would do wonders.

"Come, *mes amis*," he shouted, in his finest rallying voice, while raising his captured sword as high as the deckhead would allow. "Follow me, and the ship will be ours!"

* * *

From the quarterdeck, Lewis watched Jarvis' men descend, and could tell they were gaining ground, although forward, a similar British force under Corporal Collins was having less success. Many had made it down the hazardous steps, and were fighting a desperate action with the French below, but no progress was being made and he sensed that the attack would eventually be repelled. Several topmen had been aloft when the enemy rebelled, together with a boatswain's team that were carrying out repairs to the foremast and they were all now dropping down a variety of backstays, eager to join the fight. This would provide a reasonable force for yet another onslaught and Saunders, the master at arms who had chanced to be on deck, was calmly issuing them with small arms from the quarterdeck store. Lewis had ordered a signal to the prize but, before it could be made, the former privateer was already responding to the emergency and would be alongside in no time. That was good news indeed, although it did leave him with one difficult decision.

He might wait, and lead a counter attack with more men, or reinforce those already committed in the hope of keeping the French at bay until the prize crew arrived. Jarvis' men were making inroads at the aft companionway, whereas those led by Collins forward were definitely having problems.

He looked back at the capture which was still bearing down on them, with armed men visibly gathering at her bulwarks. The frigate's freeboard was considerably lower than that of a line-of-battleship; their prize crew might board if coming alongside, but would have to scale *Prometheus'* mountainous sides to gain access. Some might try to enter through her ports, yet those that were secured, must be forced. Lewis wondered what he would do if in charge of the boarders, and the answer came almost immediately.

Placing the frigate alongside the battleship's stern would allow them to board through the quarter-galleries and wardroom windows: access points that would be far harder to defend than any gun port or companionway. That being so, if Jarvis' force could hold the deck aft of the main mast, they would eventually be supplemented by the boarders. Which left him only one real choice, as regards his own contingent.

"Mr Saunders, take all on the quarterdeck and reinforce the marines down the aft companionway. I shall lead those on the spar deck down for'ard." The warrant officer touched his bare head in a token salute, before collecting a boarding cutlass for himself, while Lewis hurled himself down the short ladder.

But it was only as his boots hit the main deck that the lieutenant realised he was unarmed. "Come, lads!" he shouted to a bemused group of men standing in the semi-darkness under the ship's boats. Saunders would have those stationed on the poop and quarterdeck; about twelve men should make a sizeable difference. And his own force of fifteen or so was not insubstantial; so much so that being without a weapon himself seemed almost immaterial. Lewis had been a lieutenant a scant few months but the importance of leadership had been learned over many years. He may be heading for an all out scrap, but the true value of any officer lay in command, rather than combat.

As he reached them, he saw the forward steps that led below were draped with the bodies of wounded British marines and seamen. There was hardly any sound footing available, yet Lewis sensed the weight of those following, and knew that to pause would be fatal to the success of the attack: they must descend, and do so without delay.

Jumping from the top step, he threw himself down, feet first, landing with one boot on the hard deck and the other atop the torso of an unfortunate marine. He regained his balance smartly enough and immediately dodged the thrust of a pike aimed at his chest, before springing up, seizing the weapon, and tearing it free. Then it was a relativity simple matter to smash the butt back into the moustachioed face of its owner. The man crumpled to the deck with a satisfying moan as blood began to spurt, but there were more following, and Lewis swiftly reversed the pike, before pressing forward into the wall of enemies before him.

* * *

"We'll run across her stern," King bellowed, without reference to anyone else. He was standing on the very break of the privateer's quarterdeck and hanging out from the larboard main shrouds as he piloted the ship in, while the supposed captain was further aft and seemed to be taking a far more dispassionate view of proceedings. Even from a distance, and they must still be half a cable off, King could hear the sounds of a heated battle and the men already gathered on the forecastle or along *Belle Île's* larboard gangway were spoiling for a fight.

"Enter by the wardroom," a new voice commanded, and King instinctively looked behind. But Davison was standing mute by the binnacle and seemed to have lost all interest. "Ignore the captain's aft gallery," the advice continued. "The battle will be below."

King was still trying to identify the speaker; possibly a warrant officer further forward: probably on the forecastle. But with the noise of battle and murmurings from their own boarding party steadily growing louder, it was impossible to be certain. Then a more definite shout followed, and he saw Ross, the former officer, catch his eye and wave. "I shall lead the first attack, Mr King," he yelled, and it was the same voice. "Follow as soon as you are able."

There was no time to discuss the order of command and Ross certainly had the right idea: the wardroom windows would make an excellent entry point: there was no sign of fighting on the upper decks, so they would be arriving close to the centre of the action.

"Starboard a point!" King ordered, and the ship moved almost imperceptibly round to line up directly with the seventy-four's gilded stern. Now all lay in the hands of time, and what they had was fast running out. He knew he would be leaving the prize almost unmanned; a group of elderly military men from the passengers had agreed to defend the ship if the French proved successful in taking *Prometheus*. But King had no illusions: should he fail, the privateers would be in possession of the first British liner to be taken in the current war, and must also reclaim their

177

own vessel into the bargain.

But this was not the time to even consider defeat. "Starboard," he repeated, as the ship neared. Then: "starboard – hard a starboard!" and, with a drawn out groaning of wood against wood, they scraped gracefully against the battleship's ornate gingerbread.

Those on the forecastle and forward of the main mast were the first to board. Ross himself, wielding a gunner's crow of iron, smashed through the starboard wardroom windows and soon the air was filled with the crashing of glass as Flint and Harrison copied his example. Then there was a tumble of bodies landing aboard the liner, with those still in the prize eagerly pressing forward for their turn to follow.

"Avast there!" King bellowed. He was still peering over the *Belle Île's* top rail and could see that some vagary in wind or waves was forcing the two ships apart. There was now a space of several feet between them, even though both ships appeared to be relatively stationary. "Wait for the time, lads," he continued, noticing with despair, that the distance was actually widening further. This was as bad as it could be; less than half of the boarding party had made it across: unless King could follow with the rest, both parts of the now divided force were in danger of being annihilated. Some of those about him had also registered the fact and one, a young topman and unusually lithe, looked ready to leap, despite the considerable gap that divided the two vessels.

"Stand down there, Jameson!" King ordered. He had no wish to snub the man's enthusiasm but to jump, and fail, would be the waste of a life. And if he were to succeed, it might persuade others less able to follow. Jameson positively growled with anger but the two ships were now being drawn together once more, and King realised with relief that all soon would be able to follow. Then the time was right and he himself leapt the last remaining few feet, landing soundly on the stern of the battleship, and clambering up and over the wrecked windows.

* * *

But the advance party had already quit the wardroom; most of

Flint's mess were now passing out through the double doors that led to *Prometheus'* upper gun deck, and all were eager for action. They spotted a group of former prisoners who had come up from below and were in deadly combat with a small number of British men, led by Saunders, the master at arms. The new arrivals joined the fray with all the energy of those denied action for much too long. Ross threw himself at a darkly clad officer who seemed to drop to his knees at the sight of the unexpected attack, while Butler sought out the burly, ginger-haired brute currently pinning the master at arms against the capstan head. Saunders had obviously been wounded, and the Frenchman was about to deliver the *coup de grâce* with his half-pike when Butler's cutlass intervened.

"Obliged to you, Butler," the master at arms told him shakily as he staggered forward, one hand firmly clapped across a bleeding shoulder.

"Go boil your head, Mr Saunders," Butler beamed, before moving on to seek out a fresh opponent.

But there were none to be found; it had been a brief but bloody battle: within seconds the French were overpowered, and the boarding party left without opposition.

"Below!" Ross roared, pointing down the staircase and bursting the other men's moment of self congratulation. The battle was clearly still hot on the lower deck, and in no time the group had reformed and begun to tumble eagerly down to meet it.

* * *

By the time King had scrambled through the shards and splinters that had been part of *Prometheus'* wardroom windows, the rest of his party had also boarded. He glanced at the familiar canvas covered deck and was almost surprised to find himself in his old home. But there was no time to waste; the first of the boarders was already gone, and soon he too was rushing through the room and out onto the upper gun deck beyond.

There he was greeted by a space filled only by dead bodies and an assortment of groaning wounded. But further sounds from below indicated where the battle was being fought, and King threw himself down the aft companionway noticing, almost with detached interest, that the steps were damp with fresh blood.

Once on the lower gun deck it was as he expected: the fighting was indeed fierce, but it appeared as if the British were gaining the upper hand. Amid the shouts and screams of action, a wall of marines could be seen steadily advancing, and there were cries of surrender from French voices that became more numerous as progress was made. With the stimulus of action, King's mind was racing like a clock robbed of its pendulum, and he quickly retreated to be met by those still coming down the staircase.

"Go back," he yelled. "We can do little to assist here, but may be of use for'ard." His hanger was hot in his hand: it was a brand new affair, bought when *Prometheus* had been commissioned, and he held it tight as he chased his men back up the staircase. As a group they raced along the upper deck, reaching the forward companionway in seconds. A quick glance below told King his force would indeed be needed, and he plunged down the wooden steps without pausing.

Now the new blade came into its own. A Frenchman had trapped one of *Prometheus'* men against an oak knee: King gave a sideways hack with his sword, and the attacker crumpled to the deck. He glanced aft to where the van of the second party of British could be seen advancing steadily, but there were more enemy between them and him, and King raised his weapon once more.

A pike, seemingly coming from nowhere, pitched into his left shoulder, spinning him round and biting into flesh. But the turn had caused the weapon to deflect, and King was able to swing his sword in the general direction of the unseen attacker. He felt the hanger jolt, gratifying, as its blade cut first into muscle before grounding on bone, and the body fell away into the darkness.

And then, almost as if to a silent signal, noise of the fighting started to fade. All about began to lower their weapons and stare questioningly at each other as they panted in the half light. Several of the French were standing with their hands held as high as the deckhead would permit, and there were moans and cries from the bodies that seemed to be littering the deck at every station. King caught a glimpse of Sergeant Jarvis, who had blood streaming down his white shirt, and there was Lewis, also injured, although the hand held against his thigh seemed to be keeping whatever wound he had sustained closed. Then Ross appeared from aft, teeth shining in the gloom as he grinned.

"Well, gentlemen," he said, speaking in an assured voice and with a commanding manner that was previously unknown to any aboard *Prometheus*. "We seem to have settled the Frenchmen's hash adequately enough, wouldn't you say?"

Chapter Fourteen

But much remained to do. King had taken a cursory glance at his shoulder; his jacket and shirt were ripped, but the wound beneath was not deep and had already ceased to bleed so could probably be left. Marine NCOs were organising the rounding up of prisoners as British seamen and petty officers attended to the wounded. Noticing the latter, King supposed he should go down to the orlop and check on Manning. He may have been hurt during the uprising but, even if not, the surgeon would be unprepared for what was bound to be an influx of casualties.

"I have yet to rig an operating area," his friend snapped impatiently when King approached the sick berth. "There are upwards of thirty men awaiting my attention, and nowhere to place them." Manning was literally up to his arms in gore as he tried to stitch a badly cut body on his examination table while Dodgeson, one of his mates, was similarly employed on the deck of the dispensary.

"I shall commandeer the gun room," King said decisively. "Give me a spell to have it cleared, but your men can start bringing wounded to the lower gun deck straight away, and I shall direct any freshly injured there."

Manning looked his thanks, then returned to the matter in hand, while King squeezed out of the cramped quarters, glad to be free of the place.

"Take him to the gun room," he told two loblolly boys currently dragging another unfortunate towards the dispensary. "And bring any more back there."

One of the men knuckled his forehead and turned to go; King made his way past them and began to press through the temporary pens, now being refilled with the French prisoners. In action, a good proportion of the orlop would normally have been set aside for the care of wounded. Manning was used to a large working space, with at least two operating tables formed by midshipmen's sea chests, and waiting and recovery areas for his patients. But

Prometheus had been taken by surprise and the makeshift cells took up much of the deck needed. The gun room, which had a reasonably sized dining area, would have to do instead.

"Let me through, damn it," he said, reaching the end of the detention area, and noticing Chivers beginning to close the door on him. "Once you are finished here, follow me. We need to rig a temporary sick bay." The midshipman touched his hat but King was already gone.

"Good God, Michael, are you all right?" he asked, entering the gun room and almost tripping over the first lieutenant who, still strapped to the chair, had fallen to the deck in his efforts to free himself. "Here, lend a hand will you?" he snapped, noticing Judy at the other end of the darkened space. Together they released Caulfield, who stood up shakily while rubbing at his wrists.

"Do not concern yourself with her," the first lieutenant said bitterly, as King helped the woman to her feet. "Swift is also secured aft, yet she would not lift a hand to release either of us."

King made for the far end of the room where the marine lieutenant was indeed lying half under the table, his hands and feet expertly bound. They were seaman's knots; any one would have held for an eternity but, when faced with equally experienced fingers, were released as easily as they had been tied, and soon the young officer was clambering to stand.

"Is this true, Judy?" King found himself asking. The ship had been all but taken, many were dead or injured, and he had just taken part in one of the most desperate fights of his life. And yet the woman's apparent betrayal seemed almost as important.

"He said he would take me to France," she declared stubbornly, wrapping her arms tightly about herself. "Said he would care for me. That we would be safe and live together in a proper home." The girl looked imploringly into King's eyes. "And that is all I have ever wanted," she told him.

* * *

The next day Banks was feeling very much better. Once more, he had called the meeting in his sleeping quarters as the great cabin was now being used as a further extension to the sick berth. He sat alone, at what effectively became the head of the card table, with the others crowded about the other three sides. And he was in the comfortable chair that had once been considered an indulgence. Since rising for the first time that morning Banks had eaten two full meals and taken one short nap, but now the responsibilities of command were gradually returning to his shoulders, and he was feeling increasingly guilty as a consequence.

"And you believe it to be poisoning?" he asked, aware it was not the first time he had posed the question. Despite the evidence, Banks could still not believe such a thing would have taken place.

"Yes, sir," Manning replied, as patient as ever. "Saltpetre, to be precise."

"And it definitely wasn't sourced from the Indiaman," the captain questioned. Saltpetre was a regular essential often shipped from the East, so would have been an unlikely outward bound cargo. Besides, his memories of the rescue were decidedly shaky, but he could not recall any freight being salvaged.

"No sir," Caulfield replied, a little crestfallen. "We think they might have taken it from the gunner's stores."

Banks waited, and his first lieutenant continued with the painful story.

"As soon as the prisoners were established on the orlop, both magazines, and even the light room were doubly secured and placed under additional marine guard. But Mr Abbot, our late gunner, kept a storeroom, for flints, locks and other supplies. He also carried a small stock of saltpetre there, and it is believed that the fellow Carroll gained access to it."

Banks remained silent while he thought. Saltpetre was a component of gunpowder, but needed to be mixed with sulphur and charcoal before any dramatic result could be achieved. By itself, the stuff would not necessarily be considered a dangerous substance and *Prometheus* carried far worse. Try as they might, it would have been impossible to guard or remove all such items, and it was just unfortunate that their efforts in securing the ship had been shown to be inadequate. But then the act appeared to have been carried out by a man who had given his parole, so there was at least some defence.

It was less easy to excuse the girl's part in the proceedings. After accepting their trust, the tame stowaway had betrayed them; something that was regrettable on many levels. However, if anyone was to turn traitor, it was surely better for it to be an outsider, and Banks would rather deliver her to the authorities in Gibraltar than any of his own men.

"And how was it administered?" he finally asked.

"Of that we are not so certain," Caulfield confessed. "But Miss Kinnison's duties as an honorary steward gave her access to all pantries and the main galley. It is assumed she contaminated what she could of the officers' food, as well as that supplied to the marine guard and some of the hands."

Banks considered this. Manning had already stated the smallest measure of saltpetre would be needed to create symptoms of headaches, nausea and heavy sweating. Had she increased the dose, someone would undoubtedly have died, for which, he supposed, they should be grateful. From the little he knew of the woman, she was probably not intelligent enough to understand the devastating effect it would have. Neither was there reason to endanger her captors so effectively, unless...

"She was not working alone, of course," he said at last, and noted that all of the assembled officers accepted his comment.

"No, sir," Caulfield agreed, almost sadly. "I am afraid she was in league with the Irishman."

The atmosphere in the small room grew suddenly tense. They were coming to a different matter entirely and, rather than regret at knowing their trust had been betrayed, Banks found himself growing increasingly angry.

"Well damn him to hell," he said simply, as an echo of his former headache momentarily returned. "The man gave me his personal word of honour..."

"Yes, sir," Caulfield agreed, while King and Lewis looked unaccountably sad, although Banks noticed that Manning was showing no emotion.

"I did challenge him on the subject," King said softly. "He said he had agreed not to attempt escape, but there was never any mention of refusing to take up arms."

The captain snorted; it was pure semantics, of course, but such things should be expected when dealing with rogues. At least the privateer's captain had made no such undertaking: the man may be little more than a pirate in many people's eyes, but clearly held some respect for the obligations of a gentleman.

"Very well," Banks conceded at last. "You had better let me have the butcher's bill."

Manning reached into his pocket and brought out a scrap of paper. "We lost eighteen men, including nine marines and four able seamen and not counting Mr Abbot or Marine Lieutenant James who you already know about. Thirty-one are wounded and require sick berth accommodation. The French losses amount..."

"I'm not interested in the French," Banks told the surgeon bluntly. "There will be less of them to look after, and the wounded can be cared for by their own."

Manning's eyes rose up in a brief protest, but lowered again at the captain's livid expression. "And there are still twelve men recovering from internal consumption of saltpetre," he finished lamely.

Banks said no more. After his personal experience of the stuff he would have little hesitation in feeding it to Carroll and the rest of his cronies, were such a thing permitted. The illness was bad enough, but to be totally incapacitated while his ship and people were in such danger had brought out the worst in him.

"And where do we stand as far as healthy bodies are concerned?" he asked, switching his attention to Caulfield.

"Five hundred and ten," Caulfield replied crisply, and without reference to notes. "Four hundred and seven trained hands, the rest are landsmen and boys. Our marine force has been cut to thirty nine by fatalities, injury and current sickness," he glanced across at Manning. "Although I understand that most of the latter are expected to be back on duty within the next day. Mr Donaldson is still indisposed, and has expressed a wish to be exchanged when we reach Gibraltar. Until then, the marine contingent is under the temporary command of Lieutenant Swift." All looked towards the young officer who was seated with them. He had been silent throughout and now blushed at the sudden attention.

Banks closed his eyes for a moment. The headache had passed, but he was still feeling incredibly weak and hearing the number of killed and injured simply reinforced his contrasting feelings of gratitude and failure. They might have suffered far greater casualties: indeed, he could so easily have lost the ship.

"I owe you all a good deal," he said, as his eyes opened once more. "And will say as much in my report, although," and now a faint smile came to play upon his lips, "I will of course be dependant on each of you to provide the necessary details."

There was a low rumble of laughter, then Banks fixed on the second lieutenant.

"None more than you, Mr Davison," he said, and noticed that both Caulfield and King grew strangely alert. "You showed great fortitude in boarding *Prometheus* so promptly: indeed the task was done in the best traditions of the service. Had it not, we might be holding this conversation on the orlop right now."

The captain had been expecting his remark to arouse further laughter, but instead the young man grew visibly embarrassed, while King appeared positively angry. His eyes flashed from one to the other and then across to Caulfield, who simply looked resigned. Banks supposed the first lieutenant was still suffering from the humiliation of being captured so easily, whereas the two more junior lieutenants were bound to compete for battle honours. So be it. Caulfield had nothing to berate himself for, and young men would always squabble.

"Well, if there is no more," he said. It was much harder to appear formal from an easy chair, but Banks' intention was unmistakeable, and his officers rose to leave. He thought King might have been trying to catch his eye, but purposely did not respond. Caulfield had already informed him how well the third lieutenant performed during the action; King was probably just a little put out that Davison, who had not been mentioned by the first lieutenant, was receiving all the praise. But there could be no argument that the prize's intervention had carried the battle and Banks was determined to see that the young man's efforts were properly acknowledged.

"So how was it you ended in command of the fo'c's'le?" Thompson demanded, when they were back in their temporary berth aboard the prize.

"Aye, shoutin' instructions to Mr King you was like a proper Admiral of the Fleet," Harrison agreed, from the other side of the mess table. "An' 'im doin' what you said like 'e were no more than a middie."

Ross turned away from his questioners, and found himself looking straight into the eyes of Flint, the head of the mess. In the past he had thought there might be a modicum of understanding in the man, and even wondered if Flint already guessed his secret. But now the seaman was fixing him with a set stare, and appeared as interested in his answer as any of the others.

"I didn't mean no disrespect," Ross told them, striving, as usual, to ape the casual way in which they spoke. "Only, from where I was, I could see best how we might lay the ship alongside, and so board in the right place."

His reply was greeted with silence and Ross was momentarily relieved. But all were in the midst of eating their first hot meal for some time, and the questioning had only been postponed.

"There weren't any of us worrying about where the ship was to be set," Harrison continued, after he had gummed his way through a piece of gristle. "Just wanted to get our 'ands on a Frenchman."

"As did I," Ross replied, with assumed resentment. "And could see the best way of doin' it. Is there anything so very wrong in that?"

The unexpectedly sharp response surprised most although Harrison, it seemed, was not so easily dissuaded.

"But it didn't end there though, did it?" he persisted. "Once aboard the barky you went on orderin' us about. Takin' command like you was meant for the task – like you was used to doin' it."

"An' then, when it were done, there was all the back slappin' and handshakin' with King and Lewis," Butler had taken up the thread. "It were as if you'd all been thrown out of the same nanny house."

Ross forced himself to think. They had entered *Prometheus'* wardroom in utter confusion. King and Davison were still to board and, with no junior officers present, the men became confused. Some began cheering, calling out, or tripping over the furniture and there was no apparent understanding of what needed to be done. But Ross had felt far more comfortable, and was the only one with any thought for the carnage they might find beyond the closed doors.

So yes, he had taken control: had bullied them into a governable body. And when they did burst through to the fight, it was undoubtedly down to him that their force was in some form of order.

He opened his eyes and looked to Flint, trying to gauge the man's exact position. As head of the mess, Flint was senior to Ross, yet had been one of those so commanded. And, though it might be resented now, the man had performed well: they all did. Every member of the boarding party seemed to welcome the word of authority, as a frightened horse might the reassuring pressure of a rein. But that was then – now they clearly held a very different view.

"Well if I did, it turned out for the best," Ross replied lamely, before setting his attention back to the food in front of him. The strain of living a lie was starting to tell and he had already decided to find some way of leaving *Prometheus* when they reached Gibraltar. He could jump ship, or feign illness; both methods were not without their perils, and neither would be easy to pull off. But Ross felt there was little left to lose, and nothing as far as his self respect was concerned.

He had known becoming a lower deck hand would never be easy, but the reality had proved even harder than his predictions. The work was arduous, with limited leisure time, and absolutely no privacy, although such things were off-set by benefits he had equally failed to anticipate. He was now well versed in many seamen's skills, and had become foolishly proud of his abilities, although the main gain lay in something far more subtle.

Ross had always enjoyed studying his fellow men, and what

he had learned about the regular foremast Jack was utterly fascinating. In the past few weeks he had come across men who wanted for a formal education, yet possessed a different pattern of intelligence that was equally useful and actually quite formidable. Some, who could neither read or write, proved able to calculate the value of a prize, its cargo and any head money, along with the seaman's share of it. The network of communication also spread further than most in command realised, with discussions in the wardroom, gun room and even the great cabin regularly being dissected and evaluated during the same day's dog watches.

And the lower deck's corporate knowledge, which verged upon a shared understanding, was truly impressive. It had been exhibited on several occasions; from choosing mess cooks and other honorary positions, to the subtle manipulation of divisional officers. Petty thieves and other minor miscreants were almost instantly identified by the whole, despite being as sharp as any single one of their fellows.

During his time aboard *Prometheus*, Ross had become aware of several minor crimes that were hidden from authority to allow them to be privately resolved by the seamen's own, unwritten code. And the judgements that followed, together with penalties imposed, appeared far more apt than those expected from dispassionate and remote commissioned officers.

With a chill, Ross wondered if his particular case was about to come under such scrutiny; should it do so, there was no doubt they would discover his secret.

"Ask me, there's a touch more to our Mister Ross than meets the eye," Butler was saying.

"Per'aps the lower deck's not good enough for him," Harrison agreed, while he continued to gum manfully at his chunk of beef. "Maybe he's got ideas above 'is station."

"So what did I do that offended you so?" Ross demanded, looking up suddenly. "No one else was willing to take charge: you were all running about like headless chickens. All I did was take you in order – someone had to."

"Mr King was due to board," Cranston murmured. "And Mr Davison followed eventually."

"But both came with the second wave," Butler pointed out.

"Davison were in command, though" Harrison again. "It were up to him to lead us – we should have waited."

"If we'd have waited for Davison, the Frogs would have likely taken the ship," Thompson grunted, disparagingly. "He's not up to it; the man's a fool."

"Aye," Ross found himself agreeing. "I'd say he were rocked in a stone kitchen."

There was a moment of stunned silence, and the former lieutenant felt a wave of instant and genuine regret. As an officer, it had been drummed into him never to ridicule another man of similar or superior rank. It was almost a cardinal sin and, when done amongst others of a lower status, might even be considered mutiny. The gulf that separated him from Davison's position as second lieutenant was vast indeed, and he felt immediate guilt for having committed such a crime.

It was not a sentiment shared by the others, though. As he glanced along the two rows of faces there was no sign of censure; they merely appeared surprised and amused in equal measure.

"Rocked in a stone kitchen," Harrison repeated, savouring the words as much as any concept. The expression might not have been totally of the lower deck, but it was one they undoubtedly approved of and, for probably the first time since joining *Prometheus*, Ross felt properly part of the mess.

Chapter Fifteen

They raised Gibraltar at first light, four days later, and entered her harbour during the late afternoon. The sun was still bright and the wind remained in their favour as Lewis, in *Prometheus*, made her number and the private signal, before announcing the prize as their own. Hurle, one of the gunner's mates, supervised the saluting procedures in Abbot's absence: they were ordered to anchor in the lee of the new mole and, within half an hour, Banks was seated in his barge, stiff in his fresh, full dress uniform, journal in hand, and prepared to explain all to whoever received him.

And there was much to tell, he decided, as the boat skimmed across the flat waters of the harbour. Firm news that the *Duke of Cambridge* was lost, for instance: there were bound to be those in London and beyond who would probably expect her to be on the way to the East for some time to come. Even the very existence of the *Belle Île* may come as a surprise. The Indiaman had been her first victim: that *Prometheus* had already found and dealt with her so efficiently could only be greeted with relief. Shipping owners would be that much more confident of sending their charges along the Portuguese coast and across the Bay of Cádiz, while the Royal Navy had been spared a powerful and probably elusive enemy to hunt down, just when their smaller warships were at a premium. But Banks was less certain how the near loss of one of his Majesty's third rates would be received.

Any captain who allowed prisoners to take over his ship would have much to answer for, and the fact that he, and several others, were indisposed at the time, when the cause was also directly attributable to the enemy, would hardly be an excuse. To balance that, he was delivering a fine frigate, and one that was likely to be taken under the British flag. But whether or not one would equal out the other was still to be seen and, as the boat turned for the stone steps of the quay, his doubts increased.

If the Admiralty did buy her, *Belle Île* might need to return to England for refit, and some time would pass before she sailed again. The government would pay handsomely though and, when it came, Banks' personal share would be no small sum; certainly enough to see him and his family secure, should he find himself censured in any way. But were he to be sent for court martial, and if the unthinkable happened and he found himself dismissed the service, no amount of wealth could compensate for being denied the right to walk a quarterdeck again. And if his capture were not considered suitable for Navy use, she would be put up in the local prize auction, when he would be lucky to get a quarter of her value at scrap.

Now they were drawing closer to the quay and the fact that he would shortly be explaining himself hardly lightened his mood. Even if he were spared, and a blind eye turned to the uprising aboard *Prometheus*, he must still face the unhappy task of seeking further men. The losses they had suffered of late had accounted for a good proportion of what had been an enviable crew. Marines could be sourced on Gibraltar, even replacements for the two officers should present no difficulty, and there were bound to be midshipmen a plenty keen for a sea-going post. But the ordinary and able seamen were more of a problem. Their like were in short supply wherever British ships sailed and Gibraltar, being one of only two local ports serving the Mediterranean Fleet, would be no exception. Then, to top it all, they required another gunner. Abbot had been with the ship since *Prometheus* first commissioned and, old and cranky though he may have been, he carried out his duties admirably. It would be hard to find another half as good without returning to England.

"In bows," Chivers, the midshipman seated next to him, commanded. The two rowers furthest forward completed their stroke, before tossing, then boating, their oars, and standing by with the boat hook. Banks raised himself gingerly and stepped onto dry land; a fresh faced lieutenant was there to meet him and introduced himself as Hoskins.

"The Commissioner presents his compliments and apologies, sir," the younger officer informed him. "Currently he is meeting with Sir Thomas, the Lieutenant Governor, and Major Barnett: they cannot be disturbed. There is news of a further breakout of fever," he added in a softer tone and with an air of confidentiality.

"Lieutenant Governor?" Banks questioned. He was under the impression that Prince Edward, the king's son, was in command, and had been rather hoping for a chance to meet with royalty.

"Yes, sir," the lieutenant said, lowering his head slightly. "The prince was recalled, and Major General Trigge is carrying out his duties. Purely temporarily, of course."

"I see," Banks replied; he had been aware of some problem with the garrison a year or so back, and supposed it to blame. "Is there any news of the Admiral?"

"My Lord Nelson?" the lieutenant inquired. "None currently sir. *Victory* called here quite recently, but he was not aboard."

Banks looked his confusion, and Hoskins went on to explain.

"The Admiral visited us in *Amphion* in early June and brought news that we are once more at war."

"A frigate?" Banks remarked in surprise.

"Aye, sir. He'd shifted his flag to her after leaving *Victory* behind to search for Admiral Cornwallis, off Ushant."

Banks knew *Amphion*, a relatively new fifth rate. Tom Hardy had her; they'd met several years back and he remembered him as a dour fellow: surely an odd choice for such a lively little ship? And it was equally strange that a Commander-in-Chief should abandon his first rate in favour of her.

"Apparently Lord Nelson was to offer *Victory* to Admiral Cornwallis of the Channel Fleet," the lieutenant explained. "But Billy Blue turned the old girl down and sent her back to her master." Hoskins grinned amiably.

"Billy Blue?" Banks repeated the nick-name with a raised eyebrow, and the young lieutenant began to fluster: in his enthusiasm Hoskins had apparently forgotten he was addressing a senior captain.

"F-forgive me, sir; I meant no disrespect," he stammered, his face now decidedly red. "*Victory* called on her way to the Med. but did not linger more than two or three days. We believe she has caught up with Admiral Nelson and he to be off Toulon with Sir Richard Bickerton's fleet. But no official report has come through to that effect, and a neutral sighted a three decker at Malta."

Banks considered the situation. The Mediterranean Fleet was hardly blessed with ships, and could not be easily reinforced. They were also sailing in waters where much of the coast was either owned by France or heavily under her influence, yet Nelson was clearly intending to stretch his command over as large an area as possible. It was not to be surprised at; in every station where the man had served, Nelson had played by his own rules, and Banks supposed it was something he must get used to.

"Commander Stewart would be happy to speak with you in the Commissioner's absence," Hoskins continued hurriedly, having taken Banks' lack of response as further criticism. "I am sure there is much you will have to relate, and your ships clearly require maintenance..."

"Very well," Banks said, unbending slightly.

"He can speak with the master shipwright as well as arranging for any victuals you may require," Hoskins carried on eagerly. "I have a carriage awaiting that will take us to The Mount. If you would care to follow me, sir?"

* * *

"What will become of you?" King repeated the question with more than a hint of impatience. "Why on earth are you asking me?"

Her eyes fell, and she looked small and quite pathetic, seated on one of the large upholstered lockers that was about the only space free in what used to be part of the captain's quarters. Banks had decided Judy might continue to earn her keep; the girl seemed filled with genuine remorse for what she had done and incarceration would be inconvenient to all, as well as taking up valuable space aboard *Prometheus*. And so she had been set to take care of the injured although, considering her performance to date, no British life was placed in her hands. Instead she had spent the rest of the journey to Gibraltar in *Prometheus'* great cabin tending the French casualties.

Ironically, it was an area considered ideal for treating wounded prisoners. Being relatively isolated, it could be guarded easily, and even boasted separate heads and washing facilities.

Judy had seized the opportunity to redeem herself, and worked hard and well, even if none of the medical team totally trusted her and the permanent marine guard that stood sentinel were under orders to watch the woman as keenly as any of the injured.

"I am truly sorry for what I did," she said. "And had no idea it would make any of you so very ill."

"But you put poison in the food," King stated incredulously. "How could anyone think we would not suffer?"

"Davie said it would cause no harm, the powder was just something to make you sleepy," she replied. "And I didn't see how that mattered. If you'd all just dozed off, he could have taken the ship over, and no one would have been hurt at all."

"That was never going to happen, Judy," King told her, and she had the grace to nod in agreement.

"No, I do see that now, but it seemed so right at the time. Davie and I were to sail to the Tagus, and he would stay with me forever."

"Well he doesn't wish to be with you now," King pointed out.

"That he doesn't," she agreed, and her expression hardened.

"But did you not realise?" King asked, when they had been quiet for a moment. "When men started to become ill?"

"Not at first," she replied in little more than a whisper. "But as soon as I did, I stopped. And I wanted to tell you at least, but Davie wouldn't hear of it."

King sighed in disbelief; Judy, though no intellectual, was hardly stupid. In matters of the heart though, he had seldom met anyone quite so gullible.

The wounded prisoners were due to be transferred to the shore hospital that afternoon, leaving those aboard *Prometheus* with a shambles for what once had constituted their captain's finest room. All hammocks and make-shift bunks would be cleared out, and the whole place brought back to something like its previous splendour. But as soon as that happened there would be little left for the girl to do and then yes, King supposed, it would be back to the original question of what would become of her.

"You deserve to be put straight ashore and into the care of the magistrates," he said bluntly. "They will be best suited to judge the magnitude of your crime."

She winced slightly, and he felt mildly guilty. Her actions might disgust him, but it was an emotion heightened by personal disappointment, and he had not meant the statement to sound quite so harsh.

But the fact remained, a civilian court would take a far more dispassionate view than any Navy tribunal, and was best set to judge if the girl's crime were truly life threatening. If so, Judy might hang; otherwise he guessed seven years in the colonies would be more likely while, were she able to contact her former employers and if they proved to be as influential as they sounded, she may even walk free. Such was the way of the world.

The man, Carroll, was far more straightforward, and with a fate that was easy to predict. Provided the privateer papers were in order, he would be treated as a prisoner of war and could expect to be either exchanged, or live out the rest of the war in captivity. That he had contravened his parole made no difference to any official penalty; such arrangements were purely the prerogative of gentlemen. By effectively breaking his word of honour he had denied himself inclusion into polite society but, from the little he knew of him, King did not feel such banishment would be a major concern. And to confirm himself as the bounder he undoubtedly was, Carroll had dropped any affection he had assumed for the girl. King supposed him to be one of the unemotional types, the kind who barged through life with his personal welfare the only concern. He had encountered a good few like him in the past and despised such single-mindedness, even if it also left him feeling faintly envious.

Judy was still imploring him with those deep, pitiful eyes and King felt his heart soften. What she had just told him was quite significant, he supposed; a sleeping draught was a very different matter to poison, and should certainly be mentioned to the captain. And being as naïve as she was, he could quite see how an eloquent cove like Carroll might lead her astray: any fast talking man, if it came to it. Further more, Sir Richard Banks had grown more understanding since becoming a father. With luck she might simply be set ashore at Gibraltar, told to make her own way to

Lisbon, if that was what she wanted, and nothing more would be said of the matter. And she was of the type that would survive, he assured himself, and may even prosper. But as to what would finally become of her, he did not know. And neither, he told himself firmly, did he care.

* * *

At the same time as King and Judy were speaking, Caulfield happened to be with Carroll on the orlop. The improvised cells were more crowded than even *Prometheus'* great cabin, with the officers pressed up to one end to make some form of division between them and their men. Carroll was squashed into a corner next to his captain and did not appear particularly pleased to see the first lieutenant.

"I understand you broke your parole," Caulfield said, coming straight to the point. "That was hardly the act of a gentleman."

The Irishman leant back against the spirketting and gave a short laugh. "I have not behaved like a gentleman in years," he said. "That is assuming such a thing was ever in my nature."

The British officer bristled visibly; Carroll was clearly a rogue of the first order, and it was doubtless a waste of time even speaking with the fellow. But still he felt an innate compulsion to point out exactly how badly the man had behaved. It was as if he must be told, and Caulfield had been appointed to do so.

"Should such a thing become known in society, you would be ostracised," he said with restrained relish. "There would be no chance of your ever serving as an officer again, or standing in a position of responsibility, and all forms of social intercourse would effectively be at an end."

"And that would bother me greatly," the Irishman replied. His once proud uniform was now tattered and he stared listlessly up at the slick officer who stood over him. "My, you English are a race in yourselves," he said, his head set back against the woodwork. "Behave as if the world was simply provided for you alone to rule, and naturally expect all to follow in your wake."

"There is nothing wrong in assuming a man will honour his

word," Caulfield said, with only the slightest hint of doubt.

"If there not?" Carroll asked. "Well there you have the better of me; I lived for many years under the rule of English gentlemen, so know them for what they are, and would prefer to put my trust elsewhere."

"Do you think the French will treat you better?"

"The French have no use for the pitch-cap, or the triangle, or any of the other diabolical devices you have used to torture my countrymen."

The first lieutenant snorted; this was a foolish exercise, the man was clearly not worth troubling with and, despite the two burly marines that stood not two paces away, he was starting to feel just the slightest unease.

"So you would rather *Liberté, Égalité* and *Fraternité*?" Caulfield scoffed. "And that is why you sit to one end of the cells; so that you may mingle with your brothers?"

"I was in Ireland during 'ninety-eight," Carroll replied solemnly. "And can tell you much about the way the English behaved; there was little freedom, equality or brotherhood in their actions. And a total lack of honour."

"The fact remains, you deceived us," Caulfield persisted. "And should at least show some shame."

"Do you show shame?" the French captain interrupted. "Did you not fool us into thinking this ship was an Indiaman?"

"Aye," Carroll agreed, collecting the thread. "With flags and all, or so I hears. You even used children and women to fuel your deceit; was that the act of gentlemen?"

"We did not fire whilst flying Company colours," Caulfield protested. "Everything was done strictly under the rules of war – this is a king's ship: we take notice of such things."

At this the captain laughed and turned away but Carroll, it seemed, was keen to continue.

"And that is important, is it?" he asked. "You are happy to involve yourself in a war, but only for as long as you can give such an obscenity rules that are then governed by something you call honour?"

"It would be no use explaining to an Irishman," Caulfield

sighed. "What possible interest could you have in such matters? How could you know of integrity, or trust? Or loyalty, if it came to it? Why, you betrayed an innocent woman," the first lieutenant added with a scornful laugh. "I suppose you are proud of that as well?"

"I have nothing to be ashamed of, if that is what you are asking," Carroll replied. "Every promise I made to young Judy would have been met in full. Which is more that can be said of the sailor man who brought her aboard this ship in the first place. And, unless I am very much mistaken, he was an Englishman."

* * *

Actually Commander Stewart turned out to be an old shipmate, and one not encountered since he and Banks had shared a midshipmen's berth nearly fifteen years before. The Captain had been driven through the winding streets of town, and finally deposited at The Mount, a large, new and somewhat imposing building that constituted the senior naval officer's residence. He recognised the long face and lantern jaw as soon as he was shown into a welcomingly cool room and, despite the considerable difference in rank, the two were soon gossiping and laughing like the pair of lads they had once been.

"So, how come the frigate?" Stewart asked when they had finished their second pot of coffee and were finally addressing matters more pertinent. "Not every day an old battle-wagon like *Prometheus* carries such a flighty little thing."

"She was a privateer," Banks explained briefly. "We had already encountered her capture: a five-hundred ton Indiaman."

"And you retook her as well?" Stewart asked, with growing respect.

Banks shook his head. "No, she had been wrecked. But we rescued her people, and the prize crew, so were aware that a letter of marque was operating in the area. When she was sighted I disguised *Prometheus* as an Indiaman: the rest was relatively easy." Banks felt the glib words flow almost without his willing them: even now he could remember those hours of worry, with the frigate taking pot shots at his precious command. But it was good to be with Stewart again, and difficult to remain formal in such company.

"Well, easy or not, you did well and Captain Otway, the naval commissioner, will be glad to hear of it. Why, I shall send for the master shipwright immediately; she can be surveyed and, if there is chance of her being taken into the service, I am sure it will be done without delay." He paused, and bent forward slightly. "Providing that is your will, sir," he added, using the honorific for the first time. "She is your prize, after all: I had no wish to presume."

"I should be delighted, Gordon," Banks replied sincerely. "Thank you."

"Frigates are as rare as the proverbial hen's teeth at present." Stewart sat back in his chair and relapsed into the previous, easy, manner. "We could use a dozen more and not feel ourselves filled. There's talk of a sizeable squadron coming from San Domingo; nine or ten liners, so intelligence suggests; more than enough to overpower Dickie-Bickie's fleet off Toulon, if he isn't given fair warning. And with the Dons behaving as they are, we must keep check on Cádiz as if it were already an enemy port."

The commander paused and sighed. "You would have thought lessons would have been learned from the last war; but we seem just as short as ever. Nelson has but three frigates to play with at present, and I know wishes for more."

"There is further to tell, I fear," Banks said quietly.

"Of your adventures?" Stewart asked, returning to the previous subject and raising a questioning eyebrow. "How so?"

"On our way here, with the privateer in consort," Banks began cautiously, before plunging in with the awful truth. "The prisoners rose up and almost took my ship."

Stewart was listening intently but said nothing.

"They began by poisoning many of the people, myself included, and came horribly close to pulling it off, though I am glad to say, were not ultimately successful."

"Then they sound to be more enterprising than is usual in their type," Stewart said, after considering for a moment. "Though I suppose it is not to be wondered at. Whatever the government may say, private enterprise will always win out in the end." He pondered. "Poisoning, though: that is a mite unusual."

"They had an accomplice; an Irishman, name of Carroll, who was captured with the prize. He had given his parole, though did not think to honour it."

"Well, that is a sorry tale indeed," Stewart sighed at last. "But, if you will excuse me, we need not concentrate too heavily upon some aspects."

Banks regarded him with sudden interest.

"The main point must be this: his Majesty is one frigate the richer," Stewart continued, his voice and expression set firm. "Take my advice and make that the central theme of your report."

"But I have my journal with me now," Banks protested, fingering the canvas covered document on his lap.

"Forgive me, Dick, but you do not," Stewart told him firmly while keeping his eyes well away from the document. "It has yet to be written; there was simply too much depending on you during the journey back. It is a fair excuse considering the circumstances: you will be allowed a few days' grace."

Banks felt momentarily confused, although Stewart, it seemed was far more in control. He leaned further back in his chair and gave a relaxed smile. "Believe me, the difference between a shore posting and one at sea is not just a question of keeping your feet dry. There is far more to it than playing with stay-tape and buckram; you should be amazed at the diplomatic tricks and deceptions that abound."

"I am certain you are right," Banks agreed, cautiously.

"Oh, yes, and I have learned much about reports, and what happens to them, which is probably why so few of us land crabs are ever allowed back on the briny," the Commander added with a hint of regret. "But let me tell you this, one of the skills in writing such things is telling those who read them what they want to hear."

Banks found himself smiling at the man's candour, although it was clear he was speaking in all seriousness, and gave wise counsel.

"With the right emphasis, your little tale will sound fine, and might even end up in the Gazette; word it badly, and they shall be waiting upon you in court martial." Both men laughed, but in Banks' case the act was forced.

"*When* you come to submit your journal," Stewart continued, with emphasis, "don't be afraid to lean on the good points. No one shall, if you do not. There sounds to be a full butcher's bill: that never fails to impress, and who is to know if they fell in taking the frigate in the first place, or fighting off your prisoners later? And if you can single out one or two juniors to praise, do so as well." the commander gave a subtle wink. "There's something else I have learned; nothing diverts attention from a writer's deficiencies more than a commendation or two for his inferiors."

"I see," Banks said, even though he was still deep in thought. "So I should be vague?"

"Not vague, as such, but hardly too specific," Stewart smiled again. "Think of your report as a book of accounts: the end result is what really matters, how it was achieved need only be considered secondary.

"You are in profit to the tune of the crew and passengers of an Indiaman rescued, a sizeable number of privateers taken prisoner, and a very acceptable frigate captured. Against that, the loss of so many men, and maybe a modicum of equipment, must be balanced. However you choose to word it, nothing can change that bottom line and, as I have said, you can be sure it is only the nett result that our lords and masters will be truly interested in."

Banks stayed quiet, although continued to listen intently.

"You realise I would not say this to everyone?" Stewart asked in a lower tone. "There may be some who consider such an attitude to be fundamentally wrong – corruption, even, but that is another thing I have learned ashore: such things need not be so terribly bad. Why, you need only consider the problems Old Jarvie has caused in our own dockyards. Sure, the places were a mass of double dealing and jobbery in the past, but look at the mess he has made by supposedly putting things to rights."

"I must confess, *Prometheus'* condition after refit was not good," Banks allowed.

"Then you will understand," Stewart's voice rose in triumph. "And the Admiralty itself could not survive without interest in its various forms," he beamed. "Why I dare not ponder on the number of promotions and postings that are directly attributable to the assistance of friends or family connections. If rules are bent or, on occasion, disregarded, is that such a terrible thing, providing the right results are achieved?"

"But corruption..." Banks began, hardly knowing how to finish.

"Yes, perhaps that is too strong a word," Stewart conceded. "Even though we are talking of the merest hint. Perhaps it is better to think of what you will be doing as more of a favour; like taking aboard a trusted friend's son as midshipman. No one wishes to learn of a fine and mighty battleship being overrun by a bunch of pirates, so do not tell them – not directly. Or, if you do, make light of the circumstances. Write your report in the way that I suggest, and no more will be said – I am certain of it."

It was hard to comprehend how a potential disaster could be disregarded in such a way, but Banks understood the point Stewart was making. He had not asked to be poisoned, any more than Caulfield had chosen to be captured and secured so easily. And drawing attention to the act would hardly be beneficial to either of them; in fact no one would gain. A carefully worded report might well divert attention from his own, pitiful, performance without committing too many deadly sins. And when it came down to it, he himself owed his title, captaincy and every posting until the present one to his father, or rather the Admiralty and City contacts the old boy cultivated. If he were to become prim and prudish over a few carefully chosen words, and maybe a whiff of deception, he would be starting late.

"Do you eat game, Dick?"

The question came as a surprise, and Banks took several seconds to respond.

"I have done," he replied hesitantly. "Upon occasion."

"And do you prefer yours to be hung?" Stewart persisted.

"To some extent, yes." Banks eyed his friend cautiously. "The meat is more tender and flavoursome if left for a while."

The commander winked again as he poured the last of the coffee into Banks' cup. "Then surely you can see," he said.

"However terrible the word might sound, a small amount of corruption can undoubtedly be of benefit."

* * *

The surgeon woke unwillingly to the hand that persistently shook his shoulder. There was a light in his cabin, but it was moving: someone must be holding a lantern above his head and the smell was particularly unpleasant.

"What is it?" he asked, rubbing his eyes, then peering at the figure that could only be dimly seen beyond the guttering flame.

"It's the prisoners, sir," a familiar voice told him, and immediately Manning was wide awake. The first of the captured privateers had already been removed from the ship, but there were still a fair number aboard. It seemed incredible that any attempt to escape should be made now, with *Prometheus* safe in a protected harbour. But they had already proved themselves to be a desperate lot, and the surgeon supposed he should not be surprised.

"The marines," he mumbled. "They are aware, I assume?"

"Oh, they ain't tryin' nothin'," the same voice told him with a laugh, and Manning realised it belonged to Wells, a loblolly boy who also acted as his servant. "But one of 'em's been taken proper queer, sir, an' Mr Prior thought you should be aware."

Manning rose up in his cot and prepared to clamber out. "Very well," he said. "I'll come. What are the symptoms?"

Wells was lighting one of the surgeon's personal wax candles, a luxury Manning allowed himself as the berth was set deep in the ship and received very little ventilation. By the extra light he could see the man's face more clearly, and that it was smiling.

"Hardly anythin' to worry over," Wells assured him. "Mr Prior says we seen it before. He reckons a particularly bad case of saltpetre poisoning; that's all," he continued. "And that young Irish officer seems to have been affected the worst."

Chapter Sixteen

"Stern windows and quarter-galleries should not take more than a week," the elderly man who appeared to be a combination of master shipwright and dockyard supervisor, told Caulfield. "Mind, they won't be quite the fine affairs you are used to: my men can't spend time or materials on gingerbread and the like..."

"As long as any repair proves weatherproof, and can be quickly achieved, I shall not care," *Prometheus'* first lieutenant assured him.

"Then there is a touch to see to with the fittings, that larboard bulwark to scarph and refit the top rail," the older man scratched at his balding head before referring to his bundle of notes for a moment. "Nothing too burdensome about any of that, especially if your painters can clean up and make good as we go."

Caulfield nodded; considering the mess an English dockyard had made of finishing *Prometheus'* recent refit, he would actually prefer to have such things under his control.

"Riggers will have a spot to do aloft, of course, but that is another department. And we may well discover more when the ship is truly surveyed. Even so, I should say ten days to a fortnight should see you straight."

"That would be very acceptable," the first lieutenant told him, genuinely impressed. "As well as highly commendable. My captain will be sure to say as much, I am certain. And if there is any service that can be done in return, I would gladly hear of it."

The elderly face beamed back. "Kind of you, sir, to be sure. Though we are under special instructions with your vessel," the man told him importantly. "*Prometheus* is needed on station at Toulon, so there is no time to be lost: the commissioner told us to give her our utmost attention."

Caulfield was taken aback; as soon as he had discovered the ship to be assigned to the Mediterranean Fleet he had wondered about her eventual posting, but it was slightly galling to have it confirmed by a shore-based artisan.

"Many of those on blockade at present are barely holding together," the older man continued with an alarming lack of discretion. "The Admiral is supposed to be sending one in at a time for us to refit, though quite what we're to do without a proper dock is another matter. And your prize ain't going to be no holiday," he added. "We probably won't start on that until you are once more at sea. Reckon there'll be a month or so's work on her at least, even though the damage is mostly above the waterline and of no real consequence."

"She will be returning to England though, I do not doubt," the first lieutenant commented absent mindedly.

"I should think not, sir," the shipwright replied aghast. "With such a lack of ships. I'd say they'll get us to pull her together, then rustle up a scratch crew before sending her on to join Admiral Nelson."

"Indeed?" Caulfield was surprised, both at the frigate's destination, and his informant's apparent certainty of it. "So we may be meeting with her again off Toulon?"

"Maybe off Toulon, and maybe not," the old man pondered. "The Admiral's playing a long game and will probably find a nice safe place to wait out the French, if I'm any judge. Leave a couple of sail keeping watch, but with the main force available to strike when they're needed."

Caulfield was astonished. The shipwright seemed disturbingly well informed on the Navy's intended movements, and was equally unafraid of voicing his opinions.

"Oh, they might think we're blockading them, but in truth the last thing anyone wants is for the Frogs to be stuck in harbour. At present there are as many of them as us, but we can't stop Johnny Crapaud building more, an' Toulon ships are some of the best in the world," the man added with a gleam of professional appreciation. "With their dockyards in full swing and them adding to their number on a regular basis, the sooner the French are allowed out to fight, the better."

* * *

207

Once her prisoners were taken off, *Prometheus* was moved to the new mole, where sufficient depth enabled her to lie alongside and work could begin. In no time she became a mass of activity, with stages placed against her battered stern, while topmasts, only recently struck, were set up once more allowing a positive army of riggers to attend her tophamper. Within the ship, the hastily rigged pens on the orlop were removed with Roberts, the carpenter, jealously claiming back his timber. A team of dockyard workers began ripping her battered larboard prow apart and the smell of oil paint, marine glue and bubbling pitch soon permeated the warm air.

Being small, relatively confined and heavily populated by military and naval personnel, Gibraltar was a port noted for shore leave, as it could never be regarded as a popular destination for the casual deserter. On the strength of this, Caulfield had promised evening liberty as soon as the immediate work was completed. And the privilege would be repeated each night by alternate watches, for as long as no man chose to run. Consequently, all set to with a purpose. The ship was swept clean; brass work shone under the application of spit and brick dust with only the occasional surreptitious aid of a wire brush, and even the bilges were pumped dry and sweetened by a liberal dosing of vinegar.

So it was at the end of the first week, when much had been achieved and both watches were looking forward to the delights of shore, that Banks called Caulfield into the freshly cleaned and polished great cabin, and motioned him to a chair at the dining table.

"I have my report," the captain told him, holding up a large sheaf of papers. "It covers the rescue of passengers and prize crew from the Indiaman, our taking of *Belle Île* and the subsequent revolt of the prisoners." He said the last words more quietly; there were still men working beneath his stern gallery and, although the windows were firmly closed, he had no wish to draw any more attention to the incident than it had already attracted. "Considering that we were both somewhat indisposed during the latter incident," Banks continued delicately, "I propose to allow you to read that section. You shall not mind, I am sure; we have served together a fair while now, Michael and, to be frank, I would value your opinion."

"I should not mind at all, sir," Caulfield replied as formally as any first lieutenant might on being asked a favour by his commanding officer, although he was also strangely touched by the gesture.

Banks sorted through the papers for a moment, then passed across three closely written sheets that Caulfield was quick to notice were in the captain's own hand; obviously no secretary or clerk had been entrusted with such a sensitive document.

The sun was starting to lower in the sky as Caulfield began to read. Banks waited, hands drumming listlessly on the dining table that had responded so well to David's polishing, and listening to the far off hammering that, he told himself, would be the carpenter's party putting finishing touches to the larboard top rail. Despite his attempts at distraction, it was still a relief when the lieutenant finally finished, and he looked up expectantly, only to realise that Caulfield was starting to sift through the pages once more. Banks had the uncomfortable feeling he might be going to start from the beginning but instead the first lieutenant handed his report back and gave a slight nod.

"I see what you have done," he said slowly. "And can understand why the action against the privateer figures more strongly in your account. Neither of us are in a position to give an accurate report of the later uprising, after all."

Banks watched him carefully, wondering exactly how much his friend and second in command really did understand. There was silence for several seconds and the captain was about to speak when it appeared that Caulfield had more to say.

"But I think you may have made too much of Mr Davison's part in the proceedings."

"In truth?" Banks asked, surprised. He had expected more objections to his allocation of dead and wounded. To his mind, much of their success or, to be more accurate, the reason why the French had failed, was totally down to prompt action taken by the prize. Had those aboard her not been so vigilant in spotting the disturbance, or carried out such an efficient boarding, it was very likely the British would have been overwhelmed.

"I interviewed every relevant officer," the captain began to explain. "All were most forthcoming and appeared to have carried out their duties in an exemplary manner. I do not think Mr Davison's part has been emphasised unduly; indeed, his role was vital to the success we enjoyed."

Caulfield considered this; perhaps he was wrong, perhaps the captain's report was sufficiently dispassionate, and maybe young Davison had truly been as active as Lewis or King; certainly he had nothing firm to base any contrary suppositions upon. But the first lieutenant also felt he had learned a lot about the young officer, even in the short time they had served together. And he would have been surprised if the action taken by the privateer had been solely down to him. "You spoke with Mr King?" It was hardly a question.

"Tom? Indeed I did," Banks agreed. "And later learned from Mr Manning that he had been injured, though he did not think to mention the fact himself. And he spoke much in praise of an able hand, name of Ross; do you know of him?"

"He joined us in Tor Bay," Caulfield replied automatically. "Highly educated and articulate, though a little out of practice as a seaman, if I am to judge. Still, he seems popular with the men: I have it in mind to promote him and was to speak with you on the matter."

"Well, according to King he fought extremely well, and yes, we may certainly discuss his advancement."

"It was worthy of King to commend him," Caulfield said pointedly.

"Indeed it was," Banks conceded, and considered the matter for a moment before adding: "But as to the rest of the report; will it pass?"

Caulfield thought for a moment longer; there was still a niggling feeling at the back of his mind regarding Davison's conduct, even though that was probably the more accurate part of Banks' account. He had no idea why the captain had chosen to garble what had occurred; presumably he was concerned at being shown to be indisposed but, as the distortion worked in his own favour as well, Caulfield would be a fool to say so. His mind wandered on to King – it was so like the young lieutenant to discount a minor wound, and wondered if the same tendency had been responsible for minimising his part in the proceedings. Again, so like King: as it was to commend that fellow Ross. Davison still worried him, but if he really suspected any defect in performance from that quarter, it was hardly from a position of knowledge. Caulfield's own contribution had been to allow himself to be captured and tied to a chair, so who was he to comment?

"Yes, sir," he said finally. "I believe the report will be fine."

* * *

"Would you care for some coffee, sir?" the wardroom steward asked, solicitously. "Or there could be tea: I can make a fresh pot."

King loosened his stock and shook his head. "Thank you, I require nothing," he said absently, his mind being on other matters. Work on the forecastle was progressing well and that was the last of their essential repairs. The dockyard had also taken a look at the persistent leak forward of the half deck, and there were a few more small items to consider, but nothing that would prevent *Prometheus* from putting to sea. And the new wardroom windows were really rather splendid, he reminded himself, glancing across at them. Perhaps not as ornate as their predecessors, but the simpler design actually allowed more light, and he was sure the overpowering smell of linseed and marine glue would go in time.

"There's a bite of cold beef left from dinner, sir, should you wish it," the steward persisted, and King was now alerted. Wardrooms varied from ship to ship, and *Prometheus* was now blessed with one of the best he had encountered. But never before had he received such attention from a steward: certainly not one with whom he was only vaguely acquainted. And the man, though not unfamiliar, was rarely seen on service detail; King had always considered him to be one of the cooks. Apart from the two of them, the place was empty; perhaps the fellow was simply bored, or felt like a change of task, although King sensed there may be another reason.

"Potterton, isn't it?" he questioned, and the steward, who was older and far better spoken than most, nodded. "I require nothing, Potterton." King continued. "But perhaps you are wanting something from me?"

"I-I would appreciate the chance to speak, sir," the man confessed. "That is, if it be no trouble."

"You are starboard watch, are you not?" King replied. "Mr Davison is your divisional lieutenant. Ship's business is better spoken of with him."

"Yes, sir. Yes, I am aware, and have endeavoured to bring the matter up, though Mr Davison was unforthcoming. He is quite young, sir."

The last words were delivered in a whisper and King supposed there was a form of compliment in them, even if he himself were hardly much older. It would be wrong to ask the man to sit, not when it was his place of work, so King remained standing.

"Very well, Potterton; what do you have to say?"

"It was about my recruitment, sir," the older man began. "It is not that I wish to cause trouble, and am certain Mr Lewis felt it within his rights to seize me. But I think there may have been an error, sir. I am a cook: a recognised tradesman. I served an apprenticeship and have never had dealings with the sea in my life. And I am also part owner of the Three Tuns in Galmpton; it is only a share, but I have since learned that such a thing makes me a freeholder, so I surely should not have been taken."

"Whyever did you not say something before?" King asked.

"It was so sudden, sir," the man explained vaguely. "One moment I was happily at work in my kitchen, the next aboard this ship. I have only ever been in service, and was unsure of the correct procedure to protest. And, you will forgive me sir, but it does seem that those who complain or cause trouble are somewhat roughly dealt with."

King supposed he had a point: the Navy was not known for its pastoral care and Davison, Potterton's divisional lieutenant, could never be accused of having a sensitive side.

"And then, when I was posted to wardroom service, I felt it a job that needed doing. We are at war, yet the methods and facilities for serving the officers were sadly lacking. I think I have made a few significant changes there, sir," Potterton added, somewhat smugly. "It was only when we reached an English port, that I considered it worth bringing the matter up."

"You have certainly made a great improvement," King allowed. "The wardroom fare has never been so good, and you have forged a fine team from the stewards. Were you to wish it, there may be a warrant in it for you – how would you feel about being a petty officer?"

"Thank you, sir; it has been enjoyable work. But I also miss England and would prefer to be there, and in my own kitchen."

"I see," King said, although in reality he was still slightly mystified. "And what is it that you expect of me?"

"Well, as a novice in these matters, I am unsure of the exact procedure, and wondered if you would be so good as to guide me?"

* * *

"You advised him to seek legal counsel?" Davison asked, with obvious disgust. It was the following evening, and once more in the wardroom. King, in contemplation of an early night, had been yarning pleasantly with Lewis, Dawson, the purser, and Marine Lieutenant Swift when Davison entered. The starboard watch had been granted shore leave; by now all should have returned and, as the divisional officer responsible, Davison was plainly troubled. But both his presence and position struck a chord with King, who had been looking for an opportunity to speak with him all that day. Consequently he broached the matter directly, and probably without the finesse it deserved; in any case, he was somewhat taken aback at the reaction.

"If that fellow Billings has been bending your ear, I am not interested," Davison said, interrupting King's explanation. "Ever since we left Tor Bay he has been griping about being seized illegally; even brought a deputation from his mess, on one occasion. I own that he has been more quiet of late, but now I knows why: it seems he has found an ally. Damn it, King, we have few enough men aboard as it is; losing a good hand is not going to make matters easier."

"Actually it is another; a steward, name of Potterton," King replied mildly. "But if either is here in error, that should surely be corrected; no good will come of it otherwise. A pressed man is one thing, but any hand illegally detained only spreads dissatisfaction and contempt amongst the people."

"Do not take that tone with me, sir," the younger man snapped in reply. "I'll have you know I am your superior officer and entitled to a little more respect; something I have had cause to remind you of on more than one occasion."

"I am sure Mr King meant no discourtesy," Swift, the marine officer, commented soothingly.

"Indeed not," King confirmed. He felt tired, and this was hardly the restful end to a long day he had been anticipating. But Davison had already annoyed him too many times in the past, and he was determined not to let him get away with it yet again. "As the man is under your charge, I simply thought you should be aware of the situation," he said. "Indeed, any conscientious officer would surely wish to know."

"He would have been better to speak with me, and you should have told him so." Davison grumbled, having missed King's barb. "I'd have put him straight as far as any legal status is concerned."

"Then you would have brought yourself a great deal of trouble," King retorted. "It is not unknown for writs to be raised against officers, especially those who abuse their authority."

Davison flushed. King's statement, taken in conjunction with the knowledge that Potterton was seeking legal advice, had hit him in a sensitive spot. "You, sir, are an arrogant cur," he spat back, conscious, as were they both, of the sharp intakes of breath from the other officers present. "I shall thank you to refrain from meddling with my affairs and division."

"I have no wish to interfere, and will gladly allow you to settle matters for yourself," King told him.

"After setting Potterton with a lawyer," Davison gave a brief laugh. "I call that a rogue's trick, and it does you no credit."

King swallowed; Davison had now insulted him twice, but he

was determined not to lower himself to such a level. He went to speak, but was surprised to find himself beaten by Lewis, usually the least forthcoming of the wardroom officers.

"I fail to see why you are quite so concerned," the fifth lieutenant said gently. "If, as you say, Potterton has no case, then surely it can not worry you what action he brings?"

"I remind you, sir, that this is a wardroom," Davison replied, turning on the junior man. "Home of officers and gentlemen. If you wish to be considered as either, I suggest placing a guard upon your tongue."

"Mr Lewis has a commission every bit as valid as yours," King pointed out, as steadily as he could. "And I think you should apologise for that remark."

"Apologise? To a lower deck reject?"

"A gentleman would apologise," King replied. The second lieutenant had now insulted two of his fellow officers, and was definitely on dangerous ground.

"Are you saying I am no gentleman?" Davison asked.

"Let the circumstances speak for themselves," King sighed, and was disconcerted to notice a faint look of triumph appear on the younger man's face.

"Then you have affronted me, sir," the younger man stated with confidence. "And for that I shall demand satisfaction."

Chapter Seventeen

It was early morning and, from the height of the tiny plateau, the town below appeared bathed in a soft mist which had been invisible during their ascent. King climbed down from the small horse which had carried him from the dockyard and stretched his legs. With *Prometheus* still alongside the mole, there had been little difficultly in leaving the ship, and Lewis had done well in securing a guide and mounts at that hour. He secretly hoped Davison might have been less lucky. The man had been snoring loudly in his cabin when they left the wardroom: he may even over-sleep, or awaken and decide that words spoken in haste might just as easily be forgotten. Failing that, Caulfield, Banks, or even Reynolds, the new marine captain who had replaced Donaldson, might have got wind of what was about. Duelling, although still relatively common, remained illegal and was definitely falling out of fashion in the Royal Navy. King was sure that morning's example would be stamped upon, should any of the senior officers hear of it.

However the unbreakable rules of honour meant that he could not give word. And he was equally certain Lewis, his official second, or Manning, who had agreed to attend as surgeon, would never have dreamed of speaking to another of the affair. And even if there had been no horses available, or a positive ban on travelling about the rock, King knew in his heart that Davison would appear. And so, indeed, it turned out.

The first they saw of his party was a panting man who reached the tiny clearing with obvious relief, and could well have run the entire way. Then, in a shaft of sudden sunlight, Davison and his second made their entrance. They were aboard two fine cavalry horses that stood several hands higher than the sad examples King, Lewis and Manning had ridden. Both men were in full dress, whereas King had only bothered to don duck trousers and a plain jacket. Manning and Lewis were more conventionally attired; the latter wore undress tunic and second best britches, whereas

Manning was functionally smart, if mildly funereal, in his black surgeon's uniform. But all were positively shabby when viewed against Davison's tailored and flowing broadcloth, white silk stockings, and buttons that positively glowed in the first rays of what promised to be another glorious day.

"I see Davison has persuaded one of the new men to support him," Lewis whispered as the second lieutenant and Marine Lieutenant Locke dismounted. "Presumably he has not been aboard *Prometheus* long enough to judge the cull's true worth."

King said nothing, although it was somehow comforting to know he was not alone in detesting Davison. The two immaculate officers had begun a discussion with their guide that soon became heated. "And it looks as if their local man wants his money on the capstan head," Lewis added with something approaching a laugh. "For all their grandeur, he has no intention of losing a fare if Davison ends up dead meat."

King swallowed dryly. This whole matter had grown out of hand; he felt as if caught within the strands of some complex and intricate netting, and dared not make a move for fear of worsening the situation.

"I'd chance that our new friend Locke ain't too happy about being involved," Manning said, joining them. From his relaxed demeanour, King had the impression the surgeon was treating the affair as something considerably less important than a cricket match. "Davison leaned on him rather heavily, I believe; their fathers are friends, or something on that line."

"It was Locke who organised their mounts," Lewis added. "Spoke to a garrison officer, who also happens to be under the Davison family's thumb, by all accounts. Though I gather he objected more strongly when his precious pistols were requested. From the sight of them I should say both see hard wax and brick dust more often than powder."

"But reliable weapons, none the less?" King asked anxiously.

"Oh, for sure: I checked them thoroughly." Lewis assured him. "A pair of Joe Manton's finest. And flinters: no fancy scent bottle locks or exploding pellets."

King had often fantasised about owning a Manton pistol, but

the thought that he might shortly die with one in his hand was not attractive.

"I should not take on so, Thomas," Manning said, with the first signs of compassion. "The vast majority of duels end with neither party being injured." Then he considered for a moment before adding, "or if so, it is not always fatal."

"You have the letter for Juliana?" King asked coldly.

"Indeed, it is in my pocket as I speak," he agreed. "As is your will."

"Gentlemen, if all are ready I suggest we proceed," the voice of Locke, the marine lieutenant, sounded unusually loud and filled the small space easily. A detachment of naval signalmen were billeted on the rise beyond the nearby copse; King wondered if they might even hear of the proceedings and put a stop to them, before deciding that such an event was probably common place. Their clearing was one of the few level pieces of ground on what was a truly colossal hill. And when so many members of the military and naval services were crowded onto one small rock, with the addition of wives, daughters and, doubtless, lovers to make matters more complicated, they would probably be lucky to retain what was such an ideal location for their exclusive use.

"May I suggest twelve paces?" the red-coated officer enquired of Lewis.

"Indeed, sir. Shall we pace together?"

King and Manning watched in silence as the two lieutenants stepped out what seemed to be a remarkably short distance. Davison was standing alone, and apparently unperturbed.

"If you gentlemen will join us," Locke again, "we may attend to the weapons."

King stepped forward and almost missed his footing, although Davison's stride was far more confident. Each man joined his second, and for the first time since the previous night, regarded the other face on.

"As seconds, it is now our duty to inspect and load each pistol." Locke spoke no less softly. "In that time might I suggest both parties examine the motives behind this affair and, if there be a way of avoiding bloodshed, it be taken."

King continued to stare at Davison, even though the mention of bloodshed sent shivers within. He had thought this would be the moment when sheer terror took over; with the possibility that, in some way or another, he would disgrace himself. But on seeing the man properly, and in the clear light of morning, King felt far more determined to follow matters through to their logical conclusion.

The pistols were soon ready and selected by their seconds; King accepted his from Lewis, and weighed the warm, reassuring piece in his hand. It was perfectly balanced, and would undoubtedly fire as true as any weapon over such a distance. Whether either man was hit or not would depend entirely upon their opponent's aim and composure.

"Very well, if you are totally decided," Locke continued, after a suitable pause. "I will ask Mr Manning, as a neutral party, to supervise the proceedings."

"That man is no more neutral than a second," Davison protested, speaking out for the first time, and King was quick to detect a slight catch in his voice. "The two have been cronies for years; I demand that one of the guides act in his stead."

"I assure you, sir that, as a surgeon, I regard myself as completely objective, when it comes to matters involving human health," Manning stated firmly. "And may also add that, should you require my attention, it will be given readily and with my full professional competence." Davison seemed to blanch slightly at the mention of a surgeon's care.

"But this affair was to be carried out at seven," Manning continued, bringing out his watch and looking at it pointedly. "And we are still a spell light – so will wait until the time is correct."

"Not so!" Davison protested. "Seven, or five minutes to, it makes no difference. Let us be about our business!"

"We will wait until the hour," Manning repeated firmly, fixing the young officer with a harsh stare.

The time ticked slowly by, with both King and Davison flashing the occasional glance at their opponent, and the two seconds shifting their stances uncomfortably. The atmosphere was tense but, if Manning had intended the delay to break either man's nerve, he was disappointed. And finally, with what might have been slight reluctance, he looked at his watch once more.

"Very well," he said, glancing about him. "We may begin. I shall count to ten. After reaching three, either man is at liberty to fire. As soon as I reach ten, there are to be no further shots. You are both reminded that, by colluding in this affair you are contravening number 23 of the Articles of War by which we are all governed, and any officer present may be liable to stand trial by court martial." He spoke slowly and with cold authority, looking to each man in turn as he did. "That is whether or not any injury is received, while a subsequent death may see whoever is responsible speak for their own life."

Both men continued to stare at the other although King noticed that Davison was now standing side on, and altered his own stance to match.

"One."

King raised the hand that held his pistol, which had suddenly become very heavy, and lined the weapon up upon his opponent's torso.

"Two."

His own chest was starting to hurt in apparent anticipation. Then he hurriedly drew what must have been his first breath for several seconds.

"Three!"

As soon as Manning spoke, there was a flash from Davison's gun that delayed King in firing his own. An odd whirling sound instantly followed, and King was vaguely conscious of the wind of a shot as it passed close by his ear.

"A miss, by God," someone muttered, but King was uncertain who.

Now he had seven seconds to compose and fire his own pistol but, even as the relief began to flow, he wondered if he were really capable of such an act. From somewhere close by a dog began to bark, and a flock of birds, alerted by the noise, took to the sky.

"Four..."

Manning was still counting the seconds, while King continued to debate. The look on Davison's face said much. It was an odd expression: something between anger and despair. And, as a pistol remained trained upon his heart, raw fear was also becoming increasingly apparent.

"Fire, you damned booby!" the younger lieutenant ordered, just as the surgeon reached six, but everything in King's opponent, from his posture, to the terror in his eyes, said differently. The perfectly balanced pistol remained steady on Davison's chest while King considered the best way of ending matters. He could shoot to deliberately miss, but that might create more problems; Davison was quite capable of seeing the act as an insult, in which case there would have to be a further exchange of bullets.

"Seven..."

Or he could wound the fellow; it might teach the lad a lesson and would make a point – perhaps a slight nick to the arm, or the lower leg? But, despite Manning's attendance, such a wound sustained in the height of summer was likely to turn septic: amputation might then be necessary, or he could even miss and sever an artery.

"Eight..."

This was the first time King had experienced having his thoughts timed, and was amazed at how fast his brain could work. Davison had gone a deathly white, and a sixth sense said the lad might soon run. Much of his assumed importance also appeared to have been shed, even if a steady flow of defiant rubbish still trickled from his mouth. King felt as if he were watching an unruly schoolboy, one caught after having broken a window, and he unconsciously tightened his finger on the trigger.

"Nine..." Now there was only one second left; King had to decide one way or another.

"Fire, damn you!" Davison repeated, almost in a scream. Then King heard a shot that surely sounded too loud, yet seemed to come from far off. He stared uncomprehendingly at his own weapon, before realising that no one now stood in front of him, and what had been a smart officer was lying in an untidy heap on the ground.

* * *

"Well, I think both you young gentlemen owe a deal of thanks to Mr Caulfield," Banks told them sternly. It was two hours later, the sun was now properly up and shining through *Prometheus'* stern windows while, to King at least, the great cabin smelt wonderfully of coffee and recent breakfast. Neither had been offered to him or Davison however. Both stood, side by side, at the foot of the large dining table while Banks lounged in his comfortable chair at the head and Caulfield sat, more upright, to one side.

"Not only did you endanger your own lives, valuable officers were removed from their duties aboard this ship, and at a time when all were needed." The captain's expression was as cold as anyone present had seen it. "Numerous laws might have been contravened, as well as Admiralty Regulations: generally you both behaved in a manner ill-befitting the service."

He paused as all in the room took in his words, before continuing with equal gravity.

"It is only by the first lieutenant's efforts, that I am not lacking at least one senior officer. Had Miss Kinnison not overheard the whole thing and brought this foolish matter to his attention, any amount of mischief could have been caused."

In reality, young Judy's actions had done even more good than the captain was prepared to admit. Manning had already advised Caulfield of the incident, and would doubtless now be facing no end of personal recriminations for doing so. Her intervention had rescued his surgeon almost as much as either lieutenant. With that, and the severe dose of saltpetre that most suspected her of administering to the man Carroll, the girl had done much to reinstate herself, certainly as far as Banks was concerned.

"Do you have anything to say for yourselves?" he asked, maintaining the same severe demeanour.

"I am sincerely sorry, sir." King spoke clearly and the captain grunted.

"Mr Davison?" Banks enquired, after nothing had been forthcoming.

"I regret the incident," the younger man said finally, "but do not approve of catering staff reporting on private conversations. Nor the method Mr Caulfield used to disrupt what was an affair of honour."

Banks and his first lieutenant exchanged a quick look, and there was possibly a trace of humour on the captain's face as he continued.

"Do you object to the method he used?" he asked with emphasis. "Or your own reaction to it?"

King thought Caulfield might also have been trying to control a smile, even though the situation was surely far too serious for any merriment.

"The first lieutenant had just completed a very exhausting climb," Banks continued with a captain's authority. "And was quite correct in directing one of the marine escorts to fire his musket – which was surely the most immediate way of breaking up what was indeed a deplorable assembly. However I can see that Mr Davison's reaction to the gunshot might cause him some embarrassment," he added especially coldly.

"It was the shock, sir." Davison insisted. "Nothing more; I did not faint."

"No indeed," Banks agreed. "I am sure Mr Manning was quite wrong in his assertion. But I would rather we passed on to other matters," he continued, after a distinct pause.

"In view of the way you have performed, I have to ask if I wish to have such a pair serving aboard my ship in future. I would, of course, expect any animosity to have been settled by this morning's little farce but, where one disagreement has arisen, it seems likely more shall follow. Therefore one of you must leave."

King felt the tension well up inside. Of the two, he was the junior man and by rights should be the one to go. But he had served with both Banks and Caulfield for several years and in two previous ships: to leave them now would be hard indeed. And there would be no certainty of finding an alternative posting; sea-going berths for middling lieutenants being not so very common, while the captain's report that must surely follow him would hardly help in finding a new position. And he would be leaving Manning behind, and Lewis, as well as others amongst the crew that he had come to count upon as friends. The very notion of striking out on his own appalled and dismayed him in equal measure.

"I have not spoken with the naval commissioner, or indeed anyone ashore, and do not intend to do so in connection with the earlier incident," Banks continued. "As far as I am concerned, it did not take place; something you would both do well to remember. But I am aware that the *Belle Île* will be made ready to take into the service. She is my prize, so it is reasonable to assume that a recommendation from me will be properly regarded. As a new ship, it will be a fresh start for whoever I propose."

King felt his mouth go dry. A frigate of such a size would probably require three lieutenants; were he to transfer, at least it would not be a reduction in position. And a sixth rate was surely so much more the thing for the young and ambitious officer he supposed himself to be. But still the spectre of serving without his shipmates returned to haunt him and, however hard Banks might be trying to organise an alternative berth, he did so wish he might be allowed to remain aboard *Prometheus*.

Mr Davison, I shall be recommending you for *Belle Île,*" Banks said the words, uncommonly quickly, and King gave an involuntary gasp. "You will have the advantage of being on hand to supervise her repair and fitting out, and your current rank must enable a posting of second lieutenant to be retained."

Davison was silent and, from his viewpoint, King had no idea how the man was reacting to the news. But it could not be bettered, as far as he was concerned. And for the second time that morning, King felt a welcome rush of relief.

Chapter Eighteen

"Duty Midshipman," the marine sentry bellowed as the boy rapped on the outer door of the captain's quarters. Banks, in the coach, called out impatiently for him to enter: *Prometheus* was due to sail that afternoon, they still had the last ten tons of Gibraltar's scant and meanly allocated drinking water to take aboard, and there was a day and a half's worth of returns and manifests to sort, so he needed no distraction.

"Urgent message from Mr Carlton, sir," Steven said, his face flushed. Carlton was the new fourth officer; a youngster barely older than the midshipman who stood before him, although his commission still beat Lewis' by several months. Banks wondered quite what terrible new discovery the lad might have made to cause such a panic.

"*Canopus* in sight and entering the bay," the midshipman gushed. "Captain Conn, sir."

That would be John Conn, Banks soberly decided. Something of a rising star, although junior to him on the captains' list, and lucky to have a third rate with his seniority. Stewart had mentioned he was due to join them. Conn was a favourite of Nelson, and had taken part in at least two actions under the Admiral, whereas *Canopus* had been captured at Abukir Bay, so the presence of both was logical, and hardly worthy of such fuss. She was an eighty, though; still a two-decker but even more powerful than *Prometheus* and he supposed her muscle would be a welcome addition to the Mediterranean Fleet.

"Very well, I'll come," Banks told the boy as he went to replace the ledger on the shelf from where it had only just been collected.

"There's something else, sir," the lad insisted. "She's let fly her sheets."

The captain paused in his task. "Are you certain?" he asked.

"Yes, sir," the child replied earnestly. "Least that's what Mr Brehaut said, though she just looked all ahoo to me."

The ledger dropped to the deck and Steven very nearly followed it as, with sudden urgency, Banks pushed past him and out through the half opened door.

* * *

"What's about, Mr Brehaut?" the captain demanded on gaining the quarterdeck. Lieutenant Carlton was also present but Banks wanted a detailed report and from someone he could trust.

"Masthead sighted HMS *Canopus* in the bay less than half an hour ago, sir," the sailing master told him calmly. "Mr Carlton wanted to call you but I said you were probably busy, and simply expected her to enter harbour. Then, just as she was in sight of the deck, she let fly her sheets. She's recovered now, and has hauled in her wind. No wait," he added suddenly. "There is a signal."

"Where's Lewis?" Banks shouted impatiently as the duty signal midshipman levelled his glass on the bunting that had just been released. But the age old warning had actually been enough: a fleet was in sight and, for Conn to announce it so dramatically, this must be far more than just a stray East India bound contingent.

Seemingly drawn by the sudden excitement, Lewis bounded on to the quarterdeck and over to where Chivers was fussing with the code book.

"Enemy in sight, sir," the lieutenant said positively, after no more than a second's glance through the glass and without reference to his junior or any book.

"Hands to stations for leaving harbour," Banks cried instantly, adding, "Who is ashore?" to a bewildered Carlton.

"I – I could not be certain, sir," the young man began and Banks was turning away in frustration when the reassuring face of the first lieutenant appeared at the companionway.

"Mr Dawson and Mr Stone are at the victualling office," Caulfield told him crisply, naming the purser and cook. "And Mr King can be expected at any time."

"King?" Banks, snapped.

"Yes, sir. He had personal business and took one of the hands with him. Oh, and I understand Mr Swift and Sergeant Jarvis are

226

with a party of marines sent to collect the men who went adrift last night," he continued in a lower voice.

"*Canopus* is signalling once more," Chivers broke in, having spotted a second hoist. "Three ships, sou'-west by south and steering to pass," he looked back at his captain anxiously. "I cannot read the last, sir."

"Signal from The Mount," Lewis interrupted. "Our number and *Aries*; permission to leave harbour." The crack of cannon fire emphasised the importance of the last message, and Banks felt his frustration grow.

"Hoist the peter and single up to our stern cable," he snapped. Three ships could mean anything or nothing; Stewart had spoken of ten expected from San Domingo, in which case they might be battleships, and possibly just the head of a larger fleet. Otherwise it was more likely a collection that had escaped blockade, and would probably prove smaller. If frigates, they would run before the lumbering old *Prometheus* could even cast off, although liners might be a different prospect entirely. As an eighty, *Canopus* mounted much the same ordinance as *Prometheus* but in greater quantity, whereas *Aries* was little more than a sloop, and potentially even a liability. But still, handled correctly, the two British two-deckers could probably account for an enemy up to half as big again. It all depended on the final number.

"There's the marines," someone shouted from the forecastle and, sure enough, two bands of red and white could be seen marching stiffly towards the ship. A far less orderly group of seamen ambled between them wearing looks of defiant shame. Banks glared at them then turned away. The added manpower would be useful; marines were determined fighters and every hand was needed, but he was far more interested in knowing his recently appointed second lieutenant's whereabouts.

"What the devil was King thinking about?" he demanded of Caulfield. "The ship's about to sail and he's squandering time ashore."

"He has hardly taken any leave so far, sir." Caulfield pointed out. "And would undoubtedly have returned well before our intended departure time."

Banks muttered something under his breath, then shifted his gaze to where *Canopus* awaited them in the Strait. *Aries* was already preparing to set sail and, even though a line-of-battleship was probably allowed to take longer than a sixth rate, it would be at least five minutes before they would be able to follow her example. If King was not back by then, they would just have to leave without him. And it would be his loss, Banks assured himself.

* * *

But, as luck would have it, *Prometheus* sailed with all hands. Even Stone and Dawson, alerted amid the confusion of a busy market day by a dozen differing rumours, were in time to board. By three bells in the forenoon watch the ship had cleared Bleak Beach and caught the fresh east-north-easterly that had only recently risen. *Aries* was already ahead, and steadily drawing more so although Banks felt quite content to let the little frigate scud over the waves in a splendour of spray and sail. She might have all the dash and impudence of her type but, if there were to be a battle, it would be won by the brute force and solidity of warhorses such as his own *Prometheus*.

And she was being cleared for action at that very moment. The men, many of whom were still digesting the briefest of breakfasts, obviously anticipated getting to grips with the enemy almost immediately, and threw themselves into their work with gusto. Furniture was being stashed in the hold, bulkheads broken down, and every one of the many tasks necessary to turn their home into an efficient fighting machine was being undertaken with almost frantic haste.

For this had all the makings of a regular ruck, no attempt to humbug by disguising the barky as an Indiaman; no hand-to-hand combat in the cramped nether regions of the lower decks. It might hardly be a major fleet action; the British numbered three, and that was counting a jackass, but what *Canopus* had spotted bore all the hallmarks of a regular foe. A chance for *Prometheus'* big guns to speak properly and in earnest: to put their skills to the test against a conventional enemy with no attempt to deceive or delude. And, for most, the opportunity could not come fast enough.

* * *

But Banks was not so keen for action and had no intention of sending anyone to quarters for some time. He was even happy for his senior officers to remain on the quarterdeck. *Canopus* was likely to signal again at any moment and it would be better for all to be fully appraised of the situation before being confined to their stations.

King, as newly appointed second lieutenant, would command the lower gun deck; two batteries, both containing fourteen of *Prometheus'* heaviest artillery. And they were big; the largest long guns regularly used by the Royal Navy: each consisted of over fifty-five hundredweight of cast iron and he would be responsible for dispatching broadsides with a combined weight of close to a quarter of a ton. There had been little time to exercise the crews, but King knew the men were more than familiar with their weapons, and only hoped he might prove worthy of such a force.

Lieutenant Benson was equally unsure. Davison had not been easy to work with but, now the young fool had gone – flounced almost – to take up what he had insisted to be a superior position aboard the prize, his absence was being felt in a most unexpected way.

Davison's replacement, the even less experienced but far more likeable Carlton, had only been commissioned a few weeks before Lewis. This meant that Benson was now third lieutenant, and had the entire upper gun deck under his control. To date his responsibilities only extended as far as second in command of the lower batteries: now he would have the ship's secondary armament of eighteen pounders to play with, and the prospect was daunting.

This was also his first taste of being in overall charge of such a large body of men. And it would be such a public duty: were the topmen a little tardy taking in a sail, or the afterguard not quite up to scratch when it came to attending the braces, few would notice. But an ill-timed or incomplete broadside was not to be missed, and he could expect comments, derision and even censure from the captain downwards.

For Brehaut too, this would be the largest action in which he had conned a ship, although in his case there were no doubts, just a mild but genuine desire to use his expertise. The Strait was a challenging region; should the action be extended, they might encounter hazards in almost every direction. And even if they confined their manoeuvres to a small area, there was a fast running rip that would have to be allowed for, as well as the famed Levanter: that very wind that currently filled their canvas so admirably. It was potentially a devastating force and could easily run to forty knots while raising a hazardous sea. The waves at present, white capped and rolling, were of no particular danger, although Brehaut had heard tell of gale force gusts building without notice and often carrying fog and rain in their wake. But, should such a situation occur, he would be prepared for it. His chart was laid out in readiness less than ten feet from where he stood, while the previous weeks aboard *Prometheus* had been enough to instil sufficient respect for him and his abilities from every station. And Brehaut would be doing what he enjoyed most; practising a talent honed through a lifetime's usage, while testing his powers to the utmost. If he were spared and blessed with the chance, he might one day end up as sailing master aboard a three-decker, and responsible for leading a battle fleet to victory. But at that moment to have charge of *Prometheus* was sufficient; in fact Brehaut wondered if he had ever been quite so happy.

"*Canopus* is signalling..." Lewis began solidly but a younger voice interrupted him.

"Deck there, I have them!" It was Midshipman Steven, who had been placed way above at the main masthead for just such a purpose.

"Enemy is three line ships," Lewis continued. "Steering west."

"Sighting off the larboard bow; looks to be a thumper, and steering west," the lad unwittingly confirmed from his lofty perch.

"That sounds like the last in line," Caulfield commented. "And would be roughly twenty miles off, if our masthead is in sight."

"They may have been intending to try for the Med., sir,"

Brehaut agreed. "This wind has only risen in the last couple of hours. It were more southerly afore, and had blown so for a while. Such a breeze would have seen them past Gib. easily."

Banks remained non-committal. What Brehaut said was probably true and, if the French really had come from San Domingo, they would naturally have tried to head for Toulon first. But Stewart had mentioned a larger number, and no more were in sight. It was not inconceivable that a few might have become separated after such a voyage, or this could be a completely different force.

The contrary wind, combined with sighting a British line-of-battleship on the horizon, was likely to have encouraged their change of plan. And, now that it had arisen, the Levanter was likely to linger, while *Canopus* could be the head of a veritable fleet, rather than fronting what was really only a derisory force of two liners and a jackass frigate. Yes, he decided, in their position he would abandon all thoughts of a home port, and make for Cádiz: the Spanish base was considerably closer and a far more favourable option.

"I think she might take the royals, sir." Brehaut spoke gently, as was his habit when proffering a suggestion to the captain, but Banks was immediately attentive. The wind had steadied to a fine eighteen to twenty knots and *Prometheus* was making good progress, running before it under forecourse, topsails and topgallants. The addition of royals would increase their speed still further, as long as there was no strain to the top hamper.

"Do you think she can carry them?" he asked.

"Yes, sir," Brehaut replied with certainty. "At least for a spell; if it freshens I shall be sure to alert you."

"Very well," Banks murmured and the air became alive with the squeal of pipes and a bellowing of orders.

Ahead, *Aries* had caught *Canopus* and both ships sat a mile or so off *Prometheus'* jib boom. But, as the extra canvas was released and began to fill, Banks felt the deck positively buck under his feet and knew they would make up the distance soon enough.

"*Canopus* is signalling." Lewis again. "It's *Aries'* number; she's being told to close with the enemy; I think they may be speaking."

Banks watched; the two were abreast and barely half a cable apart. *Canopus* was possibly slightly slower than *Prometheus*; but a sixth rate would have the heels of them both, and it made perfect sense for her to stalk the French. If more were hidden, she would be able to report the fact, while there was always the possibility of sighting other British vessels and drawing them in to join the party.

The bell rang seven times; the forenoon watch was drawing on. Soon Banks would have to order Up Spirits, and arrange for the people to be fed. It would be a scratch meal of cheese and hard tack when, being a Tuesday, they would have woken to the prospect of two pounds of salt beef at midday. Since then the ship had sailed and was already in chase although, with such a lead, it would be late evening at the earliest before the French were brought to battle. He was well aware how tiring an all day pursuit could be, and having an empty belly would not make matters easier. They had yet to beat to quarters, so officially those of the starboard watch were below, but the ship was also cleared for action, and scant comfort would be found anywhere. Banks considered the problem for a moment: he had no wish to take unnecessary chances, but tired and hungry men did not fight well. And if he was to compromise the safety of the ship, it would be better done now than when the enemy was actually within striking distance.

"Mr Caulfield, ask Mr Stone to relight the galley fire, if you please. And he may call away his mates to assist." Caulfield looked up, but was experienced enough to cover his surprise. "We may have a Frenchman's breakfast for our dinner," Banks continued. "But supper shall be beef, and with a double shotted duff to follow, if it can be managed."

"Very good, sir," the first lieutenant replied, before flashing a look at Adams, the duty midshipman, who made off in search of the cook.

"I have another in sight," Steven reported from the masthead, confirming Bank's suspicion that they were gaining on the enemy. "Same bearing, and I'd judge her to be another liner, steering a similar course."

Banks said nothing; even if the French hove to, it would be several hours before *Prometheus* closed on them, and he was convinced that feeding the men a hot meal later was the correct decision. They would then go through the evening and part of the night with full bellies and, when action was joined, be that much the stronger for it.

In theory, the chase might continue for far longer, of course; the British may follow the entire run to Cádiz, only to be cheated of their prize at the very mouth of what purported to be a neutral port. But Banks thought not: an inner feeling, born either from experience or intuition, told him this would not last more than twelve hours. Within that time they would see action. And the French would be defeated; of that he was quietly positive, even if he could derive little pleasure from the prospect.

Instead he seemed to know already that the victory was to be tainted. However hard he may try, he could tell no more, but the feelings remained strong, and he was strangely disconcerted.

* * *

"Never gone into battle afore with duff in me belly," Harrison commented with an air of wonder. It was over six hours since *Prometheus* made her hasty exit from Gibraltar, and the men had just consumed an unexpectedly large supper. "I'm not sayin' it ain't welcome," he continued. "But it just don't feel like we're gonna do any fighting today."

Despite the fact they had still to beat to quarters and were officially off watch, most of Flint's mess had gathered about the starboard gun that several of them manned. The piece also marked the aftmost limit of their mess area; there was no table slung from the deckhead, and their benches had been consigned to the forward hold, but all were comfortable enough. Some perched on the gun carriage, others leant back against a convenient oak knee or, in the case of Butler and Jameson who were younger and far more supple than most, sat cross-legged on the deck. And they had eaten well, for the considerable meal recently issued came atop of a perfectly acceptable midday dinner of cheese, raw onions, pickle and biscuit; something which would have suited them perfectly on most banyan days.

"It was on the captain's orders," King, who was passing by, told Flint's men.

"Kind of 'im, I'm sure," Harrison replied, picking at his gums with his finger.

"Aye," Thompson mumbled. "Probably thinks we'll die better with decent scran inside us."

"Any news of the enemy, sir?" Flint asked in a clearer voice. He had known King since the officer had been a raw volunteer and, despite the fact that Flint's career had failed to progress to the same extent, there was mutual respect between them.

King paused and squatted down to speak with the mess. "I've not been on deck for an hour or more," he said. "Last I heard they were still six or eight miles off our prow."

"Travelling slow for Frenchmen," Cranston commented.

"There's some talk about them having come from the Americas, so they might not be as spry," King replied.

"Or as well manned," Ross added.

"How do you work that out?" Thompson asked, suspiciously.

"Fever," the seaman replied briefly.

"He's right," Harrison agreed. "They got all sorts out there, you can take your choice."

"Long as barrel fever's included, I'm in," Thompson commented dryly.

"So when do you think we'll meet them?" Flint asked, and King shrugged.

"Blowed if I knows. *Aries*, the frigate, was off their larboard beam earlier; trying to steal past to make sure there weren't no more hiding ahead, and one of them let off a broadside in her direction. They were out of range, but it was trained straight: if the French are short of men, they've a fair few gunners left and no lack of powder."

"How far is Cádiz?" Ross asked, and King considered him for a moment. No mention had been made to the hands about the enemy's probable destination: he had worked it out for himself. But then King supposed it was no great mystery. The man was a former officer after all and, if he had retained his commission, might even have been his senior.

"We're comfortably through the Strait by now," he replied, glancing through the open port. "If that's where they're heading I would expect us to turn north-westerly at any time. Then it can't be more than fifty miles."

"Do you think there will be British thereabouts?" Ross again and, again, an intelligent question.

"Now that is something we can only guess," King replied. "Last heard, the Dons were neutral. We may have a couple of ships keeping watch, but there'll be no official blockade."

"Fifty mile ain't far," Flint pondered.

"No it isn't," Ross agreed. "And if they've come from the Indies, the French will know less than we do. So I'd say they'll go elsewhere."

"Not make straight for Cádiz?" King asked. "Why so?"

"If they've crossed without speaking to any ship, they may think us at war with Spain," he reasoned. "Everyone knows it will happen soon enough and, when it does, there is bound to be sanctions on every Spanish port. Three big ships might make it through from seaward and take a blockading force by surprise, especially if they come by night. But if we're on their tail, we should be close enough to give warning. And with our help, even an inshore squadron would snap them up, neatly enough."

"So you think they might give Cádiz a miss?" King asked, impressed, despite himself.

"To my mind; at first anyway." Ross confirmed. "I think our friends will carry on westerly in the hope of shaking us off, which they may well do in the dead of night."

"And then what?" Thompson asked.

"Well, there's no moon at present," Ross mused. "If we get a change of wind, I wouldn't put it beyond them to work past, leaving us sailing blindly into the Atlantic while they try their luck on Cádiz without us a chasing them." There was a pause while they all digested this, and then Ross added; "Sir."

* * *

It was five hours later, the wind had indeed veered and was now blowing just as strong but more from the south-east. *Prometheus* and the other British ships remained steady on their westward course and Caulfield was just considering going below to get what rest he could. His cabin would not exist, of course. Even though it lacked a gun to encumber the space, the frail bulkheads would have been knocked down with the rest and what had been the officers' wardroom would simply be an extension to the upper gun deck. He may get a hot drink from one of the stewards, if they were serving a nearby gun, but no more. And there would be little chance of conversation, something he craved even more than any bodily need at that moment. Then he saw King clambering stiffly up the quarterdeck ladder; he and the second lieutenant had been shipmates for years and Caulfield waited expectantly in the half light of dusk.

King noticed him and walked slowly over with the air of one who had been on his feet a good while, and expected to remain so for some time longer.

"Fancied a breath of fresh air did you, Thomas?" Caulfield asked as the younger man approached.

"Thought I'd leave Carlton in charge of the deck and take a peep at the enemy," King replied. "There's nothing to be seen from below; the French are so set on our prow that even the for'ard ports don't cover them."

"Then look your fill," the first lieutenant told him, adding, "but make it your last."

King glanced sidelong at him as they moved to the fife rail at the break of the quarterdeck.

"Sun'll be setting in no time," Caulfield explained. "It'll be pitch black within the hour."

Prometheus was now sailing in line abreast with *Canopus* to starboard while *Aries* sat well off their larboard bow. The French were in clear sight but still a good four miles ahead of the battleships.

"And we're still heading west?" King asked. It was a foolish question: the lowering sun was quite obvious and almost in their faces, but he craved conversation almost as much as the first lieutenant.

"Indeed, they seem set on shaking us off, though we shall surely catch them eventually." Caulfield stated confidently.

"And you don't think they might double back, in the darkness?" his friend whispered.

"Oh, I think it very likely," the first lieutenant replied. "Doubtless Sir Richard has considered the possibility as well, and shall take measures to see they do not."

"But what can he do?" King persisted, and Caulfield sighed.

"In truth, very little. Oh, he may set us further apart, and make certain all keep a sound lookout," he continued vaguely. "Send *Aries* in as close as she can lie, without risk of trying their mettle; other than that, not a great deal. There is no moon at present and we cannot set a line between us," he tried to force a laugh; the conversation was becoming far too serious and he was mildly disappointed: usually Thomas could be counted on for a measure of banter. "But why do you ask?"

"It was one of the men," King replied guardedly. "He mentioned the possibility."

"One of the men?" Caulfield reacted in astonishment. As first lieutenant he rarely spoke with the people on matters of strategy and was almost shocked that King should think of doing so. "You mean a hand?"

"Yes," King admitted. "Ross."

Caulfield nodded. Ross, yes, that perhaps made a little more sense. "You have mentioned him before," he said. "Commended him, as I recall, for his part in retaking the ship. And was it not you who brought the man to us originally?"

"I did, though that were pure chance," King replied. "But there is something I suppose you should know." His tone was still restrained; not like the spirited young man Caulfield knew at all, and he waited for him to continue with a feeling of trepidation.

"Ross was an officer."

"Indeed?" That was probably the last thing Caulfield had expected his friend to say.

"A lieutenant," King elaborated. "First of the brig, *Wakeful*. He was broken at court martial."

"I read of it for sure – Antigua, was it not?" Caulfield muttered as the memories came back. "A sad case, and one that painted few in a good light. I thought at the time their premier seemed to have paid the penalty, but didn't expect to find myself shipping with him. And an ordinary hand, you say?" He sighed softly before adding, "how are the people taking it?"

"They do not know. No one does – and they must not," King said, suddenly guilty. "I gave my word..."

Caulfield looked at him in further surprise. "If you gave your word, Tom, why ever do you speak of it now?" he asked. The two were friends without a doubt, but that did not excuse either of them from the normal constraints of gentlemanly conduct. Why, King was behaving as badly as that fellow Carroll.

"I – I am uncertain," King admitted and the first lieutenant was forced to concede that he did seem remarkably at a loss. "I suppose it must be all this talk of the French..."

There was silence as both men considered what had been said. As far as Caulfield was concerned, the shock of discovering one of their regular hands to have been a fellow officer was nothing compared to King's apparent disregard of a personal confidence. But then he also knew the young lieutenant well, and trusted him far more than most; if King had broken his word it could only have been done for the greater good. Vague memories of a recent conversation with Carroll hovered at the edges of his mind but he instantly dismissed them. This was a completely different situation: the two did not compare in any way.

"Never fear, I shall say nothing," Caulfield told him eventually. "If Ross were concerned about the enemy we can only assume he has our welfare very much in mind. But such a man may have caused any amount of mischief amongst the people. Were you prompted to tell me at all, I would have preferred it to have been earlier."

"It was not my secret," King explained, and received a brief nod of understanding in reply.

"But be assured, we had already considered the chance the French may double back," Caulfield continued. "That, or make a move to the north-east: either is a possibility. I cannot say it will not happen, or that, if it does, we will necessarily be aware. But in any event, we do not need the advice of a broken officer, sound though his intentions may have been."

"He wasn't attempting to advise," King said hurriedly. "And does not know I am even speaking with you. In truth, there never was a more loyal hand; I doubt that I would stay so in his position."

"No indeed, I see that," Caulfield allowed. "And a first officer, you say? It shows we can never foretell what may occur."

"And probably better so," King agreed.

Chapter Nineteen

The French made their move just after two bells in the middle watch although *Prometheus'* bell had not actually been struck since dusk. The night was at its darkest, those officially below were behaving like true seamen and taking the opportunity to drift into a deep and dreamless sleep, when all became suddenly awake. The fact that they had spotted the enemy's change of course was in no way down to Ross and his predictions; the manoeuvre was actually signalled by *Aries*, who had already dodged the wrath of two further broadsides in her effort to keep in touch with the French squadron. When she was finally certain of the new heading, the frigate sent up a rocket that shone painfully bright, before being engulfed by the absolute black of night.

"Summon the watch below," Banks growled. The cry was immediately taken up, and the deck became alive with men turning up from their various sleeping places. "Master: a course for Cádiz, if you please."

"All hands – all hands wear ship!" Cartwright called out in oddly restrained tones.

"Steer nor'-east by east," Brehaut told the quartermaster then, to his captain: "That will bring us to windward of the port, sir."

"Very good," Banks agreed. It was a wise move and Brehaut had done well to consider it. Arriving with the port on their lee gave them an advantage should no British forces be on station. And it also kept them the right side of the French during any pursuit. "Make to *Canopus* and *Aries* to follow."

The deck was briefly lit by the glow of four blue lights; the night signal for a starboard turn. *Canopus* might be the larger ship and John Conn's command of her no doubt indicated his position as one of Nelson's favourites. But Banks was senior on the captains' list, and would take charge of any action that might ensue.

Those on the quarterdeck could hear the rumble of feet on the hollow deck as the afterguard rose up to their duty, but few faces could be made out in the poor light. Then, with the squeal of blocks and a good few groans from her hull, *Prometheus* began to be eased through the wind.

The manoeuvre was completed with the minimum of fuss and soon the ship settled on her new heading, although the night remained so dark that little could be seen in any direction: even the masthead lookout was invisible to those on deck.

"Well, we can only hope to be following, and trust *Canopus* and *Aries* are doing likewise," Banks said to the officers who had instinctively clustered about the dim glow of the binnacle lamp. "But send all to quarters; if we run across a Frenchman there will be small enough warning."

Caulfield hissed to a midshipman, who made off into the gloom to pass on the order. "I think most will be awake by now," he said, after the lad had departed. "Indeed, they will be eager for a fight."

Banks supposed he was right. Even after so great a delay, the men would be more than ready to see their guns put to use, although he was also aware that the ship could not remain at action stations indefinitely. Once summoned to their pieces, even the strongest nerves would be stretched. Exhaustion would soon set in, and every man's fighting ability was bound to deteriorate. And if, as he suspected, the French were intending to avoid action and simply make a run for Spain, their current game of blind man's bluff could last a good few hours yet.

But it was not to be. Within minutes, those on the quarterdeck were alerted by the sound of one of the masthead lookouts slipping down the main topgallant backstay, and all waited in expectant silence as the man made his way to the command group on the quarterdeck.

"Liner to leeward," he announced excitedly, and Caulfield remembered him as being pressed from the homebound transport before they left Tor Bay. "Just off our larboard bow," Butler added excitedly. "But they've made sail, and we're losing 'er."

"Are you certain?" the first lieutenant questioned.

"Both me an' Jameson saw 'er, sir," the lookout confirmed.

"Very well, return to your post," Caulfield told him, before turning back to the group where Brehaut was in deep conversation with the captain. *Prometheus* was riding with the wind on her beam under staysails, topsails and forecourse, but the breeze was proving fickle in both strength and direction. To constantly set and strike canvas would only cause confusion, yet the night would remain dark for several more hours, and if they did nothing the French might steal a lead that could see them safely to Cádiz. It was not a decision the first lieutenant would wish to make.

"Set t'gallants," Banks voice rolled out strong in the hushed atmosphere, and there was a flurry of movement. Caulfield watched Brehaut mark out the order on the traverse board as the topmen began scaling the starboard shrouds. The extra sails would make *Prometheus* more visible, and could even endanger her masts, if there were any repetition of the gusts experienced during the first watch. But the captain was evidently content to risk that in return for the increase in speed more canvas would bring. It was a brave move, and one that might see them separated from *Canopus,* a ship that had already proven herself to be a slow sailer.

Banks looked to Caulfield. "Reckon we're in for a bit of a chase, Michael," he told him, as if the previous hours had not existed.

"Do you think they will make safety, sir?" the first lieutenant asked. It was probably not the most professional of questions, but the captain's sudden bouts of loquaciousness always caught him off guard.

"No, I think we shall see action afore then," Banks replied, and Caulfield could see the gleam of his smile in the green binnacle light. "At least, I hope so."

* * *

"Enemy is expected to larboard," King repeated for the fifth time as he strode down the length of the lower gun deck. With ports closed but battle lanterns alight and open, what was usually one of the darker areas in the ship was unusually well lit, and the men who stolidly moved across from their positions at the starboard guns could see each other remarkably well.

"Do we have a range, sir?" Flint asked as the lieutenant passed.

"Range, Flint?" King snorted. "We can't even be sure they're there – it's as black as Newgate's knocker outside. But be ready, all of you," he continued in a louder voice. "We're liable to run them down with little notice."

The men, though tired, revived at his words, and began checking their particular pieces of equipment. Then an excited squeal took everyone's attention, and one of the younger volunteers could be seen scampering down the companionway and over to Carlton, who was second in command of the main battery.

"Captain orders the guns run out to larboard," he panted.

"Is the enemy sighted?" King shouted across the crowded space.

"I don't believe so, sir," the lad replied doubtfully.

"Very well," King glanced back along the deck. "We'll have all lanterns closed, then open ports and run out your pieces," he said, and the order was quickly passed down the line. The various pin-points of light were quickly shuttered until only the faintest of cracks could be seen, but a glow came from the two companionways that led down to the orlop, directly beneath them.

It was where Manning had his medical team waiting in readiness. And there would be at least four lanthorns burning over the operating area. To larboard, the heavy ports were being heaved up amid a cloud of oakum dust, allowing a cold breeze to banish the close, moist atmosphere all had become accustomed to. And, as the solid black muzzles of the battleship's main armament were run out to stare at the empty night, King wondered if the orlop lights might be visible to an enemy. He supposed he could send a message to Manning, or maybe even nip down himself; he had not seen his old friend for ages and Carlton was quite capable of looking after the deck for thirty seconds. He could simply check all was in order, and possibly ask the surgeon to mask a couple of lamps.

And Judy would be there: she had responded well to the second chance Banks granted. This was ostensibly for the tireless work put in with the wounded, although King suspected her action in all but fatally poisoning that blackguard Carroll might have been an unmentioned factor in the captain's decision. But, whatever the reason, she was back to her previous duties and it was always good to see a pretty face.

King actually took a step towards the aft companionway, then felt himself abruptly stop. Suddenly he had no desire to meet with Manning, or Judy, or visit the orlop. It was as if the place, and all those who worked there, had become totally repugnant to him, and should be avoided at all costs.

There was nothing so very strange about that, he assured himself. He had witnessed a crowded cockpit during the heat of battle and there were few worse stations. Of course the action had yet to begin and there would be no wounded, but still he resolved to stay well away. The cold wind was now veritably howling through the open ports; it might have been summer, but there could be no doubting the chill of early morning. And that explained why he was actually shivering slightly as he waited for the action to begin.

* * *

An hour later, they were none the wiser. Occasional glimmers from astern showed where *Canopus* was slowly being left behind. She was on roughly the same course, though and all on deck knew the battleship would catch them quickly enough should they raise an enemy. But of the French there was no sign; either they were better at darkening ship than the British, or had altered course once more, and might be heading away in almost any direction at that very moment. Marines were stood to along the bulwarks, muskets loaded and bayonets fixed. Servers crowded about their guns and anyone with the merest glimpse of the outside world appeared to be looking out to sea. But only the black night stared back. Some would spot images, faint swirlings in the mist, or a flurry of spray as the breeze woke up a particularly proud wave, but these were soon revealed as the frauds they were, and nothing solid came to take their place. Nothing worthy of report, nothing but the night.

And then, impossibly, the outline of a ship began to take form off the larboard bow.

A low murmuring accompanied the discovery, alerting all who looked in that direction and drawing those whose attention had been elsewhere. She was laughably close, less than a cable off their prow, and steering roughly the same course as *Prometheus*.

The captain was the first to react, his mind beginning to spin even before he knew it. As they were, *Prometheus* must soon be alongside and in a position to exchange broadsides. And it was quite possible the French would be caught napping, enabling the battleship to serve before she received. But Banks could see a far better way of dealing with the situation. Providing, that is, he was as sure of his ship as he truly felt.

"Starboard the helm, Mr Brehaut; take us hard to larboard," he ordered, still staring at the enemy. "And Mr Caulfield, we shall take her with the starboard battery!"

Shouts came from the Frenchman, and a musket shot rang out, but by then those aboard the British battleship were already in action. At the long guns, men once more rushed across the decks before heaving their black monsters out to greet a vacant ocean. But all knew it could not stay that way for long; even as the pieces were secured, *Prometheus* began to heel as the wind swept her prow round. One moment they were pointing directly at the Frenchman's imposing stern, the next their speed increased, and the mighty battle-wagon was running down on the enemy's larboard quarter. Points of light began to appear on the British ship's upper deck: battle lanterns were being unmasked or re-lit, and a collective cheer erupted from the gunners as they steadily approached what was probably the finest firing position any of them had ever known.

The French were first, however: twin tongues of flame licked out from their stern mounted long guns, almost blinding anyone unfortunate enough to be looking in that direction, while the silent night was split with a deafening roar. The heavy shots struck low on *Prometheus'* hull, but she had been given a task to complete and neither paused, nor deviated from her course as she performed it.

"Ready Mr Benson..." Caulfield cautioned from the fife rail, but all on the upper gun deck were certainly so, as would be those at the thirty-two pounders under King's direction. Then, with a single shouted command, *Prometheus* spoke.

The broadside was simultaneous and neatly raked the Frenchman, knocking through her stern, and creating untold carnage and terror deep within the warship's hull. Watching from his position on the quarterdeck, Banks knew that the single barrage would have knocked much of the fight from his enemy. The shots would dig deep into her very vitals, killing men and destroying equipment; any vessel treated so would take an age to recover from such a drubbing.

But in performing the action he had also exposed his own ship to danger. The night held two more equally powerful enemy war machines; they would remain hidden, but now must know exactly where *Prometheus* was to be found.

"Masthead, what do you see there?" The captain's voice had to battle against the cheering of his own men, as well as a rumble of gun carriages as the starboard pieces were served.

"What do you see there?" Brehaut repeated, with the advantage of a speaking trumpet.

"Only the immediate enemy, sir," Butler's voice came back apologetically.

"You, boy – get aloft to the masthead," Banks snapped at a nearby midshipman who was gazing, white-faced, into the night. The lad was still apparently in shock at seeing the devastating results a single close-ranged broadside could achieve. But it was possible the lookouts had committed the cardinal sin of losing their night sight, or even that this particular Frenchman had become separated from her consorts, and an extra pair of young eyes was not to be wasted.

Another flash, and the crack of a single enemy cannon, followed by two others and, after a pause, three more. *Prometheus* was now passing her opponent's larboard side, and evidently some of the French crew were sufficiently alert to reply, if only in a derisible manner.

"Take her further to larboard," Banks snarled as the deck beneath him jarred with the impact of heavy shot. *Prometheus* was a solid ship, with sides made up from several layers of oak and elm and specifically designed to take such punishment. But the Frenchman was close by, and Banks could not afford to suffer any unnecessary damage. More to the point, that single, raking broadside had started a small fire deep within the enemy battleship. By its light he could already make out their own topsails and, if they were visible to those aboard *Prometheus*, others further off would also spot them.

"Deck there, enemy in sight to larboard!" It was Adams, the midshipman he had sent aloft. The boy must have made the ascent in record time, and was already proving his worth.

"Where away?" Caulfield shouted before Banks had the chance.

"Right on our larboard beam!" Adams replied. "We're in the perfect position!"

"Ready larboard battery," the first lieutenant ordered, and there was a moment's disorder as the starboard pieces, as yet not fully served, were abandoned in favour of their opposite numbers.

"Belay that!" Banks shouted, his voice breaking in sudden excitement. He sensed Caulfield's confusion, but there was no time to explain. The captain rushed across the quarterdeck and, thrusting aside a pair of marines standing sentinel, leaned out over the top rail.

There was the ship Adams had spotted, right enough and a line-of battleship without a doubt. The lad had also been correct with regard to their firing position. The last turn had placed *Prometheus* neatly across her bows; it would only need for them to spill their wind to be able to deal a devastating blow upon the vulnerable prow.

"Is there a problem, sir?" Caulfield asked, joining his captain.

"There would be, if we opened fire," Banks replied, nodding towards the dark shape that was gradually taking form at point blank range from their loaded battery. "That's *Canopus*."

* * *

"Belay larboard and continue serving the starboard pieces," King ordered, when the message reached him. He peered through an open port, and guessed what had so nearly happened. Their consort must have increased sail on seeing *Prometheus* go into battle, and come up on their lee. Such things were hardly unusual in the confusion of battle and, given the present conditions, Banks could hardly have been blamed if he had fired on her. But serving such a devastating blow against *Canopus* would have affected *Prometheus* almost as much. A well timed broadside could only have taken out a large proportion of her crew, to say nothing of the material damage inflicted on the British liner. Once so weakened, it was extremely likely the French would have overpowered them both, even with one of their own number severely damaged.

"What do you see there?" he asked a quarter gunner who was peering through one of the starboard ports.

"The Frenchie we raked is taking fire, sir," Guillom, a seasoned hand, reported. "I'd say we hit her hard, but there's no sign of any of the others."

"What of *Canopus*?" King asked.

"She's turned to starboard and is coming past our stern; looks as if she intends finishing the Frog off."

King considered this; it was probably wise to make sure the wounded Frenchman was totally silenced although, in doing so, Conn would be exposing his own ship to the light of her flames.

"Starboard battery ready," Carlton told him, adding, "I've sent the word to Mr Benson."

"Very good," King muttered. They had done well to reload so quickly, especially with the distraction of being called to the larboard guns. *Prometheus* was once more able to deal a blow on either side, and may have to do so at any moment.

Or she might continue into the dark night, gamely feeling her way, with all eyes straining for further enemies, yet not encounter another until dawn. Really there was no telling when this game might end, but he was certain it would last a while longer.

* * *

But King did not have to wait long; no one did. As predicted, *Canopus* passed their taffrail, and took position off the wounded

248

Frenchman's quarter. The solid thump of a broadside followed, and was repeated in good time by another just as devastating. Banks, who had retreated alone to the starboard bulwark to think, watched from the darkness and relative safety that distance had bought them. He could well understand Conn's desire to involve himself in the fray, but there could be no fight left in the enemy battleship now, and every second the British ship remained illuminated by her funeral pyre, was time allowed the other two enemy vessels to re-form. And then, even as he thought, there came another call from Adams at the masthead, and Banks knew he had been correct.

"Two ships running down off our starboard beam," Caulfield announced as Banks rejoined the group at the binnacle. "I should chance it to be the French coming back to save their own."

That was exactly what Banks had anticipated, and it was a trifle annoying not to be able to say so. But, more importantly, *Canopus* might be unaware; the fire, burning so close to her, would rob those on board of any vision in the dark.

"Port the helm, take us four points to starboard," he commanded, and the orders were swiftly translated into a series of shouts and responses. There was no time to signal *Canopus*; but if he could bring *Prometheus* round in time, he may still be able to alert her to the danger in a less conventional manner.

"What of the sighting, masthead?" he shouted, as the ship was brought closer to the wind.

"First is fine off our larboard bow, and a good three cables' distance. The other I have lost for now, but she were a way behind."

Banks was satisfied; *Prometheus* had ceased to turn and would be coming on the enemy out of the darkness. He was not one to trust much to fortune but, on this occasion felt unusually confident. With luck they were heading for an encounter every bit as successful as the last.

Chapter Twenty

They had five patients so far and none had taxed them any. Manning stood up gingerly after tending to the last, his head bowed to clear the low deckhead. It had been the simple amputation of a waister's right arm that was smashed at the elbow. Before that, two men had been brought down with the self inflicted injuries that were to be expected when firing heavy cannon in dark, confined spaces. One nursed a broken leg, caused by being in the wrong place when the beast discharged while another had been careless enough to drop a thirty-two pound round shot directly onto his foot. There was also a minor splinter wound, and one of the midshipmen had succumbed to mild hysterics after a French eighteen pound ball came clean through an open port and missed his head by inches.

But from several years' service, Manning knew the party was only just beginning to warm, and a good many more could be expected to clutter his clear and still orderly space on the orlop. And he was not alone in his experience; although he had yet to see them properly stretched in an extended engagement, both his assistants had previously seen fleet action at least twice, with Dodgeson being a veteran of Copenhagen. His loblolly boys also appeared relatively practised, and were not indulging in the irreverent chatter so common in those yet to know the terrors of a crowded cockpit. It was just the girl, Judy, who caused him to worry.

With such a history he, as a professional man, had objected strongly when she was posted to looking after wounded prisoners. And even after her tireless efforts had reclaimed a measure of respect, part of him was still only prepared to tolerate her presence with a good deal of caution. The incident with the Irishman, Carroll, had hardly helped. He could appreciate the measure of poetic justice involved, but to deliberately poison a prisoner went against a score of moral and legal codes.

Yet Manning was not without compassion; Judy was hardly

the brightest of sparks, and her remorse for what she had done to her rescuers was obvious. He was also more than familiar with the numerous ways the human body could fail and, in his opinion she had simply exhibited a recurring weakness. Were her symptoms to have been physical: a deformed limb, or bouts of giddiness, the ailment would have been defined as medical, and addressed. But this was something far more subtle: Judy had shown a pathological tendency to trust.

It was hardly a major defect by anyone's standards even if, as Manning knew, the condition had already endangered her own life on more than one occasion. And, as far as he was concerned, there was no specific remedy; character faults being way beyond any correction by surgical intervention. She would either have to diagnose the disorder herself, and make the appropriate allowances, or become resigned to a lifetime of being constantly hoodwinked and beguiled. Such a prospect offered only a very poor prognosis, so he was prepared to tolerate her presence in his medical department, and even bestow on her the care and almost respect he would give any chronically ill patient.

But if Judy's character had a defect, it was balanced to some extent by an attribute that was truly valuable. Manning knew of her ability with food, and accepted this as a natural talent, but her prowess in other areas was, to a surgeon's mind at least, far more precious. For Judy had an innate understanding of the human body. More than that, she seemed able to see past physical disorders and discern a patient's inner wants, be it food, rest, or other natural requirements. This had quickly been accepted when dealing with the injured prisoners; even those without a word of English seemed able to communicate their needs to her. But dealing with patients who expected nothing from their captors was a different matter from attending her own kind. And when the English wounded began to arrive, Manning became concerned.

The first, who had broken three toes from dropping the round shot, objected strongly when Judy attempted to examine his foot. Manning swiftly intervened, but it was a similar situation with the splinter patient. From what he understood, wild stories were still circulating about the young woman who, as legend had it, had come so close to accounting for all of the officers as well as a good many bootnecks into the bargain. Only the troubled midshipman, perhaps through greater understanding or need, had shown any faith and even then seemed more inclined to believe the girl to be his mother. And soon she would be needed. There were few major actions that proved anything like as economical as the present one and Manning was not so blessed with medical staff to be able to delegate any of his team to less personal duties.

He watched her now as she sat poring over the instruments laid out ready. He had shown her the basic items, and most were now memorised, or at least she was currently making some attempt to do so; her lips moving silently as each was examined before being placed back in line. Judy may well be of use assisting him in operations, but if they became as busy as he feared, such a luxury would not be possible and her help would be needed elsewhere.

* * *

"They've finally seen us!" Lewis shouted, as the two red flashes marked fire from the enemy's bow chasers.

But he was wrong, Banks decided. Even though flames from the burning battleship were some way off, the Frenchman would have been able to make out *Prometheus* bearing down on them at a bowline snapping angle for a good while. In these present conditions that meant upwards of thirty seconds, and the enemy gunners must have been holding their fire until a better target presented.

The delay might mean that whoever commanded his current opponent was of a slightly higher calibre. Banks still could not believe the ease with which he had surprised the first liner. Admittedly *Prometheus* must have appeared like a ghost from out of the night, and the Frenchman was now offering a spirited defence to *Canopus'* subsequent attack. But, he told himself, it had still been a remarkably fortunate encounter.

The two ships were still approaching each other at a fair rate and he mentally braced himself for a more challenging duel. One of them would have to turn shortly and it was anyone's guess as to who, and which way it would be.

"Mr Brehaut, we shall be steering to larboard on my word. Mr Caulfield, kindly warn the starboard battery. And for this engagement see the lower deck re-loads with double round; we shall have bar for the upper deck and carronades, with targets appropriate."

The orders were repeated for confirmation then passed on their way. Whichever direction the enemy chose, it was wise to select his response now, so there would be no confusion. Should the French make their turn to starboard he would be presented with the ideal chance to rake the enemy's bows, whereas a move to larboard meant they must meet broadside to broadside. The latter was probably the more likely, and would also give his opponent an advantage in speed. But Banks felt in his bones that his choice was correct and soon, very soon, he would discover if he was right.

* * *

King felt the deck beneath him heel slightly; they were taking on speed and the stem was digging deeper into the waves. It was unlikely that Banks was adding additional sail so he guessed the wind had changed yet again.

"Target will be to starboard," a young voice called down from the aft companionway, and Carlton's almost equally youthful tenor repeated the information to those standing ready at the guns.

Now they had actually fired their pieces, the atmosphere had changed significantly on the lower gun deck. No longer were there any instances of chatter, inappropriate laughter, or even quiet conversation; the men were standing patiently, simply waiting for the chance to act once more. Of course a thick haze of smoke still hung in the air, and the fact that every one of them was mildly deafened was a contributing factor to their subdued behaviour, but King felt any concerns he might have had about cowardice or panic could be ignored, at least for the time being.

"Captain wants the lower battery to aim for the hull, and reload starboard with double round," the voice from the deck above continued and Carlton immediately relayed the message.

King heard the exchange, and was certain every gun captain had taken note; but only slowly, when he had chance to reflect, did he realise the importance of such a command.

Double shotting the guns would reduce their reach and accuracy; Banks must be intending closing with the enemy to such a distance that neither would be vital. King supposed such short range work was inevitable, considering the conditions, but it also meant little warning could be expected before a target was revealed while, in addition, any shot received from the French was bound to be that much more lethal. Currently there was no ship in sight, at least from the limited view provided by the lower deck gun ports, yet *Prometheus* was apparently about to go into action. So they were clearly planning to surprise their target, and might be opening fire at any time.

King managed a pace or two along the crowded deck as he considered matters; this was quite unlike any battle he had ever fought; even night-time actions, when viewed from the upper deck of a frigate, held no such mystery. The weapons under his command were of far greater power than any he had ever controlled in the past, yet he had far less of an idea how they would be used. He could only hope the enemy would not stay hidden for long and that, when they were finally revealed, he and his men would be ready for them.

* * *

But Banks and others on the quarterdeck had no such concerns. From their superior vantage point, they could see the mass of tophamper that marked out the enemy battleship fine off their bow, and hardly more than a cable away. She was sailing with the wind just forward of her quarter, and all eyes strained to see the first sign of a turn. Banks swallowed, momentarily disconcerted. If she did not alter course but continued, apparently content for *Prometheus* to slice off her jib boom, he would actually be caught out. With the starboard battery alerted there might not be time to man their larboard guns: the Frenchman could pass well within ideal range, with hardly a shot fired from the British. There were several seconds of acute worry, then the enemy's forecourse and topsail were seen to shiver, and her hull fell away to larboard.

"Turn," he snapped at Brehaut and, so ready were all for the order, that the ship began to heel almost immediately. His opponent had actually chosen the safer option, but they would be passing so close as to make any difference almost immaterial.

"Below! There's another following!" Adams' frantic call from the masthead came just as *Prometheus* had completed her turn, and was almost a distraction. But Banks' brain was accepting the information even as Caulfield called for the starboard guns to fire. Another enemy, another change of heading, and another broadside: *Prometheus* was ready and capable of all. Really, Banks felt, things could not have turned out better.

* * *

The British ship's starboard side erupted in a wall of flame less than a second before their opponent began to return the compliment. And the reply came with none of the Frenchman's usual habit of aiming at spars. Neither was it instantaneous. Delayed by her own barrage, for upwards of twenty seconds, a succession of round shot struck *Prometheus* hard and repeatedly in an area concentrated solely about the level of the lower gun deck, and at a range close enough to puncture even a third rate's substantial sides.

The well ordered structure that King supervised dissolved into carnage as the first of the French shot burst through the wooden walls. Screams from the wounded followed swiftly, although few penetrated the deadened ears of servers still trying to tame their guns. Hot iron and equally deadly splinters flew about the packed and confined space, a thick smell of burning caused men to choke, while battle lanterns were hurled to the deck, creating darkness where none was required and starting several small fires. Shot was knocked from the garlands, both fore and main masts received glancing blows, and four of the battleship's own cannon were hit.

Flint's was the first. Struck by a heavy ball, its carriage instantly disintegrated into a dozen well sized splinters while the barrel reared up and over, landing squarely on two of its carers. Thompson happened to be one: the man who had lured Judy aboard *Prometheus*, was killed outright, whereas the toothless Harrison survived, although his smashed legs lay trapped under the tremendous weight of hot iron. Further aft, another gun was hit on the edge of its muzzle, sending the still mounted cannon slewing about to point disconcertingly down the length of the deck, while further round shot entered next to number five, and accounted for an entire side of servers. Midshipman Chivers cried out and some quirk of fate allowed King to hear him amid the cacophony of destruction. He turned to see the lad drop to the deck, knowing him to be dead even before the body landed.

"Secure your pieces: sponge your guns!" King's brain might refuse to register what was happening but, so ingrained was the task, that he continued to control the men as if by instinct. "Remmer – that side tackle needs clearing - Moffat, set that round shot to order!" He paused and drew breath, then spotted something anew. "Fire party there at number seven!"

As he watched, his orders were gradually responded to and some degree of order emerged. King was well aware that *Prometheus'* own broadside should have caused every bit as much damage and confusion to the enemy, and the ultimate winner would be the one who continued firing when the other had stopped.

Forward, he could see that Carlton, the new lieutenant, was also on top of matters. The young man's voice cracked painfully as damage parties and gunners were directed in their work, but he was keeping his head and obviously understood the importance of their well practised routine beginning again. King nodded in silent approval, making a private note to mention his attention to duty when the opportunity presented. And then all such thoughts were made redundant.

For Carlton was also dead, struck by a late shot that came through an open port and left no room for doubt. King watched as the lieutenant's broken body was pushed roughly to one side and soberly accepted that he was now in sole charge of *Prometheus'* main armament.

But there was no time for deeper thought, he must take action if total chaos were to be avoided. There were still ten apparently sound guns; some might lack full teams but, with a few well chosen orders, those from damaged weapons were soon transferred.

In the midst of his reorganisation a man ran past, clutching at his shattered arm: King ignored him, as he did Harrison, a less mobile casualty, who shrieked a series of obscenities while the remains of his team tried to lever the heavy barrel from his legs. From aft came the hiss of steam: someone with an element of nouse had turned a wash-deck pump on the smouldering remains of a heavy round shot, and a team made up of one designated hand from every gun began to systematically clear the deck of the wounded and dead. And gradually all immediate dangers were dealt with: men began to return to more normal duties and finally the process of serving *Prometheus'* guns could start once more.

Within a very few minutes of receiving the French broadside, King saw the first of what shortly became several hands held high as gun captains squared their pieces. There was thunder from above: the upper deck were already releasing their broadside as he guiltily called his men to order. Benson's battery could not have been so badly hit as his own, and time had certainly been lost. But it was hardly irretrievable, and he swiftly dispatched those of his own cannon that were loaded, before abandoning simultaneous broadsides and ordering independent fire from the entire battery.

The last command had not come from the quarterdeck, but was given on his own initiative. There could be no doubt the lower gun deck had been hit especially hard. Only a few of King's crews had escaped intact; most were short of men or troubled by damage but to limit the firing rate of those unaffected to that of the slowest was madness. He supposed it was one of the advantages of being in sole command, and even smiled to himself at the thought, before snapping back to the work in hand and bellowing at a man staring stupidly at a wad hook as if wondering its purpose.

Another of the monsters nearby fired, and another after that until all the guns left intact were giving a creditable performance, and even those men detailed to deal with the dead and wounded had started to make headway on their grim task.

But the French were also active; after their first, drawn out barrage they had also apparently opted for independent fire and, from such a close distance, their shots were breaking through *Prometheus'* heavy timbers with worrying regularity. Despite this, King knew his men were performing well; they might not be setting any records for speed or efficiency but, amidst such chaos, it was surprising the lower battery worked at all.

And he was also keeping his head. King knew himself to be less than the fire-brand he tried to portray, and secretly worried about his occasional bout of soft heartedness. But in the current bedlam there was no room for such niceties and he found himself screaming at the sweating bodies to stretch themselves still further, while vehemently wishing his guns were causing similar devastation across the short stretch of dark water.

The noise was almost constant now; if a British cannon was not in the act of firing then shot was being received from the French. A thick cloud of smoke threatened to engulf what light there was from the remaining battle lanterns, and the lads carrying powder were desperately dodging unexpected obstacles as they carried their deadly loads to the waiting guns. There was no way of knowing the state of the action but this was undoubtedly warm work. Then a section of bulwark directly opposite was blown in, and the Frenchman's fire suddenly became very much more personal.

King watched, transfixed, as the heavy ball entered, even noticing the fair sized hole it punched between two adjacent ports, thus expending much of the raw energy that could have carried the thing on for at least a further thousand yards. But there was momentum enough remaining for it to rip into *Prometheus'* inner timbers, and certainly sufficient for a swath of well worn oak to be torn into a dozen deadly splinters. And King actually saw the one that made for him, felt the chunk of wood that ripped through his arm before puncturing the side of his thorax. It was just below the level of his heart and the shard was naturally sharp, entering his body with little more pain than a gentle caress.

A part of his jacket fell away, and he gasped as what felt like something large filled an important void deep within him.

Breathing became difficult, then impossible. He noticed with dispassionate interest that blood, his blood, was flowing down, staining the second best pair of white britches donned especially before going ashore the previous morning. His left arm was also bleeding and swung impotently at his side, and there was a sudden feeling of heat that came, then went, in a single instant. The sounds of hell echoed about his head before mercifully fading, to be replaced by feelings of peace, light and an odd sense of reassurance. He knew himself to be lying on the deck, although how he arrived there remained a mystery. And then, at last, came a deep and blessèd, silence.

Chapter Twenty-One

On the quarterdeck, no one was aware quite how badly the lower battery had been hit: their main concern was damage done to the enemy. Already the two ships were drawing apart on opposing tacks but, even as their opponent dwindled into the night, the changes to her tophamper were obvious. Fire from the British ship's upper deck and carronades had been both devastating and accurate; the enemy's mizzen topmast was the first to go and soon the main followed. Now, as they watched, the foremast was also apparently in danger, although all that could really be seen was the white waves of canvas as they floated down, robbed of support. *Prometheus* had inflicted definite and decisive hits to the Frenchman's hull as well; in several places adjoining gun ports had been knocked into one, both levels of the starboard quarter galleries were all but destroyed and the enemy's starboard mainchains had disappeared, meaning any sizeable wind from that side should see them totally dismasted. But however loud the men might cheer, Banks knew that no respite would be possible. There was another, undamaged and possibly more deadly, enemy following, and they must act now, or be caught napping.

"Mr Brehaut, lay her to starboard, if you please. As close to the wind as she will lie." The sailing master reacted immediately and, despite their excitement, the afterguard was not so very far behind. "What see you, masthead?" Banks called up to the invisible Adams.

"Approaching enemy is two cables off," the boy replied, timing his words between gunfire. "Steering a steady course and coming across our prow as we turn."

That was good, the captain told himself. He just hoped they could gain enough sea room before they were caught in irons. All stared forward into the gloom, but there was no sign of a Frenchman's bows.

"Even if we make it, we should soon be trapped by the wind," Caulfield voice was low but it spoke surprisingly close to him, and

Banks realised he had been standing right next to the first lieutenant for some while. "And it will be tight; no closer than a biscuit toss," he added, enunciating each word clearly, to make sure his captain heard.

Banks did not reply, but took note. More to the point, Caulfield's statement had alerted him to the fact that the two ships might run foul of the other. If their yardarms were to touch and tangle, the French could board, and he was not sure if those in *Prometheus* were ready to repel a determined attack. He wished there had been chance, and space, to tack; allowing him to present their broadside to the oncoming enemy's bows. But voicing regret would not change the wind and, even as he thought, Banks accepted the fact that it was also starting to fade.

"It will be close, without a doubt," he agreed instead. "Make certain upper deck and carronades reload with grape on round, and switch their aim for the hull; do you think we should prompt King to reload the larboard battery with double?"

"He will surely notice the distance and do so without our interference," Caulfield replied, confidently. "Why Benson has already told off his crews without our asking: see, there is grape drawn."

Caulfield was right, although Benson had a better view of the action than King, who was stuck deep below in the bowels of the ship. But then the second lieutenant was a seasoned gunnery officer, and must notice how close they were off the third target. He would reload with double round without their prompting; it was the obvious choice for anyone with experience.

* * *

But King was not on the lower gun deck; that station, arguably the most important in *Prometheus* at the time, had been without command for several minutes. His limp body was finally collected by two men detailed for just such a task and, noticing some possibility of life, they half carried, half dragged it down the aft companionway and onto the deck below.

"Another for you, witch," one told Judy pragmatically as it

was placed on the canvas covered deck beside her.

"I don't want no more dead ones," she replied with equal frankness and without taking her attention from the wounded marine that was only just being persuaded to sip lemonade.

"That one ain't dead," the second man told her, glancing back at his load. "He's an officer, an' a good one, so no messing with any of your evil concoctions or there'll be the devil to pay."

"And no pitch hot enough," the other agreed as they walked away.

She said nothing; insults from the seamen had been common since she was caught colluding with the Irishman, although Judy was stoical enough to ignore them. Besides, she had sorted the little worm's lot in a way that no one else appeared to have noticed. And, despite her apparently brusque attitude, she cared greatly for those under her charge. Her current patient had lapsed into a deep sleep and Judy gently lowered him back to the deck, before turning to assess the new arrival.

"Oh Lordy!" she said in horror, as a familiar, but whitened, face stared back vacantly at her. King's shirt was soaked in blood and a large lump of wood protruded through the torn material. "Mr Manning," she shouted at the surgeon who was bent over his operating table only a few feet away. "It's Mr King, he needs your help!"

But it was as if she had not spoken; the surgeon's total concentration remained on his current patient, and Judy wondered if she should repeat herself. Only some lengthy seconds later did Manning's gaze lift, his expression a mixture of surprise and anger.

"I cannot attend," he told her quickly. "He shall have to wait: do what you can for him."

Judy looked back at the body: it was the first patient who had been known to her. Mr King: the smart lieutenant who let her call him Tom, and she secretly found rather attractive. The one who discovered her in the forepeak, and had remained a friend since, even to the extent of speaking up to the captain when her terrible crime was discovered. In return Judy had been pleased to warn the first lieutenant about the duel, and there was nothing she would not do to help him further. But as to what, well she hardly knew where to start.

She pulled back the torn flap of blue jacket and what remained of King's cotton shirt before gasping for a second at the evil shard of oak that lay embedded in the young man's chest. The majority appeared to be pressed between his ribs and skin, although some might have bypassed the bone, and be resting inside the chest cavity. Blood continued to seep from the wound and no great medical knowledge was needed to deduce it was the wooden splinter itself that allowed such a steady flow.

There was a rag that had served her well until that moment but, seeing it was a new and special patient, she reached for fresh, and soaked it liberally in the spirit supplied for just such a purpose. Once cleaned, the wound was more presentable, although the bleeding remained constant. Desperately her gaze travelled back to the surgeons but both Mr Manning and his two assistants were far too busy to be disturbed. Then she took a firm grip on the warm fragment of wood, and began to heave.

It came surprisingly easily and was soon free, even if small remnants remained in the jaws of the lesion. Picking delicately at these, Judy repeatedly dabbed at the area with her cloth and when the two loblolly boys came looking for their next patient, she was quick to catch their attention.

"I have removed a splinter," she told the surgeon, as the body was placed on the soiled platform of midshipmen's chests that formed Manning's operating table. "Though there may be traces that remain."

Manning examined the wound, pressing it with his fingers and pulling out the occasional sliver of wood that came to the surface. "It is as clean a job as I could wish for," he told her softly, "though he requires a deal of attention."

"But you will look after him?" she questioned.

"I will," he replied evenly. "Tom is my friend as well."

* * *

The ship began to turn to starboard and Ross was at a loss. All about him men were working furiously; the guns were in the main secured, though those that had been hit still lay at odd angles, their muzzles either pointing downwards, or at an oblique slant, while his own was simply lying sideways on the ragged remains of a former messmate. Harrison had eventually been released and should by now be safe in the hands of the medical team on the deck below. In fact it appeared all of the wounded were cleared, while those of the dead who could be reached had been despatched through a convenient gun port. And with some degree of order restored, it was obvious to him that command was the next requirement.

He could hear the rumble of wheels as the larboard battery on the deck above was run out. The target to starboard was now out of their arc of fire but he could appreciate the likelihood of the third enemy being immediately behind and, with the ship turning yet again, guessed it to be to larboard. A distant order filtered down; that would be lieutenant Benson who had charge of *Prometheus'* secondary armament. When a lieutenant himself, Ross had commanded gun decks in two ships. He knew what needed to be done, and that any distraction would not be appreciated. A midshipman, if there were any left, or one of the quarter gunners may well appeal to Benson for assistance, but it was unlikely the man would have either time or energy to supervise both decks. One of the senior warrant officers, or possibly the fifth lieutenant, might be found at length, but if the guns were to continue to fire efficiently it was a job that required immediate attention. And here he was, trained, experienced, and well versed in the work: there really was no option.

"Pay attention there, secure starboard battery and attend the larboard!" his voice rang out far louder than it had for many months, and carried with it a note of command that amazed himself almost as much as those he served with. But, apart from a few foolish grins and rather more blank expressions, no one actually responded.

"Do you hear me there? Larboard battery, and now!" Desperation was giving even more authority to his words, yet still the men regarded him with little other than tolerance. "You, there: Guillom: do you see a target for'ard?"

The quarter gunner; a petty officer who supervised four thirty-two pounders and comfortably out-ranked any able seaman, stared back for a good second before dutifully making for a forward port.

"Enemy liner is in sight," he replied, turning back and looking at Ross as if having just performed some special trick. "She's a cable to larboard, and we're going to pass her close," then, still with the look of wonder on his face he added: "Sir."

A cable to larboard was tight work indeed; Ross was surprised the captain had not ordered them to double shot the larboard battery.

"Stand to your pieces," he ordered, beginning the routine, as he had a thousand times on past occasions. "Now, check your priming."

The men dutifully attended to their weapons; each captain carefully inspected the fine mealed powder that would ignite the main charge, before flipping forward the frizzen on the gun locks, and drawing back their hammers to full cock.

"I have her!" someone from far forward shouted excitedly, and a buzz of anticipation ran down the larboard side of the deck.

"Hold fast there, hold fast!" Ross snapped. He had not controlled a battery for many months and was unlikely ever to do so again: this one last chance was not to be ruined by any premature discharges. "We'll fire off as loaded, but serve the next double-shotted." There were nods of comprehension from the loaders as Ross continued. "Now, wait upon my word," he added, striding up the deck with total authority.

And they all did exactly as they were told.

* * *

There was perhaps the faintest lightening in the sky; but it was far too early for dawn and with no moon due, Banks turned back and saw the blaze from the first ship they had engaged. Beside her, but not too close, *Aries* could be seen in the process of lowering boats, while *Canopus* had moved on and was doing all she could in such light airs to close with the second Frenchman. He switched his attention back; Conn, with what must be a relatively intact eighty, should be able to deal with a damaged seventy-four without trouble, which left him free to direct all his attention to the present problem.

The enemy was hard by and, every four or five minutes, fired her bow chasers into *Prometheus*, while they replied with far more celerity and speed, using their forward facing long nines. The British ship remained underway, but was moving with such reluctance that her rudder could be of little use, and Banks knew he was relying more on a fortunate current for forward motion than any wind. But progress there was; his opponent became clearer with every gun flash and, when one particularly lucky shot started a small fire on her forecastle, it was obvious the time when they might properly exchange broadsides was near.

Presumably a similar thought had struck his opposite number. The Frenchman's helm had been put across in the hope of bringing her broadside to bear on the British ship's bows but now, as such a move was proving impossible, she was correcting, and appeared content to wait until the two met side on. Then, almost imperceptibly, the wind began to rise.

It came with hardly more force than a breath, then grew, causing men to look to each other in doubt, before peering up through the gloom to their sails. The canvas that had been hanging torpid and flat, first rippled, then flapped, and soon was billowing softly.

Prometheus responded well: there was a murmur from the stays, her rudder bit and then the quartermaster could finally make that much needed point to starboard. With the rise, the wind had also veered, giving them far more space for a considered distance, although Banks now felt there was less need for room. He had no knowledge of any deficiencies below; all damage reports so far received had mostly come from the upper deck or spars. And King was well known to him: any major problem would have been relayed promptly enough, and the lad would not bother his captain with anything less. Consequently Banks was quite prepared to match his well proven guns against any Frenchman, undamaged or not: actually he was looking forward to the prospect.

* * *

Judy had done well; the wound was clean and almost free from debris, although Manning was still not confident. Splinter wounds alone were bound to account for a good proportion of the casualties he would be dealing with that night, and carried a far greater risk of infection than the effects of more conventional weapons. Even as he worked, stitching deep into the mess of muscle and tissue that currently constituted his friend's chest, he knew he may be leaving fragments behind. Fragments that would stay hidden long enough to indicate a good recovery, when their festering presence would finally be revealed. He knew, but there was little he could do about it; King had already lost a great deal of blood and, in the make-do surgery he was forced to practise, the immediate need was to achieve a sound closure.

And so he worked, with half a brain set on the difficulties of keeping the stitches even, while the rest of his mind tracked movement all around. Of his two mates, Dodgeson was proving faster in attending to his charges, but that was in keeping with the man's more brittle personality, and Manning knew the more careful Prior would not be slacking. The flow of casualties had slowed; there were still many awaiting attention, but it was not an inordinate number and all would be dealt with, even if it took the rest of the night.

That the action was in no way over had also been noted. The ship appeared to be underway following a brief period of calm, and Manning had worked through enough major battles in the past to know the difference between an interval and the end of a performance. There was none of the excitement common when an enemy either surrendered or attempted to board, so further fighting, and subsequent casualties, could be expected.

But no part of his thinking was reserved for King the person; his best friend, and shipmate for most of his adult life. He tied off the last stitch and motioned to Judy, who appeared to have abandoned all other work to assist him. She wiped down King's chest with a liberal amount of spirit, then did so again using a cleaner piece of tow. Manning said nothing as he watched. He

267

knew he must continue to take a dispassionate view and his prognosis was exactly on those lines.

"*The patient has sustained major trauma to the upper chest, with complications stemming from the impact and removal of a large fragment of wooden debris,*" he told himself, taking refuge in the impartial prose of a surgeon's report. "*After cleansing, the wound has been closed, and it is hoped that convalescence will encourage a full recovery.*"

For a moment he stopped and thought some more: he had further to add and, despite the inevitable conclusion being painful, it must be reached.

"*There is, however, the risk that latent foreign matter remains within the lesion, which will inevitably cause an imbalance in the humors and subsequent mortification. A further operation might rid the patient of this if the corruption is not too deeply seated although, once established, the malady is likely to remain and no permanent recovery can be expected.*"

Chapter Twenty-Two

Those on the lower gun deck had long since dismissed the novelty of being commanded by an able seaman. Ross knew what he was about and, in a service where skilled men with a lifetime's experience were expected to take orders from privileged children, they instinctively sensed competence and felt comfortable in his control.

"What see you there?" he growled at Guillom once more, and the quarter gunner bent through the open port yet again.

"We got the wind, and are gaining speed," he shouted back. "For'ard broadside guns will be coming into range shortly."

Ross nodded, but did not speak further. The command to open fire would come soon enough and his true responsibilities began when the enemy started to hit back. In case of injury, men would have to be moved, making up numbers from one gun to another, while the regular supply of powder could not be interrupted. Only by constant attention could the main guns continue to fire. If they should ever stop, *Prometheus* would be taken for certain, and it was down to him to see they did not.

* * *

"Captain orders independent fire, and as you bear!"

The order was screamed down the aft companionway by a voice surely far too young to carry such a message. But it was heard by most on the lower gun deck and, at a supplementary command from Ross, all crews immediately stood to.

"Keep 'em laying straight!" he added quickly, as some captains made to train their pieces forward. Several seconds might be gained by aiming the guns so, but Ross knew the angle of impact would be altered: their shots would not penetrate the enemy's hull so easily, and might even be deflected. "Range will be less than point blank," he continued. "Should we touch, fully depress your pieces."

In a true close action, shot aimed low was more likely to sink an enemy, while endangering fewer boarders that might have been sent from the upper decks. The thirty-two pound balls would also not hull the opposing ship – passing straight through and potentially damaging friendly vessels beyond. All on the lower gun deck were aware of these basics, but there were still respectful acknowledgements from the nearest crews, and Ross felt that his authority, assumed though it might have been, was holding up well.

"Target!" Guillom shouted from forward, and the discharge from the farthest gun followed a few seconds later. The rest of the battery continued in turn, with only one, which suffered a misfire, and had need of the slow match, being out of order. Ross watched in approval as the well trained teams then went into action serving their pieces, and was wondering vaguely why there had been no answering fire when the enemy did reply. It was with a simultaneous broadside and seemed to come from so close a range that *Prometheus* was all but pressed sideways by the impact.

"Fire buckets aft!" Ross directed as a small blaze erupted close to, and above, the main magazine. "You there, the wash-deck pump and smart at it!" Directly next to the flames an unlucky hit had also killed a lad carrying two cartridges of cylinder powder and, what was even more unfortunate, spread his load evenly over the surrounding area. A circle roughly fifteen feet in diameter was coated in fine powder; if the fire was allowed to spread, the entire ship would be in imminent danger. "Fire buckets," he repeated, steadily. "Dilston, Colebrook – all those of the fire party – look to!"

His words seemed to wake everyone out of a trance. The fire itself was soon out but continued to smoke heavily and two pails of sand together with the entire contents of the scuttlebutt were subsequently poured over the grisly mess. A further pail of water was added, neutralising any remaining grains and giving a degree of grip to the barefoot men who had to tread the deck.

"No powder, no powder here!" He turned to see two groups of servers shouting from further forward. Evidently the ready-use charges were not being immediately replaced: something must have broken down in the chain of loading, and in no time other hands were calling attention to the problem. Ross looked about and realised the team of powder monkeys were gathered about the body of their fallen colleague.

"Make a move there!" he shouted in a voice that might have never left the quarterdeck, and the lads were instantly brought back to their duty. All else appeared to be in order; a man was examining his left hand, that appeared to be lacking a number of fingers, and there was some sort of argument going on within a nearby gun crew, which was instantly quelled by the strict voice of authority. Apart from that, Ross decided, the lower battery had got off remarkably lightly. Two men appeared to be missing from number eight, but the gun was being served well enough by its remaining crew. Then, even before he was considering it time, the first of *Prometheus'* thirty-twos fired in reply.

Soon the entire deck was vibrating with the rumble of trucks and erratic, but almost constant, discharges from cannon that Ross was starting to consider his own. He checked through the nearest port: they were hardly moving; apparently the captain had hauled in their wind, so now it was all down to the speed of his gunners.

Another broadside was received from the French, again simultaneous, and again the lower deck did not suffer greatly, although Ross heard the extended crash and clatter from above that might be falling tophamper. But the mere fact that the enemy was not trusting their gunners to fire independently was a strong indication of their lack of practice, and Ross was growing increasingly confident as he prowled behind his straining teams.

"You there, Carter," he bellowed, just as the nearest cannon erupted, adding, "make up as shot-and-wad man on number seven," when the deafening noise had subsided. The curly, red-haired Londoner who was part of a full team obediently presented himself to Hill, now down to five servers, and soon became integrated within his unit.

Once more there was a lack of fire from further forward; a larboard gun had been hit muzzle on, and was lying diagonally across the deck, with the remains of some who had attended it sprawled ungainly about. Hurle, one of the gunner's mates, was bellowing at a group of powder monkeys. Debris was scattered across the deck and the boys were finding it hard to pass. As Ross watched, the petty officer organised an improvised human chain that covered the explosives' final journey; the boys would be able to remain relatively stationary, and throw the charges from one to the other, rather than running with them. It was a method that had worked on previous occasions and he was glad to see Hurle resorting to it without reference to him. As soon as the charges were reaching their rightful place, Ross gave a wave of thanks to the gunner's mate. The gesture was returned by Hurle with a nod, followed by the briefest touch of his forehead that owed nothing to irony.

* * *

But none of this mattered to those on the quarterdeck; as far as the officers, now gathered about the larboard bulwark were concerned, *Prometheus* was simply fighting well. Long guns from both upper and lower batteries were keeping up an incessant pounding that was supplemented in no small way by the forecastle and quarterdeck carronades. Even her marines, rigid lined yet firing independently, seemed to be sniping effectively at any hint of movement on their opponent's deck. The flickering flares from British cannon fire cast the scene in an unearthly, ever changing, light and it was obvious to all that the French broadsides, still simultaneous even this deep into the action, were becoming slower, and less blinding. *Prometheus* was missing her jib boom, and the lower mainmast had been struck by a heavy round shot that remained partially embedded in its mass. But Banks had long since discounted any further movement; they could be kept on station easily enough with what sail-power remained and he had no wish or need to board while they could continue to hand out such a drubbing.

"Frenchie's taking damage," Caulfield bellowed, inches from his captain's ear and Banks could only agree. Discounting the hull shots, that would have caused far more injury to those within than could be seen, the two-decker was slowly being stripped of her fittings. Both anchors had been knocked clear, while the channels and dead-eyes were a tangle of wood and line to the extent that it appeared the mizzen mast at least was not fully supported. And to make matters worse, some variance in the current was steadily turning her bows away. This was forcing the French gunners to train their pieces further and further aft in order to continue firing on their tormentor, while slowly, but inevitably, their own vulnerable stern was being presented for attack.

After half an hour the French ship was apparently little more than a wreck. Banks waited until several minutes had passed beyond the time when another enemy broadside could be expected, then turned to the first lieutenant. ""Cease fire," he said, and Caulfield duly fumbled for his silver whistle before sounding three long blasts. It still took considerable time for relative peace to arrive; some of the gun crews being so immersed in their work that they had to be physically alerted to the order, and even then the ear-ringing echoes of such recent cacophony were almost deafening in themselves.

"Hail them, if you please, Mr Brehaut."

"Vous rendez-vous?" The sailing master's voice rolled over the short distance to no immediate response. Together with silence, the lack of cannon fire meant that darkness had also returned and nothing of substance could be made out on the enemy's deck. From far off came the distant sound of battle – presumably *Canopus* was engaging the second Frenchman – but little more. Then there was a muffled shout that certainly came from their enemy, followed by the continuous ringing of the ship's bell. There was no sign of further fire from the battered battleship and gradually those aboard *Prometheus* began to draw breath.

"Do we have any boats that will swim?" Banks asked, and the first lieutenant looked suddenly awkward.

"That I could not say, sir. But I'd chance we might risk a light to find out."

"Send a party across when you have," Banks agreed. "Both cutters if they survive, otherwise the launch. Marine complement, carpenter's mates and enough seamen to see them straight. I'd like at least sixty men," he added then, remembering his recent experience: "And as many French speakers as we possess; Mr Brehaut, would you oblige us?"

"I should be happy to, sir," the sailing master replied formally. There would be little called from him until morning and, although he was not a military man as such, Brehaut could not ignore the opportunity to extend his stock of charts: French cartographers being amongst the best in the world. "But I should prefer it if a regular officer accompanies me also."

"Yes, yes, of course," Banks agreed. Then, as a thought occurred, he gave a tired smile. "Be so good as to send for Mr King," he said to a nearby midshipman. "He has received so many of our captures in the past, it would surely tempt fate not to allow him the honour on this occasion."

Chapter Twenty-Three

Dawn found them victorious but exhausted. *Canopus* continued an erratic bombardment of the second battleship for less than fifteen minutes after *Prometheus'* opponent struck then, as if sensing defeat, the final Frenchman followed suit. The remaining dark hours were spent making good; carpenters, boatswains, sailmakers and their teams did what they could to secure the vessels while medical parties from all ships shared men and resources in a combined effort to save lives. *Aries* used the time clearing all from the burning French liner; a dangerous task that constantly exposed rescuers and rescued alike to the danger of explosion, and it was almost with relief that the stricken ship finally slipped beneath the waves with the first light of day. Prize crews were arranged for the two remaining captures; one was taken under tow and, by noon, the battered squadron had already set course for Gibraltar.

In *Prometheus*, much still needed to be done. The boatswain and his team had performed wonders with her tophamper; she now boasted a fresh jib boom while a series of stout splints set tight about her damaged main were judged adequate enough to see her back to the British port. And there was the usual detritus of battle to contend with: lads were sent to sluice the dales and scuppers, first with raw sea water then ever increasing ratios of vinegar. Guns were remounted, and shot holes stoppered until, by the time the bell had rung for the first dog watch, *Prometheus* was fit to fight another extended action at a moment's notice. But there was little of the usual good humour and celebration common at the end of battle.

The British were cheerful enough, and none would have swapped places with their French prisoners, but all were equally aware that victory had been won at the cost of many lives. And in addition, a good few hours' sailing would be needed to see them safely back to harbour. Once there, once they were truly safe, the celebrations could begin in earnest. Stories told, songs sung and fallen colleagues solemnly honoured, but, while a fresh enemy could be sighted at any time, this was just an interlude: the fight was not truly finished.

And for some, it had only just begun. Harrison, the toothless server from Flint's team waited several hours to meet with Mr Manning. And when he did his examination was brief, with the subsequent operation taking hardly any longer. Within ten minutes of being passed into the surgeon's care, both legs had been removed above the knee and the best Harrison could hope for was a life that could no longer include his chosen profession. Lewis too was wounded although the musket ball in his shoulder proved relatively easy to remove and, with an arm swathed in bandages and set tight against his chest, the lieutenant quickly returned to duty. But with King there was no such possibility and, as the surgeon pored over his wound under the doubtful light of the sick berth's lantern, he was not encouraged.

"He is weak and has lost blood," Manning told Judy. The woman had been working tirelessly for all the wounded throughout the night and naturally gravitated to the sick berth when the more serious patients were moved there. "I would have him wake and take proper fluid, but fear he will be in pain, which might upset the sutures," he added sadly.

"But he cannot last for long on that," she said, indicating, with disdain, the dark glass bottle Manning carried.

"I would concur: there is small enough curative power in laudanum," the surgeon agreed. "But, at this stage, oblivion is the best I can provide for him."

She nodded, although it was clear the answer had not sufficed.

"He will be well in time," Manning continued, feeling only mildly guilty about breaking his rule for honest prognosis. King's condition was not without hope, but no good would be served by being too accurate.

"And you yourself must take rest," he told her, switching his professional attention to the girl. "All are as stable as we could wish. Take a few hours, and come back refreshed; I shall authorise soup for later this morning; it will give them strength and your help would be appreciated then."

"Very well," she said, rising up from her place next to King's bunk. "But I will not feed them that portable stuff. The Dear knows what goes in to make such a vile concoction: there is likely to be more goodness in the pan that boils it."

* * *

"And you placed yourself in charge of the entire lower gun deck?" Caulfield asked flatly. They were in the chart room, which was one of the more orderly areas of *Prometheus* and, although small, proved ideal for such an interview. Ross stood to one side of the table and the first lieutenant sat back in his chair as he regarded him.

"I did, sir," the seaman replied, his eyes staring straight ahead at the spirketting above Caulfield's head.

"Rather an unusual move for an able seaman, was it not?" the officer questioned.

"Perhaps, sir," Ross acknowledged, but said no more.

"Especially one that has only recently joined the ship, and professed no prior knowledge of guns, nor their care or organisation."

This time Ross remained silent although the first lieutenant, it appeared, was not requiring an answer but seemed content to conduct the interview from his perspective alone.

"However, you are to be commended," he continued, relaxing slightly. "Indeed, from what I hears, you handled the men with all the skill of an old hand." Caulfield's attention was still upon him but Ross' gaze did not alter, and neither did the eyes flicker for an instant.

"Or is 'old hand' the wrong term?" the first lieutenant enquired. "Perhaps you may think of another?"

"I have asked for nothing," Ross said quietly. "I did what I had to because the situation demanded it; no more."

"But you do deserve recognition; a promotion at least," Caulfield allowed, and then drew a deep sigh. "Indeed, Ross, it appears we are very much in your debt," he continued. "Look, sit down man, do; this is a foolish situation."

The seaman's eyes finally fell, and met those of the first

lieutenant; then he settled himself somewhat stiffly on the only other chair in the tiny room.

"That is better," Caulfield told him, softening further. "Now, what say you tell me your story, and we shall see what can be done about it?"

* * *

"There's a Mr Markham to see the second lieutenant," the boy said uncertainly as he stood at the door to the great cabin. "I have said Mr King is not to be disturbed, and he asked to speak with you, sir. I take him to be some kind of lawyer."

"How many forms does such a thing take?" Banks asked Caulfield then, turning back to the midshipman, "Very good, Mr Adams; you may show him in."

Prometheus had been at anchor in Gibraltar's crowded harbour for two extremely busy days. In that time her hull had been surveyed and judged reasonably sound, with only minor damage below the waterline. But there was considerable work needed above, to say nothing of the fresh lower mainmast and larboard fore channel and chains. Nothing was beyond the considerable capabilities of Gibraltar's dockyard, but knowing that the ship would not be returning to open water for at least six weeks had instilled a holiday attitude in at least two of her officers.

And the caller actually turned out to be one of the better examples of his breed, causing Banks and Caulfield to be cautiously impressed. Markham was an older man, certainly sixty yet with a full head of white, unpowdered hair that emphasised his deep Mediterranean tan. Well and soberly dressed, there was the air of polite efficiency about him, and both officers recognised more than a casual interest in his surroundings.

"I am certain you have better things to do with your time, gentlemen," Markham assured them, when they were all three seated at the large table. The room, only recently returned to use as the captain's dining cabin, was splendidly lit by an afternoon sun shining through the magically unbroken stern windows, and few could have guessed that *Prometheus* had been fighting for her life

278

only a matter of days before. The lawyer opened the thin leather case in front of him and removed a sheaf of papers. "And, after such a valiant action – I must confess to feeling slightly abashed at disturbing the heroes of the hour."

"Your business was with Thomas King, I believe," Banks commented, and Markham looked up sharply.

"So it is, Sir Richard. But I understand Mr King is indisposed and, as the subject also concerns yourself, I had hoped to speak with you in his absence."

"Very well," Banks replied guardedly. If King was involved, this could only be a naval matter and presumably Sarah, or his immediate family, were not concerned. But still he disliked dealing with lawyers and, pleasant though Markham might appear, instinctively wished him gone.

"Indeed it should be addressed immediately, sir." The lawyer paused in sorting his documents to regard Banks with a more serious expression. "And would be in your personal interest if so."

"Very well," Banks replied. "Perhaps you would care to elaborate?"

"It is the case of one of your men; a Michael, Ian, Potterton; you are aware of the fellow?"

Banks looked to his first lieutenant who shrugged. "He is of the wardroom catering staff," Caulfield replied. "A cook, and a very good one; of late he has been given charge of all senior officer victualling and I was to apply for him to be warranted. But as to his personal affairs, I know nothing."

"In a ship that must hold many hundreds of men, that is no surprise, I am sure," Markham allowed. "Perhaps I should enlighten you further?"

* * *

The original mess tables had been replaced, as well as both benches, and the racks that held their eclectic selection of tableware were once more filled. Some of the latter had been confused with those of Sanderson's mess which was adjoining, but the surviving members of Flint's team soon reclaimed their own, and the rest no longer mattered.

They were actually five men down in all: or six, if Ross were counted. Thompson and Billings were killed in that first, devastating, broadside which had also wounded Harrison. He had since been transferred to the shore hospital; a place known more for receiving contributions than returning them. Potterton and Greg were missing for less dismal reasons. The former had been transferred out some while back, and now messed with the wardroom stewards, whereas Greg, only a gun room man and so not entitled to any privileges, had been called for extra duty. And Ross, though present, was also somehow absent.

Following the action, he had returned to duty as an ordinary hand, resisting all requests for explanation and even ignoring the several personal approaches from members of his own mess. Instead, he carried out his work with quiet efficiency, but kept himself at a distance, refusing to discuss any issue beyond the immediate task and blocking all attempts at conversation or discourse. Even when addressed by petty officers, enquiries were deflected by blank looks and a mumbled denial that he had done anything out of the ordinary, while deeper questioning was met with a stark refusal to explain further: something that, at other times, might have placed him on a charge for insolence. Only in his recent interview with the first lieutenant had he consented to speak further, as well as revealing more of his personal history than he wished. And when he had, there was no feeling of relief from sharing the sorry tale; rather the opposite. That someone else was now aware of his plight had not softened it at all, but only confirmed his inner fear that, inevitably, it would become common knowledge.

However, for the past few days there had been far too many calls on everyone's time to bother about a single man's behaviour. With damage both aloft and alow, *Prometheus* needed extensive work before she could set sail for home. And when that had been achieved, the not inconsiderable responsibility of two captures and the remains of three enemy crews to supervise served to make the journey back to Gibraltar exhausting for everybody. But now they were safely under the care of her dockyard and protected by mighty shore-based batteries there was slightly more time, and Ross guessed his actions would not remain ignored for very much longer.

About them, men in other messes were deep into the evening stingo; beer that had been provided by a captain suitably appreciative of their support. Soon there would be singing and probably hornpipes to celebrate the recent victory and, more importantly, each man's survival of it. But in Flint's mess the atmosphere was far more reserved. They had no less to celebrate; all present appeared sound in wind and limb and each was down to receive a goodly sum in both prize and head money, while their recent experiences would have reassured them, yet again, of their apparent immortality. But even while calculations might have been done in private, in public there was a single concern, and that was for one of their messmates.

"Any left in the pin, Ben?" Flint enquired, and the boy sprang up before collecting the small cask, and proceeding to fill each man's tankard in turn. But when he reached Ross, the seaman placed a hand over his pot.

"None for you?" Flint asked, and Ross shook his head in a silence that was becoming far too common at their particular table.

"There's a sight more space on the forms," Cranston said eventually, more in an effort to promote conversation than anything else. But he was right; even allowing for Greg's absence, and with Ben unilaterally voting himself the right to join the men at the side of the table, there was no doubting they were fewer in number.

"More will be allotted," Flint sighed, with the air of one who had seen it all before. "In a month from now there'll be new faces that we'll already be sick of, and them what has died will probably be forgotten."

"That's assuming we haven't been sent to join 'em," Jameson added brightly. There was a moment's stunned silence, then a ripple of laughter ran about the group.

But one man's' participation was noticeable by its absence, and all eyes naturally turned to him.

"You not joining us then, Ross?" Flint said, finally addressing the problem they had all been skirting. "Been as quiet as a cut-purse since the action, you has – them Frenchmen offend you?"

"T'ain't the French, nor no one present," Ross said slowly whilst staring into his mug as if it held some special secret. "And I apologise if I have offended."

"Man has a right to be quiet if he's wanting," Flint told him gently. "But if there's trouble, and he can't share it with his mess, then it's a problem indeed."

"You've nothing to rebuke yourself for, if that's what's botherin'," Jameson added softly. "We all knows what you did on the gun deck and are grateful."

"Aye, pulled us all together like a proper officer," Cranston agreed. "Like you was born to it."

"I was," Ross said, his voice equally low and the words were greeted in hushed silence. For this was the moment when everything ended.

Caulfield had been surprisingly reassuring, saying that court martial decisions could be challenged and, even if not, there was no reason why he should have to spend the rest of his life on the lower deck. Provisions could be made and rules bent. Volunteers, who wore similar uniforms to midshipmen and carried almost identical authority, were actually rated as able seamen on the ship's books; a man of his experience might be considered as such, until a more permanent solution were found.

And indeed, Ross had no desire to remain an ordinary hand; in theory at least there was nothing he would have liked better than return to his previous position: go aft and resume being an officer in a fighting ship. But his time spent as a lower deck man aboard *Prometheus* had taught him more than he would have learned in a lifetime of walking quarterdecks, and he was strangely reluctant to leave.

There was nothing unusual in any of the men; the same could be found in almost any vessel afloat and currently serving the king, yet it remained as hard to betray them as it would his own mother. And that is what he would be doing – that was what he had already done. Simply associating with officers was contrary to the ways of the lower deck; how they would react to the news they had been sharing their lives with one could hardly be imagined.

"Spent six years as a mid., and five a lieutenant," he continued, still staring fixedly at his beer. The noise was growing about them and his words were barely whispered, yet every man at the table heard and all then knew for certain exactly what they had been living alongside.

"Now why doesn't that amaze me?" Flint asked at last, and there was even a smattering of light laughter as Ross finally raised his head.

All of his mess mates were staring in his direction, but as he met each man's gaze in turn, he realised there was a total lack of revelation on any of their faces. And neither was there animosity; over the time Ross had been part of the mess, his mates had become stupidly important to him and to be ostracised or excluded would have been one of the worst fates he could have imagined. But no, they were looking upon him kindly, as those who had a shared knowledge and it was clear that, however dreadful the crime he had imagined, none seemed particularly bothered. And neither were they in the least surprised.

* * *

"I understand that Mr Potterton was one of several recruited by your Lieutenant Lewis on the night of the seventeenth of June."

"The smugglers!" Caulfield said in sudden realisation, and Markham nodded.

"Indeed so, there was a meeting at the Three Tuns, a local hostelry, and most of those present were known to be of such a calling," he replied, his eyes twinkling. "But not so my client. Mr Potterton is actually joint freeholder of the establishment and, as such, it would seem he was seized in error."

"If that is the case, I am sure it was not intended," Banks replied quickly. "You have proof, I have no doubt?"

"None whatsoever," Markham admitted blithely. "I have been informed of the fact merely by word alone, although it does bear the ring of truth. After over thirty years in legal practice one develops an ear for such things; a sixth sense, if you wish, and I would assess Mr Potterton to be of a trustworthy nature. The actual fact can certainly be tested although that would probably take some months, and my client hopes the effort will not be necessary."

"I cannot speak for his ethical status, but the man is an excellent cook," Caulfield commented quietly. "And appears totally reliable: I would not think him capable of a blatant lie."

"You will no doubt be aware that illegal impressment is a felony?" Markham continued, more delicately. "If found guilty, an offender may face a fine, or possibly imprisonment." He paused for no longer than a second but, even in that time, tension in the great cabin became almost tangible.

"My client appears capable of proving his claim, yet to do so will actually aggravate the offence, as he would need to remain in the king's service for a longer period." The lawyer relaxed in his chair and both officers sensed he was coming to a significant point. "Were you to authorise his release without putting him to such trouble, he would equally be happy to relinquish any claim for compensation; providing my office's modest fees are also met," he added, more softly.

"Well, it should be a pity to lose his services in the wardroom..." Caulfield began.

"But I am sure we do not wish to make too much of the issue," Banks interrupted. "*Prometheus* was ordered to sea almost immediately, otherwise a more detailed investigation would undoubtedly have taken place. But the service has no use for men taken illegally, and we shall be pleased to grant him his freedom without delay."

"He will also be due a tidy sum in prize money," Caulfield added. "Certainly enough to set him up for life, should he so wish."

"I am confident my client will be happy to hear of it," Markham lowered his head slightly. "But would judge Mr Potterton more than content to return to his former occupation, as he has one further request."

Once more the two officers exchanged glances, but said nothing.

"There is a young lady aboard, I believe?" he continued. "A Miss Kinnison? Mr Potterton wondered if she might be permitted to accompany him."

"The old dog," Caulfield said without thinking, then hurriedly tried to take back the remark by clearing his throat.

"Oh, I think the arrangement is purely professional," the lawyer beamed. "Mr Potterton has enjoyed working with her, and feels she would be of benefit to his business. And Miss Kinnison has expressed an interest in joining him; it is as simple as that."

Banks looked over at Caulfield. "I would say that any harm the girl may have done has been more than outweighed by her efforts with the wounded," he said.

"To say nothing of her alerting me to that foolish duel," the first lieutenant agreed. "I had already received word from the surgeon, but she was not to know that. She spoke out, when many would have held back, and may well have saved two lives."

"Then there is little left to be said." Markham began to collect his papers. "The matter may be swiftly forgotten. I can thank you gentlemen for your time, and wish you well." He stopped and regarded them both with a slight smile. "I was to have pursued a naval career myself but, alas, my father had other thoughts and it is the source of constant regret to me."

"There is one point you may be able to clear for us," Caulfield said, as the man was preparing to rise. "We were about to discuss the matter before your arrival. Are you acquainted with every aspect of Naval law?"

Markham looked suddenly alert. "I confess a working knowledge; one can hardly practice in Gibraltar without it. How may I assist?"

"It is with regard to the findings of court martial; principally the sentence," Banks explained.

"Would this concern a certain William Ross?" Markham enquired, his eyes once more alight. "And the hearing that took place in English Harbour, Antigua?"

285

"You are familiar with the case?"

"Mr Ross was to be my next call," Markham confirmed. "He is also a client although, unusually, we have yet to meet: Lieutenant King was pleased to engage my services on his behalf. I understand the gentleman is also currently serving as a seaman aboard this ship?"

"He is," Caulfield admitted, while manfully avoiding Bank's stare.

"Well, I am not at liberty to discuss the personal circumstances, but we are fortunate that court proceedings have been reported in some detail. The *Naval Chronicle* carried a significant piece in the last issue and there were also references in several London newspapers. Reading between the lines, I would say Mr Ross has attracted a deal of interest in England – as he would doubtlessly have discovered, had he delayed before accepting a berth in this ship."

"Interest, you say?" the captain grunted. He was aware that Ross had done well in the recent action, and held every sympathy for any man treated unjustly. But he was also instinctively suspicious of public attention, and certainly not sure if it were welcome on this occasion.

"Indeed, and so he might," Markham replied. "From what I read, there are a number of points regarding that particular tribunal that would benefit from professional consideration. Between ourselves, the president appears to have been wide of the mark on at least two points of law and decidedly so with regard to his summing up and sentence."

"Would you say it was a miscarriage of justice?" Caulfield asked.

"Nothing of the sort," Markham stated firmly. "Even when voiced as a casual opinion, such an assertion would be highly unprofessional. However, the verdict has yet to be confirmed by London, and that is by no means a certainty when dealing with the Leewards. Should the Admiralty see fit to do so, I feel we would have sufficient grounds for appeal. That is based on what I have already discovered: a thorough examination of the papers may well bring forth further issues."

There was a silence as Banks and Caulfield considered this, then Markham continued.

"It is a sad fact that many trials conducted on foreign stations are not carried out with strict regard to legal procedure. Indeed, there are frequently times when the facts are disregarded in favour of friendships and associations. Normally such patronage is allowed, especially when intended for leniency although, in this particular instance, it would seem the very reverse was the case."

"You believe Ross was used as a scapegoat?" Banks suggested, but still Markham would not be drawn.

"I shall say nothing further until my requested copy of the court records has been delivered," he said. "But, as I have said, the subject appears to have already attracted a deal of public sympathy. Such incidents are an embarrassment to the Admiralty and I should go so far as to predict their Lordships would greatly prefer the whole thing to be swiftly forgotten." He paused. "You would not be surprised to discover how often cases can be solved in such a manner."

The lawyer regarded both officers for a moment. It was as if his words might carry some special significance to them, although neither Banks nor Caulfield seemed particularly sensitive to their meaning.

"Do you think the court martial decision might be quashed?" the first lieutenant persisted.

"Not quashed, as such," Markham replied. "But, if confirmed, Mr Ross is probably entitled to a re-trial at the very least. However, from what I gather, there was never any question of him being dismissed the service as such: even to have his commission revoked might well be considered harsh and, as I have said, has yet to be confirmed by London. Consequently, and despite what the president might have stated, I would doubt an official block on further progress to his Naval career exists or, if it does, will be upheld."

"So I might at least appoint him midshipman?" Banks asked.

"I would be surprised if such an action were challenged." Markham's previous smile returned. "Indeed, he may well be entitled to a return of his commission. And if not, I might anticipate any recommendation from a future lieutenants' board would also be looked upon favourably. Frankly, gentlemen, I judge Mr Ross to have been abominably ill treated, and predict any truly impartial judge would have no hesitation in both agreeing, and putting matters to right."

Epilogue

"I understand Mr King is continuing to show signs of improvement," Manning said, as he followed the duty loblolly boy into the sick berth.

"He is indeed, sir," Wells agreed. "Miss Kinnison's with him now. But then there ain't so much time as she's not with one or other of the patients," he added, and Manning noted that considerably more respect was now being paid to Judy.

The ship had been at anchor for more than a week and, although the small room still held six filled bunks, its patients had less severe injuries. This was not entirely due to Manning's care; most of the more complicated cases had been transferred to the Naval hospital ashore. A few might grow better, and some could even find themselves taken aboard another ship in time. But the outlook for most of the current inhabitants of *Prometheus'* sick berth was far more hopeful. All had stated their intention of staying with the ship and most could be expected to take an active part in her future. Most, but not all, as there was still a rhetorical question mark hovering above Lieutenant King.

Without doubt he was a far stronger man than the one transferred from the cockpit nine days earlier. There was more colour in his face, and Judy stoutly maintained some weight had been added. But it was equally definite that he was not out of the woods and, in his professional capacity, Manning was forced to remain cautious. His friend had survived the initial trauma and so far the wound was mending, but experience told him there was a good way to go before he could be confident of a full recovery.

"Well, you certainly seem to be eating well enough," Manning conceded. "And soup yet again," he added, eyeing the empty bowl that Judy had been feeding King from. "Why, if you take any more chicken, I shall expect you to turn into one."

"That's not how it works at all, Robert," King replied seriously. His voice, though weak, was richer now, and this was the first time the surgeon had noticed the welcome hint of humour.

"I should have thought a medical man would have known better."

"How is the arm?" Manning asked, reverting to his professional role.

"It is much improved," King replied, flexing his left hand: the limb had been badly cut and was still swathed in bandages. "Still very stiff, and I cannot raise it."

"Then do not attempt to; the time for physical exercise will come soon enough, but better, for now, to place no strain upon it unnecessarily." Indeed, it would not, Manning thought grimly. He alone knew how piecemeal his repairs had been, although it was the chest wound that caused him true concern.

Many layers of tissue and muscle had been bound together with horse hair and catgut, in a way that would never have impressed a shore-based surgeon. But then few in general practice knew the need for tending to one patient while keeping a wary eye on those that were to follow. Over sixty men had been injured aboard *Prometheus* during the recent action, and only slightly less than half received exclusive attention from Manning himself. Yet he could have spent the entire thirteen hour spell of duty on three or four cases alone. King's wounds would normally have required the care of two surgeons, and probably an operation lasting a good deal longer than the fifteen minutes allowed.

But the end result seemed sound enough, and Manning was cautiously confident as he removed the single outer bandage that had taken the place of King's previous full chest wrap.

"Will you be travelling soon?" he asked, and it took a second or two for the others to realise he was addressing Judy.

"I – I hope to leave on Monday," she told him. Mr Potterton has arranged cabins for us both aboard the general packet. It is fortunate, she sails straight from here to Tor Bay, with perhaps only one call at the Tagus."

"That was your home, as I recall," Manning commented, as the bandage came away. "You do not wish to return to Portugal permanently?"

"No, those days are gone," she laughed. "I see my future at the Three Tuns, Galmpton; it sounds a fine place, and I know I shall be happy working with Mr P."

"And will you become Mrs P?" Manning asked, with a faint glint in his eye. "You will forgive the question, but it is what most suspect."

"Lordy, no!" Judy said quickly, and seemed to follow her words with wink at King. "There have already been three men who've let me down, so I have vowed not to trust any further until they have truly earned the privilege."

"That is indeed a worthy undertaking," the surgeon replied seriously. "And if your cooking enjoys the same success in Galmpton as it has aboard this ship, I see a rosy future for all."

He removed the small patch of gauze and was finally able to examine King's wound. The edges were slightly blackened, as was to be expected, and his entire chest area remained discoloured in the deep and varied colours of bruising. But there were also positive signs that all would be well and, as he relaxed, Manning realised quite how concerned he had been.

"So, who shall look after you when she is gone?" the question was now very definitely directed at his friend, and King grinned back from his pillow.

"Whoever it be, they could not do a better job," he said, and Manning nodded in silent agreement as he ran his fingers over the chest area. It was perhaps, a trifle hot; again, not to be surprised at, but he would have preferred a cooler skin. And then, quite suddenly he stopped.

"Whatever is the matter? King asked, instantly alerted. Manning realised he had leaned nearer to the wound and his change of expression appeared to have betrayed him.

"It is of no consequence," the surgeon replied automatically while forcing a smile, although he already knew the statement to be a lie.

For what he had discovered was substantial indeed: to most medical men it sounded an alarm as significant as 'deck there!' called from the masthead, or 'fire!' shouted below. Manning studied the wound more closely while being careful not to show any further emotion. No proper examination should be confined to merely sight and touch, and in this case it was the scent of King's wound that had signalled the warning. And sadly he was not wrong, the sign was undoubtedly there – not visibly obvious perhaps but, to one in the know, unmistakeable.

"Is there something amiss?" Judy asked with her customary lack of tact, and Manning gloomily conceded his professionally neutral countenance was not as convincing as he had thought. He shook his head, but did not trust himself to reply. The girl was clearly fond of King, and he knew his friend well enough to guess there might be more between them. But as his surgeon, he hoped not. As his surgeon he could only wish her gone; her presence could not improve matters, and may well cause Thomas even greater distress.

And gone she would be in two days: it was a short enough period and likely one in which both would remain convinced King was to make a full recovery. Manning reached for a fresh patch of gauze and began to replace the bandage as he thought. If she knew different Judy might decide to stay, but there would be little point in that; not when a new life and future awaited her in England.

He might apply to the hospital for a second opinion; maybe even consult with one of their physicians. But there could be no doubting what he had discovered – Manning had encountered it far too often in the past and knew, only too well, the probable consequences. It was the scent of corruption; a faint yet distinct deviation from that of a healthy lesion and even such a subtle hint told him his friend was likely to remain healthy for no longer than a week. After that, he could hold out very little hope.

Glossary

Able Seaman	One who can hand, reef and steer and is well-acquainted with the duties of a seaman.
Back	Wind change; anticlockwise.
Backed sail	One set in the direction for the opposite tack to slow a ship.
Backstays	Similar to shrouds in function, except that they run from the hounds of the topmast, or topgallant, all the way to the deck. (Also a useful/spectacular way to return to deck for a topman.)
Backstays, Running	A less permanent backstay, rigged with a tackle to allow it to be slacked to clear a gaff or boom.
Banyan Day	Monday, Wednesday and Fridays were normally considered such, when no meat would be issued.
Barky	*(Slang)* Seamen's affectionate name for their vessel.
Barrel Fever	*Slang)* Illness brought about from excessive alcohol consumption.
Belaying Pins	Wooden pins set into racks at the side of a ship. Lines are secured about these, allowing instant release by their removal.
Bilboes	Iron restraints placed about an offender's ankles, allowing him to be of some use, picking oakum, *etc.*
Binnacle	Cabinet on the quarterdeck that houses compasses, the deck log, traverse board, lead lines, telescope, speaking trumpet, *etc.*

Bitts	Stout horizontal pieces of timber, supported by strong verticals, that extend deep into the ship. These hold the anchor cable when the ship is at anchor.
Block	Article of rigging that allows pressure to be diverted or, when used with others, increased. Consists of a pulley wheel, made of *lignum vitae*, encased in a wooden shell. Blocks can be single, double (fiddle block), triple or quadruple. The main suppliers were Taylors, of Southampton.
Board	Before being promoted to lieutenant, midshipmen would be tested for competence by a board of post captains. Should they prove able they will be known as passed midshipmen, but could not assume the rank of lieutenant until they were appointed as such.
Boatswain	*(Pronounced Bosun)* The warrant officer superintending sails, rigging, canvas, colours, anchors, cables and cordage *etc.*, committed to his charge.
Bob	*(Slang)* A trick.
Booby	*(Slang)* A lout, clodhopper or country fellow.
Boom	Lower spar to which the bottom of a gaff sail is attached.
Bootneck	*(Slang)* Term for a marine.
Braces	Lines used to adjust the angle between the yards, and the fore and aft line of the ship. Mizzen braces, and braces of a brig lead forward.

Brig	Two-masted vessel, square-rigged on both masts.
Bulkhead	A partition within the hull of a ship.
Burgoo	Meal made from oats, usually served cold, and occasionally sweetened with molasses.
Bulwark	The planking or wood-work about a vessel above her deck.
Canister	Type of shot, also known as case. Small iron balls packed into a cylindrical case.
Careening	The act of beaching a vessel and laying her over so that repairs and maintenance to the hull can be carried out.
Carronade	Short cannon firing a heavy shot. Invented by Melville, Gascoigne and Miller in late 1770's and adopted from 1779. Often used on the upper deck of larger ships, or as the main armament of smaller.
Cascabel	Part of the breech of a cannon.
Caulk	*(Slang)* To sleep. Also caulking, a process to seal the seams between strakes.
Channel	(When part of a ship) Projecting ledge that holds deadeyes from shrouds and backstays, originally chain-whales.
Channel Gropers	*(Slang)* The Channel Fleet.
Chink	*(Slang)* Money.
Chips /Chippy	*(Slang)* Traditional name for the carpenter. Originally from the ship builders who were allowed to carry out small lumps of wood, or chips, at the end of their shift.

Close Hauled	Sailing as near as possible into the wind.
Coaming	A ridged frame about hatches to prevent water on deck from getting below.
Come-up Glass	A device using prisms and lenses that can detect the speed at which another vessel is gaining or falling back.
Companionway	A staircase or passageway.
Counter	The lower part of a vessel's stern.
Course	A large square lower sail, hung from a yard, with sheets controlling and securing it.
Cove	*(Slang)* A man, occasionally a rogue.
Crapaud (Johnny)	*(Slang)* Popular derogatory name for an Englishman to call a Frenchman.
Crows of Iron	Crow bars used to move a gun or heavy object.
Cull	*(Slang)* A man.
Cutter	Fast, small, single-masted vessel with a sloop rig. Also a seaworthy ship's boat.
Dale	Drain aboard ship, larger than a scupper.
David's Sow	*(Slang)* Describes a high degree of drunkenness (from a popular story of the time).
Dead Donkey	Parlour game in which the winning participant is the one who stays still for the longest time.
Deadeyes	A round, flattish wooden block with three holes, through which a lanyard is reeved. Used to tension shrouds and backstays.
Ditty Bag	*(Slang)* A seaman's bag. Derives its name from the dittis or 'Manchester stuff' of which it was once made.

Driver	Large sail set on the mizzen. The foot is extended by means of a boom.
Dunnage	Officially the packaging around cargo. Also *(Slang)* baggage or possessions.
Fall	The free end of a lifting tackle on which the men haul.
Fetch	To arrive at, or reach a destination. Also the distance the wind blows across the water. The longer the fetch the bigger the waves.
Forereach	To gain upon, or pass by another ship when sailing in a similar direction.
Forestay	Stay supporting the masts running forward, serving the opposite function of the backstay. Runs from each mast at an angle of about 45 degrees to meet another mast, the deck or the bowsprit.
Frizzen	The striking plate that encourages the spark in a flintlock mechanism. Also known as a steel.
Futtock	A lower frame in the hull of a ship (similar to a rib). Futtock shrouds run down from the edge of a top to the mast.
Glass	Telescope. Also, hourglass: an instrument for measuring time (and hence, as slang, a period of time). Also a barometer.
Gobbler	*(Slang)* Derisory term for a revenue officer.
Gingerbread	Common term for the ornate carvings common on larger ship's sterns.

Gun Room	In a third rate and above, a mess for junior officers. For lower rates the gun room is the equivalent of the wardroom.
Go About	To alter course, changing from one tack to the other.
Halyards	Lines which raise yards, sails, signals *etc.*
Hammock Man	A seaman or marine unofficially employed to tend the hammock of a junior officer.
Hanger	A fighting sword, similar to a cutlass.
Hard Tack	Ship's biscuit.
Hawse	Area in the bows where holes are cut to allow the anchor cables to pass through. Also used as general term for bows.
Hawser	Heavy cable used for hauling, towing or mooring.
Headway	The amount a vessel is moved forward (rather than leeway: the amount a vessel is moved sideways) when the wind is not directly behind.
Heave To	Keeping a ship relatively stationary by backing certain sails in a seaway.
HEIC	Honourable East India Company.
Holder	One aboard ship who spends much of his time moving stores in the hold.
Idler	A man who, through his duty or position, does not stand a watch, but (usually) works during the day and can sleep throughout the night.
Interest	Backing from a superior officer or one in authority, useful when looking for promotion.
Jemmy Ducks	A traditional name for the hand who looks after poultry aboard ship.

Jib-Boom	Boom run out from the extremity of the bowsprit, braced by means of a Martingale stay, which passes through the dolphin striker
Jimmy Leggs	*(Slang)* The master at arms.
John Company	*(Slang)* The East India Company.
Junk	Old line used to make wads, etc.
Jury Mast/Rig	Temporary measure used to restore a vessel's sailing ability.
Landsman	The rating of one who has no experience at sea.
Landshark	*(Slang)* Popular smuggler's euphemism for land-based revenue officers.
Lanthorn	Large lantern.
Larboard	Left side of the ship when facing forward. Later replaced by 'port', which had previously been used for helm orders.
Leaguer	A long cask with a capacity of 127 imperial gallons, normally used to hold water.
Leeward	The downwind side of a vessel.
Leeway	The amount a vessel is moved sideways by the wind (as opposed to headway, the forward movement, when the wind is directly behind).
Liner	*(Slang)* Ship of the line (of battle). A third rate or above.
Linstock	A forked staff to hold a lighted slowmatch. Using a linstock enables a gun captain to fire his weapon from a distance, without the aid of a gunlock.
Lobster	*(Slang)* Soldier.
Lubber/Lubberly	*(Slang)* Unseamanlike behaviour; as a landsman.

Luff	Intentionally sail closer to the wind, perhaps to allow work aloft. Also the flapping of sails when brought too close to the wind. The side of a fore and aft sail laced to the mast.
Manger	Area aboard ship where livestock are kept.
Martingale Stay	Line that braces the jib-boom, passing from the end through the dolphin striker to the ship.
Nanny House	*(Slang)* A brothel.
Orlop	The lowest deck in a ship.
Pariah (Mess)	A mess made up of those rejected by others.
Packet / Packet Service	The HEIC maintained a number of fast sailing vessels to maintain communications and carry light cargo.
Peter (Blue)	Introduced in the 1750's as a blue flag with six white balls. The later version, which replaced the balls with a white square, became the signal to recall everyone to the ship.
Phyz	*(Slang)* face.
Pipeclay	Compound used to polish and whiten leatherwork.
Point Blank	The range of a cannon when fired flat. (For a 32 pounder this would be roughly 1000 feet.)
Portable Soup	A boiled down mixture of beef and offal that could be reconstituted with water.
Preventive Service	The customs (or excise) service; at the time both acted independently.
Pushing School	*(Slang)* A brothel.
Pusser	*(Slang)* Purser.

Pusser's Pound	Before the Great Mutinies, meat was issued at 14 ounces to the pound, allowing an eighth for wastage. This was later reduced to a tenth.
Quarterdeck	In larger ships the deck forward of the poop, but at a lower level. The preserve of officers.
Queue	A pigtail. Often tied by a seaman's best friend (his tie mate).
Quoin	Triangular wooden block placed under the cascabel of a long gun to adjust the elevation.
Ratlines	Lighter lines, untarred and tied horizontally across the shrouds at regular intervals, to act as rungs and allow men to climb aloft.
Reef	A portion of sail that can be taken in to reduce the size of the whole.
Reefing points	Light line on large sails, which can be tied up to reduce the sail area in heavy weather.
Reefing Tackle	Line that leads from the end of the yard to the reefing cringles set in the edges of the sail. It is used to haul up the upper part of the sail when reefing.
Rigging	Tophamper; made up of standing (static) and running (moveable) rigging, blocks etc. Also *(slang)* Clothes.
Rondy	*(Slang)* Rendezvous. A recruitment point and base for the press for men joining a ship.
Rummer	Large drinking glass originating in Holland.
Running	Sailing before the wind.
Salt Horse	*(Slang)* Salt beef.

Scarph	A joint in wood where the edges are sloped off to maintain a constant thickness.
Schooner	Small craft with two or three masts.
Scran	*(Slang)* Food.
Scupper	Waterway that allows deck drainage.
Sheet	A line that controls the foot of a sail.
Shrouds	Lines supporting the masts athwart ship (from side to side) which run from the hounds (just below the top) to the channels on the side of the hull.
Six an' Eight-Pence	*(Slang)* A lawyer or attorney (from a commonly charged fee).
Smoke	*(Slang)* to discover, or reveal something hidden.
Soft Tack	Bread.
Spirketting	The interior lining or panelling of a ship.
Spring	Hawser attached to a fixed object that can be tensioned to move the position of a ship fore and aft along a dock, often when setting out to sea. Breast lines control position perpendicular to the dock.
Sprit Sail	A square sail hung from the bowsprit yards, less used by 1793 as the function had been taken over by the jibs although the rigging of their yards helps to brace the bowsprit against sideways pressure.
Stay Sail	A quadrilateral or triangular sail with parallel lines hung from under a stay. Usually pronounced stays'l.
Stern Sheets	Part of a ship's boat between the stern and the first rowing thwart and used for passengers.

Stingo	*(Slang)* Beer.
Strake	A plank.
Suds (in the)	*(Slang)* To be in trouble.
Tack	To turn a ship, moving her bows through the wind. Also a leg of a journey relating to the direction of the wind. If from starboard, a ship is on the starboard tack. Also the part of a fore and aft loose-footed sail where the sheet is attached, or a line leading forward on a square course to hold the lower part of the sail forward.
Taffrail	Rail around the stern of a vessel.
Thumper	*(Slang)* A third rate or above.
Ticket Men	Hands employed aboard a pressing tender to replace those crew seized, and see the vessel safely to harbour.
Timoneer	One who steers a ship.
Tophamper	Literally any weight either on a ship's decks or about her tops and rigging, but often used loosely to refer to spars and rigging.
Tow	Cotton waste.
Trick	*(Slang)* A period of duty.
Veer	Wind change, clockwise.
Waist	Area of main deck between the quarterdeck and forecastle.
Watch	Period of four (or in case of dog watch, two) hour duty. Also describes the two or three divisions of a crew.
Watch List	List of men and stations, usually carried by lieutenants and divisional officers.

Wearing	To change the direction of a square rigged ship across the wind by putting its stern through the eye of the wind. Also jibe – more common in a fore and aft rig.
Wedding Garland	An actual garland that would be raised when a ship was expected to remain at anchor for some while. It signified that the ship was not on active duty and women were allowed aboard. This was considered a preferable alternative to granting shore leave, a concession that was bound to be abused.
Windward	The side of a ship exposed to the wind.
Yellow (Admiral)	The rank of Admiral was achieved solely through seniority. Following a man being made post (captain) he gradually rose on the captains' list as those above him died, retired, or were promoted. On attaining flag rank he would normally be appointed Rear Admiral of the Blue Squadron, the lowest level of flag officer other than Commodore. But should the officer be considered unsuitable for such a position, he would be appointed to an unspecified squadron; what was popularly known as being yellowed, and a disgrace to him so honoured.

Character List

HMS *Prometheus*

Captain:	Sir Richard Banks
Lieutenants:	Michael Caulfield, Davison, Thomas King, Benson, Lewis, Carlton
Sailing Master:	Brehaut
Master's Mate:	Cartwright
Midshipmen and Volunteers:	Bruce, Chivers, Sutton, Franklin, Adams, Steven
Surgeon:	Robert Manning
Surgeon's Mates:	Dodgeson, Prior
Loblolly boys:	Macintosh, Wells, Mercer
Purser:	Dawson
Boatswain's Mates:	Simmonds, Clement
Master at Arms	a.k.a. "Jimmy Leggs": Saunders
Gunner:	Abbot
Gunner's Mate:	Hurle
Quarter Gunner:	Guillom
Cook:	Stone
Carpenter:	Roberts
Sailmaker:	Stevenson
Captain's Steward:	David
Davison's Steward:	Hughes
King's Steward:	Keats
Poulterer:	"Jemmy Ducks"
Seamen:	Jenkins, Todd, Marne, Dilston, Colebrook, Carter, Sanderson, Jeffrey, Hill, Remmer and Moffat
Flint's mess:	Flint, Greg, Potterton, Cranston, Butler, Billings, Harrison, Jameson, Ross, Thompson and Ben (boy)
Marines:	Captain Donaldson,

Captain Reynolds, Lieutenant James,
Lieutenant Swift,   Lieutenant Locke,
Sergeant Jarvis, Corporal Collins

And:

Supercargo: Judith Kinnison (Judy)
Wife of carpenter: Mrs Roberts

Belle Île

Captain: Agard
Prize Master: David Carroll
Seamen: Manasse, Molony

Gibraltar

Naval Commissioner's Staff: Captain William A Otway,
                                    Commander Gordon Stewart,
                                    Lieutenant Hoskins
Garrison Commander: Major Barnett
Solicitor: Markham

Also

Captain: HMB *Wakeful*:   Commander Harker
Captain: HMS *Canopus*: Captain John Conn
**Admiral commanding
convoy**:   Rear Admiral Ford
King's estranged wife: Juliana

About the author

Alaric Bond was born in Surrey, and now lives in Herstmonceux, East Sussex. He has been writing professionally for over twenty years.

His interests include the British Navy, 1793-1815, and the RNVR during WWII. He is also a keen collector of old or unusual musical instruments, and 78 rpm records.

Alaric Bond is a member of various historical societies and regularly gives talks to groups and organisations.

www.alaricbond.com

About Old Salt Press

Old Salt Press is an independent press catering to those who love books about ships and the sea. We are an association of writers working together to produce the very best of nautical and maritime fiction and non-fiction. We invite you to join us as we go down to the sea in books.

www.oldsaltpress.com

More Great Reading from Old Salt Press

Blackwell's Homecoming by V E Ulett

In a multigenerational saga of love, war and betrayal, Captain Blackwell and Mercedes continue their voyage in Volume III of Blackwell's Adventures. The Blackwell family's eventful journey from England to Hawaii, by way of the new and tempestuous nations of Brazil and Chile, provides an intimate portrait of family conflicts and loyalties in the late Georgian Age. *Blackwell's Homecoming* is an evocation of the dangers and rewards of desire. ISBN 978-0-9882360-7-3

Britannia's Shark by Antione Vanner

"Britannia's Shark" is the third of the Dawlish Chronicles novels. It's 1881 and a daring act of piracy draws the ambitious British naval officer, Nicholas Dawlish, into a deadly maelstrom of intrigue and revolution. Drawn in too is his wife Florence, for whom the glimpse of a half-forgotten face evokes memories of earlier tragedy. For both a nightmare lies ahead, amid the wealth and squalor of America's Gilded Age and on a fever-ridden island ruled by savage tyranny. Manipulated ruthlessly from London by the shadowy Admiral Topcliffe, Nicholas and Florence Dawlish must make some very strange alliances if they are to survive – and prevail. ISBN 978-0992263690

The Shantyman by Rick Spilman

In 1870, on the clipper ship *Alahambra* in Sydney, the new crew comes aboard more or less sober, except for the last man, who is hoisted aboard in a cargo sling, paralytic drunk. The drunken sailor, Jack Barlow, will prove to be an able shantyman. On a ship with a dying captain and a murderous mate, Barlow will literally keep the crew pulling together. As he struggles with a tragic past, a troubled present and an uncertain future, Barlow will guide the *Alahambra* through Southern Ocean ice and the horror of an Atlantic hurricane. His one goal is bringing the ship and crew safely back to New York, where he hopes to start anew. Based on a true story, *The Shantyman* is a gripping tale of survival against all odds at sea and ashore, and the challenge of facing a past that can never be wholly left behind. ISBN978-0-9941152-2-5

Eleanor's Odyssey by Joan Druett
It was 1799, and French privateers lurked in the Atlantic and the Bay of Bengal. Yet Eleanor Reid, newly married and just twenty-one years old, made up her mind to sail with her husband, Captain Hugh Reid, to the penal colony of New South Wales, the Spice Islands and India. Danger threatened not just from the barely charted seas they would be sailing, yet, confident in her love and her husband's seamanship, Eleanor insisted on going along. Joan Druett, writer of many books about the sea, including the bestseller Island of the Lost and the groundbreaking story of women under sail, Hen Frigates, embellishes Eleanor's journal with a commentary that illuminates the strange story of a remarkable young woman. ISBN 978-0-9941152-1-8

Water Ghosts by Linda Collison
Fifteen-year-old James McCafferty is an unwilling sailor aboard a traditional Chinese junk, operated as adventure-therapy for troubled teens. Once at sea, the ship is gradually taken over by the spirits of courtiers who fled the Imperial court during the Ming Dynasty, more than 600 years ago. One particular ghost wants what James has and is intent on trading places with him. But the teens themselves are their own worst enemies in the struggle for life in the middle of the Pacific Ocean. A psychological story set at sea, with historical and paranormal elements. ISBN 978-1943404001

The Guinea Boat by Alaric Bond
Set in Hastings, Sussex during the early part of 1803, *The Guinea Boat* tells the story of two young lads, and the diverse paths they take to make a living on the water. Britain is still at an uneasy peace with France, but there is action and intrigue a plenty along the south-east coast. Private fights and family feuds abound; a hot press threatens the livelihoods of many, while the newly re-formed Sea Fencibles begin a careful watch on Bonaparte's ever growing invasion fleet. And to top it all, free trading has grown to the extent that it is now a major industry, and one barely kept in check by the efforts of the preventive men. Alaric Bond's eighth novel. ISBN 978-0994115294

Lady Castaways by Joan Druett

It was not just the men who lived on the brink of peril when under sail at sea. Lucretia Jansz, who was enslaved as a concubine in 1629, was just one woman who endured a castaway experience. Award-winning historian Joan Druett (*Island of the Lost, The Elephant Voyage*), relates the stories of women who survived remarkable challenges, from heroines like Mary Ann Jewell, the "governess" of Auckland Island in the icy sub-Antarctic, to Millie Jenkins, whose ship was sunk by a whale. ISBN 978-0994115270

The Torrid Zone by Alaric Bond

A tired ship with a worn out crew, but *HMS Scylla* has one more trip to make before her much postponed re-fit. Bound for St Helena, she is to deliver the island's next governor; a simple enough mission and, as peace looks likely to be declared, no one is expecting difficulties. Except, perhaps, the commander of a powerful French battle squadron, who has other ideas.

With conflict and intrigue at sea and ashore, *The Torrid Zone* is filled to the gunnels with action, excitement and fascinating historical detail; a truly engaging read. ISBN 978-0988236097

The Beckoning Ice by Joan Druett

The Beckoning Ice finds the U. S. Exploring Expedition off Cape Horn, a grim outpost made still more threatening by the report of a corpse on a drifting iceberg, closely followed by a gruesome death on board. Was it suicide, or a particularly brutal murder? Wiki investigates, only to find himself fighting desperately for his own life. ISBN 978-0-9922588-3-2

Hell Around the Horn by Rick Spilman

In 1905, a young ship's captain and his family set sail on the windjammer, *Lady Rebecca*, from Cardiff, Wales with a cargo of coal bound for Chile, by way of Cape Horn. Before they reach the Southern Ocean, the cargo catches fire, the mate threatens mutiny and one of the crew may be going mad. The greatest challenge, however, will prove to be surviving the vicious westerly winds and mountainous seas of the worst Cape Horn winter in memory. Told from the perspective of the Captain, his wife, a first year apprentice and an American sailor before the mast, *Hell Around the Horn* is a story of survival and the human spirit in the last days of the great age of sail. ISBN 978-0-9882360-1-1

Turn a Blind Eye by Alaric Bond
Newly appointed to the local revenue cutter, Commander Griffin is determined to make his mark, and defeat a major gang of smugglers. But the country is still at war with France and it is an unequal struggle; can he depend on support from the local community, or are they yet another enemy for him to fight? With dramatic action on land and at sea, *Turn a Blind Eye* exposes the private war against the treasury with gripping fact and fascinating detail. ISBN 978-0-9882360-3-5

Captain Blackwell's Prize by V.E.Ulett
A small, audacious British frigate does battle against a large but ungainly Spanish ship. British Captain James Blackwell intercepts the Spanish *La Trinidad*, outmaneuvers and outguns the treasure ship and boards her. Fighting alongside the Spanish captain, sword in hand, is a beautiful woman. The battle is quickly over. The Spanish captain is killed in the fray and his ship damaged beyond repair. Its survivors and treasure are taken aboard the British ship, *Inconstant*. ISBN 978-0-9882360-6-6

Blackwell's Paradise by V. E. Ulett
The repercussions of a court martial and the ill-will of powerful men at the Admiralty pursue Royal Navy Captain James Blackwell into the Pacific, where danger lurks around every coral reef. Even if Captain Blackwell and Mercedes survive the venture into the world of early nineteenth century exploration, can they emerge unchanged with their love intact. The mission to the Great South Sea will test their loyalties and strength, and define the characters of Captain Blackwell and his lady in *Blackwell's Paradise*. ISBN 978-0-9882360-5-9